# UNTIL TH

CW01083700

**The first in the Downf**
**thriller of crir**

**Addiction. Obsession. Jealousy. Murder.**
**No one can be trusted in this train wreck of a life.**

Seth Wright and Jane Ellerton are messed up. *Really* messed up.
Their violence and love of excess makes them a perfect match.
Together or alone, they will do anything to ensure no one gets in
their way. Life should be good in their screwed-up world, but it's not
because there are many people who have an agenda.

Drugs, guns and murder - along with Seth's escalating paranoia and
Jane's erratic behaviour throws them further into chaos, madness and
debauchery and their promise to love one another until the end of
time turns into a war. A war not just against everyone around them,
but with each other.

Can they get their lives on track or will one of them finally snap,
meaning they will both forever have to live with the aftermath?
After all, obsession is a deadly downfall and love does not
necessarily conquer all. Especially when it is well and truly warped.

**What readers are saying about *Until the End of Time*:**
- *"Brutal, vicious, shocking... A cataclysmic novel of life in its most
raw form..."*

- *"I couldn't help but think of Seth and Jane like the couple in the
movie Natural Born Killers..."*

- *"If you aren't afraid to dive into a world of sex, drugs, and
violence, you'll love this one!"*

- *"A rollercoaster of a book..."*

- *"A gripping tale of love skewed through the lens of drugs, alcohol,
and duress..."*

*\** *This book contains written depictions of graphic violence, sex and strong language. It also
contains some themes that may be uncomfortable for certain readers.* *\**

# UNTIL THE END OF TIME

## TIME

### DOWNFALL SERIES #1

## EDIE BAYLIS

ATHAME
press
· LONDON ·

Athame Press
Unit 13230 - PO Box 6945 – London – W1A 6US

# Part One

PAUL THOMPSON LOOKED at his reflection in the window of the Black Eagle. *He looked fucking good even if he said so himself.*

Glancing around the small tap room with its old wooden tables and psychedelic carpet, he stared mesmerised at the flashing lights of the dilapidated fruit machine leaning at a funny angle at the end of the bar.

These new tablets had done the trick and something was finally working. In fact, they'd worked so well, the hospital had released him to get on with his life. *See! It was all fine now.*

He smiled as he fiddled with the lacing on the side of his leather trousers. That bloody idiot cousin of his, Stuart, saying they'd released all patients back into the community due to lack of funds was bollocks, but it didn't really matter. Not now he was back to normal. Besides, he couldn't have stayed in hospital indefinitely. He needed to be around for the public because he had gigs lined up, or he would have shortly.

Looking towards the bar with its collection of real ale, Paul wondered whether to treat himself to a roll from the selection in the plastic bread bin. There might be a cheese and onion one in there and he was pretty hungry, but spotting the landlady glaring in his direction, he changed his mind and quickly looked away. *What was everyone's problem?*

Paul instead turned his attention towards a group of old men sitting on a scuffed wooden settle. What the hell were they staring at him for? Sat there with their bloody trilbies and snuff boxes like the three monkeys.

Self-consciously touching his head, he was glad the bald patch had finally grown back enough to blend in with the rest of his hair, which reminded him that he could do with a bit more black dye.

Turning his head from side to side in the reflection of the window, he inspected his roots. *What if someone wanted to take his picture and his roots were showing? That would never do.*

He picked up his pint of cider and wondered where his mates were. It was almost like everyone was avoiding him and he wasn't sure why. The only person he'd really seen was Stuart, but it was no secret they'd never liked each other much.

He hadn't played with the band for ages either. They needed to practice and catch up for lost time, but he hadn't heard back from any of them, even though he'd left several messages. It was all very strange. They'd better hurry up though as he'd get the booking for their UK tour confirmed soon.

Paul sniggered to himself. He'd phoned up his agents in London last week and they'd pretended they didn't know who he was! They'd actually thought he was *joking* when he'd said he was Alice Cooper. *Who on earth did they think he was then, the bunch of jokers?*

Sipping his pint, he took a cigarette from the packet. He needed to see Jane. He'd missed her and wanted to speak to her, but he hadn't seen her anywhere.

He'd heard she was still wasting her time with that stupid gorilla. His eyes narrowed angrily. What on earth she was doing with that nutter, Seth, he had no idea, but it wouldn't last. Not once she knew *he* was back.

Paul exhaled slowly, refusing to get stressed. Once he'd asked Jane to marry him again, it would all work out. Then they'd get back to normal like before.

He grinned, thinking back to when she'd finally agreed to go out with him. Admittedly, she'd taken a bit of persuasion, but after several weeks of chatting her up at the Ten Barrels and many crates of cider, he'd managed to win her over. It might have been his motorbike that had finally clinched it - which reminded him, where was his bike? Did he still have it?

The other factor was the band. Now he was famous, she'd *definitely* want him back, wouldn't she?

Paul smiled, picturing Jane in her skin-tight shiny leggings or tiny leather skirts, then frowned. Those type of clothes were too much to wear off the stage. *Far* too much. He'd kept telling her, but would she listen? *No, she fucking well wouldn't.*

He took another swig of his pint.

'Alright, Alice?' someone shouted, laughing loudly.

Paul ignored them. *Some fans were just plain weird.* He was beginning to get used to this strange adoration and just let it wash over his head these days, realising he needed to get used to this fame thing.

Finishing his pint, he walked up to the bar and shouted up another.

'Alice! Alice! Who the fuck is Alice?'

Baring his teeth, Paul made a growling noise as the jeering chorus began again from the group around the bar. He knew his full-faced black eye makeup and white powder sent the fear of God into everyone. Sneering, he turned his back on the laughter and returned to his seat. *Let them laugh. It was him who was moving on to better things.*

His relationship with Jane had been great until she'd started getting the hump, saying she didn't want to go out with him anymore. Apparently, he kept on about her clothes being too revealing, that she wore too much makeup and that she couldn't talk to anyone without him moaning.

He didn't understand what her problem was. Buying her an engagement ring, he'd explained quite clearly she didn't need to wear that stuff anymore. Not now she had him. She could also take her makeup off.

He'd thought her completely insane when she chucked the ring away and said they were over. *Finished.*

Then she'd refused to talk to him at all. *How could they be over? They were getting married, for God's sake.*

Clearly he'd needed to sort the situation, so after giving her chance to calm down and see the error of her ways, he'd walked into the Barrels. He'd wanted to surprise her, so he'd waited in the women's toilets. That way they could talk and sort everything out.

He'd waited for over an hour before she'd finally appeared, but it seemed she hadn't learnt anything. She'd been wearing those skin-tight leather trousers again and *everyone* had been looking at her.

She didn't need to do that for him and so he'd said so. Why that had upset her so much, he didn't understand. After all, surely it only proved how much he'd loved her, otherwise he wouldn't be bothered, would he?

Jane had stormed out of the Barrels across to a block of flats opposite. He'd run after her, but she'd just screamed at him to leave her alone.

He hadn't meant to push her down the steps though. *Everyone knew that, didn't they?*

Neither had he meant to break her cheekbone – that was the sort of thing that happened sometimes with those sort of accidents, but even that had made her angry.

Getting off the floor, she'd grabbed his hair and ripped a big clump directly out of his scalp as she'd smashed his head through the glass door of the flat's entrance.

However, the fall had also taken a big chunk of skin off her face, so at least she couldn't wear makeup for a while. *Silver linings and all that.*

Besides, that was ages ago and she didn't even have a scar anymore, so it wasn't like it was a big problem. Even so, he'd tried to make it up to her by following her around. He'd even bought her flowers, but she hadn't liked that either.

The thing was, he'd have done *anything* if it meant she'd take him back. He still would. Being without her had made him quite sick.

Taking a swig from his new pint, Paul glanced out of the window, wondering whether he should get some more fags, but decided against it in case he got mobbed by fans. *That seemed to be happening more and more lately.*

He breathed out angrily. Eventually someone had got cross with him following Jane about and had thrown him down the steps of the Barrels. The fact he'd had his arm broken hadn't particularly fazed him, but not being able to play his guitar for a while had completely pissed him off. It hadn't changed his feelings for her though.

But then some fucker had tried to run him over. He'd been walking down the road back from town one night when he heard a car screaming at full throttle towards him out of nowhere. It mounted the pavement and he'd had to jump over a wall otherwise he'd have been totally mangled. The car had then pulled back on to the road and sped off as if nothing had happened!

Of course, there must have been something wrong with that motor. Perhaps the steering? It had been weird though, because for a minute he'd been *sure* it was Jane's car. Obviously, it couldn't have been because she wouldn't have done that to him.

He'd been overjoyed however, when after he'd been home an hour, he'd opened his bedsit door to find her standing there. He'd invited her in, but she didn't look well. Her eyes were glazed and she'd seemed angry. She was saying really confusing things, like it was *him* who'd upset her and that he'd got a problem. How could he have upset her? He *loved* her.

All he could remember after that was smiling as she'd stepped towards him. *He'd waited a long time to get her back.*

Paul shook his head. He didn't really like thinking about what had happened after that.

Waking up in the hospital, he'd been subjected to loads of questioning by the police, who wanted to know who'd attacked him. He'd no idea, but knew he'd been lucky because he'd been found within minutes of being thrown in the canal. Apparently, he'd been knocked unconscious and should have drowned.

The strange thing was they'd found a weird carving on his shoulder. Paul fingered the 'J' shaped scar absentmindedly. He must have got cut on something as he'd fallen.

*Yes, that was exactly what must have happened.*

The police though had other ideas and had kept on and on at him. In fact, he was convinced the constant hassle and pressure from them was what caused him to lose it and end up in hospital. All of this was *their* fault.

Paul looked down at his pint again and smiled. It was all going to be ok now he was well and back in town.

## ONE

**1991**

DEBBIE DIXON FUMED AS she stomped into the small kitchen of her grubby first floor flat. Accidentally kicking an empty tin of cat food on the floor, it rolled into the corner and came to rest against a pile of cereal, plastic tubs and jumbo packets of toilet rolls. She stared miserably, realising that getting a staff discount on top of the special offers at the supermarket was sadly the only bonus of working in the crummy place.

Scowling at the dirty plates and sticky glasses piled in the sink, her pudgy nose wrinkled and she pulled the waistband of her faded black leggings up over her ample backside. *The fucking dump was driving her mad. Like everything else.*

As she squeezed into the small hallway and shuffled past piles of dirty clothes stacked against the skirting board, she sighed and self-consciously yanked her pink T-shirt down in an attempt to cover the rolls of fat on her belly. Getting distracted meant she'd forgotten to get herself a drink. She must be losing the plot. *Damn him and damn that fucking freak whore too.*

Giving up finding anything clean, she poured cider into one

of the less offensive glasses, before sitting her heavy frame down on the leather sofa in the lounge. She glanced at her watch and smiled. She'd got half an hour before she was due to meet Ned for a special delivery which she certainly didn't want to miss because this one would sort her life out once and for all.

Absentmindedly kicking a pair of dirty knickers across the carpet, Debbie picked up a purple plastic-framed mirror from the coffee table and peered at her reflection. Even though she plastered the mascara on, she'd been cursed with short, straight eyelashes and they ended up looking stupid, rather than devastatingly lush like the eyelashes of that psycho bitch.

She glugged down a second glass of cider and pulled her hair back. Focusing critically, she turned her head from left to right in the mirror and eyed the flat mousy mess. At least she looked like a *real* woman though, not some freaky plastic doll.

Against her will, she couldn't stop thinking about Jane and inwardly seethed because the name she hated more than *anything* was bouncing around in her head. Ok, so Jane was pretty and thin, with curves in the right places, but she was still a fucking freak. *And* a psycho.

Opening a packet of biscuits, Debbie angrily crammed some into her mouth and shook with rage. *She HATED Jane-fucking-Ellerton.*

Debbie would be the first to admit she'd been systematically trailing Seth Wright for over two years and had been crazy over him since the first time she'd laid eyes on him. Tracy kept on that he was bad news and to leave him alone, but what did she know? Tracy might be her sister, but that didn't give her the right to tell her what to do, did it? She scowled angrily. She knew full well Seth was a hard case, but that was what she liked about him. A *proper man,* rather than a wimp.

She'd hang around the bar at the Ten Barrels every night he was working instead of sitting with her mates, but despite her repeated offers of meeting up, he'd never agreed. *Apparently he didn't do relationships.* That was fine. She'd happily take a few rounds with him. After all, once he'd sampled her, he'd be back for more.

A frisson of excitement ran though Debbie's body as she imagined running her hands through Seth's long hair and peeling the clothes off his muscly six foot three frame.

All things considered, she'd thought she'd been in with a very good chance. *Until he'd got with that bitch.* Not into relationships? He could have fooled her. Him and that bloody Jane were joined at the hip.

Smiling sarcastically, Debbie popped the last biscuit into her mouth. After tonight it was just a matter of time before she could put her plan into action and then everything would fall nicely into place.

Glancing at her watch once more, Debbie hefted herself off the sofa. It was time to meet Ned.

· · · ·

SITTING IN THE passenger seat of the white Transit, Seth impatiently glanced at his watch. 'What time did Phil say this bloke would be here?' he muttered, getting more and more agitated.

Digger shrugged his huge shoulders and mindlessly strummed his thick fingers on the steering wheel. 'Any time now.' He glanced at Seth and even in the gloom of the twilight, could see the green of his eyes getting darker, which always signified danger.

Seth sighed and slipped a pill into his mouth. He swallowed it dry and continued getting himself in to the zone. He needed to get this wrapped up quickly because there was a party on tonight and he wanted to spend some time getting drunk first.

Looking out of the window, he trained his eyes on the alley between the two ramshackle buildings that led into the car park where they were waiting and weighed up the surroundings. He decided the corner between the half-derelict remains of an old shop would do just nicely. It was out of the way enough should someone else be stupid enough to wander into the car park whilst he was delivering what was needed.

Sparking up a cigarette, Seth took a deep drag and tried to regulate his breathing as he pictured what Jane was doing in the interim.

Clenching his teeth together he tried to remain rational. In his minds' eye he visualised the long tendrils of her dark wavy hair running down to her waist and his muscles tightened thinking of her blood-red lips. The lips he immediately wanted to crush his mouth onto. He'd felt exactly the same way ever since the moment he'd first clapped eyes on her and admitted his feelings for the woman scared the shit out of him.

Seth sighed resignedly, wondering why he had to be so totally, utterly and crazily in love with her. It made him weak and he didn't like it. Spiralling out of control emotions could make him careless and he was getting on quite nicely at the moment.

Aside from his bar job, he'd developed a damn fine reputation for his ability to sort situations out and was getting more and more in demand. The cuts he took from the money he collected were gratefully received, not to mention the *extras*. Smiling, he patted the large bag of coke in his pocket that he'd got as a bonus from yesterday's job.

Before Jane had steamrollered into his life a year ago, he hadn't given a flying fuck about anyone and he didn't want emotions getting in the way. The trouble was, he knew there was no way he could be without her. He wanted to marry her, for God's sake. He'd asked her twice now, but she'd laughed each bloody time.

'Here he is!'

Digger's gruff voice snapped Seth from his thoughts and without another word they both pulled their sawn-offs out from under their seats.

. . . .

THE SHORT MAN with no discernible neck and a long scar running across his face was taken by surprise when seemingly from out of nowhere he was unceremoniously dragged around the side of a building. He barely had time to react before he was thrown roughly into the battered remains of a shopping trolley by a six foot four bloke built like a brick shithouse, sporting a short Mohican. To his horror the other man, who was almost as tall with long curly hair and a feral expression across his face, delivered a swift kick to the side of his jaw, shattering it on impact.

'You owe people money, don't you?' Seth roared, sneering at the man on the floor as blood, bits of teeth and saliva poured from his shattered mouth.

Digger stood to one side and watched Seth jump astride the man and tighten one hand around his throat.

'Well?' Seth screamed, whilst pointing the sawn-off. 'Cat got your tongue?'

The man's piggy eyes darted frantically from left to right to avoid staring down the barrel of a gun six inches from his face. 'I-I'll get you the money,' he stammered. 'I know I'm late with the payments and I'm sorry…'

Eyes wild with rage, Seth jumped to his feet. Keeping the gun trained on the man's face, he grinned savagely, his teeth flashing brightly in the moonlight. 'Let's just say we've been sent to pick up the money you owe. *All* of it.'

'Please don't kill me,' the man wailed, panic wracking his being. 'I'll get it. It'll all be there!'

Digger leant over the man's shaking body. 'I don't think you understand, dickhead. We need it *now*, plus interest…'

The man shook his head as much as he could muster. 'I-I can't. I don't have it.'

Seth grinned. *The prick was lying*. Phil had told them this twat was on his way back from a deal and had the readies on him. The fuckwit didn't have the nous to realise it wasn't the best idea to walk through the back streets with three grand burning a hole in his back pocket. Especially when he was late with loan payments to the wrong people. Still, that was this moron's problem, not his.

'You must think we came down on the last fucking branch!'

17

Seth roared, moving the barrel of the gun away from the man's face and stopping at his kneecap.

Realisation dawning, the man attempted to sit up, his eyes pleading through his ruined face. 'No wait! *Wait*! I....'

'Too late! You've lost your chance to walk away from this decently now,' Seth growled.

A high-pitched wailing noise emanated out of the remains of the man's mouth as one and then the other kneecap were blown away.

'Go through his pockets,' Seth muttered. *He needed to finish this. The fucking screeching coming from this prick's gob was setting his teeth on edge.*

Holding the writhing, screaming man down with one beefy hand, Digger extracted the wad of cash from a back pocket and grinned. *Phil would give them a nice cut from this.* He stepped away. 'The money's here. Let's go.'

'Ok,' Seth winked, swiftly unloading the gun into the man's chest.

Digger raised his eyebrows questioningly. *What the fuck was Seth doing? They'd got the money, hadn't they?*

Seth smiled coldly. 'What's the problem? His wailing was getting on my nerves, ok?' Without a second glance at the man on the floor, he began walking. 'Let's get a move on. I need to go and find Jane.'

Sighing, Digger followed Seth back to the van.

## Two

JANE PARKED IN AN immaculately pruned flower bed in front of the large, imposing white house and got out of the car, whilst Seth retrieved a crate of beer from the boot. They entered the house through an open door into a kitchen, sporting polished granite countertops, littered with piles of bottles, cans and lines of coke.

Jane wandered past a large bong smoking silently on a snooker table. Someone lay next to it, naked apart from an afghan coat.

Seth leant against the wall and watched Jane flit around the room. He loved looking at her, especially when she didn't realise he was watching. Shaking his head in an attempt to clear the ringing tones of a sitar playing from the top of the range stereo piping music into all rooms via built-in speakers, his brows furrowed together.

He knew how *he* felt but for all his bravado, even after a year together, he was still unsure how Jane felt about him and it was playing with his mind. Cutting two lines of coke on a table, he quickly sniffed one before beckoning her over.

Smiling, Jane snorted the line through the rolled-up fiver Seth handed to her and stretched on tiptoe to kiss him before disappearing back into the void of the large room.

Seth reached after Jane as she slipped away, wanting to hold on a moment longer, but forced himself not to follow. Instead, he concentrated on the projection of pulsating plasma on a far wall and gladly accepted the bong handed to him.

Finding a place on the floor next to Digger, he rested his head against the cool wall and humming along to the music, sniffed another pinch of coke. He needed to keep his head on his shoulders.

'Hiya!' Debbie yelled brightly, pushing her backside between the two men.

Digger rolled his eyes as he was forced to move up before his leg was crushed.

'Try some of this!' Debbie exclaimed excitedly, thrusting a small screw-topped bottle at Seth.

Taking the bottle, Seth turned it round in his hand. 'What is it? If it's that mushroom wine, I've already had far too much thanks!'

'No,' Debbie smiled, her eyes gleaming. '*This* is the elixir of life!'

Seth cocked an eyebrow. 'What? What is it really?'

'It's good stuff. I had some earlier,' she lied. 'Brings you up nicely. You're looking a bit stoned, so thought you could use some.'

'I'll have some!' Digger quickly took the bottle.

Debbie snatched it out of his hand. 'NOT YOU!' Passing the bottle back to Seth, she shot Digger a glare. 'You can wait your turn.'

Seth unscrewed the bottle. *He certainly was stoned.* That bong had knocked his bonce off and the coke hadn't touched the sides either. He definitely needed something to bring him back up. Raising it to his mouth, he tipped the contents down in one.

'Hey!' Digger growled, 'Where's my half?'

'I've got some more in the car. I'll get you some next time I get up.' The lies flowed easily off Debbie's tongue and she took in a deep, satisfied breath.

*All she had to do now was wait.*

· · · ·

JANE TIPPED HALF a bottle of mushroom wine into her mouth and let the rancid gloopy liquid slip down her throat. She picked her way around the room, stumbling over grinding couples on the floor. A collection of 60's head music pounded and she stepped across a man busily vomiting into a bowler hat, whilst a woman's bare foot rubbed against the side of his face. Another man sat naked and cross-legged sucking from a bong bubbling away on a gold edged coffee table, his hand pumping furiously on his cling film-wrapped cock.

Everything tilted at a strange angle and Jane's feet sank into the carpet as she pulled herself up the stairs. She took a swig from her vodka bottle to try and steady the rushing in her head and ignored the man rubbing himself up against the back of her skirt.

Laughing, she moved away from the swaying naked body, the man's concentration now locked on a moth flying around the light and mindlessly wondered how long the banging in her head had been going on for.

Suddenly out of the corner of her eye she saw someone who reminded her of somebody. *Somebody she didn't want to be reminded of.*

Flicking her head around quickly, she realised nobody was there. She must be off her bonce. *It couldn't have been him anyway, could it?*

Taking another swig of neat vodka, she walked unsteadily back down the stairs, the music pulsing through her nerve endings and looked for Seth.

· · · ·

SETH CONCENTRATED HARD on the bottle of whisky as he brought it to his mouth. The room was well and truly hanging on its axis and Debbie's voice sounded like white noise. He exhaled slowly as she droned on. He couldn't face listening to the boring bitch much longer.

Irritably pushing Debbie's hand off his thigh, only for her to immediately replace it, he shook his head and attempted to pull his consciousness back together. The song playing earlier in the car was repeating in his mind and he wished it would stop.

Sensing Jane's presence without seeing her, Seth opened his eyes and found he was right. Putting his hands out, she took them and he pulled her down astride him, seeing a smile twitch at the corner of her mouth when Debbie pushed her bulk up and moved away muttering.

Seth carefully moved Jane's hair away from her eyes and cupped her face gently. He said nothing - there was no need. She was sparkling like a diamond. As he pulled her closer and kissed her, he flew down a twisting, turning tunnel where death lurked at the end. He didn't care. He'd quite happily die for her. *Crazy wildflower! How he loved her.*

Feeling someone staring, Jane pulled away from Seth and squinted at the figure in the corner of the room, trying to get a clear picture into her spinning mind. With a jolt, she realised it *was* him. *That fucking imbecile. That piece of shit.*

She stared at Paul, his waist-length black hair hanging limply around his gaunt face painted thickly with makeup. *He was supposed to be under observation at the hospital, so why the hell was he here?*

Bile rose in her throat. She shook her head and looked again. It was *definitely* him. The hatred rushed back like a rollercoaster as if it were yesterday and she pulled her eyes away from the figure attempting to dissolve into the shadows.

'Who the fuck are you staring at?' Seth slurred angrily.

'No one,' Jane muttered. The last thing she wanted was Seth kicking off. Seeing Eliza wander over she quickly got up, needing to get away for a while.

Eliza and Jane moved into the garden where music was also being loudly piped. There were lots of people milling around, some twirling in circles, others lying on the grass naked and a few splashing about in an ornate pond. A girl Jane didn't recognise sat in a bush crying and pulling clumps of her hair out.

Fairy lights twinkled from the hedges, each with a kaleidoscopic halo and the grass felt like Astro-turf as it brushed Jane's bare feet. 'Come on! Dance with me!' she shouted, grabbing Eliza's hand.

Quickly stripping off, they gyrated to the music, spinning around faster and faster, whilst laughing and screaming. More bodies joined in and arms snaked around each other as they swirled, twisted and writhed whilst the beat went on.

Clint wrapped himself tightly behind Jane, his arms encircling her waist and his lithe body followed her moves. Eliza pressed herself up against Jane's breasts, her arms stretched up towards the sky and a woman with blonde hair ran her hands over all of them.

Jane looked up towards the stars as the darkness rushed down in torrents and she rested her head back against Clint's shoulder, feeling his erection hard against her naked back. His long hair fell over her arm as his lips trailed down her throat. Laughing, she span around and took his hand.

Suddenly dragged backward with force, she lost her footing and crashed to the floor. Scrambling to her feet, she looked around in shock. *What the hell was going on?*

Seth swayed in front of her snarling, his eyes spitting fire. Panting, he wiped away a small trail of spittle from his beard with the back of his hand. 'What the fuck are you doing?'

Ignoring him, Jane stormed towards the house, picking her clothes up as she went, but by the time she'd reached the back door, Seth had caught up and pinned her to the wall by her throat.

When he raised his fist, she ripped his hand away, her eyes defiant. Pushing him hard, he staggered back. 'Don't even *think* about it, Seth!' Jane hissed.

Stalking inside the house and quickly slipping on her clothes, she took a large slug of rum from a random bottle and glared angrily out the window, seeing Seth sitting on a low wall with his head in his hands.

Feeling eyes on her back, she turned just in time to see Paul making his way towards her. Grabbing her bag, she left the house as fast as she could and her car sped off down the driveway towards town.

• • • •

SETH WOKE FACE down in a bedroom with fuddled memories. The last thing he remembered was trying to transmit his thoughts via the ether into Jane's head, willing her to come back. He wouldn't have hit her. He didn't have a clue as to why he'd even raised his fist.

His head felt like someone was whacking it with a sledgehammer. *Who had Jane disappeared with*? *If it was that prick Clint, he'd fucking kill him!*

Scowling, he realised his jealousy had outstripped him yet again and now he was here without her. With some difficulty he turned over onto his front. His muscles felt flayed. *What was wrong with him?*

Another memory suddenly leapt into his head like a bolt of lightning and he sat upright, head pounding with the sudden surge of blood pressure. His eyes darted to the other side of the bed but there was no one there. *Oh God, it was all coming back...*

In his dream Jane had appeared in a floor-length blue satin dress. Her long raven hair flowed down to her waist and her arms were stretched out towards him. He'd kissed her. *It had felt so real.*

The shock had then hit him that someone was *really* kissing him, but the lips on his weren't Jane's. His eyes had shot open to find Debbie lying over him, her chubby face inches from his.

He'd jumped to his feet, but found his legs were unreliable. Crashing into a chest of drawers, he'd stared at Debbie, her face awash with shock and disappointment. 'What are you doing?' he'd screamed.

'I-I thought you wanted me?'

Finally standing upright without support he'd laughed incredulously. 'Are you *mad*?'

'You brought me upstairs with you.'

The vague memory of being manhandled up the steps by Digger and Tony flashed into Seth's mind. He'd looked at the flab hanging below Debbie's top with disgust and wanted to smash her head down her neck. 'I certainly did *not*!'

Debbie had looked like she was going to cry. 'But you *did*.'

'Just get out!'

Clambering off the bed, Debbie had wrapped her arms around his waist. 'Come on, babe?'

Gripping her wrists tightly, he'd pushed her away, revulsion coursing through him. 'Don't! I'm with Jane.'

Visibly flinching at the mention of Jane's name, Debbie had approached him again, her hand touching his chest. He'd thought he was going to be sick.

Slowly bringing his mouth towards hers, Seth had watched Debbie's bottom lip quiver with anticipation. He'd placed his hand around the side of her face, his eyes narrowing. 'I've told you once. I won't tell you again. Now get the *fuck* off me, you beast!'

With full force, he'd tightened his grip and pushed Debbie backwards over the bed into the door frame. Landing in a crumpled heap, she'd frantically scrabbled around like a beetle stuck on its back, abject horror etched in the pudgy mess of her face.

Seth's cold eyes had watched as she'd pulled herself up, grabbed her bag and ran from the room sobbing.

Putting his head in his hands, he sat on the edge of the bed, his heart racing. He scrubbed his mouth desperately with his shirt, still able to taste the fat bitch. *He wanted to go home.*

• • • •

AFTER WALKING with some difficulty to the King's Head, Seth staggered down to the basement where he and Jane had lived for the past year and found the light still on. Jane lay fully clothed on top of the mattress with stains of mascara down her cheeks. He felt a lump form in his throat. *God, he loved this woman.*

Sensing his presence, Jane's eyes snapped open. 'Decided to come back?' she slurred, trying to focus. 'Got bored with whoever you were fucking?'

Seth blanched. He wanted to get into bed with her, not have an argument, but he couldn't help himself. His brain felt addled and his temper frayed. 'Where were *you* when my lights went out then and what was all that shite with that prick, Clint?'

As Jane's glazed eyes narrowed, jealousy stabbed like a knife to Seth's heart. Turning on his heel, he began to walk back up the stone steps away from her, but the sound of bottles smashing against the basement wall stopped him in his tracks. His rage was at boiling point. *She was playing him, wasn't she? She knew full well how he felt about her.*

He stormed back into the room. 'What the fuck are you doing now?' he spat as Jane stood up and glared at him, her red lips parting defiantly.

Jane smiled wryly at the fire in Seth's eyes. *He was even more attractive when he was angry.*

Moving forward quickly, Seth's hand twisted in Jane's hair. 'Save your smiles for me, Jane. You're *mine,* remember. MINE.' He brought his mouth down crushingly hard onto her velvet lips and feeling her yield, electricity surged through him. Cupping her face with his hands, he pushed his body against hers, his kisses urgent.

As Jane's fingers wound in his curls and pressed her body back into his, Seth groaned against her mouth, his desire torturous. Controlling his ragged breathing, he pulled the ribbon on her top to reveal her small pert breasts, the nipples erect with want. Encircling one with his thumb, he took the other into his mouth and she moaned softly.

Freeing himself from his jeans, he found her mouth again and ran his fingers over the lace of her knickers. Feeling her readiness through the silky material, he quickly yanked them to one side and pushed her to her knees. Grasping her hips, he slammed into her. 'Tell me you love me, Jane,' he growled, his voice raw with lust.

Jane remained silent apart from her gasping breathing. She concentrated on staying conscious whilst waves of pleasure hurtled through her body. As Seth drove into her relentlessly, she desperately tried to contain her quickly building orgasm, resenting the innate ability he had to render her helpless for him within seconds.

'Jane,' Seth groaned, one hand moving from her hips to circle his thumb rhythmically on her aching clit. 'TELL ME!' Rotating his hips, he ground deeper. Feeling her tighten around him, he slammed into her harder and sank his teeth into the side of her neck.

Jane's senses sped out of control. Legs shaking as the burning waves of climax rose from the core of her being, she arched her back and cried out. Unable to control herself any longer, she exploded around Seth in waves of rolling pleasure.

Seth smiled watching Jane's body writhe. He loved having the same effect on her as she did on him. He wanted *everything* with this woman. *Marriage. Kids. The works.*

Digging his fingers into her hips, he groaned, the throbbing ache for release agonising. 'You and me against the world, Princess. Love you till the end of time, remember?'

With an animalistic roar as his own orgasm rushed through him like an express train, Seth spilt into her. He'd get his way somehow because he always did.

*Then Jane would remain his.*

# THREE

'HURRY UP!' JANE muttered to herself through gritted teeth and tapped her fingers on the steering wheel. She didn't mind doing this, but *did* mind that she'd been dumped with such a crap motor.

Why on earth they'd chosen that bloody Datsun Seth had won at cards last week for this job when they'd got a whole host of motors at their disposal was totally beyond her. *It had as much poke as a cow pat.*

She wasn't happy about the dodgy plates either. She'd got several which had already proved to be safe, but now not only was she driving a bag of shite, but one with crap plates. *Apparently, it was an emergency.*

Revving the engine, she sparked up yet another fag and rolled her eyes. *Come on, come on!* How much longer would this take? Her fingers drummed again on the leopard-skin steering wheel cover as she glanced into the rear view mirror. No police so far, but it was only a matter of time.

Spotting movement from the door of a terraced house opposite, Jane left the engine running and jumped from the car to open the boot. After the struggling, trussed-up man had been unceremoniously dumped inside, everyone got in.

'Floor it!' Seth shouted as he hopped into the passenger seat.

Quickly glancing in the rear view mirror, Jane slammed the accelerator to the floor. With a screech of tyres, the car flew off the kerb and swerved onto the road, whilst Digger and Dodge frantically tried to close the back doors.

Smiling, she took the corner at a ludicrous speed and raised her eyebrow mischievously on hearing the cargo in the boot slam into the wheel arch.

Reaching the lane to the woods ten miles away, Jane killed the headlights and manoeuvred the Datsun down the dirt track as best as she could by the moonlight. The contents of the boot kicked from the inside and she sighed, hoping this wouldn't take long. She'd had a long day.

After planting a quick kiss on Jane's lips, Seth got out of the car and Jane watched in the rear view mirror as his fist slammed down within the contents of the boot.

The men passed by the drivers' window dragging the unconscious man by his feet across the ground as he began his final journey and as they disappeared into the woods, Jane swigged from the quart bottle of vodka she'd had the sense to bring.

She rummaged blindly in her bag and locating some pills, she held the bottle up in the moonlight. Unable to decipher the label in the gloom, she shrugged and tipped a few into her mouth and sat back to wait.

• • • •

SETH SCOWLED AS they walked into the bar at the King's Head. The scruffy room was even gloomier than usual, thanks to the blackout blinds and tightly closed moth-eaten curtains used for hiding the nightly lock-ins. Despite the late hour, many people populated the blue upholstered bench seats and rickety wrought-iron tables.

He glanced at his watch. He was stressed. *Really fucking stressed.* He'd only got five hundred quid for offloading that bloke tonight. If people now expected him to deliver that sort of thing rather than collect a bit of cash or gear, then he'd put his prices up. Still they were back now and thankfully when Lee had clocked Jane reversing the Datsun into one of the lockups out the back, he'd started pouring the drinks.

From his place at the bar, Seth noticed that Dodge and Digger had moved to the dartboard and picked up the darts to have a game. Well, they could come over and get their own drinks, he thought angrily. *He wasn't a fucking waiter.*

Sparking a fag up, he willed himself to get out of this goddamn awful bloody mood and glanced at Jane sitting on one of the bench seats, putting on lipstick. He grinned, but then his smile fell. It wasn't just the money for the job that was stressing him out. It was more to do with he knew he should tell her what had gone on earlier, but didn't know where to start and just wished he hadn't spoken to that stupid bitch, Debbie, this morning or in fact, *ever*.

He'd guessed Debbie had a thing about him, especially after that party a few weeks ago, but he'd managed to completely avoid her since then - until today. He'd even got one of the others to serve her in the Barrels, but he hadn't thought in a million years she'd pull a stunt like this. The girl was totally cracked.

But what if Jane didn't believe him? She'd go berserk and leave him for sure. The story was feasible after all, so he couldn't risk it. *Not in a million years.*

Seth ran his hand through his hair. He should have told her about this in the first place, but it was too late now.

Lifting the drinks from the sticky beer towel, he walked over to Jane. Placing himself beside her, he took a gulp from his pint and languidly draped his right arm around her shoulder. Kissing the side of her head, he stared straight ahead, whilst absentmindedly fiddling with a lock of her hair.

Jane looked up. 'What's the matter?'

'Nothing.' Seth's smile didn't quite reach his eyes. He was worried. *Very* worried. If he didn't nip this in the bud, Debbie would balls his life up and then he'd have to kill her.

Taking another slug of lager, he wiped his mouth on his sleeve as waves of sickness washed over him.

He'd walked up from the basement into the bar this morning for a cup of tea after Jane had left for work and that stupid slag had literally jumped on him.

Debbie had looked up at him with her ghastly panda eyes and rested her hand on his arm. 'Are you ok?'

Jerking his arm away, he'd glared at her.

'Look,' she'd hissed, her eyes flickering slightly. 'I need to talk to you.'

'What about? I don't think I've anything to say to you.'

'Can we go to your room or something?'

*Yeah, right! Nice try!* 'No, we can't. If you've got anything to say, talk to me here.'

Debbie had bit her lip and glanced around the bar. 'I don't really want to talk in front of everyone.'

He'd looked at her with a bored expression. 'What's the problem?'

She'd touched his arm again. 'Please....'

Seth had sensed people beginning to glance over. 'Come over here.' Grabbing his tea, he'd walked to a small wooden table near the dartboard and sat down stretching his long legs out. 'Right. What do you want?'

Fumbling with her bag clasp, Debbie hadn't been able to look him in the eye.

'Well?' Seth had prompted, getting annoyed. He hadn't time for this.

'I'm pregnant.'

'And?' *What the fuck was she telling him for?* He hadn't been in the mood to counsel some dopey tart. Especially *her.*

Debbie had paused. 'And it's yours…'

Seth had laughed loudly. 'What in Christ's name are you talking about?'

'It's yours.'

*Was he hearing things?* 'How the hell can it be mine, you silly bitch!'

'Don't you remember? A few weeks ago? Back at the party?'

'Now, hang on a minute!' he'd yelled, before reining himself in and lowering his voice. 'Nothing happened!'

A small smile had formed on Debbie's fat lips. 'Oh yes it did. Don't pretend you can't remember. It happened alright and you fucking loved it!'

Seth had sat back in confusion. *What the fuck?*

'I'm most definitely pregnant and it's most definitely yours!'

'You must be imagining it!'

'It's *you* who's imagining nothing happened. You certainly weren't imagining it that night, I can tell you!' she'd whispered whilst Seth's fist had clenched under the table.

'Now, how will you explain this to Jane?' Debbie had smirked. 'Or shall I tell her for you?'

Standing up, Seth had swiped his pint mug of tea from the table, leaving it to smash on the floor. 'You fucking well leave Jane out of this. I don't know what game you're playing, but I wouldn't if I were you.'

Giving her one last look, he turned and walked out of the bar, slamming the door and knew that everyone had looked up when Debbie burst into tears.

• • • •

'PENNY FOR THEM?' Jane's finger traced the line of Seth's jaw through his neatly-trimmed beard, snapping him from his thoughts. 'Are you *sure* you're ok?'

Seth planted a kiss on her lips. 'I'm fine,' he lied. Fine was the blatant opposite of how he felt. He'd spent hours today going over the night of the party. Over and over and *over*. Maybe Debbie *had* been in there for ages and Digger and Tony had got it wrong? His forehead glistened with beads of sweat at the thought. *NO! He hadn't touched her!*

He wasn't sure what sort of game the tramp was playing, but he intended to find out and *fast*. He needed to tell Jane what had *really* happened, but what would happen if she didn't believe him?

Seth closed his eyes in frustration. He'd be the first to admit he wouldn't believe *her* if it was the other way around.

'Seth, what's wrong?' Jane asked.

'Stop going on, will you!' he roared, immediately regretting it. 'Sorry. I'm sorry, baby.' Seth ran his hand gently down Jane's face. 'I'm just hungover and tired. Another drink?'

Without waiting for a reply, Seth walked to the bar, feeling Jane's eyes on his back. She knew something was bothering him and he needed another drink. *He needed more than fucking one.*

As he waited for the drinks, he came to the conclusion he should forget all about Debbie. Why was he letting her stupid games bother him anyway?

*The stupid bitch was obviously mad.*

# FOUR

DEBBIE SAT ON THE park bench, sipping at a can of coke and wished she'd got something to put in it, like vodka. Or better still, Bacardi.

It had been a few weeks since she'd told Seth she was pregnant and he'd avoided her like the plague. To be truthful, she wasn't remotely happy how things had panned out. She'd thought it would be relatively simple, but it hadn't.

Picking at a chewed fingernail, she scraped at the chipped pink polish. She'd expected him to believe her, convinced he'd been fucked up enough from Ned's stuff to ensure he'd have had no memory whatsoever. But then, maybe he'd been bluffing? He might have just *pretended* he thought nothing had happened. Besides, if she'd had a bit longer to work her magic before he'd told her to get lost, she was sure she'd have successfully slept with him anyhow.

Debbie's cheeks burned with angry humiliation as she recalled that night. When he'd put his hand on her face, his lips an inch from hers, she'd been so sure he was going to kiss her. *God, how she'd wanted him.*

She'd nearly passed out with the anticipation of him pressing that mouth of his onto hers and then pulling her onto the bed.

Slowly peeling her clothes off and making love to her whilst whispering how much he loved her.

Instead, he'd crushed her face in his hand and launched her over the bed onto the floor. She'd seen the revulsion in his eyes. *He'd completely broken her fucking heart.*

She'd initially tried to convince herself he hadn't meant what he'd said or done, but slowly and painfully the truth had dawned. All that time she'd allowed herself to believe he wanted her, when he hadn't. *Ever.*

Debbie squirmed, feeling desire throb and realised angrily that even after everything, she still wanted him desperately. Tears welled up in her eyes and she fished a damp tissue from her pocket.

She'd locked herself away for two weeks, refusing to go anywhere at all. She'd even lost her job and although she was broke, she couldn't face looking for another one. What was she supposed to do? Go and work in the factory and see that Psycho Bitch every day?

She hadn't even told Tracy about her abject and total downfall. She'd explained the bruise on her face was where she'd fallen into the door, which was *partly* true, but gradually the embarrassment had turned to anger which festered like a sore at the base of every fibre in her body. *This was all Psycho-Bitch's fault.*

Debbie had known Jane since she'd arrived on the scene like a whirlwind five years before. Well, not *known* her, but seen her about and knew enough to know she'd got a screw loose. Oh yes, she knew *all* about Jane. Knew about all the stunts she'd pulled and the people she'd given a kicking to, even if no one else did. Well actually, everyone *did* know, it was just that no one would dare say anything in case the freak kicked off. Well, *she* wasn't scared of Plastic-Fucking-Fantastic, even if everyone else was.

She seethed. *Jane with her high bloody morals. Yeah right!* It was hardly a secret that Jane had done Paul over. Even the police knew this, but he was so bloody deluded he hadn't pressed charges. The poor guy had done nothing to deserve it - apart from love that psycho desperately.

Debbie felt the anger building further and her head felt like it was going to implode with rage. She'd even fancied Paul at one stage herself, but he wasn't interested in her, was he? Oh no, because he was far too busy with that cow. Now the poor bastard had gone stark raving mad, thinking he was a rock star or something. It was a crying shame.

*Jane needed to be locked up, not revered.*

When Debbie had the brainwave of telling Seth she was having his baby, it was all supposed to fall nicely into place. He was a decent bloke and even though he wouldn't remember the act, he'd have insisted on standing by her. He'd dump Psycho-Bitch and promise to look after her and the baby. He'd have been good like that, she just knew it.

Alright, so there was no baby. Not unless there'd been an immaculate conception, but that could have been easily rectified. It was only a matter of weeks since the party and once Debbie had got him, it wouldn't have taken him long to bed her. He was a man after all. Soon she'd have been pregnant for real and then it would have been plain sailing. It was easy to pass a couple of weeks' difference in the dates by having an overdue baby, wasn't it?

*Except her plan hadn't worked and worse still, he was still loved up with Psycho Bitch.*

Debbie glowered at a buttercup on the grass beneath her feet, wanting to grind its pretty little head into the ground.

Ned had *ensured* her that stuff he'd given her was the real deal and promised it would do the trick. Well, it hadn't, had it? *Not even slightly.*

Scowling, she wrung her pudgy hands together. Maybe she should go and see her brother. He'd have an idea of what to do. The trouble was she hadn't seen Ian for ages as he was too busy with that awful Maggie woman. Obsessed with her, he was and the final insult was that she was one of Jane's friends. *How typical was that?*

*Wait a minute…* A small smile twitched at the corners of

Debbie's lips. All may not be lost. It was only Seth's word against hers. There'd been plenty of people at the party that night who had seen him go upstairs and then seen *her* go upstairs, but had anyone actually noticed her come down? She didn't think so, sure everyone had passed out by that point.

Debbie picked frantically at her fingernail. It was time to implement the backup plan. She wasn't prepared to take this crap anymore. She'd serve revenge on Jane, big time and would enjoy it more than she'd enjoyed anything for ages. That bitch had a weak spot and she knew *exactly* what it was. For all Jane tried to hide it, she was as much in love with Seth as he was with her.

The way they looked at each other made her fucking choke. A manic coked-up version of Romeo and bloody Juliet. *Not for long though... Not for fucking long...*

A smile spread over Debbie's tear-stained face. She would ensure she ruined it. Jane's feelings for Seth would be her undoing and when it was all over, she'd get the Psycho-Bitch locked up where she belonged.

Starting with Tracy and her Aunt Barb, she'd very convincingly play the 'betrayed woman' act. She would, of course, *beg* them not to say anything to anyone. *Wasn't she humiliated enough as it was by Seth's rejection after he'd had his way?*

Obviously, neither of them would be able to keep their big gobs shut, therefore it wouldn't take long for word to get around and then the sparks would fly; Psycho-Bitch would bin Seth off for sure and that alone would be victory.

Once everything had been achieved, she'd suffer the most devastating 'miscarriage' caused by all the stress. That's if she needed to. She might be pregnant for real by that point.

Debbie rubbed her fat hands together, pleased she'd finally come up with a solution to rectify the situation. Finishing her can of coke, she smiled. The pub would be open by now.

# FIVE

SETH GRADUALLY OPENED his eyes with some difficulty. *Where was he?* The green curtains weren't theirs and the wallpaper *definitely* wasn't. He squinted his eyes against the sun shining through the open curtains and wiped his hand across his forehead, feeling like death.

Deciding he should look on the carpet to see if there was anyone lying on it, he turned and peered over the side of the bed, but the excruciating pain ramming through his brain put paid to that idea.

Gingerly rubbing at his temples, he grabbed a bottle from the bedside table and swilled the beer around his mouth to try and get rid of the foul taste. *Ah yes, this was Digger's place, wasn't it?* The vague recollection of taking a taxi after they'd left the King's Head last night seeped into his mind.

Seth turned over and focused on Jane curled up with her back to him, naked apart from the little skirt she was still wearing. Seeing the rip, he groaned inwardly. He hadn't been able to work out how to unzip it last night, so he'd torn it. Furthermore, they'd been so drunk they'd burnt fag holes in the sofa, and knocked curry face-down on the cream carpet.

Seth grinned shamefacedly. Digger was going to kill them.

Tracing his finger down Jane's back, Seth wished she'd wake up and do something with his hard-on. Impatiently he began kissing her neck and she awoke as he pushed into her. 'Morning baby,' he murmured, his hand teasing her nipples into hard aching points.

Hearing Jane's breathing quickening whilst she clutched at the cotton sheets, bunching the crisp material in her hands, Seth lengthened his thrusts. Moving his hand from her breasts, he splayed it over her stomach. 'So….' he growled, rotating his hips mercilessly. 'Isn't it about time I got you pregnant?'

Jane stiffened, her impending climax disappearing at the rate of knots. *Not this again.* Sighing angrily, she moved forward, freeing herself.

'Shit, Jane!' Seth yelped as his throbbing erection was forced from her velvety wetness to rebound against his stomach. Grabbing her hips, he tried to push his aching cock back into her. 'What the fuck's the matter with you?'

Jane sat up angrily. 'I've told you before, stop going on about babies!' she snapped. They were screwed up and lived in a basement for God's sake. Plus there was *far* too much grief going on. For all her bravado she still wanted the fairy-tale; for things to be the right way, not like *this*. She loved Seth with a vengeance, not that she'd ever tell him that of course, but a child? The way they were? It just wasn't right.

'Ok, OK! I'm sorry,' Seth muttered, turning on to his back. He stared at the green-fringed lampshade hanging from the pendant in the centre of the room. *Fuck. He'd misjudged that one, hadn't he?*

Running his fingers through his hair, he glanced at Jane and passed her a bottle of beer from the bedside table. Was it so wrong that he wanted to see her belly full of his baby? *Maybe then she'd marry him?*

Jane wished Seth would stop looking at her like that. Taking the cigarette he handed her, she gave him a small smile and got up from the bed. After rolling her eyes at her ripped skirt, she picked up his shirt from the floor and slipped it on. 'I'm going downstairs to get another drink.'

When Jane left the room, Seth lay back resignedly and exhaled smoke in a long stream. He ran his hand over his aching cock, frustrated. Resisting the urge to relieve himself, he jumped out of bed and pushed himself down rather painfully into his jeans.

Time for a line or a joint. *Preferably both.*

• • • •

IN A LAYBY ON a backroad, Jane swigged from a bottle of vodka and sighed. Pulling down the sun visor, she pushed back the cover over the little vanity mirror and peered at her glazed eyes.

After leaving the bedroom this morning she'd walked into the lounge and smiled seeing Eliza asleep on the sofa and Lee lying face down on the carpet in nothing but a pair of dodgy pants covered in curry. When she'd heard the floorboards creaking overhead, she'd realised Seth would be on his way down and an overwhelming feeling of needing to get away had enveloped her.

Grabbing a couple of unopened bottles of cider, she'd taken her bag and quickly left the house. She'd known she'd looked a right state in a ripped skirt and a man's shirt as she'd run up the street, but she hadn't cared. Quickly flagging down a taxi, she'd sped back to the King's.

Once she'd picked up her car, Jane had spent thirty minutes in a burger bar throwing up her hangover before parking up in a layby, unable to face going home where Seth would undoubtedly have been by that point.

Taking another long slug of vodka, she looked at the half empty bottle dispassionately. Coupled with the cider she'd drunk when she'd parked up this morning, the constant noise in her head would soon be gone.

She frowned. She needed to sort herself out. She knew she'd overreacted when Seth had said about getting her pregnant, but she was scared shitless. She didn't like having an Achilles heel and knew he was hers. How come she'd allowed herself to fall in love with him?

*There. She'd said it.*

Putting yet another cigarette to her mouth with shaking fingers, Jane exhaled loudly. She didn't like being out of control of her feelings and wasn't used to having emotions. That way of living had always served her well. *Until now.*

Oh, she knew how Seth felt about her, but she just couldn't bring herself to deal with her own feelings. Angrily raising the bottle back to her lips, she slipped a few more pills into her mouth and took a big gulp of the spirit.

*Fuck it. She couldn't help it.* She'd just have to live with the fact that she needed him as much as he needed her. It didn't mean she'd have to tell him though, did it?

Feeling better than she'd done all day, Jane snorted another fat line of coke off the dashboard and then fired the engine.

• • • •

SETH WAS CROSS. *Very* cross. It had gone 8 and there was still no sign of Jane. He hadn't seen her since she'd disappeared from Digger's this morning and she'd given no explanation for it either. She'd just *gone.*

He'd waited agitatedly the rest of the day and eventually, for want of nothing better to do, had put away fifteen pints since he'd got to the bar.

As he'd got drunker, he'd got angrier. His brain was driving him mental, betting she'd gone off with someone else. He'd been waiting for something like this to happen. Just *waiting* for it. *Fuck. Fuck. FUCK!*

With his blood pressure through the roof and adrenaline physically pounding through his veins, he looked down at his shaking hands and glared at anyone who dared to look in his general direction.

Sparking up another fag, Seth's eyes were suddenly drawn to the man lurking by the jukebox. *It was that wanker who thought he was Alice Cooper, the fucking prick.* He knew all about him and what he'd done to Jane. The man could certainly use a damn fine kicking, but there were more important things to think about right now.

Closing his eyes, Seth took a deep breath. *Christ, he couldn't take this! Where the hell was Jane*?

He pushed himself to his feet and forced the rest of his pint down his throat. That was his plan for tonight. He'd drink himself to death. *Right. Fucking. Now.*

Seth walked out of the bar into the empty toilets and leant against the cold tile wall. Punching the cubicle door off its hinges, it landed with a crash on the floor. His knuckles hurt, but he didn't care.

Turning on the tap, he splashed cold water on his face and from his reflection in the cracked mirror, he wasn't much impressed with what he saw. His green eyes were bloodshot and his beard too long. He looked like shit. *Total shit*. No wonder Jane hadn't come back.

*Sort yourself out Seth*, he muttered. Pulling a wrap from his pocket, he quickly cut two lines on the side and snorted them through a rolled up twenty. Sniffing hard, he felt the rush hit his brain. He needed to sober up fast because when Jane returned, he was going to ask her to marry him again and *this* time she was going to say yes.

Yanking the external door to the Gents, it slammed noisily against the wall and Seth walked through the bar towards the jukebox.

As he was grabbed around the throat, Paul stared up at the crazed man who had appeared from nowhere trying to choke him and saw nothing but pure hatred. *So, this was what the infamous Seth looked like close-up? This was one mad fucker.*

He sighed. He'd have to speak to Jane later. She wouldn't be happy to hear Seth had treated him like this, but maybe it would be the crux needed to prove she was better off without the nutter.

Paul's train of thought was interrupted when he was lifted off the floor and slammed against the wall. Struggling to breathe as the vice-like grip tightened around his windpipe, he blinked and a glimmer of fear radiated from deep down in his stomach.

'Listen to me, dickhead,' Seth growled, 'and listen well.' He smiled as Paul slowly raised his eyes. 'I'm going to kill you. Not now, but soon.'

Releasing his grip, Seth casually continued on his way as if nothing had happened and Paul slid slowly down the wall. He raised his hand to his throat, hoping his makeup hadn't smudged. It had taken him *ages* to get it right.

It was happening again, wasn't it? The room had gone from loud and clamouring laughing voices, to silence and everyone was looking at him. It was madness. If they wanted his autograph, all they had to do was say.

Pulling himself to his feet, he stepped back behind the jukebox where it was darker.

· · · ·

THE COKE HAD DONE its job and Seth was on a roll. He'd had a cold shower and pulled himself together. Admiring himself in the mirror he smiled, exposing his straight white teeth, happy with his newly trimmed beard and moustache.

Better. *Much* better.

Shrugging on a long-sleeved white cotton shirt, he slipped solid silver cufflinks through starched cuffs and pulled on his nicely pressed black suit trousers. Tucking his shirt in, he did up the silver buckle on his black leather belt and looked in the mirror again.

*Not bad. Seth, you can still definitely work it.*

Adjusting a slim grey tie around his neck, he slipped on his black double-breasted suit jacket and admired his wide shoulders in the reflection. 'Now turn me down, woman!' he muttered to himself.

Slicking his hair back, he tied it into a ponytail and walked into the bar with a spring in his step, feeling good. Tonight he would get *exactly* what he wanted and get it good. 'Lee, I'm going up the Barrels. You coming?'

Lee did a double take. 'Bloody hell!'

Eliza stared at Seth and drank in his wide back, accentuated by the shoulders of his jacket and sighed. She dared to glance up at his bright green eyes. *He was even more gorgeous in a suit.* She squirmed uncomfortably on the seat and hoped no one could read her thoughts.

Seth turned his wide shoulders towards the landlord, Benny, sitting with a group of regulars, his big belly straining against his beer-stained shirt. 'Benny, when Jane comes in, tell her I'm at the Barrels, will you?' he yelled.

Shaking his head in disbelief, Benny winked. 'Will do.' Even *he* had to admit Seth looked good. 'You scrub up well, son.'

Lee scowled and glanced down at his scruffy jeans and ripped polo shirt. Pulling Eliza to her feet, he wished she'd roll her tongue back in.

• • • •

JANE TANKED DOWN the road, her mind racing as fast as the speedometer. She needed to get home. *She needed Seth.*

Pulling into the car park, she abandoned the motor and ran into the bar, her eyes searching the room.

'Alright J?' Benny winked, signalling she'd got a drink in, whilst his other hand kneaded himself through his tan-coloured chinos. 'Fancy some lovin'?'

Rolling her eyes, Jane walked to the bar and picked up the freshly poured glass of vodka, downing it in one. *Where was Seth?*

'He's not here…' Benny said, reading her thoughts.

'I can see that!' Jane snapped as he refilled her glass. 'Where is he?'

'He's just this minute left.'

'Left? Why?' Jane's heart skipped a beat. Looking at Benny, she searched his eyes.

'He's gone to the Barrels with Lee and Eliza. Looking rather dapper, even if I do say so myself!'

Paranoia rushed through Jane's brain and she glanced at the

clock on the wall. *What was Seth doing? Why hadn't he waited?* Draining the refill, she walked towards the door, pretending to be happier than she felt.

As she reached for the handle, Paul emerged from behind the jukebox and grabbed her arm. Seeing his garishly made up face leering from the shadows, she recoiled instinctively.

'I need to talk to you,' he hissed.

'Get fucked!' Jane snarled, ripping her hand as far away as possible and disappeared out of the door. She felt sick just looking at him. *Why had she ever let that thing put his dick in her?*

Grabbing some clean knickers and clothes from the basement, she rushed up the stairs to the bathroom. Turning the shower on, she slipped under the water, relieved to wash the day down the plughole.

Drying off quickly, Jane pulled on a black basque, fishnets and a ruched velvet figure-hugging skirt. After reapplying her makeup and some thick red lip gloss, she stepped into her black stilettos. Popping a pill into her mouth, she ran down the stairs and out into the night.

· · · ·

SETH WAITED PATIENTLY at the Ten Barrels. He'd heard on the grapevine Jane was back. News always travelled fast in this town.

Swigging from his pint, he fingered the box containing the full carat diamond ring and smiled. It had cost him a fortune, but he didn't care. He'd get her without fail tonight. If she turned him down again, he'd have to kill her. Even that would be better than losing her.

Jane pushed open the double doors of the underground bar into the pumping music. She wanted to drink and dance, but most of all she wanted to find Seth. Her eyes flitted around, spotting Eliza and Lee frantically waving to get her attention. *But where was Seth?*

Spotting Jane straight away, Seth purposely turned his back

on her and lined up a drink.

With a jolt, Jane saw Seth and took in a breath. She'd have recognised him by his shadow alone. *Fuck, he looked good.*

As she reached his side, Seth's hand moved to the small of her back and Jane felt herself go weak at the knees. Chastising herself silently, she glanced sideways as his free hand pushed her drink towards her. Pulling herself together, she took the drink and turned to walk away.

Seth immediately swung around and grabbed her. 'Where are you going?'

'To the other side of morning,' Jane replied evasively, a trace of a smile on her lips that needed his kiss.

'Then I'm coming with you,' Seth growled and pulled her towards him. Bringing his mouth down onto hers he held her tight, his tongue working its magic in her mouth. 'Where have you been?' he rasped huskily. 'I've been worried.'

Watching Seth's brows furrow, Jane smiled and ran her hand down his thigh feeling his hard muscles underneath the soft material. 'Nowhere important...' *She'd explain later, but right now she wanted to enjoy herself.*

She traced her finger along his cheekbone. 'I can see your face again.' Jane pressed herself up against his body. 'And I like it….' *God, she wanted him.*

'Love you, Princess,' Seth murmured. Giving her a lazy smile, he picked up his pint.

• • • •

JANE SPENT THE rest of the evening unmolested by Seth's temper. He either propped up the bar, leaving her to do her own thing for once, or sat in the corner with Lee whilst she and Eliza danced on the tables.

When the lights went on at the end of the night, she was proud to take his hand as they staggered up the stairs onto the pavement.

Smoking a joint outside, Jane was chatting to Digger when she heard Seth shout her name. *Where on earth was he?*

'Look!' Eliza screamed, pointing.

Following Eliza's gaze, Jane saw Seth standing on the top of a telephone box. The crowd was eerily silent, waiting in expectation for the shit to hit the fan like it usually did. Walking forward, she wondered what she'd done this time. 'What are you doing, Seth?'

'Come up here!'

*What? Was he mad?*

'Digger! Get her up here!' Seth yelled.

Dutifully lumbering over, Digger grabbed Jane and hoisted her onto his massive shoulders. Her legs splayed either side of his thick neck and she clung on for grim death as he stood to his full height.

Seth span around on top of the phone box with his head towards the sky, his eyes closed and arms outstretched. His hair, now free from the ponytail, blew loosely in the wind.

Jane's heart beat like a drum when Digger lifted her up and Seth grabbed her arms, pulling her up to join him. He quickly lifted her to her feet and grabbed her face with both hands. She swayed, feeling very drunk as the fresh air hit and stared at Seth's intense expression. *How she loved him.*

Everyone was looking at them - including the police, who'd moved slightly closer, but so far were just watching.

With her eyes alight with excitement, Jane stared at the crowd, feeling alive. As they started cheering, she turned to see Seth down on one knee. *Oh God.*

Taking her hand, Seth's green eyes were serious. 'Well, come on then. Will you?'

Jane wanted to run her tongue across his eyelids, taste the salt of his skin. Melt into him. 'Will I what?' she teased, her heart thudding painfully.

Seth's eyes narrowed slightly but held his unblinking stare. He sighed impatiently. 'Ok… For you… Once more… Jane Ellerton, will you marry me?'

'Come on, don't be crazy!' She tried to pull her hand away, feeling embarrassed.

'Answer me,' Seth muttered quietly, a nerve twitching in his neck. '*Now.*'

Jane felt like she would pass out as he continued to stare intently, his eyes stabbing into her soul. It was completely silent as everyone waited for her answer.

'Well?' he whispered.

'OK.'

'OK, what?'

Jane broke into a wide smile. 'Yes, I'll marry you.'

A huge cheer erupted around them and even the police were clapping when Seth pulled himself to his feet, kissing Jane passionately. He slipped the gorgeous diamond on to her finger. 'Trust me,' he whispered.

Raising Jane's arms over her head, Seth lowered her over the side of the phone box. She smiled. She already trusted him more than he knew.

Winking at Jane standing on the pavement below, Seth launched himself off the top of the phone box. 'I LOVE YOU JANE ELLERTON!' Rolling onto the floor, he pulled her on top of him.

Ignoring the pain as her knees hit the pavement, Jane wound her fingers in Seth's hair, kissing him hungrily and started pulling his shirt from his trousers.

A policeman nudged them. 'Come on you two, get a room!'

Smiling, Seth and Jane dragged themselves to their feet and staggered back towards the King's Head.

## Six

AUNT BARB HAD BEEN steaming when Debbie had told her about Seth's rebuff after what had 'happened' at the party. She'd wanted to give him what for, but thankfully she'd talked her out of it, instead successfully blaming Jane for his attitude.

Since then, Aunt Barb had launched a hate campaign at the factory, messing up Jane's work and dropping her in it with the foreman. She'd managed to well and truly get her constantly in the shit.

Taking another crisp out of the packet, Debbie sucked her fingers and smiled. *It was the little things in life.*

Tracy had also been horrified by Seth's disdain and had wanted to have a pop at him as well, except she wanted to reason with him. Would he not even pay for the abortion?

Debbie scowled. *What fucking abortion?* As if she'd actually even *consider* getting rid of his kid! It was her ticket to everything, after all. Well, it would have been if there had been a kid…

A small part of her wondered whether she should have even started this. It should have been done and dusted by now and she wasn't sure how it was going to end. She certainly didn't want to be outed for what she'd done or it be known that she'd made the whole thing up because she'd be a laughing stock.

No, it *had* to pull off soon because she was starting to forget what she'd lied about and that alone was dangerous. She couldn't afford to balls this up. It should have been all over the factory that Seth had got Barb's niece pregnant, yet it appeared nothing had been said.

Debbie had been in the pub for the last three hours and was fairly drunk, but fully intended to continue until either her money ran out, or she could find someone who'd pay to replenish her glass.

Looking around the Black Eagle bar, she saw Paul in the corner staring glumly into his pint. His makeup was smudged and she was sure he'd been wearing that T-shirt for two weeks. Maybe she should go and speak to him to see if he was ok?

Glancing at her pint of cider, Debbie decided she'd just finish her drink first.

Tracy had hardly been able to wait to tell her that Seth had proposed to Jane in front of everyone. The thing was, Debbie already knew, but no one had noticed her standing in a shop doorway witnessing it. Neither had they seen the tears streaming down her face or heard her punch the window over the bloody cheering, had they? Not that it mattered. No one ever noticed her anyway.

It should have been *her* on the phone box with Seth, not Jane. Tying the empty crisp packet into a greasy knot, Debbie tipped the remainder of the cider into her mouth and scowled.

• • • •

PAUL WAS OFF WITH the fairies. He had no idea how long he'd been sitting with the same pint. It could have been days for all he knew, but he didn't care.

Pulling his eyes away from the Boddington's beer mat, he stared at the toothless old man looking at him gormlessly from the other side of the table with a long trail of dribble hanging from his hairy chin.

*For fuck's sake*, Paul thought, getting crosser by the minute.

He was a rock star, so why was he surrounded by these dregs of society? He should be living it up in swanky city bars with beautiful women pawing at him. *Something was obviously very horribly wrong with his life.*

He'd tried to speak to Jane about Seth's behaviour, but she'd told him to get lost. Could she not see how that lunatic had treated him? Did she not care? The overgrown orang-utan had clearly brain-washed her and he wasn't going to put up with it much longer.

'Hi Paul!'

*Oh no. Who wanted a piece of him now? Another bloody autograph? He really must get a minder or something. This was beyond a fucking joke.*

'It's me, Debbie. Remember? We went to school together.' Sitting down uninvited, Debbie struggled to keep her arse cheeks levelly balanced on the narrow wooden stool. 'I just wondered how you were, you know…. since, erm, you got out of hospital?'

Paul slowly lifted his head and looked at the woman blankly. Actually, he *did* remember her from somewhere. 'Hi…' his voice was flat.

'So, er, are you, er… ok now?' Debbie asked.

'Ok?' Paul looked puzzled. 'Yes, of course. Why wouldn't I be?'

'Oh, you know… all that stuff with Jane…' Feeling a little awkward, Debbie began to wish she hadn't started the conversation. 'The canal stuff….?'

Paul blanched. He didn't want to think about that. He'd worked very hard to ensure he hadn't. Very, *very* hard. He glared at Debbie. 'I don't know what you're talking about.'

Quickly realising she wasn't going to get anywhere with that subject, she changed tack. 'I wonder if we'll get invited to the wedding? Heard it's going to be a big one.' Fiddling with her new drink, she watched carefully for a reaction.

Paul looked confused. 'Whose wedding?'

Debbie smirked knowing this would set him off. 'Jane and Seth's wedding. Just about *everyone's* talking about it….'

Paul had heard about it alright, just hadn't wanted to believe it. Jane was supposed to be marrying *him*. How could she be marrying that shit-for-brains bastard? He wouldn't allow it. Not in a million years. He feigned indifference. 'Oh that…'

'Aren't you bothered? Thought you two were supposed to be getting married?' Debbie pushed.

Despite his pretence, Paul suddenly felt desolate. 'We are…. We were…. I don't know. I just don't know….'

Well, Debbie knew. She'd followed Jane and Seth the night of the bloody phone box proposal - at a distance of course so they hadn't noticed her. Not that they'd have noticed *anyone*. They hadn't even got half way down the street before they'd diverted down an alley.

Hanging back, she hadn't meant to watch, but out of morbid curiosity she'd forced herself. In fact, she needed to see for herself - to hurt herself more than she already hurt. Sticking her head around the dingy alleyway mouth, she'd crept along and concealed herself behind a jutting wall.

It had been disgusting. They'd been rutting like animals. Jane's legs were around Seth's hips, her skirt up around her waist and a stiletto dangled off the end of her foot. His suit jacket was in a heap in a puddle and his shirt tore as her fingernails clawed his back. He'd slammed into her repeatedly, pulling her head back by her hair and biting her throat. He'd been groaning her name over and over as he'd fucked her hard. '*Jane, Jane, JANE….*'

Much to Debbie's abject shame, she'd got turned on. In fact, she'd got so horny she'd felt sick and didn't know whether to be jealous or disappointed. She'd always imagined Seth to be a gentle lover, not the wild animal she'd witnessed, but either way, she hadn't been able to take her eyes off them.

She'd eventually run from the alley with tears pouring down her face. *Why couldn't it have been her?*

'I love her you know… I still love her…' Paul's voice broke the silence. 'I can't cope with it anymore.' A tear ran a furrow down his white face paint.

Realising Paul was staring, Debbie snapped back to reality. She knew she was drunk and should concentrate on what she was doing, but she couldn't help herself. It was just *too* tempting to offload everything on someone and here was that someone. *It was perfect.*

Smiling, Debbie placed her hand over Paul's. 'I'm going to let you into a little secret….'

Over the next few hours Paul listened avidly as Debbie got steadily drunker and told him everything. He could hardly believe his ears when she admitted what she'd done, her obsession with Seth and her utter hatred for Jane.

Paul now knew for certain that whatever anyone said, he wasn't *that* mad. This one was definitely a lot madder.

Studying Debbie's face, he realised it was *her* he'd seen in another doorway whilst he'd been watching Jane leave the King's Head the other night. Now it all made sense. She'd been watching too. The woman really was barking mad. He might have had a bit of a strange time lately, but he wasn't stupid by any stretch of the imagination. *Unlike this one.*

Trying to read Debbie's manic eyes as her mouth jabbered at one hundred miles a second, Paul realised with a smug smile that if she was being straight about all of this, then he could use it to his own advantage.

Getting up from his seat, he walked over to the bar to get some more drinks. *Oh yes, this would sort it. This would definitely sort it.*

'Thought you'd gone,' Debbie slurred when Paul returned with two fresh pints.

Paul felt saner than he had done for a long time now the light at the end of the tunnel had finally become achievable. 'I'm not going anywhere. Now, tell me the rest.'

Sitting quietly, he allowed Debbie to continue rambling. He'd come to a decision. He'd got nothing to lose. His life was going nowhere and something had to change. If that meant taking a risk, then so be it.

'Listen,' he said, getting Debbie's attention and watching as she raised her bloodshot eyes to his. 'I'll help you.'

There was a confused pause. 'What do you mean?'

A smile formed on Paul's mouth and he reached for Debbie's greasy hand. 'Exactly what I said. I'll tell Jane myself.'

Debbie's slack mouth fell open as she attempted to focus on Paul's painted face. *Had she heard correctly?* 'You'd do that?'

'I *will* do that. There'll be no more waiting then. It'll either work or it won't, but either way, something will happen. The worst case scenario is I'll get killed or at best, your plan will work. If it does, that means you get *him* and I get *her*...'

Raising her glass, Debbie pressed it towards Paul's and smiled, happier than she'd been for ages. 'Deal!'

## SEVEN

JANE GLANCED AROUND Mudflap's poky bedsit as she lowered herself into the bath for a most welcome soak. Closing her eyes, she let the warm water lap around her body. She wasn't confident Mudflap would keep schtum on her whereabouts, but she hadn't had much option. She'd had nowhere to go and furthermore, she'd had to trust *someone* to fetch her things. She couldn't survive with nothing and it had been *days* now.

After it had kicked off in the King's the other night, Jane hadn't cared where she'd gone. All she'd known was that she'd had to get out of there, away from the treacherous bastard she was in love with.

Jane shook her head. *Don't think about Seth.*

She just couldn't work out how that stalking bastard, Paul, had managed to get in for the lock-in, but much to her misfortune, he had. When she'd spotted him lurking in the women's toilets, she'd tried to walk out but he'd grabbed her arm. He'd said he needed to warn her about what Seth was really like before it was too late.

Jane hadn't believed what he'd said to start with, but as he'd continued, it all started to tie up with months' worth of unexplained comments. Stuff at work that had made no sense at the time had slowly slotted into place.

As she'd thrown her guts up in the sink, Paul had held her hair out of the way. Despising that he was witnessing her pain, she'd locked herself into a cubicle, willing him to leave her alone. She'd needed to think, but he'd kept talking, talking, *talking* and repeating things she didn't want to hear.

Paul had said what Seth had done to Debbie was well out of order. He'd *pleaded* with her to believe him and not to marry Seth - after all, the bastard had been told of the pregnancy months ago and *everyone* knew about it. What sort of a man was he, he'd said.

It had been that bit that finally tipped the load. *Seth had got that bitch pregnant?*

White-faced with rage, she'd shoved past Paul and slammed him into the door, failing to notice the wide smile on his face.

Seth had been busy putting chalk on the tip of his cue when she'd stormed back in to the bar and punched him square on the jaw.

Dropping the cue in shock, Seth had tried to grab her but she'd continued smacking him in the face. Snatching up the cue, she'd whacked him across the side of the head again, again and again. His face had been a mask of hurt and confusion, but his expression had only made her more livid.

Jane let the welcome warmth of the bath water lap around her body and soothe the pain her memories was causing. She desperately tried to stop the tears which were threatening to fall. Everything that had been said she could remember in exact detail. It had been burned into her mind.

'Did you think you'd get away with it?' she'd screamed at Seth. 'Did you *really* think I wouldn't find out?'

When she'd thrown herself at him for the third time, he'd successfully grabbed her arms and shook her, his right eye swelling and beginning to close.

'It's bollocks, I *swear,* baby. I never touched her. I never fucking touched her!' Seth had yelled, blood running from his split lip.

Jane had struggled to free her arms, feeling like she would have a heart attack. 'So you *did* know about it then, you bastard!'

'Please, Jane. It's not true. The woman's fucking mad!'

Raising her knee, she'd slammed it into Seth's crotch and he'd crumpled forward, retching. She'd then driven her knee into his face before screaming at the spectators. 'ALL YOU FUCKERS HAD A GOOD LOOK? YOU HAPPY NOW?'

Swiping a table full of drinks onto the floor as a parting shot, she'd run full pelt out of the front door into the night and didn't stop until she could no longer hear Seth roaring her name.

It had been irrelevant where she'd gone. There had been only one thing on her mind - which was to seek total oblivion. She'd gone off with the first person she'd bumped into. Her life had been removed in one whack, but it didn't matter now.

It was over. *Done.*

Jane stared at her toes poking out of the bath water and frowned. Then there was work…

She was unsure whether she'd even attempt to return to the factory. That bitch Barbara would be having a field day. If she hadn't already lost her job, it was only a matter of time and she'd no longer be able to let the old bag's snide comments ride over her head. She'd have to silence the cow once and for all.

She should have *guessed* Debbie was Barbara's niece. They were both fucking fat, ugly bastards, but one thing was certain and that was she'd find the bitch and rip her fucking head clean off.

Swallowing the lump in her throat, Jane looked down to where her engagement ring had been and pushed the unwelcome guilt for chucking it down a drain out of her mind. There was no time for regrets. *She didn't need the ring anymore.*

*Stupid, stupid bitch for letting your heart have a say*, she seethed. All of this had only proved Seth was like everyone else. *But doing the dirty on her with that piece of shit, of all people?*

With some difficulty, Jane sat up in the bath and began soaping her body down. Hearing the door slam, her heart jumped into her mouth. *Please don't let this be Seth…*

'Hello?' came a voice.

Jane remained silent, unsure whether to answer or not.

'Hello? Anyone here?'

'Is that you Owen?'

Pushing open the door, Owen walked in, his eyes nearly popping out realising Jane was in the bath, naked. 'Or, er, sorry… I was looking for Mudflap.'

Jane laughed. 'It's fine!'

'How are you?' Owen asked, sitting on the toilet lid and trying not to look like he was drinking in every inch of Jane's flesh, even though he was *and* she knew it.

'I'm ok, thanks. In fact, yeah, I'm fine,' she lied, eyeing him closely. *She needed to get back into the swing of things and he may well be the way to do just that.*

'Think it's time you came out for a drink, girl!' Owen grinned, almost able to read her mind.

Jane studied her toes in the bathwater and looked up slowly. 'Think you might be right!'

Hearing the front door slam once more, Jane stiffened.

'It's only me,' Mudflap called.

Wrapping herself in a towel, Jane cracked open a can of Fosters and walked out, breathing a sigh of both relief and disappointment to see Mudflap was alone.

Owen blew a plume of smoke slowly towards the ceiling as he fell into a chair. 'Well? Did you see him?'

Placing three bin bags of Jane's belongings down on the floor, Mudflap wiped his hand across his brow. 'No.' He fished his cigarettes out of his pocket. 'He's gone.'

A cold wave ran over Jane. 'Gone? What do you mean?' Unable to hide the panic in her voice she silently berated herself once more for being even slightly bothered and tried to deflect this by rummaging through one of the bin bags.

The truth was, she *was* bothered. *Very* bothered. She needed to get over Seth, but wasn't sure how to.

• • • •

SETH LAY FACE DOWN in the single bed at Dodge's house, struggling to come to terms with everything. He'd nowhere to live, but worst of all, he'd lost Jane. *For what? Fuck all.*

Even thinking about it made him want to smash the place up, but he had to control himself somehow. Dodge's missus had been good to him over the past couple of days, given the circumstances. She hadn't had to take him in - after all she hardly knew him.

After the shit had hit the fan at the King's, he knew he'd gone completely berserk because he'd smashed the place to pieces. First, he'd looked for that fuck-head Paul, knowing he'd had something to do with it, but the weasely little shit had conveniently disappeared.

Seth scowled. He hadn't finished with him by a long shot and would hunt the little cunt down and slowly rip him to shreds if it was the last thing he did.

Even more fuelled with rage, he'd then up-ended the pool table and most of the other tables before moving behind the bar and smashing every optic like a madman. Benny, Tony and a couple of others had attempted to drag him into a corner, but he'd turned on them, punching Tony in the face and head-butting Benny. It had not been good.

Storming down to the basement, he'd then trashed his and Jane's room and repeatedly head-butted the door until he was half-conscious. The others had found him collapsed in a heap in the corner with tears rolling down his face.

He'd offered no resistance when he'd been roughly thrown onto the street. He'd expected nothing less. Even though he'd apologized to Benny the next day, he hadn't asked to come back and neither had it been offered. He'd burnt his bridges at the King's Head but that was just how it went sometimes.

Gritting his teeth Seth grimaced, confident he'd worn most of them down over the last couple of days from gnashing them. However, on the upside, his eye although nicely black, was no longer swollen. *Fuck, that girl could pack a punch.*

A smile erupted, before quickly disappearing. Christ, how

the hell would he put this right? As for that piece of shit, Debbie, she was a dead slag walking.

Having already done his homework, Seth knew where she lived and he was going to throttle her. He'd *never* whacked a woman, but for that bitch he'd make an exception and after stamping on her ugly fucking head, he'd enjoy throwing her in the rubbish to be eaten by rats.

Anger seeped out of his pores like poison. He tipped half a bottle of whisky down his throat and wiped his mouth with the back of his hand.

For the last three days he'd put Digger and some other scouts out to find Jane, but unusually for them, they'd failed. No one seemed to know where she was. Either that or someone knew and wasn't talking.

Seth ran his tongue over the cut on his lip, his head thumping. He'd have to put pressure on some people if this wasn't rectified soon and then he'd make sure the whole shit house went down in flames.

*Then and only THEN would he kill that fat fucking slag.*

He stared at the dog curled up on the bed next to him and the whisky bottle which was virtually empty. He didn't feel even slightly drunk. His head was working way too fast for the alcohol to stick to the sides.

Propping himself up, he revisited the urge to punch the wall again out of frustration and instead cracked his knuckles, focusing on a damp patch on the wall at the end of the bed.

He frowned. *Maybe he should attempt to pay that fat bitch another visit?* She hadn't been in last time he'd tried, but she'd be in at some point and she wasn't intelligent enough to hide. He'd torture the fucking truth out of her and once she'd admitted it, he'd drag the lump of lard to Jane so she could hear the truth directly from the horse's mouth. *Then she'd believe him, wouldn't she?*

Sparking up his last fag, Seth pushed himself to the edge of the bed and extracted his boots from under a pile of crumpled clothes. Doing his laces up, he sighed.

When he discovered who'd been sheltering Jane, he'd teach them a lesson they wouldn't forget in a hurry. In fact, he'd punish everyone he possibly could until she was back where she belonged. *With him.*

On the upside, Digger had slipped him Paul's address, so he'd pay that twat a visit and find out exactly what his involvement was in all of this mess.

Standing up, Seth shrugged his coat on, muzzled the dog and walked from the room.

# Eight

SETH DROVE HIS Senator V6 around the back of the old red-brick factory which hosted a collection of cheap bedsits and was pleased to see a parking space free next to the back door. Glancing at his watch, he smirked. Nearly midday. Thanks to his homework, he knew Paul had his lunchbreak at 12 and would therefore be back any time now.

Sparking up a cigarette, he leaned back in the driver's seat to wait, then sat up slightly when a motorbike turned into the car park and pulled up in a wooden lean-to. He watched Paul dismount and take his crash helmet off.

Seth stifled a laugh watching Paul shake his hair and admire his reflection in the bike's wing mirror. He decided to give the prick time to get in before he made his move. *He didn't want to be rude now, did he?*

Feeling adrenaline pumping, he rubbed his hands together. *He was looking forward to this.* Glancing in the rear view mirror he saw the heavy metal door was ajar as arranged. *Well done Digger*, he thought, checking his watch again.

*Ok. That was long enough.*

Running up the stone steps with the dog following faithfully at his side, Seth pushed the metal door open. Slipping inside easily, he glanced around the dark and musty hallway and his eyes flicked from side to side, searching for number five.

Walking over the cracked floor tiles, he banged on the chipped wooden door with his fist, making sure he was out of the way of the spy hole. Not that the thick fuck would have the sense to look through it. Paul wouldn't be expecting a visit at lunchtime.

After a pause, the door opened slightly and Seth quickly shoved his foot in the gap.

Paul didn't get a chance to react when he was grabbed around the throat and manhandled quickly into the room.

Kicking the door shut behind him, Seth smiled with a glint in his eyes. 'Good morning, Paul. Got a moment?'

Unable to disguise his shock and horror, Paul wondered what he should say, but before he could think of anything, a fist connected with the side of his head. Crashing backwards across the room, he landed painfully against the wall next to the small kitchenette.

*Keep your head*, Seth chanted silently, determined not to knock the dumb fuck out straight away. *He needed answers first.*

Walking over to where Paul lay dazed, Seth squatted on his haunches and smiled coldly. 'Thought you and me could have a little chat. Bring me up to date on some things, perchance?'

Paul rubbed the side of his head as he pushed himself up onto his elbows and nervously eyed the dog. 'What do you mean?'

When Seth dropped forward off his haunches and slammed onto Paul's shins, pinning him firmly to the floor, his face twisted in pain realising this had been the entirely wrong answer. He now wished more than anything that he'd remained at work for his lunchbreak. Even being ignored and laughed at by the others on the shop floor would have been better than this.

Grabbing both hands, Seth bound Paul's wrists together in one fast motion using a large roll of duct tape pulled from his coat pocket.

Paul watched Seth tear the tape with his teeth and a horrible sinking feeling spread down to the centre of his stomach. Unless there was some type of miracle, he was well and truly fucked.

Flipping Paul face down, Seth bound his ankles, then placed his size twelve boots inches from his face. 'Now,' he said quietly. 'I suggest you tell me what's been going on. By that, I mean as to what you know about Debbie and her little plan.'

Dragging Paul by his hair, Seth lifted him to a standing position and then launched him backwards - his fall broken by his head smashing against the wall. 'I mean, like telling me *now*!'

Sitting casually on the end of the bed, Seth looked down at Paul lying on the floor. 'You see, although I knew about the stunt that slag was trying to pull, I'm still not sure how *you* fitted into all of it.'

Paul swallowed. How would he work his way out of this one? He'd had nothing to do with what Debbie had done, but he *had* been the one that spilt all to Jane. *Shit.*

Aware that Paul was thinking of something to say, Seth decided it was time to help him along and pulled a pair of long-nose pliers from his pocket.

Paul's eyes widened in fear as his boots and socks were yanked off. 'NO! Don't do anything stupid! I'll tell you what I know!'

Seth glanced up. 'First things first. I *never* do anything 'stupid.' Just helping you out because you seem a bit stuck for words. This should make it easier for you to tell me everything, shouldn't it?'

Smiling brightly, Seth moved to a small stereo and slowly flicked through a pile of LPs and picked one to play on the turntable. As Paul's first toenail was ripped from its root, his screams were drowned out by the sound of Pearl Jam.

Spilling his guts like verbal diarrhoea, Paul explained how he'd talked to Debbie in the Black Eagle and how she'd told him what she'd done at the party.

'And what exactly was she trying to achieve?' Seth growled, removing the second and third toenails.

'S-She thought you were doped up enough to sleep with her.'

'Yes, and....?'

As the remaining toenails on his left foot were deftly pulled from their beds, sweat poured from Paul's face. Shaking uncontrollably, he embellished further. 'When you didn't sleep with her, she had to rely you wouldn't remember and believe it was your baby. Then Jane would dump you.'

Seth rolled his eyes, his anger increasing. 'I suppose she's told everyone this version of events?'

Paul nodded and looked at the blood pooling on the floor around the mess of his feet. He felt like he was going to be sick.

Wracking his brains, Seth frowned. *Did this cunt just mention something about doping up?* Getting down closer, he stared darkly into Paul's watering eyes. 'What did you mean by 'doped up enough'?'

Paul panicked further. Dropping that silly cow in it was one thing, but he really didn't want to involve anyone else. For fuck's sake, at this rate he would be a dead man walking. He smiled wryly. He pretty much was anyway, given his current situation.

'What the fuck are you smiling at, you greasy bastard?' Seth roared, grabbing Paul's wrists and pulling off the thumbnail on his right hand.

Paul howled in pain and promptly vomited all over himself.

'YOU DISGUSTING PRICK!' Seth roared, removing the nail off Paul's index finger. 'WHAT THE FUCK DID YOU MEAN? TALK!'

Panting and sweating, Paul spilt the rest out. 'Ned. It was NED! Debbie bought the stuff off him.'

Seth sat back, genuinely shocked. The memory of Debbie handing him a small bottle at the party flooded back. *Oh, Jesus. Now it all made sense. No wonder he'd been so messed up, the dirty bitch. And Ned? That dim-witted gyppo? He'd fucking kill him!*

'Ned didn't know it was for you,' Paul gibbered.

'I don't give a flying fuck if he knew who it was for!' Seth screamed. 'That bastard still gave her the ability to mess my life up!' Seth was furious and wanted to take his rage out on Paul, but reined himself in. He still needed him for a while longer, at least.

Grabbing Paul around the throat once more, Seth pulled him to his feet and crushed him against the wall. 'But none of this answers *your* part in it though, does it?'

*This* was the bit Paul had been dreading. He'd hoped Seth had forgotten about it, but should have known better. His eyes darted frantically from side to side and with final humiliation, wet himself.

'I suggest you fucking well tell me,' Seth snarled, looking at Paul in disgust as the stain seeped through his jeans. 'Well?'

Taking a deep breath, Paul knew he was pretty much finished. *He may as well just get it over with.* 'I had a deal with Debbie to make sure Jane found out.' Closing his eyes, he waited for the inevitable. 'So, I told her…'

Paul expected to see stars, blackness or both, but didn't expect there to be nothing. He waited, but still nothing was forthcoming. Taking the risk, he slowly opened one eye to find Seth quietly scrutinising him.

'You do realise between the two of you, you've fucked my life up, but I'm sure that was exactly your intention, wasn't it?' Seth muttered.

Paul was unnerved. He'd expected Seth to go mental, not come out with something meaningful. 'I-I'm sorry,' he garbled. 'I-I still love Jane and I thought if you weren't on the scene, she'd come back to me.'

Seth stared at Paul. 'By rights I should kill you stone dead for what you've done,' he whispered. 'However, I'm not going to.'

Paul's body visibly sagged with relief.

'But,' Seth continued and tightened his grip. 'There's something you're going to do for me to put this right.'

'Anything. I'll do anything. I'm really sorry. I'll do

*anything.*'

Seth dragged him towards the door. 'You're coming with me.'

Paul nodded. The prospect of spending one more second with this nutter was not high on his agenda, but figured he'd got off pretty lightly, considering.

'First, one last thing before we go.' Seth raised his fist. 'This,' he smiled, 'is from Jane…'

As the punch shattered Paul's cheekbone, stars of pain shot through his body. He was dragged through the door and shoved fully-clothed into the shower down the corridor. Feeling even sicker as vomit and blood sluiced down the plughole, he hoped the duct tape would come loose in the water, but he wasn't that lucky.

Minutes later, Paul was unceremoniously bundled, soaked through and in agony into the boot of Seth's car. The last thing he heard before he finally passed out was the engine start.

# NINE

AT THE GREEN DRAGON, Seth sat uncomfortably, unsure of how he felt. He'd heard Jane was in the Ten Barrels, but despite the need to see her, he'd refrained. He was nervous. *What if she rejected him?*

His scouts had finally come up with the goods and unbeknownst to Jane, Seth had watched her go into Mudflap's place with that Owen bloke. His blood had run cold watching her kiss him. It had taken all his power not to launch himself out of the shadows, punch the wanker's teeth out and pull her towards him, wrapping her back in his life. Instead he'd stood silently torturing himself, his heart splitting in two.

He'd needed the last piece of the jigsaw in place before presenting her with the evidence, but now he'd got it, he would deliver. It would have to be tonight. *Time was of the essence.*

Meanwhile, walking hand in hand with Jane out of the Barrels, Owen was unable to wipe the wide grin off his face. He couldn't believe his luck. He hoped a repeat performance of last night would be on the cards because the sex had been mind-blowing! He just wanted Jane to be his girl now, but had to contain his eagerness and settle with whatever she was willing to give until she was ready. He'd put her off otherwise and he didn't want that.

As they walked with Eliza down the High Street, Jane attempted to shake off Owen's hand and hid her irritation with a forced smile. She knew full well she'd accepted the inevitable when he'd pulled his hard, muscular body over hers last night. Although he was a nice guy, she just didn't want him. *He wasn't Seth - but then nor was anyone else.*

She'd spent all evening watching the double doors of the Barrels, both hoping and dreading Seth would walk in, but she needn't have bothered because he hadn't. It had been over a week since she'd seen him and the fact he hadn't even come to look for her spoke volumes.

Debbie hadn't been seen either but that was ok. She'd bide her time and sort it properly.

Jane felt sick. She'd no idea how to get over him. Finding some uppers in her bag, she quickly swilled them down with a swig of vodka and tried to pull herself together. She needed to get on with her life. What there was of one without Seth.

Eyeing the queue snaking out of the chip shop, she groaned, not relishing waiting ages, only to find there was only half a steak and kidney pie left by the time they got served. 'Shall we bother?'

Owen tugged her arm. 'C'mon babe, let's just get in there. I'm starving!'

Jane protested as she was swung around and pushed through the doorway, but stopped dead in her tracks seeing Seth leaning against the counter. She saw a soft smile twitch in the corner of his mouth as he regarded her with amused eyes. His stare blazed into her and she concentrated on the lips she'd dreamt of kissing every night in his absence.

'Jane,' Seth murmured softly, then turned his gaze to Owen, who'd frozen in his tracks.

The tension was tangible in the crowded space whilst everyone waited to witness the kick-off.

'Alright, Seth. How you doing?' Owen uttered, his voice sounding like someone had crushed his balls.

Seth stared intently at Owen. 'Oh, I'm fine,' he drawled, smiling coldly. 'Apart from that you seem to have run off with my wife.'

Jane stepped forward, her dark eyes spitting venom. 'I'm *not* your wife.'

People shuffled uncomfortably in the queue behind, whilst Eliza sighed and waited for the inevitable. *It was always the same.*

'Oh, but you will be, Jane,' Seth whispered, bringing his face closer.

Feeling the pull, Jane wanted to melt into Seth's arms and bury her face in his soul, but she wasn't going to let him do this to her. Not going to let him do this at all. Except she was and she knew it and as he placed his fingers around her wrist, her heart raced.

'Jane,' Seth whispered. 'I didn't do anything and I'll prove that to you. Tonight. *Please?*'

*Go on… Beg, you bastard. Fucking BEG me*, Jane thought, but finding an inner resolve, turned to Owen. 'Right, come on! Let's forget the food. I'm not hungry.'

Owen faltered, not sure what to do. He'd seen the way they'd looked at each other and his heart sank. He knew he'd lost.

Seth twisted Jane's arm around and pulled her towards him. '*I'm* hungry, though,' he growled.

When Seth crashed his mouth down onto hers, Jane desperately willed her body and mind not to respond. But what was the point? This last week she'd died a little more every second she'd been away from him. She couldn't ever love anyone else like this.

Seth folded Jane in his embrace and she pressed herself up against his body, breathing in his scent. Her arms moved around his neck and she wrapped his familiar curls around her fingers. The background noise disappeared into a seamless void and little stars shot through the darkness behind her closed eyes, hearing only her own heartbeat thundering along in her chest next to his.

'Erm….' an apologetic voice came from behind them. 'Your food's ready.'

Pulling away, Seth turned to the man behind the counter and smiled. Taking the carrier bag, he turned to Jane and holding out his hand, raised an eyebrow.

Giving Owen an apologetic shrug, Jane took a deep breath and took Seth's hand.

• • • •

SETH GLANCED AT JANE. Not a word had been uttered in the five minutes since they'd left the chippy. He hadn't expected it to happen like this. He'd planned on psyching himself up beforehand. Seeing her unexpectedly had caught him off guard, but he was extremely pleased that it had.

Gripping her hand tighter, they carried on walking and he sneaked another look at her. It was taking all his power not to go berserk, however all he really cared about at this point of time was her, so that would have to wait.

'Why have you been avoiding me?' Jane snapped, staring at Seth's clenched jaw.

'I wanted to get enough proof that it was lies before I came for you,' Seth sighed. He hadn't wanted to discuss this until he'd shown her. He knew it would cause another argument.

'Yeah, and you haven't been able to? There's a surprise….' The hurt of the past week flooded back through Jane's veins and she yanked her hand away from his. 'Look, this is a mistake.'

'NO!' Seth pulled her around by her shoulders. 'It's *not* a mistake. You're NOT leaving me again, Jane.' Bringing his lips down onto hers, he felt her body respond to his hunger. *God, he'd missed her.*

Jane knew resistance was futile. She ran her hands down Seth's back as his lips bruised hers, his want for her hard against her stomach. 'Where are we going?' she asked breathlessly, pulling her mouth away from his. 'Thought you were living at Dodge and Mary's?'

Seth gave her a slight smile. 'Ah, so you knew where I was?'

'I heard, yes, but I wasn't exactly going to come running after you got someone pregnant, was I?' Jane spat, her eyes narrowing.

'At least I didn't fuck some muppet!' Seth roared, spitting fire. *Shut up! Shut up! SHUT UP*, he screamed to himself. He'd promised to keep a lid on it but was failing miserably.

'You bastard!' Jane screamed, slapping Seth hard around the face.

'Stop this NOW!' Seth slammed her against the railings and held her arms by her sides. 'You listen to me, Jane and you listen good. I won't be punished for something I haven't done.'

Jane fixed his glare with one of her own, but felt unable to walk away. She didn't *want* to walk away.

'It's a set up! That Debbie's fucked in the head and I'll prove it. I love you. Love you more than anything. Till the end of time, Jane. Remember?'

Jane searched Seth's eyes. She wanted to believe him. *Really* wanted to believe him.

'I'd die for you, baby,' Seth whispered softly, finding Jane's mouth.

Clinging onto Seth, Jane's hand moved to his face, her fingers running over his skin needing to touch him, but he stopped her and pushed a wrought iron gate open.

'Why are we going in here?'

'My absolution, Jane, that's why...'

Jane stared at the large detached Victorian house on one of the town's poshest streets and looked thoroughly confused.

'House sitting,' Seth winked. 'Friend of a friend.' Grinning, he led her up a small path under an archway covered with foliage and stopped at a dark green front door.

As Seth opened it with a key from his pocket, Jane followed him into the wide entrance hall. Flicking on the light, she squinted up at the chandelier hanging from a high pendant. 'Very nice,' she murmured, slipping off her jacket.

Seth ran his eyes over her, the ache in his groin relentless. 'Drink?' As he grabbed her hand, his eyes narrowed seeing her ring was missing. *He'd deal with that later.*

Opening a thick oak door with a steep set of steps leading down to a cellar, he smiled. 'Come with me.'

Walking down the stone steps, Jane gasped. It was a wine cellar. Judging by what could be seen from the rows of bottles in their individual holes in the bespoke wooden compartments, it was obviously horribly expensive.

Seth grabbed two identical expensive vintage wines and placed them on an upturned keg.

'Start as you mean to go on!' Jane laughed and lined up two long lines of coke on a marble table next to a group of cask barrels.

Seth took the rolled up note Jane handed him and took a deep sniff of cocaine. He placed his hands on her shoulders, his lips brushing gently against her earlobe. 'Now baby, there's something I need you to see.'

'What's that?' Jane didn't particularly want to look at anything else apart from him, but he moved to the far side of the room. He opened a small wooden door set in a recess which dragged noisily against the stone floor, revealing a dark, narrow cupboard.

Leaning against the marble table, Jane watched Seth bend down and disappear inside. She peered into it but could see nothing but darkness. After a moment or two, Seth backed out of the small cupboard pulling a bloodied and trussed up Paul by the hair across the floor.

'What the fuck is this? Is this a wind up?' Jane screamed, quickly taking in the state of Paul's hair stuck to his head and the dried blood crusted around his bound hands and feet.

She could not believe she'd come to some stranger's gaff with Seth, only out of all the people to be concealed in a fucking cupboard in a huge wine cellar would be *Paul*.

Seth pushed Paul forward and he landed in a heap a few feet from Jane. 'No, this isn't a wind up. Our *friend* here has some stuff he wants to bring you up to speed with.'

Jane glanced at Seth and then looked back at Paul. She

folded her arms and sat on the table. 'Ok. I'm listening...'

With a concerted effort, Paul turned onto his side and was dragged into a sitting position against the wall.

Jane listened with mounting anger as Paul spoke and felt sick, realising she should have trusted Seth. *She was going to crucify that fat bitch.* 'And you told me all of that to split us up and back up Debbie's bullshit?'

Watching Paul nod, she walked over slowly and stared into his haunted eyes. 'But why?'

A tear ran down Paul's bruised face, his broken cheekbone horribly swollen. 'Because I wanted you to dump *him*,' he glared at Seth. 'I want you back, Jane. I love you...'

Jane stared at Paul incredulously as his bloodied hands raised in an attempt to touch her. 'But I don't love you. Never have and *never* will.' Batting his hands away, she punched him hard in the mouth.

Paul spat blood and his front teeth out onto the floor as Jane launched at him again.

Seth gently pulled her to one side. 'Don't waste your energy.' Dragging Paul to his feet as he frantically tried to scramble out of the way, he swiftly brought his head down onto the bridge of Paul's nose and dropped him in to a heap on the floor. 'Thanks for spilling your guts for the second time today, wanker! NOW SHUT THE FUCK UP!'

Turning back around, Seth shook his head. His voice was soft as he tilted Jane's face up towards his. '*Now* do you believe I didn't do it?'

Jane nodded. 'I'm sorry...'

'No need,' Seth smiled, exhaling with relief.

'I need to go and sort that bitch out,' Jane muttered savagely.

'Not right now, you don't!' Keeping his gaze on her, Seth expertly opened another bottle of wine and lifted the bottle to Jane's lips. Tipping it up, the red wine ran in rivulets over her chin, her throat and down her top.

Jane gasped, swallowing as much as possible. Grabbing the bottle, she laughed as it smashed on the flagstones.

Hearing Paul groan from his place on the stone floor, Seth turned towards him, 'Shut up, dickhead!'

He'd instructed Digger to appear at some point over the next day or two to remove Paul and give him a 'top-up' pasting on the off chance he needed one. He'd then be dropped off somewhere to pick up his shattered life, so that part was sorted.

All that was important now was Jane and getting their life back on track. *Everything else was irrelevant.*

Seth took a long draught of wine whilst Jane undid the buttons of his shirt. Pulling her top over her head, he encircled her nipple with his finger before teasing it with his teeth as she kneaded the tight muscles across his shoulder blades and slipped his shirt off.

'Now I'm going to fuck everyone else away, baby,' he murmured.

Lifting Jane onto the edge of the marble table, Seth trembled with the need to possess her. *To claim her back as his.*

Pushing her backwards, he freed himself from his jeans and raised her knees up towards her chest. Sliding inside easily, he groaned, feeling her close around him.

'I've missed you,' Jane gasped, unable to help herself.

Seth smiled. 'Let me refresh your memory.' Thrusting in delicious long, slow movements he drove deeply, grinding against her expertly with each stroke.

Raising her hips higher, Jane gripped his buttocks. She'd missed him alright. *All of him.*

'Let's fuck it all away, baby. Come on, come with me.' Seth felt his orgasm rush up on him. This would be a quick one for both of them.

As their moans of pleasure filled the space, Paul sobbed loudly behind them.

· · · ·

AFTER LOCKING PAUL in the cellar, Seth and Jane moved to a dimly-lit, sumptuous attic bedroom. Its huge skylight was surrounded with heavily embroidered drapes of many colours.

Seth sat cross-legged on an intricately carved emperor bed, covered with a thick dark purple velvet bedspread in the centre of the room and rolled a joint. He eyed Jane kneeling naked next to a music system that rested on top of a carved Indian bench.

Slicing off the foil wrapped around the head of a bottle of Bollinger with his blade, he twisted the wire cage away from the cork and prised it up with his thumbs.

As the cork slammed into the far wall with a bang, Jane looked round momentarily to check neither of them had been shot. *Weirder things had happened.*

Seth couldn't take his eyes off Jane as she selected an album and then jumped on the bed to snort a line of coke. The need to bury himself in her again was intense. He lifted her on top of him and enfolded her in his arms, wrapping himself around her body and holding her tight.

He'd no idea how long they lay there for, it may have been minutes or hours. Time stood still when he was with her and was of no importance or consequence. Like a continuous acid trip, his mind was overloaded with desire, love and madness. He needed Jane running through his veins.

Seth trailed his fingers down her body and slipping into her again, picked up a gentle pace. The music reverberated around the high-ceilinged room as she dug her long nails into his back, pulling him deeper. *This was good. Real good. Christ, how he loved her.*

Seth shuddered with pleasure but forced himself to keep it slow. He wanted to watch her face as he gave her the best prolonged orgasm ever. *He needed to remind her that she was his.*

Feeling her begin to pulse around him, he kept the pace leisurely, slowly bringing her closer and closer.

As she arched her back, he traced a line down her jaw with his tongue, stopping at her mouth. Biting her lip, Seth's breath hitched sensing the first waves of her orgasm approaching. When she cried out into his mouth, it took all his power not to join her.

'Oh God,' Jane cried, finding herself immediately building

into another climax when Seth ramped the pace up. As it exploded around her, she went into freefall and didn't come down. It ran and ran and ran.

'Seth...' The uncontrollable rushing in her head was getting louder. Her senses were on fire and she came up again, like a roller coaster.

Seth watched Jane's total abandonment into full chaos. Feeling her muscles tighten around him he fell over the edge and with an animalistic growl, came hard and long, whilst Jane released herself around him once more.

After what seemed like an eternity, they collapsed in a pile of sweat.

# TEN

MAGGIE WAS A BAG OF nerves. She'd always been over-emotional, but this crap with Ian had really taken the wind out of her sails. It had only been a week since she'd found the courage to leave him, but since then, she'd been constantly on edge waiting for him to show up.

She'd thought him gorgeous with his long, straight dark hair and big bike, but his excessive dope intake had made him paranoid. He'd given her constant grief about everything - from what she wore, to where she went. Eventually she'd believed she was fat, ugly and stupid and that no one liked her.

It had finally got to the point where it had just been easier to stay in the flat, watching him and his revolting mate, Teddy, getting stoned and drunk whilst listening to Gong over and over.

Maggie had been with Ian for over a year and had spent most of that time like a slave in his crappy flat with its ripped carpet, moth-eaten sofa bed and light-green peeling wallpaper. A bare forty watt light bulb hung from the damp artexed ceiling in the centre of the room and the bright orange and green flowery-patterned curtains draped from the sagging rail held together in the middle with sellotape.

The kitchen had been part of the main room and consisted of

a two-ring camping stove balanced on a melamine-topped free standing kitchen cupboard and a rusted metal sink sunken into the top of another. The fridge had stood randomly in one corner of the lounge and the only form of heating was a two-bar electric plug-in heater that rarely worked.

*Who'd needed drugs*, Maggie thought bitterly. Five minutes in that place was enough to send anyone off their head. She'd hated that fucking flat. *Hated* being there and thanks to Ian, her free spirit had gradually disappeared. *She'd felt like she was going mad.*

Then there was his horrible sister, who never ever hid her hatred. It was almost like she was *jealous* of Maggie's relationship with Ian. The two of them used to disappear into the bedroom for hours to talk. Probably about *her*, Maggie thought angrily, shuddering. She'd tried to go in once. After all it was *her* bedroom too, but the door had always been locked. Thankfully, she didn't have to put up with any of it now.

Ian had always said he'd kill her if she ever left - not that he'd thought she'd have the guts to, of course. Well, she had now, hadn't she? *Thanks to Jane...*

Maggie had missed her friend desperately in the year she'd been holed up with Ian. When she'd met Jane two years previously, she'd been instantly drawn to the confident wild girl in the corner of the Ten Barrels who everyone wanted a piece of. They'd clicked straight away and she'd been taken on a crazy roller coaster ride. The downside was there was *no way* she could keep up with her. The amount of stuff that girl put away was legendary, to say the least.

Jane would pop all manner of potions, powders and pills 'just to see what would happen,' but if there was ever any grief, Maggie could rest assured she'd appear from out of nowhere, quickly despatching whoever was kicking off with a quick smack to the jaw, a head-butt, or a timely chuck down the stairs. In fact, Jane had got her out of so many scrapes and bad situations she'd lost count and now she'd come up trumps again.

She knew Jane had previously tried to find her, but Maggie

hadn't had the chance to tell her exactly where she was living when she'd moved in with Ian. She'd seen her from the window asking around though. She'd tried to get her Jane's attention, that was until Ian had dragged her away from view. None of the neighbours had probably even realised she was there. Not that they'd have cared anyhow. It was like that round there.

Ian hadn't wanted her having anything to do with her 'old life.' Apparently, she didn't need mates now she'd got him and it had only been by chance Jane had been outside that day when Ian and Teddy had smoked so much gear, they'd passed out and she'd managed to call out of the window. After a whispered conversation, Jane had promised she'd get her out of there and true to her word, within a week, she had.

Admittedly, Maggie knew she probably wouldn't ever have left if Jane hadn't sorted it by buying her a caravan and towing it onto the traveller's field. Ok, so the van was falling apart and she got the creeps at night, but at least the other travellers were close by, so it wasn't like she was completely on her own.

She glanced towards Ned and Zed sitting a few yards away attempting to cook something over the campfire. Ned was so stoned he was putting food around the edge of the pan rather than in it.

Turning away to light a cigarette, Maggie tried not to laugh, but picking up the scent of burning, she turned back to the fire where thick, acrid smoke rose from the contents of the pan. Zed had wandered off and was having an in-depth conversation with a tree and Ned had passed out.

A fat bloke with matted green hair was propped against one of the old camper vans playing with himself, not giving a fuck it was broad daylight. He was surrounded by people taking it in turns to drunkenly throw stones at him and he appeared not to notice the rocks bouncing off the top of his head. He just continued staring at the sky whilst his arm stretched over his large belly, his hand pumping furiously up and down.

Maggie grimaced and turned away. *There were just some things that were just too gross.*

She tried to remember whether she'd got any dope left. She could do with a bit of a toke to calm her nerves. Picking at her fingers, she absentmindedly wondered what Jane and Seth would do now.

Apparently, they'd been living in the car since being kicked out from where they'd been staying. The police turning up and arresting them for something to do with a house had been the last straw, it seemed. They'd already been keeping the family up half the night with their constant slanging matches and noisy sex. The dog had howled all day and the kids had freaked out by the constant stream of 'weirdos,' as the woman had put it, which were coming round. They'd been given their marching orders and that had been that.

Maggie couldn't help but smile. They should have put the rest of the money Jane had won when she'd bet her car at poker on a deposit for a flat. Instead, true to form, they'd gone on a bender and blown the entire lot in one weekend. They'd drunk the pubs dry, snorted enough coke to finish off a football team and then rolled up to the poshest hotel in town in the middle of the night, demanding a room. They'd spent the remainder of the weekend taking more drugs and racking up complaints from the rest of the guests and when they'd left, they'd grabbed as much stuff as they could carry and jumped out of the window.

Admittedly, she didn't know Seth too well as she'd disappeared with Ian not long after he'd got with Jane, but knew he was just as crazy. Those two loved each other passionately, but their combined volatile personalities were dangerous. It was unsurprising people hung around to see what would happen when they kicked off. *It was like a fucking film.*

Maggie's attention was suddenly diverted by Seth's Senator roaring into the field. Watching Jane emerge from the car, she ran over.

'Brought you a smoke,' Jane grinned, hugging Maggie and handing her a large reefer. 'Let's get it going.'

Smiling, Maggie grabbed Jane's hand as they walked across the field. 'What you doing here?'

Jane glanced back at Seth who was following them. 'Oh, just passing….'

Maggie looked nervously at Seth. He didn't look very happy. 'Is everything alright?' she asked Jane timidly. 'Seth looks a bit… erm…'

Jane smiled. 'Yeah, of course. He's fine. Don't worry about him, he's just going something he needs to sort out.'

Nodding politely at Maggie, Seth continued towards the campfire where Ned was lying, unsuspecting that his deliverance had arrived.

# ELEVEN

JANE LEANT BACK IN the car seat and blew smoke slowly out of her lungs. The music playing on the stereo was tripping her out and she needed to change it, but couldn't cope with rummaging around in the glove box for a different tape.

Looking out of the window into the gloom of the night, she stared at the towering chimneys from the derelict factory opposite that cast long-fingered shadows onto the car park and sighed. They seriously needed to find somewhere else to crash. Hopefully it wouldn't be too long before they'd get the money for a flat.

Glancing over at Seth in the passenger seat, Jane smiled. His eyes were closed and his legs were stretched out as far as possible. Zoned out, a soft smile played on his lips and the moon cast weird reflections on his face making it appear to sparkle. Even after all this time, she found him beautiful.

One thing was for sure and that was she couldn't smoke any more dope. She was at risk of falling asleep and they had stuff to do. As Bob Dylan's voice continued to thrum through her body, she fiddled with a tassel on her jacket and desperately tried to concentrate.

At least she wasn't working at the box factory anymore.

She'd binned off her new job after a week, courtesy of the perverted foreman who'd tried to stick his hand down her top. He was probably now on Seth's list of things to deal with, but she didn't care either way. The only score she was hell bent on settling right now was with Debbie and being as Ned had now been offloaded, it was *her* turn to shine.

She'd spent the last few days clocking Debbie's movements and as far as she was concerned, it was game on as soon as possible. In the meantime, she'd gone for an interview for a receptionist. *Well, why not? She'd see what happened.*

Taking a swig of vodka from the bottle, Jane banged down a couple of uppers and nudged Seth.

Seth was off in a world of his own and inwardly accepted they shouldn't have smoked the fourth joint. Squeezing Jane's hand, he tried to pull himself together.

Clumsily he pulled her over the gearstick and ran his fingers down her face. 'Let's get some fresh air,' he murmured against her lips.

Teasingly nibbling his bottom lip, Jane opened the passenger door and fell laughing onto the grass verge. Rolling himself out of the car and on top of her, Seth pushed her knickers deftly to one side.

• • • •

IN THE HIGHWAYMEN'S Chapter House, Phil sat with his back to the bar and a pint of lager in his hand. He glanced between the thick steel bars over the window and fingered the roll of money in his pocket, hoping Seth would be on time. The boys had more work for him if he wanted.

Running his thick fingers over the stubble on his shaved head, he glared at the pair of Capuchin monkeys in their glass-fronted case set into the wall. He hated monkeys at the best of times and this pair were looking at him. He didn't like anyone staring at him, *especially* monkeys.

Quickly moving his eyes away, he resumed gazing out of the window and checked his bike parked in the middle of the long row outside the converted semi-detached house. Clocking the cop car cruising slowly past for the third time in the last ten minutes, he hoped Seth wouldn't be too drunk when he rocked up. He didn't want him getting a tug.

· · · ·

'SETH, WHY DO WE have to go tonight?' Jane whined as they pulled into the estate. 'I know you've got to pick the cash up but couldn't that wait until tomorrow?'

Turning towards her, Seth smiled. 'You'll see. It's a surprise.'

Jane wasn't convinced. It wasn't that she minded going to the Chapter House. In fact, she loved it there and thought the world of Phil. It was just she could have done with another round of the roll-around on the grass. The reduction in their sex life since living in the car was getting frustrating to say the least.

As they pulled up alongside the collection of heavily chromed-up machines lined up outside the Chapter House, she wondered whether they could book into a hotel for a couple of days with the money they were collecting.

Phil opened the door and grinned, exposing his gold teeth. Stretching his arms out towards Jane as they walked up the narrow garden path, he swept her backwards and planted a sloppy kiss on her mouth.

Smacking Seth on the back, he pumped his outstretched hand. 'Come in, come in. Let's have a fucking beer or ten, eh?'

Following Phil inside, Seth watched Jane hug some of the other Highwaymen and pulling up a stool, he eyed the monkeys in their glass prison. 'See the monkeys are still watching you, Philip?'

'Hmm,' Phil grimaced, his bulging blue eyes rolling with mock disgust. Fishing in his pocket, he handed the wad of notes to Seth. 'Yours, I think?'

Seth nodded, quickly placing the roll into his shirt pocket and picked up the pint poured by the biker behind the bar. 'Thanks, mate.'

'Some more work, if you want it?' Phil muttered quietly.

Seth cocked his eyebrow at his friend and gave him a lopsided smile. 'You know me…'

'That I do, Seth. That I do.'

Seth grinned at Jane perched on Wazza's lap and laughed as she played with the big biker's hair. God, he loved that woman. Now he had the readies, he'd get that flat. Then they could be together without being beholden to any other fucker.

He'd also booked the hand fasting ceremony. Ok, he knew she kept saying they didn't need a piece of paper to prove how they felt, but he wanted to do it properly. *First the hand fasting, then the church.* Happily slugging down the rest of his pint, Seth replaced his glass on the bar.

Feeling Seth's eyes burning into her back, Jane fought against the urge to turn and look at him. Draining her glass of vodka, she locked her eyes onto Wazza's beard and pretended to listen as he droned on about the latest Motorhead concert. She was running out of excuses not to go back to the bar now her glass was empty, but before she could get up, Seth appeared.

Smiling, he swapped her empty glass for a full one. 'I've got some news.' Flicking his tongue in Jane's ear playfully, he sauntered back towards the bar, knowing she'd follow.

'Excuse me one minute,' Jane muttered to Wazza, who smiled benevolently as she lifted herself off his lap.

At the bar, she wrapped her arms around Seth's neck, resisting the urge to unbutton his shirt and trail her mouth down his chest. 'What's the news?'

Seth patted his chest pocket. 'Looks like we've got our flat.'

Jane's eyes moved to the fat roll of notes and arched an eyebrow. The job must have been a big one to pull in that sort of cash. 'Fucking brilliant! When can we get it?'

Seth's mouth reached for hers as he pulled her forward. 'I'll phone them tomorrow.'

Phil laughed. 'For fucks sake! Can't you guys get a room?'

Seth's eyes sparkled. 'That's *exactly* what we're doing, mate and some!' Moving his lips to Jane's ear, he whispered, 'Our wedding's in two weeks' time. That ok with you?'

Smiling, she looked into his green eyes, her heart hammering with excitement and nodded. *She couldn't wait to marry him.*

Seth grinned at Phil. 'We're getting married in two weeks, mate and you're invited!'

Phil laughed, watching Seth invade Jane's mouth hungrily. He loved those two.

# TWELVE

DEBBIE BREATHED A SIGH of relief. Well almost. She'd still got ten minutes until the end of her shift at the new bakery job and she'd had one of *those* days.

No amount of paracetamol had shifted the bloody headache she'd woken up with this morning. It might have been something to do with the eight pints of cider she'd put away at the Black Eagle last night, but on the other hand, it may have been because she hadn't gone to bed until 4am. She couldn't sleep and had just about had enough.

She'd been trying to get in touch with that mental case, Paul, for three weeks, but couldn't find the fucker anywhere. She'd last seen him a couple of nights after he'd pulled off their plan at the King's Head.

Debbie's smile had been so big, it felt like it might split her face in two. She'd been more than pleased with the details Paul had recounted - it had been *much* better than she could have hoped for. Apparently, Jane had royally lost the plot and it looked like she'd lost her job as well.

Seth had been kicked out of the King's, but he could come and live here with her. Debbie smiled. Waking up next to him in the morning was *definitely* something she wouldn't be complaining about. She'd been confident she wouldn't have to wait too long before he came to sort things out because, according to the woman downstairs, a tall bloke with long hair had previously banged on her door. It *had* to be him and she could have cursed herself for going to the shop to get more fags that night, because if she'd waited another ten minutes, she wouldn't have missed him. Still, he'd come round once, therefore he'd do so again.

Except that hadn't happened and now Paul was off the radar too, so she had no idea what was going on.

When she hadn't seen him in the Eagle, she'd gone round to his place and banged on the outer door for what felt like ten years. Finally, a greasy fat twat in a string vest had opened it. Running his tongue over his lips, the man had stared at her like a bloody retard, but eventually she'd deduced Paul had moved out one night without warning.

Frustrated, she'd then gone to Paul's work and learnt from a man smoking outside that he'd buggered off from there as well. He'd disappeared one lunchtime and never came back.

She'd been even more pissed off to learn that Seth was back with Jane. *Had all her hard work and planning been for jack shit?*

Gritting her teeth, Debbie slammed the metal tray she was holding onto the work surface. A couple of minutes left before she could leave. *Come on, she needed a bloody drink.*

• • • •

WALKING HOME IN HER bright green uniform, Debbie was still fuming. Stopping at the corner shop, she picked up a pack of fags, a ready meal and another two litre bottle of cheap cider. She'd only got two bottles left and she'd need *lots* tonight. Her plan was to get really drunk. All this crap was starting to make her ill.

It was bad enough fending off Tracy and Aunt Barb's questions about the pregnancy. She still hadn't feigned the 'miscarriage' and knew they were starting to wonder, but she wasn't going to worry about that now. She just wanted to get drunk and punch someone. *Like Jane.* All of this was *her* fault.

Finally reaching the flat, Debbie groaned. Her feet were killing. Putting the key in the lock, she pushed the door open and kicked it shut with relief.

Tripping over an empty box and a pile of dirty washing in the hallway, she swore under her breath. *Now to bung this chicken curry thing in the oven for half an hour and make a start on the cider.*

Flicking the light on, Debbie ventured into the kitchen, promptly dropping the bags on the floor in shock. The bottle of cider landed on the curry, splitting the cellophane packet open and the messy contents spilled over the cracked lino. 'What the…?'

Sitting at the chipped table, Jane looked up slowly and smiled. 'I trust I need no introduction?' Picking up a glass of cider, she took a swig. 'Is this *really* all you've got to drink in this filthy shit-hole, Debbie? Cheap cider?'

Debbie was so gobsmacked to see the Psycho-Bitch sitting in her kitchen, she couldn't answer the question. Her fat mouth flapped up and down silently. *Come on get a grip. Do something,* she thought to herself. All of her previous bravado had vanished and although she didn't want to admit it, she felt extremely uncomfortable.

'Oh, I know,' Jane's cold eyes glanced at the glass in an expression of disgust. 'I didn't particularly want to drink from one of your glasses either.' Her eyes travelled back to Debbie. 'But I was thirsty. I've been waiting a very, *very* long time for you.'

'How… How…?'

Lighting a cigarette, Jane blew the smoke directly towards Debbie. 'How did I get in?' she smirked. 'It was extremely easy. If you know what you're doing, that is.'

'Wh-What do you want, Jane?'

'What do I want?' Leisurely taking a couple more drags from the cigarette, Jane ground the remains directly onto the table top. 'Not much, really.'

With the speed of a panther, she jumped from behind the table like a coiled spring and pinned Debbie to the door, crushing her windpipe. 'Just wondered why you thought you could fuck with my life, you fat slut!' she screamed, her voice rising.

'I… I….' Debbie stammered, her eyes wide with terror as she gasped for breath and tried to prise Jane's vice-like grip away from her throat.

'Thought you could make up bullshit and fuck me over?'

'C-Can't breathe,' Debbie wheezed, her eyes bulging.

Jane smiled sarcastically. 'That's the general idea, you thick bitch!'

With her free hand, she yanked Debbie's head backwards and held it steady. 'Do you know how fucking easy it would be to slice your throat? Have you any idea how much I want to kill you?'

Feeling a tell-tale trickle between her legs, Debbie wondered if this could get any worse.

Jane's grip tightened. 'Thought you could drug up my man did you, you dirty bitch?'

Unable to move her head to nod or shake it, Debbie scrunched her eyes shut instead.

'DID YOU?'

Trying to swallow, Debbie found she couldn't do that either and turned light-headed. Hearing white noise as well as a funny whistling sound in her ears, her head thumped. As the room started to spin, she realised she was going to hit the deck. Suddenly the pressure lifted as Jane let go. Slumping forward, she staggered towards the table, desperately gulping in air.

Leaving Debbie to wheeze and retch, Jane folded her arms. 'You *disgust* me!'

Weakly looking up, Debbie was unable to retaliate. If she moved, she'd shit herself, pass out or both. Her eyes were watering and most of the blood vessels in them had broken under the pressure of the stranglehold.

'Did you really think you could break us up for long?' Jane

smiled. 'Oh, and it appears you've pissed yourself.'

'I'm sorry,' Debbie whispered, not knowing what else to say. *Could she get a knife out of the drawer without Jane getting there first?*

Unfortunately, her eyes must have unconsciously moved with her thoughts because Jane immediately turned towards the drawer and opened it.

Pulling out a carving knife, Jane turned it slowly around in her hand, the blade glinting in the light. 'After one of these, by any chance?'

Seeing the panic across Debbie's face, Jane smiled. 'You've got to be a lot better than that to outwit me, bitch. And a damn lot fucking *quicker*!'

'I-I wasn't goi....' Before she'd even comprehended that Jane had moved, Debbie was pushed back against the door. 'No... NO! Don't!' she blubbered, starting to cry. *Why the fuck had she started this? Everyone had been right, she shouldn't have gone there. Jane was a fucking psycho.*

Grabbing the front of Debbie's uniform, Jane sliced between the two collars with the knife. 'Let's see exactly what Seth's missed, shall we?'

As Debbie screamed, Jane laughed heartily and placed the knife on the table. Grasping the collar, she tore the material hard and the uniform fell to the floor into the puddle of piss.

Standing back, her eyes roamed slowly up and down Debbie's dirty grey stretchy bra and pink piss-drenched knickers. 'Dear, oh dear...' Tutting loudly, she counted the rolls of fat. 'You don't look pregnant to me. Just fucking fat and dirty!'

Debbie burned with humiliation and shame. 'I'm not pregnant...'

Jane laughed. 'Yeah, I know that too. Paul told me you made the whole thing up, you stupid, *stupid* bastard!'

Debbie closed her eyes and felt even sicker.

Jane's voice returned to screaming pitch. 'You nearly fucked everything up for me, you bitch!'

Debbie closed her eyes again. *How long was this going to go on for? Couldn't she just get it over with?*

'Take them off.'

Debbie's eyes snapped open. 'W-What?'

Jane lit a fag, her eyes burning black pits of anger. 'Take the rest of your kit off. NOW!'

Shakily unclipping her bra, Debbie pushed her knickers down and kicked them away. Her veiny pendulous breasts sagged down to her belly button and hung either side of her bloated stomach.

'Holy fuck!' Jane grimaced. 'Even worse than I'd imagined.'

Debbie's eyes darted around in blind panic.

'You tried to fuck with me, now I'm going to fuck with *you…*' Jane pulled a large glass bottle of tomato sauce off the countertop. 'With this…'

Smiling at her horrified expression, Jane slowly finished her cigarette and then ground the butt out on Debbie's breastbone, watching as her face contorted into a grimace of pain and fear. As her skin sizzled loudly, a howl escaped from Debbie's mouth.

'For fuck's sake, do you *really* think anyone would go near your dirty cunt? Now shut the fuck up.' Jane smashed her fist into Debbie's face and she fell heavily to the ground onto her piss-soaked uniform.

Dragging Debbie the other side of the kitchen by her hair, Jane dropped astride her and held her face steady with a hand around her throat before delivering series of ruthless punches to her eyes.

'No! Stop! Please! I'm sorry. I'm sorry!' Debbie screamed.

Jane scowled down with pure hatred. 'You will be….' There was no stopping now, her temper was blown. Punch after punch rained down into Debbie's face and blood gushed from her badly broken nose.

Sitting up straight to catch her breath, Jane stared in revulsion at the shaking figure in front of her. Debbie's matted hair was stuck to her face with sweat and blood ran from a deep cut over her right eyebrow into her swelling, already blackening eyes,

Jane smirked. 'Want some more?'

Debbie thrashed from side to side, screaming when her head was pulled up by her ears and then slammed down onto the floor. 'Be QUIET, bitch! You're giving me a fucking headache!'

Jane hoped Debbie hadn't passed out when she fell silent. She hadn't *anywhere* near finished. Reaching for the new bottle of cider, she slowly poured the contents over Debbie's face.

Spluttering and coughing, Debbie tried to raise her head, but Jane kicked it back down. 'I'm doing you a favour! You need a wash, you dirty bitch.'

Debbie froze and looked up at Jane, who was positively manic. *Was she going to die naked on the floor, covered in cider, blood and piss?*

Jane began systematically destroying every cupboard in the kitchen by swiping the contents out onto the floor and covering Debbie in broken crockery. 'Woken up yet?' she called, upending the table into the cooker.

Kicking some broken fragments of plate out of the way, she knelt down and poked Debbie hard in the cheek. 'You're going to put the record straight and tell everyone the fucking truth... Do you understand?'

Barely able to see through the swollen slits that had once been her eyes, Debbie swallowed the blood running down the back of her throat.

'DO YOU UNDERSTAND?'

Debbie nodded as enthusiastically as she could muster.

'And,' Jane whispered, jabbing Debbie in the throat. 'I'll be watching you.' Sticking her fingers into her swollen eyelids, she forced them apart. 'LOOK AT ME!'

Howling, Debbie's blood red eyes bulged out of their sockets. All she could focus on were the dark manic eyes burning into hers.

'Don't forget, I have absolutely *no* morals... NOW GET UP!'

Wriggling onto her side, Debbie forced herself onto her hands and knees and tried to push herself into an upright position.

'Ah wait….' Jane said, delivering a perfectly aimed upper cut to Debbie's jaw that knocked her clean off her feet to land with a crash in the pile of broken crockery.

'Perfect!' Smiling, she stamped on Debbie's rib cage, feeling several ribs snap under her foot. 'Stay there,' Jane snarled as she walked into the other room.

Pulling herself into a foetal position, Debbie howled with pain and tried to raise her hand to her face. The bottom part of it hung loosely and she couldn't close her mouth. *Oh, Jesus Christ. The psycho had bust her fucking jaw.*

Debbie desperately tried to stop the vomit coming up, but it was too late - it sprayed out of her mouth onto the floor. *Oh God. She was going to die, wasn't she?*

Wishing she could pass out and stop the pain, Debbie's stomach heaved again, the muscles pressing against her broken ribs and bile stung the cuts in her mouth.

Hearing Jane's return, she tried to open her eyes but they'd swollen completely shut. *What was that smell?*

'*Don't* try and turn me over again, you fat bitch,' Jane whispered.

Debbie shook her head as much as she could. If she got out of this she was never doing this to herself again. *Ever.* Not in a million fucking years.

'Good,' Jane muttered, 'but just to make sure…'

Debbie felt more cider being poured over her. It stung her face, eyes and cuts. *No. NO! That was petrol! It was fucking PETROL! What the fuck? No. No. NO!*

Thrashing around on the floor, Debbie tried to move, to escape. The smell was overpowering. A horrible strangulated screaming noise emanated from her broken mouth.

'Now,' Jane muttered, watching Debbie scrabble around in a pool of her own blood. 'Where are the matches in this dump?'

'You need matches, Princess?'

Debbie froze. She knew that deep voice. *Seth! He was here?*

'Fuck me, Debbie. You look even worse than usual. I didn't

think that was possible!' he drawled.

Debbie heaved and retched again, but there was nothing left to come up.

'I've been having a very nice time sitting in your lounge listening to everything,' Seth growled. 'I could have done without seeing you with no kit on, though!'

Winking at Jane, he shook the box of matches right next to Debbie's ear. 'Let's hope you understood everything my beautiful missus said to you?'

Jane glanced at Seth and felt her heart start to race. *When they'd finished here, she was going to fuck his brains out.*

'I said, DID YOU UNDERSTAND?' Seth roared.

Debbie's heart broke for the second, third, fourth and fifth time as the penny finally dropped. The man she was so in love with, hated her fucking guts. He was standing in *her* flat, laughing at her wrecked face and naked broken body and she realised once more that she'd *seriously* underestimated the situation. With total shame she accepted her obsession had blinded her to reality and that she'd orchestrated her own downfall.

Jane's voice broke Debbie out of her train of thought. That and a sharp kick to the side of the head. 'I didn't hear you answer him?'

Debbie struggled to remember the question…. *Quickly, quickly, think, think, THINK! What was it?* 'I did understand, I'll remember,' she mumbled and held her breath. *Don't let them light the match. Please, PLEASE don't let them light the match.*

Jane's arm snaked around Seth's waist and he smiled. She'd done a corking job on this piece of shit alright, he thought looking into her bright and sparkling eyes. *Too bright. Alive. Fuck, she was far too much like him!*

He felt a familiar ache in his groin and couldn't wait to get the keys to the flat. No more sleeping in cars. No more bullshit. It would all be good from now on.

Turning to Debbie, Seth whispered in her ear. 'Suggest you get cleaned up. And remember…'

When Jane traced her fingers over his belt and down to his crotch, Seth shuddered with need and placed a hand on the small of her back. 'Time to go.'

Without a second glance at the bloodstained, broken body lying sobbing on the floor, the crunch of crockery underfoot faded away.

The front door had hardly slammed before Jane unbuttoned Seth's jeans, her mouth hungrily reaching for his. Pulling at her clothes and raising her skirt, Seth pushed her against the wall.

# Thirteen

SITTING IN THE OAK APPLE with the others, Jane tapped her foot impatiently and glanced at her watch. *Where the fuck was Seth?* He'd explained he'd got to do a quick job, before flashing his killer smile and leaving the flat, but he'd said he'd meet her at the Oak at 8. *That was over two hours ago...*

Everyone had been having a dig at her for being miserable, but she didn't care. The first night in their new place and he'd gone AWOL.

It had been two o'clock this afternoon by the time the last item had been deposited in their new flat. Straightaway, Seth had balanced the stereo on a tea chest and wired it in. He'd opened the large lounge windows that looked down on to the high street five storeys below and they'd got nicely stoned listening to a Led Zeppelin album.

Jane had wandered from room to room, marvelling at the space. Ok, so it wasn't a big flat and it was a dump, but it was *theirs*.

The dirty magnolia lounge walls were chipped and scuffed, with horrible dark brown curtains and the kitchen was sparse, to say the least. There were a handful of stained white kitchen wall units, a rusted old sink and a cooker so crusted up with food it looked like it had been used as an incinerator. The main bedroom was at the end of the hallway and was big, although it didn't have a wardrobe or curtains. The second bedroom was small, but they didn't need it anyway.

'I'll sort some carpet out this week, baby,' Seth had muttered, hefting one end of the bed frame onto his shoulder.

Jane had walked down the hall eyeing a pile of TVs and stereos stacked up on top of each other, then made her way into the kitchen. She'd opened one of the cupboards but the door had fallen off and crashed to the floor with a thud. Muttering, she'd kicked it aside to wipe down the internal shelf, scraping fossilised remains from the laminated wood.

She'd then returned to the bedroom with two beers. 'Thought you might want anoth...' Jane had stopped, seeing Seth naked with his arms outstretched.

He'd raised an eyebrow. 'Time to christen our new place...'

A smile had played on Jane's face as she'd quickly knelt down and took him into her mouth.

Pulling her back to her feet, Seth had pressed his mouth hungrily down onto hers and removing her thin cotton halter neck dress, thrown her roughly onto the bed. Pushing her thighs apart with his knee, he'd followed her down onto the mattress.

That had been earlier, but this was *now*. Jane glanced around the bar once more. *Where was he?*

Sparking up yet another fag, she swallowed a couple more pills, alternating between being angry and worried. It wasn't like him to be late for *anything*, especially where she was concerned. She hoped nothing had gone wrong.

Slugging down the rest of her drink, she ignored the drivel Jake was spouting. She couldn't be bothered to even listen. Forcing herself out of the seat, she stumbled unsteadily towards the toilets.

When she came out, she saw Seth's familiar figure leaning against the bar with his back to her. Storming over, she poked him hard. 'Where the fuck have you been?'

As Seth turned to face her, Jane's anger abated at the sight of the swollen, blackening flesh around his eye. She reached up and touched his face, making him wince. 'What happened?'

'Not now,' Seth passed her a vodka and frowned. 'How drunk are you?'

'Drunk enough!' Jane snapped, her temper flaring at Seth's questioning. *It was her who had the right to ask questions, not him.*

Pouring the pint of lager down his throat, Seth waved the empty glass in the direction of the barmaid, who scuttled off to refill it.

'Are you going to tell me what's going on?' Jane hissed through gritted teeth.

Glancing at the two men stood to one side staring, Seth dug his fingers into Jane's shoulder. 'Listen, I told you *not now*. We'll discuss it later. I just want a fucking drink, alright?'

That job had proved to be a bit trickier than he'd expected. Still it was sorted now.

*Almost.*

Running his fingers through his wayward curls, Seth glanced at his cut knuckles.

When he'd got back to the flat, he'd ripped off his blood-stained shirt, launched it into the corner and run into the bathroom. He'd pulled on a clean T-shirt and eyed the swelling flesh around his left eye and scowled. *That bastard had somehow managed to get one on him.*

After sluicing cold water over his face, he'd come straight back out. He'd known Jane would be worried, but all she could do now he was here, was have a go at him?

Snorting at Seth's attitude, Jane took her glass and walked out the door for some air. She stood around the side of the pub and breathed the cool night into her lungs in an attempt to calm down.

Seth watched Jane disappear. *What was she playing at?* He didn't need her kicking off. He knew he'd fucked up by doing that job tonight, but he wouldn't put up with her pulling a paddy.

Pouring the remains of the fresh pint into his mouth, he

slammed the glass onto the bar and rapidly moved across the room.

• • • •

AS PAUL MADE his way up the Black Eagle, he'd been glad to see Jane stumble out of the Oak Apple. Whatever that nutter, Seth, had done or threatened him with, it hadn't changed his feelings. He still fully intended to get her back.

Having had a fair bit of time to reflect on life whilst his feet and hands healed, he'd reached the conclusion there would be no more 'Mr Nice Guy.' Furthermore, he'd heard what had happened to Debbie, but then, who hadn't?

After she'd finally got out of hospital, she'd had to admit her whole plan to all and sundry. *And the state of her. Dear God.*

Ok, so their plan had gone horribly wrong, but he was damned if he was giving up that easily. He'd give the fat cow a bit more time to lick her wounds and then get her back on side. After all, it was more than personal now. He owed Seth, big time and would reclaim what was rightfully his. And if Debbie had any sense, she'd be right with him.

Paul fumed silently, watching as Seth moved quickly towards Jane. She'd been standing against the wall almost *waiting* for him to approach her, but now that cunt had shown up and ruined everything. *As usual.*

He ran his shaking fingers through his lank hair. Now he'd have to go and visit his twat of a cousin.

Swallowing nervously, Paul flattened himself further against the alley wall before slipping away.

• • • •

GRABBING JANE'S FACE, Seth slammed her against the wall. 'Where the fuck do you think you're going? Leaving me again, are you?' Grasping the back of her hair, he crushed his body into hers.

Like a drug pumping through her veins, Jane's anger diminished feeling Seth against her. She held on to him tightly and sighed. *Why was he so goddamn paranoid? She was crazy about him!*

A smile passed fleetingly across Seth's mouth. 'I'm probably going to piss you off a lot more later.'

Pushing away slightly, Jane's eyebrow arched. 'Why?'

Seth leant down to kiss her. 'Don't worry about that now.'

'What is it this time?' she snapped sarcastically, moving away. 'Got someone else up the duff?'

Seth's face darkened as he dragged her into one of the many back alleys. 'That's not even *slightly* funny, Jane.'

'You going to murder *me* now then? Well go on, big man! You sure there's room in the boot?' Jane laughed cruelly and delivered a hard slap to Seth's face. 'Come on then!'

Seth placed his hands around Jane's slender throat. 'I'd *love* to kill you, Jane, but you know as well as I do, that I can't live without you, so I'm going to fuck you hard instead.' Freeing himself from his jeans, he pulled her dress up and pushed her back against the wall.

Inhaling sharply as Jane's hand ran firmly up his length, Seth pushed his fingers roughly into her, finding her ready. 'The only person I'll be getting pregnant, sweetheart, is you.'

# FOURTEEN

DIGGER TOOK A LONG swig out of his can and eyed Seth suspiciously. 'You ok, mate?'

Seth snapped himself out of his thoughts. 'Yeah, just thinking.'

'That's a dangerous pastime!' Digger muttered, watching the expressions passing over Seth's face. He could guess what the man was thinking.

Digger knew first-hand that Jane had the knack of turning a previously self-controlled man into a paranoid gibbering wreck, because he'd become one himself during his brief relationship with her a few years ago. He'd only managed to keep hold of her for a couple of months before his constant questioning had driven her mad and she'd binned him off. He'd never quite forgiven himself for fucking it up with her, but Seth *really* needed to chill the fuck out or he'd lose her too.

He smiled. He'd be more than happy to pick up where they'd left off if Seth did finally drive Jane away. Not that he'd tell *him* that, of course. Besides, he'd been enjoying himself recently. There was a nice bit of shit going down and he was more than happy to help out with more gun-running or whatever came in. He didn't care what it was.

Digger glanced at his watch, thinking he should perhaps make a move. He didn't want to be hungover tomorrow. Whether he liked it or not, Seth and Jane were getting married and the least he could do was make sure he was compos mentis.

'Going to shoot now, mate,' Digger extended his hand to Seth. 'See you at your wedding!'

Watching Digger stand up from the armchair brought Seth's attention back to reality. Shaking his hand firmly, he grinned. 'You will indeed!'

'Behave tonight, yeah?' Digger smiled.

As Digger disappeared through the door, Seth listened out for Jane. She should be back any time soon. He'd explained the other night he'd be doing a lot more work for The Highwaymen, but knew she hadn't been happy and hadn't liked the look on her face.

At the end of the day, he knew they needed more money than a straight job could pay and he was nothing if not resourceful.

Opening another can of beer, Seth glanced up hearing the front door open and eyed Jane suspiciously as she walked into the lounge with Eliza in tow.

'You're late,' he said abruptly. 'Get caught up with your cameraman, did you?'

Jane threw her jacket across the chair and motioned for Eliza to take a seat. 'Don't start, Seth,' she snapped. 'You know it's not like that.'

Although Seth moaned incessantly about her photo shoots, she'd been doing them for years and she wasn't about to stop doing them for anyone, including *him*.

Ok, so he didn't like the fact that she posed seductively across shiny black Harley Davidsons, arching her back and fluffing out her hair. Neither did he like that her tight leather skirt always rode up to expose the tops of her fishnet stockings, but he was hardly holier-than-thou with his line of work. Besides, they needed the money.

To make things even more depressing, she'd been really

chuffed when she'd landed that office job too, but not all things were what they seemed. Her new boss was creepy and the place did her head in. It didn't even pay very well, so the extra cash from the photo shoots was gratefully received.

Seth's mouth set in a thin line. He was tempted to get another dig in, but thought better of it. He didn't want to cause a row the night before their wedding. They'd got the pub and a party to get through yet, plus Jane still hadn't quite forgiven him when she'd discovered he'd still had someone in the boot of his car the night they'd moved.

He'd given her the choice of either helping him drag the body into the flat or driving to dump it. She'd been so pissed she hadn't fancied driving to a dumping point, so had agreed to put the stiff in the flat.

It had taken them *ages* to drag the fat bastard out of the car and up four flights of steps. He'd launched the body into the spare bedroom, under Jane's strict instructions for the dead guy to be gone by the time she'd got back from work the next day. This he had made sure of.

Since then, he'd made a concerted effort not to fuck up again and there had been no more bodies in the flat, only boxes of guns. And more televisions, but she'd just have to put up with those.

Jane chucked the wad of cash she'd got from the photo shoot onto the coffee table and then hastily snorted a line of coke.

'You got everything sorted for tomorrow?' Eliza asked, eyeing Jane's lounge carpet, which consisted of ill-fitting pieces of underlay Seth had fished out of a skip.

'What's there to sort? It's all pretty much done,' Jane smiled. She'd picked up her wedding dress from a cool shop in the city that sold second hand clothes and it was nice.

Seth scowled. 'The only jacket I could get is four sizes too small!'

Watching Jane's eyes narrow, Eliza interrupted to try and divert another impending argument. She handed over a box wrapped in purple tissue paper. 'Bought you guys a present.'

'What is it?' Jane asked.

'It's for tomorrow. Thought you could use it. Open it.'

'It's too small for a machine gun,' Seth laughed, sprawling back on the sofa to put a fat joint together.

Jane pulled at the tissue paper, revealing a black box. Intrigued, she opened it, and then gasped. 'Oh, it's beautiful, Eliza! Thank you! Look, Seth!'

Taking the opened box, Seth looked inside, seeing a beautiful pewter Athame with an intricate handle, inset with an oval amethyst. Running his finger lightly over the razor sharp three inch blade, he reached over to Eliza and kissed her on the mouth. 'Thank you.'

'You're welcome.' Eliza blushed furiously at Seth's mouth on hers. *How she wanted him.* Not that she'd ever act on it. She was Jane's best mate, after all and they'd done everything together for nearly ten years. Nevertheless, she still wanted Seth and sometimes couldn't help feel a bit resentful because Jane had it all.

Settling on Seth's lap, Jane ran her fingers through his hair. Breathing in his scent, she kissed his face. 'We're going out now, baby. See you up there later. Come on, Eliza, we need to go and meet Maggie.'

Seth turned the blade over in his hand. It was indeed lovely. Leaning his head back against the sofa cushion, he sparked the large joint up and smiled.

• • • •

'EVENING, GIRLS!' Davis grinned, running his eyes appreciatively up and down the women as they rocked up at the Barrels.

Spooner kissed Jane on the cheek. 'You're all looking ravishing, as usual.'

'Of course!' Jane laughed teasingly, placing her hands on his shoulders. 'Wouldn't want to let you boys down, would we?'

Standing behind her, Davis pulled Jane backwards and pressed against her. 'Can't imagine you'd *ever* let us down.'

Maggie's mouth pursed in irritation, still half-stoned from earlier. She needed to sort her head out.

She glanced down at the white lycra leggings she'd put on and forced herself to get a grip, but her mind kept wandering back to Bryn who she'd hooked up with last week. She was crazy about him, but admitted she'd been going especially soppy since Jane and Seth had got engaged. Now they were getting married, it was even worse. *Maybe she'd marry Bryn? Should she ask him?*

Twisting her hair around in her fingers, Maggie realised it might scare him off if she started talking about getting married after a week. However, Davis had been eyeing her up lately, so maybe she should go out with him instead? Or was he now too interested in Jane to notice her? *Maybe she should have just married Ian?*

Almost slapping herself, Maggie hastily reminded herself what being with Ian had been like. But she'd loved him. Well, at least she *thought* she had. Oh, she just didn't know anymore. *She must stop doing drugs. They fucked her up.*

She watched Jane free herself from Davis' grasp and decided she'd step in. *Wasn't she entitled to some attention as well?*

Wrapping her arms around Davis' neck, she fiddled with his bow tie. 'I like a man in a suit,' she purred, fluttering her long eyelashes and running her hand along the broad shoulders of his jacket.

'Do you now?' Davis smiled. 'Go on. Go and get yourself a drink.'

Davis turned back towards the door and Maggie scowled. *Was she losing her touch?* She huffed petulantly, realising Jane and Eliza had carried on down to the bar without her.

· · · ·

DOWN THE DRAGON, Seth sat on a wooden bench. He'd had a fair few pints so far. Fifteen to be precise and after the joint he'd smoked, he was well on the way. He turned towards Phil who was staring at him intently. 'What?'

'You've said nothing for twenty minutes. Are you ok?' Phil asked.

Seth sparked up a fag and glanced at his packet, seeing he'd only got a few left. 'I think so.'

'Nervous about tomorrow?'

'No, of course not!' Seth laughed and looked away. If he was honest, he *was* nervous. *Nervous that Jane wouldn't go through with it.* 'Another one?'

Levering himself off the wooden seat, Seth moved towards the bar and shouted up the drinks. He'd just have this one and then get himself up the Barrels for the last hour before the party.

Meanwhile, back up the Barrels, Jane was getting irritated. When Maggie was stoned, she was even more paranoid than usual and so far, she'd had to spend half the evening convincing her that Ian wasn't there.

'Are you *sure* that's not him over there?' Maggie shouted over the music, directly down Jane's ear, gesticulating to a dark corner near the cigarette machine.

Peering over the sea of grinding bodies, Jane could only see the normal bunch of punks and travellers and certainly not Ian. 'No, babe, it's not him.'

Maggie pointed to someone else with long hair and pulled at Jane's top. Guessing what had been asked, Jane shook her head and continued looking for more pills at the bottom of her handbag, a wide smile breaking across her face spotting Seth's familiar silhouette approach the double doors.

This time tomorrow she'd be joined to him for ever.

# FIFTEEN

THE HIGH PRIEST LOOKED from Seth to Jane and then back to Seth. 'Welcome friends, family and loved ones. We're here today to witness Seth and Jane join hands and be bound together by their love, now and forever.' Casting the circle, he directed the group of people standing behind the couple to move to form a large semi-circle around them.

Maggie swallowed the lump forming in her throat and felt horribly envious watching Seth drink Jane's every move into his soul. She sighed, desperately wishing someone loved *her* like that.

Eliza tried to keep the smile fixed across her face. She was jealous, there was no doubt about that, but equally she could have done without getting so trolleyed last night. Her tongue was still partially stuck to the roof of her mouth.

It hadn't helped either that she was knackered beyond belief. At least when Seth and Jane had *finally* finished arguing and then screwing last night, everyone else had got a bit of bloody peace. Those two were obsessed with each other and she was sure it was all going to end in tears, but only time would tell. Either way, they were getting married.

The High Priest continued loudly, commanding everyone's

attention. 'We acknowledge Thy Presence and Thy Power, Blessed Spirit. We give thanks these two souls have been drawn together by divine appointment and will be held together by the power of divine love.'

Jane's mind faded out. She tried to concentrate, but couldn't and ignored the panic rising within her. The lager, pills and coke she'd had first thing had barely done anything to take the edge off her Grade Nine hangover. She wanted to do this, of course she did, but she didn't know how the hell she was going to get through it feeling like death.

Taking a deep breath, she focused on the Priest's ceremonial robes and hoped she wouldn't pass out. She looked around the little clearing in the woods where huge old oaks and silver birches formed a bower overhead. Sunlight filtered down in dappled rays, casting beams of light across everyone's faces. The mossy floor was spongy and the birds sang along with a gentle hum of insects. The spot Seth had picked for the ceremony was lovely.

A pause in the speaking caused Jane to glance up. *Fuck! Was she supposed to have said something?* The thick white candle on the small table in front of them was lit and she tried to breathe, but her lungs were locked. She glanced at Seth, the movement making her head spin.

'Now the betrothal,' the Priest turned towards Seth. 'What's your name?'

Seth shifted his focus away from Jane and looked directly ahead. 'Seth Wright.'

'And what's your desire?'

Looking down with warm eyes, Seth smiled. 'To join with Jane, whom I love.'

Jane felt herself go red. She hoped she could remember what she was supposed to say. She couldn't remember her name, right now, let alone anything else. She couldn't even remember how the hell she'd got here.

The Priest stared at Seth. 'Will you seek to do her harm?'
'I will not.'

'But if harm is done, will you seek to repair it?'

A fleeting smile passed across Seth's mouth. 'I will.'

'Will you seek to be honest with her in all things?'

'I will.'

'Will you support her in times of distress and temper your words and actions with love?'

'I will,' Seth murmured.

There was a long pause as the High Priest slowly opened his eyes. 'These things you have promised before this company and the Gods. May you ever be mindful and strive to keep the vows you've spoken.'

Seth nodded and looked at Jane intently. *She'd best get through this.*

• • • •

WHEN JANE UTTERED her final vow, Seth exhaled with relief. This morning on their way back from that party in the van he'd stolen the night before, she'd started having a bit of a meltdown.

As they'd hurtled along the road, he'd watched her forcing pills down with lager and muttering. After she'd unsuccessfully attempted to reapply her eyeliner, he'd handed her another wrap of coke. She'd still had a couple of hours left to sort her head out, but he'd been worried she'd hit the deck during the service and it wouldn't go ahead.

He'd held his breath throughout the ceremony, scared that if he breathed, she'd run away. He couldn't have dealt with that. Not now he'd come this far. *Still, she was here and the ceremony was almost done.*

Seth looked down at Jane, who smiled shyly before looking away and Seth thought his heart might burst with happiness.

The High Priest glanced around the circle. 'May we please have the rings?'

Digger stepped forward. Rummaging in his pocket, he fished out two gold bands. Grinning, he put them on the table next to the candle.

Pointing his dagger, the Priest touched the rings in turn. 'May these rings be blessed with Air for hopes and dreams, Fire for the spark of love, Water for harmony and healing and Earth for strength.'

He moved the dagger in the direction of the four elements. 'The circle is the symbol of peace and of the Sun, Earth and the Universe. Let these rings be the symbols in which your two lives are joined in one unbroken circle. Wherever you go, return unto one another and to your togetherness.'

Seth picked up Jane's ring and locked eyes with her as he pushed it neatly onto her finger. He then placed his hand over hers so she could put his wedding band on.

The High Priest raised both arms to the sky. 'By the exchange of these tokens, your lives are interlaced. It is now time to seal the Union.'

Jane's heart thudded like a drum, each beat reverberating in her temples as Seth picked up the new Athame from the table. Pulling his cuff up, he made a small incision causing the blood to drip freely into a pewter goblet.

Taking the Athame, Jane deftly cut her wrist and let her blood collect into the same goblet.

'I ask you to cross your hands over each other's.' The High Priest wrapped a red cord around their wrists and tied a knot. 'This ritual is not to be taken lightly. Do you understand and accept that by ingesting the combined elixir of life, you'll be bound to each other for eternity. Through life, death and beyond.'

'I do,' Seth answered.

The Priest turned to Jane, awaiting her response. *This was it. No going back...* She looked at Seth. 'I do,' she whispered.

Nodding, the Priest passed the goblet to Seth who took a sip. Licking the residue of their mixed blood from his lips, he passed it to Jane who, resisting the urge to neck the whole lot, sipped it before handing it back to the Priest.

'You're now bound together for all eternity. Your lives and spirits joined in a union of love. You hold in your hands the making or breaking of this union, but nothing can ever sever it. Space, nor time.'

The Priest let go of their joined wrists. He closed his eyes and raised his dagger towards the sky. 'May the God and Goddess bless this union. May your lives be full and your hurts be few. By the winds that bring change, by the fire of love, by the seas of fortune and the strength of the Earth, I bless this union.'

Slowly bringing his arms down to his sides, he opened his eyes and looked first to Seth and then to Jane before untying the cord binding their wrists. 'The knots of this binding are not formed by cords, but by your vows. I now pronounce you husband and wife.'

As a loud cheer erupted from behind, Seth grabbed Jane's face with both hands and kissed her hungrily. Maggie was crying and Eliza had managed to retain her huge smile. Soon they were swamped in a deluge of hugs, kisses and backslaps.

Seth's hands were shaking as he grabbed the cigarette from Digger's mouth and took a drag. 'Fuck! My nerves are shot to hell!'

'Not like you to be nervous!' Digger teased. 'Too late to go back now. It's forever and eternal!'

Looking at the blood stain on his starched white cuff, Seth grinned like a Cheshire cat. 'I don't want to go back! Fuck me, I certainly don't want to go back!'

'That was a bit hard-core, wasn't it? Why can't you have a normal wedding?' Eliza yelped.

'I thought it was romantic,' Maggie added.

'You would!' Eliza quipped. 'They're fucking nutters!'

Jane laughed. Thanks to the three fags she'd just smoked and the vodka Maggie had had the sense to bring, her heart rate was returning to normal.

Picking Jane up around the waist, Seth span her around. 'Come on, we've got to go. There are cars waiting to take everyone into town.' He looked towards the others. 'Jump in whatever you can. We'll meet you there.'

Placing Jane to the ground, Seth pulled her in the direction of the lane in which their car was parked.

• • • •

DIGGER COULD HARDLY see where he was going for the foam on the Senator's windscreen as he led the convoy into town. The cans tied to the car dragged on the road behind them and made a loud grating noise.

In the back, Seth wrapped Jane in a bear hug so tight she could hardly breathe, but she didn't mind. She was quite happy being in his arms.

Swerving into the British Legion car park, the rest of the cars and bikes carried on towards town. She craned her neck out of the window. 'What's going on?' she glared at Seth. 'Don't tell me you've got to do a job?'

'Hardly!' Seth laughed as the car pulled to a stop. Jumping out, he ran around and opened Jane's door. Doffing his top hat, he bowed theatrically as he took her hand and gestured behind him. 'For you M'lady…'

Jane's mouth dropped open seeing a trap reined with two black horses and festooned with flowers.

Lifting her up onto the bench seat, Seth jumped up beside her and placed his arm around her shoulders. 'Let's go!'

The cart lurched towards the road and Jane stifled an excited scream. 'I can't believe you organised this!'

Seth pulled her towards her. 'I'd do *anything* for you, Jane…'

As the trap cantered down the hill, Jane felt deliriously happy. Cars beeped their horns and people watched at the sides of the road, waving. Seth kissed her passionately and she clung onto him as the trap swayed down the road.

# Sixteen

DAVIS WAS THOROUGHLY pissed off. He'd only agreed to pick up the dough as a favour because he'd always got on with Seth, but now the guy was beginning to fuck him off. Who did Seth think he was getting him to do lackey work? *He was Davis, not an idiot.*

Touching the tender flesh over his right eye, he winced and knocked back a whisky. Ok, so it was early, but he needed a drink to calm himself down.

He'd been ten minutes late last night, but it wasn't exactly his fault a fight had kicked off at the Barrels which he'd had to sort. Then he couldn't find the fucking Chapter House. He'd driven round that poxy estate for bloody yonks before he'd found it.

Brushing back his light brown hair, Davis peered at himself in the bedroom mirror of the small rented flat. Bloody hell, his eye was already going black. *Yeah, that looked just brilliant, didn't it? A bouncer with a black eye…*

He just wished he'd kept his gob shut when that fat prick had asked why he was late, grudgingly admitting his response of, *'It's only ten minutes, you cunt,'* was probably not the answer the guy was expecting. On the same vein, he hadn't appreciated being questioned. He wasn't used to it.

When he'd clenched his fist in frustration, the fat bastard had clumped him and the rest of the bearded wonders had stood up. Much to his utter chagrin he'd found himself having to back down and accept defeat. Then, to add insult to injury, Phil had pulled him to one side, telling him to fuck off and not to come back.

There was no chance of that. That was definitely the first and last time he'd be roped into anything like that again.

Glaring out of the grimy window onto the street below, he scowled watching someone in a grubby vest trying to bump start a Metro. *He'd have Seth for this somehow.*

'Don't be asking for a favour again, mate,' Davis muttered to himself, reaching for the whisky to top his glass up.

He hoped Seth choked on his fucking money.

• • • •

JANE OPENED HER EYES sleepily. Smiling, she twisted the gold band around on her finger. Feeling somewhat fragile she carefully moved Seth's heavy arm off her stomach, but he moved it back in his sleep, his large hand splaying out as if to reassure himself she was still there.

She looked up at the ornately carved ceiling of the room and relished the cool crisp feel of the thick white cotton sheets beneath her. The heavy gold bedspread was rumpled at the bottom of the bed and their clothes lay in a messy pile on the curved-legged boudoir chair to the right of a huge gold velvet-draped window.

Arriving at the Green Dragon after the ceremony yesterday, they'd done a pub crawl, ending at the Barrels. Jane had thought she'd been dreaming, when at the end of the night Seth had flagged down a taxi, telling the driver to take them to The Castle.

She let out a contented sigh. They'd had drinks in the luxurious bar with its tail-coated waiters and sat on deep leather chesterfield sofas. She'd *always* wanted to stay at The Castle, but never thought in a million years she would get to walk up the thickly carpeted, sweeping staircase leading to the bedrooms.

Taking a deep breath, Jane slowly exhaled, feeling like total shit, but more than happy. She turned over to face Seth and studied him. His eyelashes fanned over his cheeks and his hair spread over the pillow. The gold chain around his neck lay in the little hollow of his throat that she loved kissing.

She drank in the stubble covering his sculptured cheekbones and as she traced her finger lightly down the ridges on his stomach, he let out a soft murmur and turned towards her.

Seth groaned feeling Jane fit around him like a glove as he pushed into her from behind. 'You're insatiable, you are,' he smiled, kissing her neck. 'I love you, Mrs Wright.'

'I love you too,' she gasped, while he rotated his hips deliciously.

'Just the church now,' Seth whispered, trying to keep a lid on his raging desire.

'Not yet, though.'

Seth stopped abruptly.

'What's the matter?' Jane asked, turning around as much as possible.

'Why not yet? Don't you want to?'

Jane cupped Seth's face, wishing he'd shut up and carry on what he was doing. 'Don't be crazy! Of course I do! You know how I feel.'

'Not really.'

'Oh Seth, I'm too tired to play your insecurity games today,' she sighed. 'Come on, you know yesterday was a big deal to me.'

Pulling out, Seth jumped from the bed and glared at her.

'SETH!' Jane reached for him, but he brushed her away. She rolled her eyes. One day in and there was going to be a row already. She'd thought they might at least last until they'd got to the pub. 'Well, if you're going to be like that, then fine!' she snapped, lying back against the pillow.

Finally, after a long stand-off silence, Seth sat on the end of the bed. 'You're still doing the church?' he muttered.

'I said so, didn't I?'

'Well, I'm going to book it.'

'As you wish.'

'I DO wish!'

Seth's brows knitted together and he shook his head, finally smiling when Jane lifted the cigarette from his mouth and took a drag. 'I'm booking it, Jane...'

'Whatever makes you happy, darling.'

'Don't you *dare* be facetious with me, woman!' Stubbing the fag out in the ashtray, Seth pulled Jane across the bed and rolled himself on top of her.

• • • •

MAGGIE SAT STOCK STILL. She'd been like this for what seemed like hours, but hadn't yet found the courage to come out from under the scratchy blue woollen blanket, let alone peep through the closed caravan blinds in case he was still there. *She felt sick to her stomach.*

Unable to remember too much of last night, apart from Seth and Jane dancing in the Barrels, the rest was a bit of a blur, but due to the uncomfortableness between her legs, she was pretty sure it had involved a fair bit of sex.

Bryn had left for work early even though it was a Sunday, but a couple of minutes later there had been a knock at the door. She'd reluctantly dragged herself off the bed, presuming he'd forgotten his fags, but something made her peer through the blinds first. She was glad she had because Ian had been standing outside.

'MAGGIE! Open the fucking door. I *know* you're in there!'

Shrinking back onto the bed, Maggie had hidden under the blanket. It wouldn't have made any difference if Ian chose to rip the door off its hinges, but it had made her feel slightly more in control. It also helped muffle her loudly hammering heart.

Ian had knocked for ages, moving around the caravan and peering through the windows, whilst Maggie had remained motionless, trying to control her shaking, convinced she was going to have a heart attack. She'd no idea how much time had passed before he finally stomped away. *But had he given up? He might have just pretended.*

Feeling the familiar waves of fear rise in her chest, Maggie made a concerted effort to calm down before she spiralled into another full-blown panic attack. She'd had enough of those recently. *She needed another Valium and fast.*

According to Jane, all she had to do was to show Ian she wasn't bothered - then he'd get bored and stop. All very well, Maggie thought, chewing at her fingernails, but how the hell was she was supposed to accomplish that? He scared the living daylights out of her.

# SEVENTEEN

PLACING HER HANDBAG down on the desk, Jane flicked her cigarette in the ashtray to the right of her telephone and sighed.

The events of the past few days now sadly seemed like a thousand years ago. Had it really been only *two* days since she'd been at the Castle laughing hysterically as Seth had sipped out of the champagne flute with bubbles piled all over him. Lying back at the other end of the sumptuous bath complete with gold taps, she'd taken sips from her glass whilst eyeing their third bottle of ice-cold Moet. *She could have got used to that sort of lifestyle.*

Scraping the bubbles from his beard, Seth had winked, then carefully placed his glass on the wide-tiled surround. Reaching underwater, he'd grabbed her ankles and pulled her swiftly towards him through the frothy water. She came to rest astride him, finding him more than ready for her and as he effortlessly lifted her onto him, she'd sunk down onto his hardness, picking up a steady pace. She'd never get enough of that man.

Seth's shoulder muscles had flexed, his full lips slightly parted. 'Jane,' he'd groaned, his eyes opening slightly to reveal a flash of green. 'Kiss me...'

*How could she have refused?* Meeting his mouth, she'd known there was no doubt she would happily spend the rest of her life in a bathtub drinking champagne with Seth. Sadly, that seemed as remote a possibility as her becoming a nun now things were back to normal.

Jane glanced irritably around the office. This job really was not working out, but what could she do? She didn't have a lot of choice but to get on with it – at least until she found something else.

Seth would go mental if he knew her new boss had asked her to do nude photographs for the magazine, but she hadn't told him. Even though she'd declined the request, he'd still beat the fuck out of the man and she needed the job.

Although Seth was pulling in a fair wedge with his jobs, they never had any money and she didn't want to get to the point where they had to rent out the spare room. As it was, the place was like a motorway half the time with people coming and going, without some other fucker living there too. They may as well have stayed in the car for the amount of privacy they had.

*And then there was Stuart.* If she'd have known that dickhead lived next door there was a very real possibility she'd have waited until somewhere else had come up, however much she'd wanted a proper place.

· · · ·

SETH GLANCED BEHIND him for the second time as a double precaution. Why he was asked to do these type of jobs in broad daylight was beyond him. He just hoped the information was correct and there would only be two gophers here and not a whole bunch of heavies.

Despite his morning whisky, he was still hungover and could do without resorting to the backup plan. He touched the sawn-off concealed in his large inside pocket and his other hand tightened around the baseball bat as he raised his leg to kick the door down.

Two doped-up, hungry-looking men stared in shock, one dropping a sawdust-filled crate when Seth crashed through the metal door, roaring like a rabid animal.

Glancing around, Seth smiled. It appeared the intelligence had been correct. It was just these pair of dipsticks who were about to get the fluffy end of the lollipop. Even though he felt slightly unreasonable delivering debilitating cracks to the skulls of both men, he watched expressionless as they crumpled to the dusty floor.

Standing over the inert bodies, he looked for the crates he needed. There were *dozens* of them stacked against the walls. *For fuck's sake. It was supposed to be a simple 'pick up and take' job for ten boxes, so which ones were his?*

Looking for the branding he'd been told marked the correct crates, Seth kept an eye out for any sign of movement from the men on the floor. He'd been instructed not to finish anyone unless absolutely necessary, but he'd be the judge of that and the baseball bat remained raised in readiness, in case either of them required a second whack.

Seeing the required symbol on the side of at least a few crates, Seth pulled one towards him and levered up the lid with a spanner from the nearest workbench. His heart beat faster as he pushed the straw aside and clocked the shiny barrel of a gun.

He pulled it carefully from its hiding place. *Was this what he thought it was?*

Handling the polished wood and silver casing, Seth turned it around in the light of the fluorescent strips. This wasn't just any old gun, it was a Beretta. A very nicely, exquisitely sawn-off Beretta. *These models were worth a fucking fortune!*

Lifting the crate down to the floor, he stuck his hand back in and felt around. *Fuck!* There were at least ten or fifteen of them in this one crate alone. If they were all Berettas and if all of the crates contained these… *Fucking hell!*

Seth smiled, immediately deciding he'd be asking for one of these beauties as part-payment for the job.

• • • •

ELIZA TRUDGED UP THE hill towards her parent's house, getting slower and slower as she went. It had started to rain and she was getting soaked. She glanced at the road ahead, feeling sick from the memory of waking up next to some random bloke's puny white body and worse, the knowledge that everyone knew what she'd done because they'd all been there.

Completely lost in dismal thoughts, Eliza didn't notice the car pulling up beside her. Only the horn blasting caused her to jump and turn around.

'Do want a lift or not?' Seth shouted through the Senator's window.

Eliza gratefully ran around the other side of the car as Seth leant to open the passenger door. She'd hardly closed it before he screeched off. 'Thanks for the lift, I'm bloody soaked!'

'Where to?' he smiled.

'Home.' Eliza glanced sideways. Seth's hand was on the steering wheel and the other on the gear stick inches from her leg. A trademark fag hung between his lips and she tried not to stare. *Christ! Stop it*, she thought. She clearly needed to pull someone decent this weekend because the sexual frustration was obviously getting to her.

'What you been up to, Eliza?'

*Oh, just thinking what it would be like to sit on your face*, she thought silently, hoping the blush creeping up her went unnoticed. 'Not a lot - apart from berating myself for my crap choice in men!'

Taking his eyes off the road, Seth turned to her. 'What happened with you and Lee? Thought you two might become an item?'

Momentarily mesmerised by the green of his eyes, Eliza attempted to formulate a sensible answer, feeling guiltier by the second about having carnal thoughts about her best mate's fella.

'I don't know. I liked him.' Eliza looked back towards Seth. 'Things just tailed off a bit, I guess.' When he raised an eyebrow questioningly, her stomach flipped. *Stop it Eliza. Stop it now!*

Pulling up outside Eliza's parent's house, Seth yanked the handbrake on. 'There you go!'

*Oh, damn. Were they here already?* Eliza smiled brightly

and opened the passenger door. 'Fancy a cuppa?'

'Yeah, why not!' Seth had been on his way back from the drop-off and hadn't had a drink for hours. His mouth was like the bottom of a bird cage. Despite this, he'd been more than happy to be handed seven hundred notes and even happier to also be the proud owner of one of those bloody lovely Berettas.

Eliza felt her colour rise noticing her mother eyeing her from the kitchen window as Seth followed her up the path to the front door.

'Hi!' Joy called as they stepped into the hall. 'And who's this?' She eyed Seth mischievously. 'Ooh, you're a nice specimen, aren't you?'

Eliza cringed. *Was it not bad enough that she was still living at home, without being treated like a fucking teenager?* 'MUM! You know full well who this is.'

'Yes I know, I'm teasing. Just wondering when you're going to get a nice one?' Joy smiled as Seth took her hand, kissing it lightly and then flashing her one of his winning grins.

Eliza sighed at her mother's swooning expression. If the woman knew what this man was *really* like, it would shut her up once and for all.

# EIGHTEEN

THE SUN BLAZED THROUGH the curtains onto Stuart's face. This wasn't completely surprising, as they were as thick as that bloody awful bog roll found in public toilets. There was also a quite obvious fundamental flaw in that they were six inches too narrow for the window.

Feeling like the top three layers of his skin were burning off, he turned over and pressed his face into the lumpy pillow. It was like trying to sleep on a bag of fucking marbles and the whole thing was pissing him right off.

As he plumped up the pillow, a spring from the second-hand mattress poked him in the ribs. Growling in anger and frustration, he threw himself over onto his side, his hair hanging in a greasy mess.

As the usual thumping noise began from next door, Stuart gritted his teeth and scowled even harder, hearing Jane's muffled voice through the wall.

*Shut the fuck up, bitch*, he thought savagely. The last thing he wanted to hear was her. It consistently annoyed him that Seth and Jane had moved next door. Nearly three months now he'd put up with their nightly arguing and then the headboard banging. On and on and *on* half the night, only to begin again first thing in the morning.

*Thump. Thump. Thump. THUMP.*

Oh what was the point? Pushing himself up to a sitting position, Stuart heaved himself to the edge of the bed and pulled his sleeveless T-shirt over his skinny chest. What he needed to do now was get out of here before that idiot showed up again.

Time and time again he'd spelt it out to Paul that if he came round and Jane and Seth caught sight of him, he wouldn't be able to help anymore. He'd explained these things took time to come to fruition, but Christ, the prat was impatient.

Why the fuck he'd ended up with that retard as his cousin he'd never know, but as long as no one found out they were related, he wasn't too bothered. Besides, the only reason he was going along with it wasn't because they were family, but he'd actually thought Paul's plan was pretty damn good and echoed his own feelings.

*Thump. Thump. Thump.*

Stuart scowled. At least it was Saturday and he wouldn't have to wind himself up watching the stupid tart walking to her silly fucking car. All self-important because she now worked in an office.

The only bonus of them moving in next door was that he was getting nicely in with Seth. Although they'd always been on speaking terms, they'd never been 'mates,' but over the last couple of months, he'd found if he came out of his front door at the same time, he could strike up a friendly conversation. It had got even better when after a few days he'd been invited in for a smoke and a beer.

When Jane had returned from work to find him sitting on their sofa, her face had been a picture. Stuart smiled. Especially as Seth had been thoroughly stoned and was laughing helplessly at his jokes. Since then, he'd timed his subsequent visits very well - each time pissing Jane off further.

The other night he'd spent *hours* settled on their sofa, making sure he was part of every conversation and when he'd finally left at 2am, they'd been having a row. *Perfect!*

Stuart didn't know why they bothered with each other anyway. They were always arguing. Most of the arguments, apart from being about him, were over Jane's job or Seth's dealing and from what he'd heard through the cardboard walls, she hated people round the flat. This was of course why it was even more enjoyable to invite himself round on a regular basis.

Stuart rubbed his hands together. If Jane had a problem with people being there, then she'd have even more of a problem it being him. He knew she despised him and the feeling was mutual.

With any luck, his presence would help split them up; along with the bits of information he'd been feeding Seth's paranoid mind to get him thinking... Those little seeds of doubt about Jane, which caused him to pick even more fights with the snotty cow. *It was all good.*

Congratulating himself for his good work, Stuart looked around the messy room for his shoes. Locating them under a pair of jeans, he jumped off the bed with a spring in his step.

The sunlight wasn't annoying him anymore. It was a beautiful day.

· · · ·

ROLLING HERSELF OUT OF bed into a standing position, Jane's mind caught up with her head in a nauseating cerebral lurch. She stepped over a man on the floor with grungy ginger dreadlocks, only to stumble over someone else.

Studying the man with his shaved head and patched denim a little harder through her blurred vision, she wasn't sure if she recognised him. She certainly didn't recognise the other one.

Grabbing one of Seth's crumpled T-shirts from under the fat skinhead, she dragged it out from under him and glared as she pulled it over her naked body.

Propping himself up in bed, Seth put together the third joint of the morning and looked at Jane with a nonplussed expression. 'What's the matter with you? You should be radiant and glowing with happiness after that good seeing to I just gave you.'

Jane glowered as Seth felt around on the bed for his Zippo. He *knew* she was sick of waking up with people lying on the floor at the bottom of the bed that hadn't been there the night before. Her brows knitted together in frustration. It was *him*, not her who insisted on leaving the front door on the latch so people could come and go as they pleased.

A curl of blue smoke escaped from between Seth's lips and twisted its way towards the ceiling as he studied Jane's expression. 'You *know* we need to do this. We need the money.' Holding the smoke in his lungs, he tried to bring his high back up. He was nowhere near as mellow as he wanted to be and her scowling face was winding him up. *For fuck's sake, it wasn't like he hadn't been straight with her, was it?*

He'd explained that in addition to the work from the Highwaymen, he'd be dealing too. It was hardly like she could have too much of an aversion. She took enough gear to sink a fucking ship.

However, he admitted he wasn't bringing in half as much as he'd planned. Between them, they were taking most of it themselves, rather than selling it, hence why he had to implement an open door policy to shift as much as possible.

Seth felt his temper rising further at Jane's glaring face. 'Who the hell's going to buy it if we never answer the fucking door? Tell me that!'

Jane felt like smashing Seth's face in as he took toke after toke of the joint. *Was he not going to offer it to her?* 'Don't be sarcastic, you piece of shit!' Her anger flared like a beacon. 'None of this was supposed to be going on from here. That's what we agreed, was it not?'

Pushing himself forward, Seth leant on his thighs and glanced up with a sneer plastered across his handsome face. 'No. *You* agreed that, not me. Who are you? Miss-High-And-Fucking-Mighty?'

'And as for that twat next door. Why do I go to work while you sit here getting wasted with that piece of shit? He might as well move in!'

The bodies on the floor stirred with Jane's raised voice. 'I mean,' she prodded the ginger one with her foot, 'who the fuck is this?'

Seth shrugged and ground the joint out into the ashtray. 'You think that's all I do is it, you stupid bitch? Whilst you're sucking that fat cunt off at work?'

'You what?' Jane screamed, her dark eyes blazing.

Seth smiled nastily. 'If I find out you've done *anything* like that, it will be the last thing you do!'

'Don't you *dare* threaten me, Seth Wright. Go fuck yourself!' Jane stormed towards the bedroom door, only to trip over a piece of underlay. Swearing loudly, she regained her balance and stalked out of the bedroom, slamming the door on Seth's laughter.

Fuming, Jane made her way down the hallway, noticing a new box shoved against the wall which hadn't been there the day before. Bending down, she leant against the wall and lifted the flap of the box with one hand.

*More guns.*

Picking one up, Jane tested its weight. It looked like a nice one. She pulled back the chamber, hoping by some miracle it was loaded so she could shoot the giggling bastard. *Typical. Not loaded.*

Chucking the gun back into the box with a clatter, Jane pushed the lid down with her foot and carried on down the hall, feeling horribly sick. She swallowed a few times in quick succession to quell the rising bile and continued into the kitchen.

Eyeing the devastation which greeted her, she leant against the sticky worktop and tried to stop herself from heaving by taking deep breaths.

Taking a fag from one of many half-empty cigarette packets strewn around, she lit it, her heart banging and her mind speeding. Closing her eyes, she immediately wished she hadn't and opened them again quickly.

Jane peered into one of the cupboards for the vodka, but saw nothing in there apart from a tin of unpleasant-looking soup and used pieces of tin foil to make pipes. Sighing, she opened the fridge where a collection of used tea bags sat on one of the shelves. *What the fuck were they for?*

Swaying slightly, she reached for a bottle of lemonade sitting dejectedly in the fridge door and took a swig before spotting the vodka by the sink, shining like a beacon behind a pile of half-crushed beer cans and an open tin of dog food.

Making her way over, Jane narrowly missed treading on a chunk of broken china from the mug she'd thrown at Seth during yet another argument and crammed a handful of pills into her mouth, swallowing them with a large gulp of neat vodka.

Seth staggered in bare-chested, looking as rough as hell and gave her a bloodshot stare.

Cutting him a filthy look, Jane stomped out of the kitchen, feeling there was more chance of calming down and getting some peace if she sat in the lounge. This was scuppered on finding three bombed-out people spark out on the floor.

Indignantly she opened the plywood hatch between the lounge and kitchen and pointed wildly around the room at the various bodies. 'Who the FUCK are they?'

Poking his head through, Seth surveyed the people on the floor. Shrugging, he shut the hatch in Jane's face to continue rolling another joint.

Past caring, Jane stepped over the bodies and switched the stereo on full blast. She looked down at the Saturday morning shoppers going about their business, blissfully unaware that Planet Zog existed above them.

As she sang along loudly to Led Zeppelin, Jane noticed no one on the floor had moved, despite the thumping music and her raucous singing.

*Maybe they were all dead, including her?*

Seth entered the lounge and smiled, listening to Jane sing. He could never stay angry with her for long. Although he should perhaps find out what these people were doing on his floor, he figured he'd deal with her first.

Wrapping his arms around Jane's waist tightly, he whipped

the fag out from between his lips and chucked it to the floor. He wasn't anywhere near finished with her yet. Feeling her anger dissipate, he tilted her face up and pulled her impatiently towards him.

'Seth…' Jane tried to push him off and avoid his mouth as he slipped his hand between her legs. She was still cross with him. *Sort of.*

Seth ripped the T-shirt Jane wore clean down the middle and dropped it on the head of one of the men on the floor.

'What's going on?' the stranger slurred as Seth and Jane stumbled over him.

'Ignore him,' Seth panted, his fingers making Jane more than ready for him.

As desire took Jane over like a train, she ignored the people watching and moaned with pleasure as she fell back on the sofa, Seth's mouth on hers.

# Nineteen

ELIZA STARED AT JANE. She looked great, but had a face like a slapped arse. *For Christ's sake.* It was *her* bloody birthday and she could do without her night being ruined.

Pouring the remains of her pint of cider down her throat, she watched as Jane looked towards the bar. 'Just leave him to it,' Eliza snapped, wishing Jane and Seth would just get over their row. 'Let's get wasted!'

'Did you realise when I got back after dropping you off, that wanker was round again? Seth knows I fucking hate him, yet he *still* lets him in,' Jane moaned.

Eliza sighed. She'd heard it all before. In fact, since Jane had moved into that flat, she'd heard just how much she hated Stuart *every day* and she'd just about had enough of listening to it.

'Yeah, you told me already,' she muttered, for what seemed like the tenth time in the last hour. 'Don't let the twat ruin my birthday. Let's just have a laugh.'

Jane wasn't in the mood for having a laugh, being rational or even listening. 'Seth doesn't give a shit how I feel about *anything*!'

Eliza groaned. *Fuck it.* She was going to enjoy herself, even if Seth and Jane wanted to sulk all night.

EDIE BAYLIS

Watching through the flashing lights as Jane's face seethed whilst she knocked back glass after glass of vodka, Eliza got up to join the others.

· · · ·

DAVIS POPPED HIS HEAD around the doors of the underground bar and scanned the room. He'd left Spooner on the door upstairs for five minutes during a lull to take the opportunity to go for a piss, but couldn't resist having a quick check downstairs.

Spotting Jane in the corner, he eyed her expression and frowned. She'd been on one when she'd arrived and his normal banter and inherent flirting had gone down like a lead balloon. It didn't take rocket science to work out it was something to do with Seth.

Glancing towards the bar, he watched Seth flashing his winning smile at a gaggle of admiring girls and bristled. It had taken days for his black eye to heal and he'd been mercilessly ripped to shreds by just about *everyone* for getting a whack.

Even Seth had the fucking cheek to laugh and he'd been forced to swallow the overwhelming urge to smack the prick in his straight teeth. Then to make matters worse, Phil had blanked him, looking at him in that condescending way reserved only for wankers.

Clenching his jaw, Davis continued to stare over the crowd as Seth casually poured four pints at the same time. *God, he really thought he was something else, didn't he, the smug bastard.*

Ok, so he was useful from the brute force side of things, but he was still a twat. Davis frowned. He knew that Seth dealt gear from the vantage point of the bar, but he couldn't use that one against him without dropping himself in it. He, himself, confiscated dope and then resold it.

Maybe he should have a word with one of the coppers that raided this place? That would piss on Seth's bonfire somewhat, wouldn't it? Or he could 'accidentally' let slip to the gaffer that the man had his fingers in the till? The trouble was the tills always balanced, so how Seth managed that was a mystery.

It was no good. He'd have to put more thought into it. He didn't want the reputation of being a grass. His life wouldn't be worth living. Maybe he'd have a go on Jane? That would destroy Seth, would it not?

Jane looked up from where she was sitting and Davis raised his hand in a wave, giving her one of his best smiles. *Yeah, he'd love a piece of her.*

· · · ·

ELIZA SAT ON THE bench seat, trying to ignore Jake's advances. She wasn't interested. She was too pissed off. Jane's constant scowling had put her in the *worst* mood ever.

She'd even had to put up with Digger twirling Jane around and treating her like something special, in an attempt to cheer her up.

*It was her birthday. HERS.* She should be having a top night, not babysitting Jane's anger problem or her and Seth's fucked up relationship.

Glancing at a figure in the shadows partly obscured by the wall, she squinted and tried to focus. Who was it and who the fuck was he looking at? He was definitely staring over here. *Christ, he was creepy!*

Looking over her shoulder, she followed the lurking figure's stare, realising he was actually staring at Maggie. With a bolt of recognition, she realised it was Maggie's nutter ex. She struggled to think of his name. *Ian! That was it, Ian.*

Involuntarily shuddering, Eliza pulled her eyes away and attempted to coordinate her hand through her drunkenness into her bag for a cigarette, but as Digger sauntered back over, her stomach somersaulted. She'd made it clear on several occasions she'd like a tumble with him, but it was obviously not reciprocated. She'd even thrown herself at him once, but he'd been having none of it.

Eliza felt her temper spike again. She didn't usually have

this problem getting men, unless of course they wanted someone else more and there was no guessing as to who that was in Digger's case.

She knew Digger still held a torch for Jane and that was probably the real reason he wasn't interested. Yes, she'd bet her bottom dollar that was it. *In fact, look at her. She was encouraging him right now.*

Digger continued to push his way through the crowds towards Jane and Eliza felt like crying with rage and frustration. Her anger flared even further when she saw him hand over another drink. For God's sake, Jane had been given drinks all bloody night. How many more did she fucking want? It was her birthday, not Jane's!

The cow was taking the mick right in fucking front of her. Besides, why had Jane even gone out with Digger in the first place? Jane knew she'd always liked him, but she'd had to snap him up first. *As usual.*

*Thank you very much, Jane. Why don't you just fuck everyone's lives up, yeah*, Eliza thought bitterly. Wasn't it enough she had Seth, without keeping all the other eligible men hankering after her too? She'd just about had enough of it.

Knocking the rest of her cider down her throat, Eliza slammed the glass down carelessly on the table and unsteadily pushed herself to her feet.

Jane was far too busy shouting something down Digger's ear to have any warning before the back of her hair was grabbed.

'You fucking bitch!' Eliza screamed, pulling Jane's head around.

Reacting instinctively, Jane grabbed Eliza's arm and twisted it painfully.

'What the fuck are you doing?' Digger roared at Eliza. It had taken him a good while to lift Jane out of her bad mood. Seth had blanked her all evening, having made no attempt to sort out whatever had caused the argument they'd obviously had. In fact, he'd looked over several times to see if she'd noticed him flirting with girls at the bar, but Jane had refused to rise to the bait. At least, after a bucket-load of double vodkas, she'd finally cheered up. But now *this*?

Shocked by the unprovoked attack from Eliza, Jane stared incredulously at her. 'What the hell are you doing, you silly cow?' she yelled. 'What's the problem?'

Eliza tried to focus, her face contorting in a mask of rage. 'It's YOU!' she spat, taking an unsteady step forwards. 'You fuck everyone's heads up and it isn't right.'

Jane was starting to lose her temper. 'Don't be ridiculous! I don't know what you're talking about!'

'Oh yes you do! You've got Seth, so don't pretend you want Digger too. Although you're probably fucking him as well!'

By now everyone had caught wind something was going down and had stopped to watch. A steely glint formed in Jane's eyes. There was only so much she was prepared to take. 'Shut the fuck up now, Eliza, before I shut you up…'

Out of the corner of Jane's eye she could see Seth making his way over from the bar and Davis step through the double doors. *Here we go*, she thought smiling. It was funny how quickly word spread when trouble kicked off.

'Oh, so you think it's funny, do you?' Eliza spat, reaching for a bottle on the nearest table. 'You're nothing but a *whore* and I'm sick of your miserable face. It's supposed to be my fucking birthday!'

The music cut off mid-track and the lights flicked on just as Jane lost it. Not waiting to get glassed, she delivered a right hook to Eliza's jaw, knocking her clean off her feet and over a table.

As Eliza landed unceremoniously on the floor, Jane moved forward, but was held back by Seth, Davis and Digger. She thought she'd done well keeping her temper for so long, but now she was being stopped from meting out justice to the stupid mare.

'Leave it!' Seth growled.

'Why the fuck should I?' Jane screamed, watching as someone knelt down on the sticky carpet next to Eliza and mopped at the thin trail of blood seeping from her mouth.

*Let her fucking bleed*, Jane thought savagely as she shook Davis off her arm. 'And you can fuck off as well!'

'What did you start on her for?' Seth spat. 'She's supposed to be your friend!'

Digger moved forward, sensing the rage crackling between the pair of them. 'Eliza started it, Seth.'

'Yeah, yeah, course she did,' he sneered, not believing a word. He knew what Jane's temper was like.

Jane clenched her teeth hearing someone shout for an ambulance, whilst Eliza rolled around wailing about her face and her ruined birthday. *Ambulance? For one fucking punch?*

She wrestled herself from Seth's grip. 'Fuck you, Seth. FUCK YOU!' Jane glared between him and Davis. 'Enjoy the rest of your night, yeah?'

Seth gritted his teeth, battling with himself not to give Jane a slap and seethed with rage as she stalked towards the doors.

Digger faced him. 'Don't worry, mate. I'll make sure she's ok.' *If he could get her out now, then by the time Seth got back they should have both calmed down. It was worth a try anyway.*

Even though he'd fucked up his chance with Jane, he hadn't been surprised when she'd got with Seth - they were well-suited. It was just a shame their tempers, excessive booze and drug intake got in the way. It needed to stop before it fucked everything up.

As Digger rushed after Jane, the rest of the group reluctantly followed, leaving Seth to glare in their wake.

## TWENTY

JAKE SAT ON THE muddy floor covered in rubble, unable to stop the tears from flowing.

Maggie leant her head against his chest and sighed. 'Come on, babe,' she soothed, trying to form her words coherently, smiling as he wiped a grubby hand over his face, leaving a streak of dirt across his cheek.

'S-Sorry,' Jake stuttered, bursting into a fresh round of loud sobs which racked his entire body. 'I don't know what's wrong with me.'

Digger scowled impatiently. *That bloke was an idiot.*

After Jane's impromptu exit from the Barrels, they'd staggered down the high street into the Oak Apple for a few before last orders, but ended up having more than that. It had taken a further half an hour to calm her from spitting venom over Eliza and Seth, but finally she'd got so drunk that nothing registered.

But then Jake had lost it and after last orders, they'd found themselves side-tracking into a derelict cottage down an alleyway to save him from having an embarrassing public meltdown. The inside was nothing more than an old squat, illuminated through the hole where the window had once been by the dim light from the street lamp at the far end of the alley.

Leaning against the cold brick wall, Digger fidgeted. The wall was not just freezing cold, but wet. He irritably shifted his weight from one foot to the other and glanced dispassionately at Jake's shaking body. He knew what was wrong with him. It was always the same. Every time he got plastered, he had a hysterical crying fit and tonight was no different. *No different at all.*

Jane stood quietly. She was no longer cross about Eliza's unexpected outburst, just hurt. She knew her friend's trap ran away with her when she'd had too much pop, but she'd never turned on her before. *Was what she'd said, really what she thought?*

She didn't know what to think anymore, besides she was far too drunk to think about anything properly. As for Seth, well, it was *his* fault she'd been in a foul mood in the first place. For him to automatically blame her for the shit with Eliza, said it all really. That and how he hadn't bothered to even come after her when she'd left the Barrels.

*Fuck him. It was quite obvious he didn't give a shit about her anymore.*

Digger wrinkled his nose, feeling sick. God only knew what that bloody awful smell was. It was overpowering, like rotten animals. He'd better not step on a dead badger or something like that, otherwise he'd definitely lose his temper.

'What the hell's that?' Jane suddenly screeched. 'I've just trod on something.'

Moving towards her vague outline in the gloom, Digger flicked on his lighter, illuminating a carrier bag on the floor. Squatting down, he peered at it and picked at the knot of the bag.

Maggie looked worried. 'What is it?'

'Don't know yet, but it fucking stinks!'

Jane lent down, placing a hand on Digger's broad shoulder and screwed her face up in disgust. 'Urrgh! That's bloody hideous!'

Digger peered into the bag. 'It's meat.'

'Eergh! Don't tip it out!' Maggie screamed.

Digger eyed the fleshy greying lump of meat and a man's hand lying in the dirt on the wooden floor and paled in the dim light. 'HOLY FUCK!'

Half of the forearm was still attached and dried silvery sinews trailed from the stump. A gold ring sat on the middle finger of the hand.

'Oh Christ!' Jane swallowed down the bile threatening to rise up from the smell assaulting her nostrils.

'What? What is it, babe?' Maggie squeaked.

'An arm and,' Digger scrutinised the greying lump, 'a liver perhaps. Been here for a while, I'd say.'

Maggie jumped to her feet and flapped her arms furiously. 'Oh my God. OH MY GOD!' She started crying. 'What if the rest of the body's in here? What if I've been sitting on it?' Leaning over, she vomited violently onto the floor.

'Calm it down, Mag. It's obviously been here ages!' Jane snapped, pushing herself away from Digger's shoulders.

Digger steadied Jane as she wobbled precariously and found himself concentrating on her mouth. He realised with a jolt he badly needed to kiss her and would find it difficult to stop himself. Sweat began to bead on his brow. He knew his feelings would get too much eventually, but he couldn't do that to his mate, could he?

The thing was, he missed Jane desperately and couldn't get her out of his head. It was torturous seeing her with Seth all the time. With his head swimming, he tried to block the feelings swamping him.

'I've got to get out of here!' Maggie screeched, peering through glazed eyes to try and locate the body parts. She zig-zagged blindly across the floor, screaming as Jake dragged her towards the open doorway.

Jane moved away from Digger. She'd seen how he'd just looked at her and knew she was too drunk to be rational. Taking in his bulging muscles and massive chest, she swallowed. She had to get out of there before she took him up on what she could read in his eyes. It would be so easy to go with it. Seth didn't give a shit anymore and she could do with some strong arms around her right now.

Digger watched Jane waiting to pass through the doorway and glanced at Maggie, standing white-faced at the bottom of the stairs, hyperventilating. He was torn. He knew what he wanted to do and knew it was wrong, but if he didn't move now, it would be too late.

Digger's heart lurched painfully in his chest when Jane stepped forward to take the stairs. Before he could change his mind, he reached through the doorway and grabbed her arm.

Confusion flashed momentarily through Jane's drunken eyes as Digger pulled her towards him, before silencing anything she could possibly say with his mouth.

• • • •

SETH PACED UP and down. It was gone 1am and Jane *still* wasn't back. *Where the hell was she?* Even the Oak Apple kicked out at 12.30, so she should have been back by now.

Grinding his cigarette out on a bare floorboard, he scowled. The whole place might as well be an ashtray, anyway. It was like living in a fucking underpass.

He'd been pacing up and down for nearly a goddamn hour and his feet were hurting.

Picking at his fingers, he wished he could stop thinking. It wasn't doing any use and just driving him mad. Maybe he should go to bed?

*No! Not without her.*

Peering out of the window, he glanced down on the high street for the eighteenth time and made the decision that Jane had ten more minutes before he'd go to find her. Plonking himself down on the sofa, he sparked up another fag and knocked back a couple of pills.

He accepted things hadn't been going too well lately and took the majority of the responsibility for that. He was letting the drug thing overtake stuff and admitted he was more out of control than usual, but he couldn't help it. It was like being on a roundabout that wouldn't stop.

All this shit would have to be rectified somehow. He wasn't prepared to lose her again.

• • • •

DIGGER GRABBED HARDER onto Jane as he took her against the doorway. He thrust into her, his free arm holding her tightly. 'You've no idea how much I want you,' he growled.

Jane relished Digger's familiar driving pace with wild abandonment. She needed it. The only thing putting her off slightly, was the bag of human remains sitting three feet away and Seth, who kept flitting into her mind.

Deciding not to dwell on either of those subjects, she fixed her concentration back to Digger as his body stiffened and slammed into her for the final time, releasing himself with an extremely loud groan.

Doing up his jeans, Digger smiled. 'I enjoyed that, Jane. A lot.'

'Best we keep this to ourselves,' Jane whispered, rearranging her clothes. Turning away, she walked through the doorway.

'About time!' Jake winked as Jane made her way unsteadily down the stone steps. 'We were about to give up and go home!'

Digger followed, his face guilty even in the dim light of the streetlamp. He didn't give a shit if Seth started on him, but the last thing he wanted was Jane to get grief because of him.

Maggie's first thought as the police car pulled up next to them as they walked up the high street was that they'd found the rest of the body. 'Oh, shit!' she muttered. 'Pretend we know nothing about it.'

Jane continued walking, 'About what?'

'The body, you idiot!'

Jane was still laughing at Maggie's paranoia when the police jumped from the car and blocked her path.

'Finally caught up with you then, Ellerton? Knew you'd be lurking around somewhere, but at least you've saved us the trouble of going to your flat.'

Jane stared at them. 'What are you talking about?'

'Jane Ellerton. I'm arresting you on suspicion of actual bodily harm.'

'What the fuck? We didn't do it!' Maggie screamed.

Jane shot her a look, guessing this was nothing to do with the carrier bag of body parts, but *everything* to do with that silly cow, Eliza. *So she'd gone to the cops, had she?*

A policeman reached towards Jane to place the handcuffs on her wrists. 'You do not have to say anything, but it may harm your defence if you do not mention, when questioned, something you later rely on in court.'

Jane instinctively pulled her arms away, only to be grabbed from behind by a second officer.

'Anything you do say may be given in evidence.'

Jane twisted away. 'How about, 'FUCK YOU!' Will that do?'

As she was hastily tackled to the ground with one policeman pressing his knee into the small of Jane's back, Digger stepped forward. His bulk dwarfed the two policemen eyeing him suspiciously. 'What's this about?'

'An incident up the Ten Barrels tonight, Sir. We're taking Miss Ellerton in for questioning.'

With some difficulty, between them the police managed to get the cuffs on Jane's wrists. She glared at them with narrowed eyes as she was unceremoniously hauled to her feet. A hand pushed down on the top of her head and shoved her into the back of the car.

'Someone tell Seth, otherwise he'll go fucking mental,' Jane shouted as the doors slammed.

• • • •

DIGGER PROCRASTINATED for quite some time before banging on the door of the flat. Seth opened it quickly and Digger clearly saw the disappointment flash across his face when he realised it was him, rather than Jane.

A fresh wave of guilt swamped him. He knew more than

most how crazy this man was over her and he'd gone and done to Seth what he was always worrying about.

The problem was, for however much Seth was in love with Jane, he was too and there was nothing he could do about it. If only she'd have him back, he'd prove to her that he'd learnt his lesson. He wouldn't give her grief this time.

Unfortunately, he knew in his heart that Jane didn't want him. She only wanted the man that stood before him now. She'd just been extremely drunk, angry and hurt. *He was a revenge fuck and he knew it.*

Digger tried to smile, quickly explaining Jane had been arrested again. Seeing the anger and frustration on Seth's face, he was glad to leave and flinched when the door slammed with force behind him.

Seth walked back into the lounge and glared at the dog. Before he could stop himself, he slammed his fist through the door in frustration. The splintered wood flew in sharp pieces onto the floor and a new crack ran up from the gaping hole.

*Fuck that hurt*, Seth thought, shaking his hand gratefully. He needed the pain to take his mind away from the shit mess his life was becoming.

*Still, at least he'd got his mates.*

## TWENTY ONE

IAN LAY BACK ON the sofa bed, ignoring the remains of last night's kebab and relished the myriad of colours flashing in beautiful patterns behind his closed eyelids.

He let the rhythmic pulsing and beat of the music from the turntable thrum through his addled mind and his breathing quickened as he increased the speed of his hand working his cock.

He was fucking Maggie. Fucking her hard and making her bleed. He smiled to himself. She was sobbing as he twisted her breasts, digging his fingernails into her flesh and drawing blood. He grabbed the back of her head and yanked her hair, seeing it straining at the scalp as he gave her a slap. *Oh, this was good! Really good.*

His hand moved faster and faster as he imagined the fear in her eyes as he forced her to look at him. He was scaring the fuck out of her and looking every inch as deranged as he felt. Spittle sprayed in his beard as he slammed into her arse harder and groaned loudly.

'Take it, bitch! You know you want it. BEG ME!' Ian shouted, imagining Maggie whimpering.

'I love you, Ian. I've *always* loved you and I'm sorry for

leaving you. Fuck me. Fuck me harder,' she would scream. *He could hear her saying it quite clearly.*

Panting loudly, his brain rushed as the orgasm approached. He'd remind her what she was missing. Oh yes, he'd remind her.

*The cheap... Dirty... Little... BITCH!*

As the hot fluid shot out in a torrent and flowed onto his undone jeans, Ian's hand gradually slowed to a stop and he tried to regain control of his ragged breathing.

'Enjoying yourself?' Teddy laughed from the flea-infested armchair opposite. 'Isn't it time you got yourself back with her? That's the third time this morning you've had one off the wrist and it's starting to make me horny!'

Ian opened his stoned eyes and grinned. 'I'm working on it, mate. Working on it.'

• • • •

DAVIS PULLED HARD on the wrench and applied more force to the nut. *Why was it always the last one that was so bloody stubborn?*

Frustrated, he threw the wrench onto the concrete floor of the garage and wiped his hands down his oily blue overall. Stomping over to the workbench, he picked up the fags he'd sat on earlier and flicked his lighter into life.

He was knackered, thanks to last night's card game. He shouldn't have got involved. Nor should he have lost a bloody wedge he couldn't afford. The only reason he'd been playing in the first place was to win some dough, not bloody lose it. After all that, he hadn't even got home until 3am and it wasn't like he was going to be able to get an early night because he'd taken on extra shifts on the doors at the King's. Working full time in the car garage as well was taking its toll on his energy levels.

Running his hand through his floppy hair, Davis sighed and decided he really needed to sort something out. He fiddled with a screwdriver on the workbench.

He needed a good woman. And had he got one? No. In fact, he hadn't even got a bad one. As a bouncer he should have his pick of the girls. It wasn't like he was short and fat like Spooner.

Glancing at what he could see of his reflection in the grime-covered window, Davis scrutinised his well-built frame. He peered at his face and turned it from side to side. It wasn't bad at all. In fact, he was pretty damn attractive, if truth be known and he looked damn fine in his bouncer's suit, even if he did say so himself.

• • • •

JANE TOOK YET another call from a man enquiring when some items he'd ordered would arrive. 'It should be with you tomorrow at the latest,' she smiled, trying to keep the boredom out of her voice.

She was sick to the back teeth of this place. Actually, she was sick to the back teeth of *everything*, but at least she'd avoided the Spanish inquisition from Seth the other week. Being arrested had conveniently diverted any overspill from the incident with Digger in that cottage.

However, on arriving at the nick, she'd been placed in the holding cell where she'd been unceremoniously handcuffed with her arms over her head to the wire. After an hour, the door had opened and she'd immediately recognised the scowling copper to be a particularly sarcastic, slimy individual that even the other coppers hated.

PC Ginning had smirked in her face with his little squinty piggy eyes and at close quarters he was even more revolting than when seen from afar.

Jane shuddered. He'd made her skin crawl. She'd sarcastically informed him if he was unsure what she'd been pulled in for, perhaps he should look at her notes which would bring him up to speed.

The ugly fuck had taken umbrage at this and wasted no time in crushing her into the wire fencing and roughly shoving his hand between her legs. As he'd pushed his fingers into her, he'd whispered if she cooperated, he could get the charges dropped easily.

Jane smiled ruefully. There'd only been one answer to that, which had been to knee him hard in his visibly engorged crotch. The stupid bastard had obviously forgotten that although she had her hands cuffed and chained, her feet and legs weren't attached to anything...

Dropping to the floor, Ginning had howled and rolled instinctively into a foetal position, clutching at his genitals. Funnily enough, by the morning, the charges had been dropped and Jane had been released at 6am.

*Yeah. Whatever.*

Needing some caffeine, Jane opened a can of coke and took a swig. She had to find something to concentrate on before she lost her temper. Eliza better have a good reason, both for doing what she'd done in the Barrels *and* for involving the cops.

Swallowing a couple more pills, Jane took a deep breath as the phone rang again. She picked up the receiver, then quickly slammed it back down on the cradle. She couldn't talk to anyone. Not until she'd calmed down.

• • • •

IN THE BLACK EAGLE, Paul eyed Debbie quizzically as he waited for her response. He pushed his hair out of his eyes and sighed, getting impatient. 'You can't let what's happened stop us getting what we want, Debs. Look at what he did to me and *I'm* still going for it.'

Turning her cider around on the sticky table, Debbie raised her eyes. It was alright for Paul - he was bloody tapped, but *she* wasn't.

As it was, since that incident with Jane, she'd had to move in with her brother. There had been *no way* she could remain in the flat on her own now. 'It wasn't Seth who fucked me up though, was it? It was *her*. Besides, he doesn't want me.'

Paul had to think fast. This wasn't going quite to plan. He tried to make his face look as incredulous as possible and grabbed Debbie's pudgy hand across the table, giving it a squeeze.

'Are you *serious*? I've seen the way Seth still looks at you. He *does* want you, trust me. He's just under Jane's spell, but together we can fix that.'

*Ok, he knew full well Seth didn't want Debbie. Who bloody would?* He eyed her fat hanging in a large pasty roll over the waistband of her leggings and scowled. He had to be careful. He didn't want to make out that Jane was the problem and certainly didn't want to slag her off, but he had to make this work somehow.

'If we can just split them up properly this time, then he'll definitely come to you.'

Debbie's heart raced as she studied Paul's face. *Was it possible? Had she really been scared off that easily?* She unconsciously ran her finger down her slightly misshapen jaw. *Maybe he was right?*

Seeing Debbie's slight change in demeanour, Paul smiled, realising he was getting somewhere. He wasn't about to tell her he only wanted to fuck Seth up so that he'd be in no fit state to have any form of relationship with *anyone* ever again because then there would be no incentive for her.

'I've already told you, I've got my cousin Stuart on side. He's in the perfect location next door to them and has been working hard to put the spanner in their relationship and he's only just started!'

Paul grinned, seeing Debbie waver further. 'What we need to concentrate on, is fucking it up for them from every angle possible, without either of us being personally involved, right? We need them to end up despising each other but feeling they've broken up naturally. Then we're as good as there!'

Debbie felt a warm glow spread over her. *By God, he was right!* All this time she'd been heartbroken, but she now realised she'd just approached this from the wrong angle the first time around.

Tipping the rest of the pint into her mouth, she smiled. 'I can't believe I've wasted so much time. You're right. Get us another drink, babe. I've just thought of something *really* good to help our cause.'

. . . .

SETH'S DAY HAD GONE too fast. He hadn't had time to swing a cat and the stress crept up him like a red line. Burning a finger on the end of his cigarette, he swore and yanked the car window down to throw the butt out.

Scowling at the bloodstains on his jeans, he grabbed the quart bottle of whisky balanced between his legs, whilst pushing his foot down further on the accelerator.

*For fuck's sake. All he wanted was to get to the pub, but now he'd have to change first.*

Running his hand over his beard, Seth took a slug of spirit. He was always on edge these days. He felt like a coiled spring. Scrunching his face up, he slammed his hand on the horn as a white van pulled out of a side street. It took all of his power not to throw himself out of the car and strangle the driver.

*Calm down! Calm down*, he chanted silently and tipped the remains of the whisky down his throat. Chucking the bottle over his head into the back seat, he turned the car hard into the high street.

Seth roared out of the window as he mounted the pavement to avoid hitting someone who'd stepped out into the road and his scowl deepened, seeing it was that tosspot, Ian. Did he have time to handbrake the car and mow him down?

*Fuck it. He wanted a drink more than wasting time on that prat.*

Ian smiled at the van which had narrowly missed him. Even almost being run over couldn't divert him from what he was doing. *It was too important.*

He was on a mission. He needed to get himself in situ before Maggie came back and judging on the days and times he'd collated on her movements, she *never* returned to her caravan before 9 on a Wednesday. That gave him more than enough time to position himself in the hedge and get settled in for an hour or so. Plus, he'd got a couple of joints to keep him going and he might even get back to the Dragon in time for last orders after he'd finished, if he was lucky.

He couldn't wait to watch Maggie through the blinds of the caravan again. Ian resisted the urge to knead the hardness growing painfully in his jeans. With any luck, she'd start playing with herself, like she had the other day. He ran his tongue over his lips, betting she'd been fantasising over him.

He'd also finally made a decision about the date for the big one. The date he'd been waiting a long time for. The date he'd teach Maggie who was the fucking boss and the date he'd get her back for good.

*He hadn't got long to wait now.*

## Twenty Two

NOW THE PLATES had been fixed on the white Triumph Stag, it was ready to roll. Leaning impatiently against the wing of the car, Seth smoked a cigarette and waited.

Just as they'd been about to leave, Eliza had turned up to try and straighten things out and he'd been surprised Jane hadn't lamped her the second she'd walked in.

He'd impatiently paced around the kitchen as Eliza profusely apologised, insisting it hadn't been *her* who had called the cops. After giving Jane a blatant, 'We're going to be late,' nod through the hatch, he'd left the flat to let them finish up.

Glancing at his watch, Seth tapped his foot. Every second felt like an hour. They couldn't be late. If they were, a lot of people would be behind schedule and the window of time on this job was narrow enough as it was.

Hearing the clacking of Jane's heels on the concrete, he was relieved to see her hurrying towards him.

'All sorted with Eliza?' Seth asked as they got on the road.

'I suppose so.' Jane looked out of the window as they sped towards the address they'd been given. 'What's the crack then?'

Taking his eyes from the road, Seth glanced in her direction. 'Relatively simple. They owe money and I'm collecting it.'

'But…?'

Lighting up another cigarette, Seth changed down gears to take the roundabout, thinking for a moment before answering. He knew full well Jane was watching his every move.

'I haven't had confirmation how many of them there are,' he glanced towards her. 'There should only be one guy, but if not and I get jumped, we're fucked. Also, like I told you, there might be a bird and if so, I want you to deal.' *He may be a lot of things, but whacking women wasn't on the list.*

Reaching over, he pressed a couple of buttons on the radio, hearing white noise. 'You stay in the car until you're needed, yeah?'

Jane studied Seth's side profile, the vein in his neck pulsing. 'You're joking, right? I'm coming in!'

'I don't want you involved unless you're needed.'

'Involved? I've *always* been involved! Don't be such a fucking martyr!'

Seth sighed resignedly. He knew this would happen. It wasn't a secret Jane was way more useful, reliable and certainly more trustworthy than half of the people he knew. It was another thing he loved about her, but he still wanted to protect her.

She was one of the only women to ever be accepted into this shit, but she was still a woman. More importantly, she was *his* woman and he was uncomfortable taking her into something where he was unsure of the score. Still, there was little point in arguing once her mind was made up.

Giving her a hooded stare, he smiled. 'As you wish.'

Jane noticed the first slight colours of autumn tinting the trees as she absentmindedly stared out of the window.

'Also, I don't want you working for that prat anymore.' Seth muttered.

Snapping out of her autumnal daydream, Jane whipped her head around. 'What?'

Seth's eyes remained firmly fixed to the road. 'I said, I don't want you worki…'

'I heard what you said!' she interrupted. 'That's a bit out of the blue, isn't it? Where did that come from?'

'I've said it before. There's something about that bloke I don't trust.'

Neither did Jane. She fully acknowledged her boss was a total and utter wanker, but that wasn't the point.

Seth's green eyes flashed with ill-concealed annoyance. 'He's a seedy bastard and he'll try to drag you into the shit. I *know* he will.'

Jane gritted her teeth. 'So, you think I'm that fucking pathetic I'd take my kit off for that twat, do you? Thanks a lot!'

Shrugging his muscles to release the tension quickly building at the back of his neck, Seth turned to her. 'Oh, don't start. I'm not saying that, am I?'

'What the fuck *are* you saying then?'

Although he didn't want a row, Seth had recently done a bit of digging on that man Jane worked for and didn't like what he'd found. He wouldn't put up with her working there for much longer, whatever she said. Gripping her hand, he pulled his eyes away from the road. 'You're mine, Jane. *Mine*. You're my business and therefore what you do is too.'

Jane wrenched her hand away. 'Fuck you, Seth. No one tells me what to do!'

'What is it you don't understand? I don't like him and I don't want you working there anymore. GOT IT?'

Jane was riled. If she could have got out of the car and walked off, then she would have. '*Got it*? Who the hell do you think you are? I'm not a bendy-spined little girl. I won't take your demands up the arse and say, 'Yes Seth, no Seth.' Besides, what fucking choice do I have?'

She jabbed his arm. 'You're not holding it together right now, are you? Snorting and drinking all the money along with that wanker next door.'

Seth's eyes flashed with rage. 'And you don't, you stupid bitch? Just me, is it? Sort yourself out, girl and stop bringing Stuart into everything. He's got *fuck all* to do with anything, he's a nobody.'

He grabbed her hand. 'We're getting two grand for this job and we'll be alright for brass, so don't try that old chestnut. Besides, when have I *ever* failed to come up with the goods?'

Snatching her hand away, Jane glared out of the window. She folded her arms tightly across her chest whilst Seth sulkily turned the radio up. Staring fixedly at the road, he stamped on the accelerator.

• • • •

AS THEY PULLED UP outside the address they'd been given, Seth reached underneath the driver's seat for his sawn-off and Jane watched impassively in the twilight as he loaded it. 'Ready?'

Nodding, Jane opened the passenger door and jumped out, following Seth up the rubbish-strewn path to the ground floor flat. She could almost hear the adrenalin pumping through her veins as she waited in anticipation for the off.

With a last glance up and down the road, Seth gave her the nod. Knowing the drill, she stepped back, giving him enough room to deliver a well-aimed kick to the insubstantial wooden door.

With an almighty crash, he rushed into the small hallway with its torn and threadbare carpet. A twenty-watt bulb hung from a bare flex on the ceiling, dimly illuminating the outline of a rusty-looking push-bike propped against the brown and yellow ripped wallpaper.

Bolting through a door off the hallway, Seth found two men frozen in shock along with two scantily-clad women. One man with closely cropped blond hair sat on the sofa, his white shirt unbuttoned and his jeans pulled down to his ankles. A girl with bleached hair in a bright pink tube-dress knelt between his legs, her mouth frozen open.

A second man stood agape, his cock hanging pathetically out of his grubby boxer shorts as he was interrupted from giving a red-head a seeing to over the backrest of the sofa.

Wasting no time, Seth quickly despatched one of the men

with a swift punch which sent him flying and coming to rest in a crumpled heap on the floor, his trousers still halfway down his legs.

Jane gripped the blonde woman around the throat and slammed her into the wall, then delivered a head-butt to the bridge of her nose. The blonde crumpled to the floor screaming, blood spurting through her hands from her nose over her pink dress.

'Shut the fuck up!' Jane hissed. The silly cow's screeching was giving her a fucking headache, but at least she wouldn't be going anywhere for a while.

Jumping onto the brown velour sofa, Seth grabbed the second man by his shirt collar and dragged him over the back. 'Where the fuck's the money, you cunt?'

The man's eyes darted from left to right in panic, his mouth quivering. 'W-What money? I don't know nothing about no money?'

Seth shook him roughly and increased his grip around the man's windpipe. 'I think you do and you'll be sorting it out, won't you?'

'We don't have nothing!' the red-head screamed. 'Leave us alone.'

*One doth protest too much*, Jane thought unmoved and glanced back at the blonde on the floor.

'You must have the wrong address,' the man muttered in a strangulated voice, trying in vain to prise Seth's fingers from around his neck.

'That I doubt,' Seth snapped, getting impatient.

Jane could see the vein in Seth's neck throbbing fast and knew it wouldn't be long before he delivered. Suddenly out of the corner of her eye the red head made a swift movement towards Seth with a stiletto.

With the speed of light, Jane grabbed the woman's arm and twisted it back painfully. 'That was silly, wasn't it?' she whispered, yanking the arm down and smiling as the bone snapped.

Jane pushed the screaming woman by the back of the head as hard as possible, leaving her to crash into a cheap two-seater dining table wedged into the far corner and crumple to the floor, making a horrible screeching sound.

'SHUT THE NOISE!' Seth roared and the wailing immediately reduced to a series of quiet racking sobs as the woman clutched her arm and rocked back and forth. Pulling out the sawn-off from his inside pocket, he raised it towards the other man who'd begun to get to his feet. 'OK. Time's up!'

Registering the barrel of the gun, what colour left in the man's face drained, only emphasising the purple bruising spreading across his shattered cheekbone.

'Fucking hell, Martin! Just give them the money! It ain't worth it!' the blonde gibbered, dragging herself to her feet.

'I'm waiting, *Martin*…' Seth growled, staring the man directly in the eyes.

'I think they're taking the piss!' Jane smiled.

'I think you're right…' Head-butting the man with the speed of a panther, Seth smiled, exposing his straight white teeth. 'Now, where were we? Ah yes, you were going to get me that twenty grand, weren't you?'

• • • •

DIGGER WAS HALF an hour early, but being as he'd had nothing else to do, he'd thought he may as well head toward the rendezvous point.

He didn't, however, want to attract attention by hanging around, even though it was well off the beaten track, so he'd taken the opportunity to have a cruise around the nearest town first on his bike. After all, he might as well see if there was any talent hanging around. *There was no harm in looking, was there?*

Pulling up at a set of traffic lights, he revved the throttle impatiently and glanced at a group of three girls wearing tracksuits, each with a pushchair and eating chips on a bench outside McDonalds.

Scowling inside his crash helmet, Digger came to the

conclusion there was more chance of him becoming Colonel Gadhafi than finding any remotely acceptable women in this dump. *For fuck's sake, it was like the gathering of the Ugly Convention. Dear God! No thanks!*

Grateful the lights had now changed to green so that the image of those revolting creatures weren't forever indelibly ingrained on his retinas, Digger kicked the bike into first gear and shot up the road, hoping Seth and Jane would be on time.

He needed to deliver the cash by 9 and then he'd got to go to the city for an appointment with some old bird. She was a fucking pig, but pleasant enough. Besides, he didn't really care because she paid handsomely.

All she wanted was for him to accompany her to some bash at a casino, which was just fine by him. At the end of the day, if he had to shag her afterwards to keep her happy, then so be it.

There were worse things he could do after all. *Like fuck his mate's wife, for a start!*

• • • •

SETH SMILED. It had been pure genius on Jane's part when she'd looked in the thick brown envelope of cash to exclaim the money was short. He knew she was calling their bluff, but the dozy tart with the bust arm went into panic mode.

'Give them the coke, Martin. Just give it to them.' Shoving her good arm down the back of the grubby sofa, she rummaged around.

'SHUT UP, YOU STUPID BITCH!' Martin screamed, the whites of his eyes bulging with pure terror.

Seth looked at Jane with interest. 'What do you think, baby? Will that make up the shortfall?'

Folding the wedges of cash over in her hands, Jane looked thoughtful. 'Oh, I don't know. Depends how much coke there is.' She glanced at the wad of money. 'There's a fair bit missing here.'

'YOU SILLY FUCKING SLAG!' the man screamed to the red-head, watching as she pulled a large plastic bag from behind the sofa cushion. He looked towards the other man for assistance, but this was a pointless exercise because he was still out cold.

The red-head held the bag towards Jane. 'Just take it, will you and then fuck off and leave us alone.'

'No need to be rude!' Jane smirked, taking the bag. 'I'll just check it. It could be flour, for all we know.'

'We're hardly going to put fucking flour down the back of the sofa are we, you silly cow!' The man tried to break away from Seth and move towards Jane. 'You can't have that. I haven't paid for it yet. I'll get fucking killed!'

Turning the gun around, Seth swiftly whacked the man in the temple with the butt. 'Don't be rude to my wife, you cunt!' His eyes narrowed as he squatted closer to the man who'd collapsed to his knees. 'I don't give a shit if you've paid for it or not. That's *your* problem.'

'Ok, Ok. I'm sorry, I'm sorry,' he gibbered. 'But *please* don't take the coke. They'll kill me!' His voice rose to an almost ear-splitting crescendo. 'The money's all there too. I'm sure of it.'

Seth shook his head and tutted. 'Dear, oh dear. Are you calling my wife a *liar*, as well?'

'No. NO! I-I didn't mean it like that!' he stuttered and glanced at the red-head who looked like she was going to pass out.

Jane dipped her finger in the bag and rubbed some white powder onto her gums. She nodded at Seth. *It was coke, alright. Pure, uncut Columbian. What a total fucking result. There was at least two kilos there.*

'You don't want to be playing games,' Seth whispered, watching the man attempt to pull himself unsteadily to his feet. He smiled as he pulled the trigger, ridding him of his left kneecap.

The red-head began screaming all over again as Seth stepped over the writhing man. 'See you later,' he growled, taking Jane's hand.

Shutting the door of the flat behind them, the engine of the Stag roared back into life bang on time.

• • • •

DIGGER PULLED HIS BIKE into the well-concealed layby down the country lane arranged for the meet. Turning the engine off, he walked the bike backwards until it was half-hidden under the heavy foliage.

Removing his crash helmet, he hung it over the handlebars and unzipped his leather jacket, pulling his fags out of the inside pocket. Seeing lights appear, he looked at his watch and sat alert as the Stag pulled into the layby.

'Everything ok?' Digger asked as Seth handed him a brown envelope.

'Absolutely,' Seth smiled. 'I've taken my cut, but the rest's in there.'

After they'd left the house, they'd pulled into a grotty housing estate a mile away and counted the money in the envelope, finding the full twenty grand inside, as expected. Seth had put his two grand cut safely in his inside pocket and chopped a fat line from the bag of coke. *Jane had been right – the stuff was top notch.*

He hadn't minded when she'd set up two further lines. After all, it was only right they should test it out properly themselves before thinking about selling any of it on, wasn't it?

Besides, they wouldn't be mentioning it to anyone. After all, it wasn't part of the job and so therefore it was all theirs.

Digger looked between Seth and Jane. 'Right, I'd best be off and get this dropped back.'

'Catch up with you soon,' Seth said, jumping back in the Stag.

Once Digger had departed, Seth and Jane turned down a path into the woods and found a clearing.

Seth grinned mischievously and took Jane's hand. 'Let's move. I'm far too wired to drive right now.'

Pulling Jane out of the car, he hoisted her over his right

shoulder and she screamed with amusement as he ran off into the woods.

While police sirens wailed in the distance, Seth set Jane down at the base of a large old oak tree and swiftly unbuttoned her jeans.

Plunging himself deep into her as she leant against a tree for support, he smiled.

*They worked far too well together.*

# TWENTY THREE

ZED HAD ALMOST given Maggie a heart attack when she'd returned to the caravan. She gripped both hands around the cheap white wine he'd given her that he'd found when getting his giro. She hoped by holding onto something tightly it would stop the consistent tremoring running through her body.

She'd thought Zed might have hung around for a while to keep her company, but instead he'd headed straight back to his tent.

Maggie stared miserably at the bottle, unsure whether her shaking fingers could cope with unscrewing it. She didn't want to drop it on the floor. She needed something because she'd run out of dope.

Finally summoning up the courage, she moved her fingers up to the lid.

*What was that?* Maggie's body froze. Holding her breath, she strained her ears. She couldn't hear anything now. She must be losing it. Swallowing hard, she screwed her eyes up to try and stop the forming tears from falling.

She couldn't go on like this, seeing and hearing things all the bloody time. She was convinced someone had been following her for months.

Shaking her head slightly, she tried to rid the image of Ian from her mind. A few weeks ago, he'd cornered her down the Dragon and grabbed her wrist. He'd whispered he'd be watching her until she came back to him. The mouth she'd once found so attractive had twisted into a nasty sneer and he'd spat that if she didn't return, he'd kill her.

Maggie shuddered. Whilst she was feeling brave, she twisted the bottle top off. Raising the warm wine to her lips, she slugged down half the bottle in greedy gulps.

Ian hadn't killed her yet and surely if he was going to, he'd have done it by now? But what if he was biding his time? She knew what a fucking nutcase he was.

*What had she ever seen in him?*

Desperate for his attention, she knew she'd played down his freakish idiosyncrasies until it had been too late. By that time, he'd got her well and truly in his clutches.

She knew she was driving everyone crazy with her insistence he was everywhere she went, but she was sure it was him. Maybe she was crazy? *Oh God. Stop it. STOP IT!*

Jane must have been right. She was imagining it. She *had* to be.

Taking another long swig from the bottle, Maggie tried not to retch as the sickly sweet liquid ran down her throat. At least it was Friday and it wouldn't be long before she went out. That's if she could pluck up the balls to step out into the darkness.

She glared at the lantern, sure it was flickering and fumbled in her tapestry bag for her cigarettes. *There was that noise again! Or was it just the wind? Enough! She'd go dolally at this rate.*

Glad her fingers had stopped shaking, Maggie finished the wine and placed the bottle on the side. With an edge of confidence, she decided to flirt with Davis later and see where that led. She might as well. She hadn't seen Bryn for ages – no doubt he'd got fed up of her too.

She began sifting through her clothes looking for a sexy number.

• • • •

JANE WAS ON A mission to get slaughtered and was already struggling to keep her balance. She'd put away a concoction of pills, several pints and had lost track of just how many vodkas she'd had so far, but she couldn't care less. All she cared about tonight was drinking herself unconscious.

Leaning against one of the huge speakers on the floor, she relished the thumping beat of the music, even though she had the mother of all headaches.

As she glanced at Eliza getting it on with a guy with long blonde hair and a silver-studded leather fringed jacket in the corner, Jane felt Seth's eyes burning into her from the bar. She wouldn't rise to his constant staring. *Where the hell did he get off?*

She'd got to work this morning to find the whole building cordoned off and knew straight away it had been Seth's doing. Struggling to conceal her anger, she'd jumped straight back in the car and driven home like a bat out of hell.

Stalking into the flat, she'd kicked open the bathroom door to find him sitting on the toilet reading the paper. Without saying a word, she'd stormed up to him, ripped the paper from his hands and belted him round the face.

Eventually Seth had sauntered into the lounge. He'd sat in the opposite armchair, cocking his eyebrow questioningly and had the cheek to ask why she was back early. *As if he didn't know?*

After much shouting, he'd finally admitted that when she'd mentioned her boss was working late the other night, he'd paid him a visit. Now she now no longer had a job.

*Thanks, Seth. Thanks very fucking much.*

She couldn't think about this anymore. It had taken all day to calm down and that was mainly due to loads of tranquilisers. So much for the heart-to-heart they'd had the other day when he'd agreed the drug stuff was overtaking things and they'd get things back on track. He'd even promised they'd go away at the weekend for a break and also promised to stop dictating to her.

*And now this?*

Jane rubbed her temples, attempting to override the banging pain and necked the remains of her vodka. If she could prise Eliza away from that blond guy, she'd get her to go up the bar for refills. She refused to talk to Seth until she had to.

• • • •

'HEY, VERY NICE!' Spooner remarked appraisingly, his eyes travelling up and down Maggie's shapely legs encased in skin-tight shiny black lycra as she sashayed up the steps to the Ten Barrels.

Smiling and batting her eyelashes coquettishly at both men on the door, Maggie sidled up towards Davis and leaned towards him flirtily, giving him the opportunity for an eyeball down her low-cut pink top. 'What do *you* think?'

On cue, Davis' eyes travelled down Maggie's cleavage and then back to her face. He gently traced his fingers across her jawline. 'You look lovely.' Planting a kiss on her cheek, he smiled. 'Beautiful!'

A shiver ran through Maggie's body as Davis' fingers connected. With any luck he'd take her back to his place, which meant one less night on her own in that van.

She felt substantially better since the bottle of wine had kicked in. Plus, she'd cadged several tokes of a joint from some bloke she'd bumped into. But best of all, she'd managed to blag a lift into town and now it seemed like Davis was definitely interested in her.

Smiling at him from under her fluttering eyelashes, she continued downstairs.

'I think that one's up for it with you, mate,' Spooner said, nudging Davis with his elbow.

Davis smirked. 'Perhaps. I'll see how I feel later. I might get a better offer. I'll let you have this one, though.' He nodded towards the woman approaching the Barrels.

'Christ!' Spooner muttered. 'I'll pass on that!'

Debbie smiled as she walked up the steps. She'd seen the expression on Jane's face as she'd watched her make her way up the street earlier. It wasn't difficult to guess that her and Seth had been arguing.

She'd known she wouldn't have long to wait before the perfect opportunity arose. To make things even better, Ian was due his night with that awful Maggie and she'd just seen her go inside, so if this went according to plan, it would work out a treat.

Reaching the top of the steps, Debbie beckoned Davis over.

Davis scowled. He desperately needed a woman as it had been far too long. His balls felt like they were going to burst, but there was no way he wanted *this* one. 'What's up?'

Glancing over her shoulder to make sure no one else was listening, Debbie pulled Davis down towards her and whispered in his ear. 'Message from Jane. She wants to meet up with you after hours.'

Davis frowned. *Jane? Why on earth would she be sending a message via this thing?*

'We've sorted all that old stuff out now.' Debbie garbled, reading his thoughts. 'It was less obvious if I told you, rather than one of her usual mates.'

She glanced around quickly, relieved to see Spooner was taking no interest in their conversation. 'She's having a hard time with Seth and wants some fun.'

Davis stood back and scrutinised her. *Was she serious? This was great!*

He'd always thought Jane might be up for some with him and there was *no way* he'd miss the opportunity of getting his end away tonight. Especially with her! Feeling his groin beginning to ache, Davis grinned. *It would piss on Seth's chips as well.*

Debbie lowered her voice further. 'Don't mention anything though. Jane said it's important to just tag along after close, and then you guys can play...'

Davis winked. 'Understood. Leave it with me. Thanks.'

Smiling, Debbie continued down the stairs to the bar, hoping the stand-off between Jane and Seth would drag out long enough for this to pull off. In the meantime, she'd go and find Ian.

. . . .

TAKING DOWN ANOTHER pint glass from the brass rack above his head, Seth craned his neck and sighed. *Where had Jane gone now?*

There were far too many people in here tonight. He'd only offered to do the Friday shift at last knockings because he hadn't seen her since she'd walked out first thing and figured if he was working, at least he'd see her. He'd spotted her the second she'd come through the doors in her tight red basque, tiny skirt and black lace jacket and his stomach had flipped, reminding him of the strong effect she had on him.

He'd planned what to say when she came to the bar, but this had been ruined when she'd sent Eliza up instead. Jane had since ignored him the entire evening so far. Worse still, it was so busy he hadn't had a second to leave the bar to go and speak to her.

Holding a pint under the Carling tap, Seth set another one off under the tap next door and quickly tipped his own drink down his throat. He frowned watching Jane lean unsteadily against the side of a bench seat, talking to a man. *Who the fuck was he?*

He wasn't in the mood for this. Why was she so upset about the stupid job, anyway? Did she really think he'd wait until that gimp had tried to fuck her?

Well, it was done now and that fat bastard wouldn't be around anymore, so she'd just have to get over it, wouldn't she?

## TWENTY FOUR

DAVIS WATCHED JANE as he pretended to do a casual inspection of the busy bar. She looked completely trolleyed. His attention was suddenly diverted when Seth beckoned him over and a familiar rush of anger flooded him. *Was he clicking his fingers?*

He studied Seth's face, deciding he'd snap his fucking hand off if he kept on.

Making his way over with difficulty, he moved people out of the way so he could squeeze through the crowd. He gritted his teeth. *This had better be good.*

Scowling as a drunken skinhead spilt a pint down the front of his suit, Davis pushed the man roughly out of the way and tried to hide his rage. 'What's up?' he mouthed to Seth as he got closer.

Seth smiled when Davis appeared behind the ramp. 'Cover for me for five, will you?'

'WHAT?'

'The others are changing barrels and I really need to do something.' Seth vaulted the bar before Davis could respond and people immediately heckled to be served.

'New job?'

'Been demoted, Davis? Ha Ha!'

'COME ON! I haven't got all day!'

'Three pints of Carling, mate.'

Davis stared blankly. He could not believe this was happening. He was not anyone's mate! Demoted? Did he look like a fucking barman? He'd kill Seth for this, the cheeky bastard. This was the *last* fucking straw.

*Don't worry, mate. I'm going to make your woman scream with pleasure tonight*, he thought watching as Seth moved through the crowd.

'Did you see him looking at me, babe?' Maggie screamed down Jane's ear. 'Davis was staring at me. I'm definitely in with him tonight. I really like him, babe.' She pulled at Jane's lace jacket. 'He's *ever* so handsome, isn't he? Do you think he likes me?'

Jane struggled to concentrate, only able to focus on Seth approaching.

'JANE?'

'Sorry, Mags. Yes, he likes you.'

Jane attempted to turn her back on Seth, but he swung her around to face him. 'You going to ignore me all night?'

Jane scowled. He was acting like nothing had happened. Like it was all one big bloody joke. Well, *she* wasn't laughing. 'Go away, Seth!'

Seth rolled his eyes. 'Come on, baby. You're being stupid!'

'Being stupid?' Jane screamed. 'Why don't you just fuck off! What are you going to do next to try to control me?' Her eyes burnt into his. 'Go on, get back behind the bar and stalk someone else. Someone that might be fucking bothered, yeah?'

Seth stared at Jane a moment longer, before turning on his heels and walking away.

Jane was now even angrier than before. She hated it when it was like this. She'd wanted him to say he'd stepped over the line and kiss her, then everything would be back to normal, but he hadn't done that, had he? Nor had he even tried.

She knocked back another drink before she burst out crying

and showed to all and sundry how she really felt. That Seth made her feel out of control and made her feel things she didn't want to feel.

*Like emotion.*

Unable to help herself, she loved him desperately, regardless of how much she didn't want to.

• • • •

IAN PAINSTAKINGLY FINISHED his drink, savouring every mouthful. *It was time.*

He'd seen Maggie over in the corner but she hadn't seen him. She must feel that he'd forgotten about her by now, but that wasn't true. He'd *never* forget about her and he'd told her that. *She should have listened.*

Ian glanced at his sister. She knew what he'd planned and had agreed the stuck-up bitch needed to be taught a lesson, but didn't understand why he wanted Maggie back.

In his opinion, he thought Debbie was jealous. She'd always got funny when he had a girlfriend and had never liked any of them, but she hated Maggie the most. She'd even accused him of being too obsessed!

Ian had to admit Debbie was not the most attractive woman in the world with her pasty skin and buck teeth, but she had no need to be jealous of him being with someone else. It wouldn't change anything *they* had.

He eyed her ample backside straining through her black leggings and thought she could do with losing a stone or two. Still, for all her faults, it had never put him off.

He knew a lot of people wouldn't understand their unconventional relationship, but a woman was a woman, right? Debbie obviously didn't mind either, otherwise she'd have said something over the last ten years he'd been screwing her.

Besides, he didn't care what anyone thought. *He* knew what he wanted. Placing the bottle on the bar, Ian made his way towards the double doors.

• • • •

'JUST POPPING TO THE offy to get some fags before it closes, babe,' Maggie shouted.

'Wait for me. I'll come with you.' Jane replied.

Unable to hear over the music, Maggie stumbled unsteadily up the sticky steps towards the front door. Cheekily pinching Davis' backside, she skipped down the stairs towards the off-licence.

From his position in the alleyway, Ian watched Maggie stumble past. He smiled. He'd known if he bided his time he'd catch her, but this was better than he'd imagined. He'd presumed he'd have to wait at least another hour down this stinking alley until kick-out before getting his chance.

Maggie was rummaging for her purse when she was dragged backwards into the dark by her waist. She didn't have time to react or even scream when Ian clamped his mouth down over hers and pushed her against the cold, slimy brick wall.

Through her drunken haze, she looked into Ian's bloodshot eyes and saw the twisted sneer on his lips. A tight knot of terror formed in the pit of her stomach as she realised with dread, her paranoia had been well-founded all along.

Trying not to gag from the strong smell of fags and piss emanating from him, her eyes darted from left to right. Not another soul had passed the alley, let alone looked down it and the town would be empty until kick-out time, which was *far* too long.

'Missed me?' Ian growled, a trail of saliva hanging between his lips.

Frozen with shock and fear as he pressed his hand tight over her mouth, Maggie was unable to do anything, apart from stare into his eyes and listen. She felt like she was going to pass out.

'I'm going to make you wish you'd never left me,' Ian sneered, his free hand sliding inside the waistband of Maggie's leggings and down her knickers.

Feeling his cock throbbing painfully, he could hardly contain himself as he rubbed her clit hard. *He'd have to show her what to do and lead her like a horse. As usual.*

Rounding the corner, Jane walked unsteadily towards the off licence to catch up with Maggie, but was surprised to hear Debbie's voice.

'IAN!' Debbie screamed into the night as she ran down the steps from the Barrels. '*IAN!*' She'd clocked Jane moving across the room towards the stairwell and if she'd gone outside, that would fuck things up for Ian. She wasn't sure where he was, but knew he wouldn't want to be interrupted.

Immediately sobering up, Jane rushed towards Debbie. Grabbing her wrist, she pulled her backwards. 'What the fuck are you doing?' she yelled, slamming Debbie's head into the wall.

Blood streamed from a gash on Debbie's head as Jane grabbed her around the throat. 'Do you want to tell me what's going on?'

Debbie stared petrified as Jane's eyes burnt into hers. She couldn't go through this again. She was supposed to be keeping it non-personal and didn't want to make her suspicious. *Shit. SHIT.*

Suddenly Davis appeared and grabbed Jane with both arms.

'What the hell are you doing, Davis? Fuck off!' Jane screamed angrily.

'Calm down!' Davis cried, struggling to hold Jane, giving Debbie the opportunity to run off down the road, sobbing.

'I'll fucking find you!' Jane shouted, venom dripping from her voice at the retreating figure but missing Ian running from the alley.

'Get off me!' Jane yelled when Davis pinned her arms down by her side. As he pulled her backwards tightly against him, she ignored the erection she felt against the small of her back.

Turning her around, Davis tried to keep the want out of his voice. He'd no idea how he would wait until later until he could take her. He gripped the top of her arms and wished she'd just put her hands on his throbbing cock. 'You don't need to overplay this, Jane. Later will be good, yeah?'

Wrenching her arms free, Jane stared at him, confused. 'What are you talking about?'

'Jane! *JANE*!' Maggie squeaked, running from the alley with tears rolling down her face.

Forgetting about Davis' strange comments, Jane stared at her friend in shock. 'What's happened?'

'It was *him*! He pulled me down the alley!'

'Who?'

'Ian…' Breaking down in a fresh bout of sobs, Maggie's eyes were wild with fright. 'His hands were down my leggings.' She leant against Davis for protection, but he moved away and placed his hands on Jane's shoulders instead.

'Let's get you two back inside for another drink,' he smiled.

Maggie scowled as she walked up the steps. It was *her* that had got attacked, not Jane.

In the top bar, she glared at Davis back on the door, before turning to Jane. 'I *told* you Ian was following me and I could have sworn I heard his sister calling for him.'

Jane gulped down one of several vodkas and scowled. 'Nah, that was that fat fucking stalker, Debbie, showing her ugly face again. God knows what she wanted.'

Maggie raised her eyebrows. 'What, the one you told me about? That shit with Seth? That was *Debbie*?'

Jane stopped mid-drink. 'Yeah, that's the one. Why?'

'But babe, Debbie's Ian's *sister*.'

• • • •

AS THE LIGHTS CAME up at the end of the night, Seth eyed the pools of beer and smashed glass on the floor and frowned seeing Jane fall against a speaker.

He admitted he'd launched into her when she'd shown her face back downstairs. As it was, he'd been going off his nut worrying where she'd gone and when he'd heard she was up the top bar with Maggie it had wound him up even more. Especially when he'd heard about the shit which had kicked off outside. *Why did she have to get involved?*

Seth sighed. All he cared about now was getting out of here and taking her home.

As Jane unsteadily made her way towards the doors, he slammed the drip tray down on the bar. For God's sake, she was so drunk she could hardly stand.

Grabbing her arm just as she reached the doors, Seth swung her around, pulling her off balance. 'Where are you going?'

'Away from you!' Jane snapped, attempting to focus her glazed eyes.

Seth dreaded to think how much she'd put away. *She was paralytic.* 'I don't want you going anywhere like this.'

'You don't. *You* don't!' Jane slurred. 'That's all I ever hear from you? What *you* want. What you don't want!' Pulling her arm away, she overbalanced. 'I'm sick to death of you trying to control me!'

'You can hardly walk. Just wait!'

'I'm with my mates. You know… *mates.* Now fuck off, Seth and leave me be!'

'Fuck you, then!' Seth screamed, storming back towards the bar. Angrily picking up the broom, he began brushing the smashed glass into one big pile.

# TWENTY FIVE

STANDING AT THE BARRELS door, Davis fidgeted and self-consciously straightened his bow-tie. Ok, it hadn't quite gone to plan last night, but he'd got what he'd wanted in the end, plus, it had the added bonus of getting one over on that wanker, Seth.

What that fat Debbie bird had told him had been kosher, alright. Jane and Seth had definitely not been getting on and when his mate San had turned up to give him a lift home at closing, that dippy Maggie had asked if they'd wanted to join them for a smoke over the park.

Davis had grinned. So that had been Jane's plan? *A bit of al fresco? Perfect.*

He'd planned to offload Maggie onto San as soon as he could so the stupid tart would stop trying to cling on to his fucking arm. He'd hardly been able to contain his enthusiasm as he and San had followed them over town. Luckily his double-breasted suit jacket hid the arousal which had plagued him all night.

Once they'd had a smoke at the park, Davis had wondered when Jane would give him the nod, but she'd soon got up, saying she was going to the toilet. He'd given it five minutes, so not to make it obvious, but when he'd walked around the side of the park's toilet block, he'd been surprised to find her crashed out on the floor. It hadn't been a problem.

Unzipping his flies, he'd freed his rock-solid cock and wasted no time in pulling Jane's knickers to the side, quickly pushing himself into her. *God, she'd felt good.*

Thrusting harder and harder, Davis had fast felt himself start to build, but had seen shock flash through Jane's eyes as she'd returned to consciousness.

'What the fuck are you doing?' Jane had screamed, clawing at his face, until he'd silenced her with his mouth.

She'd been a fiery one alright, but the game she'd been playing had only heightened his arousal. Ripping her top open, he'd bitten down hard on her breasts.

'DAVIS!' she'd screamed. 'Stop this!'

It was only then he'd realised Jane was being serious. He'd felt a bit bad, but by that point was too turned on to care whether she'd been up for it or not. *Besides, she'd get over it. She liked him, didn't she?*

The only trouble was, her shouting and screaming had been getting on his tits, as had the clawing at his face. Holding her down by her arms, Davis had forced his tongue back into Jane's mouth to shut her up, but then he'd come so hard, he'd been unable to stop himself crying out with one of the most intense orgasms he'd ever had and she'd started shouting again.

His cock had barely stopped unloading, when out of nowhere San had grabbed Jane's hair. Swiftly smacking her head down hard on the pavement several times, he'd knocked her out cold.

'That's better! What's her problem?' San had muttered. 'Come on, Davis, shift over. My turn.'

• • • •

ELIZA GLANCED AT JANE and smiled sadly before returning her eyes to the television screen.

She felt like shit for two reasons: one - she was completely hungover and two - because she couldn't remember why she'd got so drunk she'd been unable to see what had being going on. Jane was her best mate, after all and she should have been there for her.

She'd desperately tried to find an excuse for her lack of ability. She just hadn't been thinking straight. *Surely that counted for something?*

Jane ignored Eliza's sympathetic expression, not wanting it and certainly not needing it. It would have been more helpful for her to have been there when it had mattered. *But she hadn't, had she? Nor had any of the others.*

Swallowing down the bile rising uncomfortably in her throat, Jane took another swig out of the bottle of homemade wine. It was disgusting but she was past caring.

She hadn't wanted to stay at Eliza's last night, neither had she wanted to stay at Maggie's, but she'd had to stay somewhere. There had been *no way* she could have gone back to the flat to deal with Seth. She didn't know when she'd be able to deal with him, but would have to soon.

Eliza looked up again. 'Are you going to call the police?'

Jane almost laughed, but found clenching her teeth helped her maintain a blank expression. Call the Police? Looking the way she looked and the state she'd been in last night? With her past, the record she had and with the people she knew? No, she'd sort it out herself and face it alone - like she always did.

Her head pounded, but she refused to think about this anymore. *Couldn't* think about it. She needed to hold it together.

Jane took a deep breath to try and quell the speeding in her head which threatened to rush over and send her gibbering in panic out of the room. The longer she allowed herself to think, the more the panic rose and spread through her mind like a virus.

She felt guilty. Firstly, because she felt *nothing* about what had happened. Not angry or surprised, not even upset.

*Just nothing.*

Secondly, if she hadn't been so mashed it wouldn't have happened. Or maybe she could have stopped it before it had gone that far?

Shakily lighting up a fag, she felt sick to the stomach. She'd never have got so paralytic if she'd realised her 'friends' would have stood around doing nothing whilst she'd been raped. She shuddered, finding it difficult to swallow that none of the people she'd classed as friends, seemed to be and she wondered again how on earth she would tell Seth. *If she told him, that was...*

'Is it ok if I go for a bath?' Jane asked. She desperately needed to wash the filth from those bastards off her. She wanted to scrub herself with bleach. *Anything* to remove the memory and any trace whatsoever.

Finishing the rest of the wine, Jane climbed the stairs towards the bathroom and gagged as the sediment flowed down her throat. She smiled slightly. A couple more bottles of this and she'd be drunk enough to go out.

• • • •

SETH SAT AMONGST a pile of empty beer cans. He hadn't even got any whisky left because he'd finished the entire bottle last night waiting for Jane to return. He'd waited all night and had she shown? *Had she fuck.*

Grating his teeth, the vein in his temple throbbed painfully. Where the fuck was she? He'd kill her when she finally showed up. *If she showed up.*

A wave of panic flooded through his system. She couldn't leave him. She was his fucking wife, for God's sake. She couldn't just disappear. He could also definitely have done without Stuart inviting himself round last night for a smoke either.

The prick had seemed almost *pleased* Jane had gone AWOL and banged on how he was better off without her. She'd probably gone off with someone else again, he'd said. Hadn't he seen Jane flirting with that bloke with the long brown hair?

*What bloke?*

In the end, he'd told Stuart to leave. The man wasn't helping by making stupid fucking comments.

Staring at the ceiling, Seth rolled his eyes. Jane was probably right about Stuart. Not that he'd any intention of telling her that. He cracked his knuckles and wished he hadn't punched the wall.

Draining the dregs of another can, he threw it angrily across the room and grimly surveyed the damage he'd done. He'd ripped the lounge door clean off its hinges and the bedroom door was in the same state. The bathroom and kitchen doors were also unusable, as he'd kicked them to smithereens and a big chunk of plaster was missing out of the wall, where he'd hurled the television, now lying on its back in the corner of the room.

It was a bloody good job Jane hadn't shown up. He'd probably have throttled her if she had.

Feeling the rage ramping up again, Seth reached for another beer. So, help him, when he found out who she'd felt the need to spend all night with, he'd kill him and then after that, he'd kill *her*. He'd had enough of her games and all this shit. It would have to stop.

# TWENTY SIX

MAGGIE WAS GLAD JANE was too busy putting together the third joint since arriving to notice her staring. When she'd heard a car pull up outside the caravan at midnight, she'd initially thought it was Ian again, but was relieved to see Jane fall up the steps, drunk.

As she'd ushered Jane onto the bench seat, Maggie wondered how on earth she drove in that state and forced herself to ask how she was, even though she didn't want to hear the answer.

She watched Jane light the joint, her glazed eyes focusing on somewhere that didn't exist and exhale a thick stream of blue smoke that drifted up to form a heavy cloud near the roof.

Biting her bottom lip to postpone the tears pricking at her eyes, Maggie studied the fresh red welts around Jane's throat and wrestled with the feelings of guilt and anger she'd had all day.

She'd been over the moon when Davis had agreed to come to the park last night. As they'd made their way across town, she'd swayed against him laughing, watching Jane weave along the road with her shoes in her hand and Eliza staggering behind.

She hadn't liked that Davis hadn't taken his eyes off Jane though. *She* was the one who had been supposed to get his attention.

Once they'd reached the park and had a smoke, Maggie had forgotten what she'd been sulking about. Realising she hadn't seen Jane since she'd staggered off to the toilet block, she'd decided to hide and jump out at her.

Giggling with the prospect of giving Jane a fright, she'd tiptoed around the corner, but her smile had immediately vanished seeing her on the floor with Davis on top, rutting like an animal.

Overcome with jealously and humiliation, Maggie had stared uncomprehendingly at Davis' mate, who'd also been watching, then flounced back to join the others.

*Always Jane. Jane, Jane, Jane!*

Shifting her weight on the seat, Jane waved the joint in Maggie's direction. Mechanically leaning over and forcing a small smile, she took the joint, noting half of Jane's long red nails had snapped.

A fresh wave of guilt rushed over her. She'd heard Jane scream and seen her claw Davis, who'd had his hands around her throat. She'd then seen his mate knock her unconscious and take over.

*Fuck! She'd watched them do this and hadn't done a thing.*

Maggie passed the joint back to Jane and watched her pull a bottle of vodka from her bag.

Gingerly touching the red welts on her throat, Jane swallowed. Getting very drunk to block out all thoughts hadn't worked. She didn't know exactly how she felt about Maggie or any of her friends yet, but that was the least of her problems right now.

As for Seth, well, she couldn't make up her mind whether he'd reacted worse, better or exactly as she'd expected. She shivered. All she wanted to do was switch her fucking head off.

After suffering the indignity of Davis acting normally on the Barrel's door earlier, for once in her life, she'd been unsure how to deal with the situation. When she'd blanked him, he'd just grinned and shrugged his shoulders, as if last night had been a standard occurrence.

Surrounded by the people she'd once trusted, Jane had somehow got through the evening, but by 10 had been relieved to see Seth enter the bar, his eyes scanning the room for her. Her heart had been in her throat. She'd been dreading this moment, but knew it had to be done.

Agreeing they needed to talk, they'd left the Barrels and driven to a car park. Seth had scrutinised her silently with a murderous expression on his face the whole of the journey. He knew he was waiting to hear something he didn't want to, but it was only when she'd killed the engine, did he turn the car stereo off.

He'd turned in the seat to face her. 'So... Where have you been?'

Jane had sat a further minute in silence, unable to start the conversation she didn't want to have. Knowing there'd been little option, she'd falteringly begun to tell him what had gone down. She'd glanced at him as he sat immobile, his steely eyes fixed on her.

'For fuck's sake,' Seth had finally muttered through his clenched jaw, the anger rising off him in waves. 'I said you were too pissed to leave without me.' His voice had been dull. 'Why the *fuck* didn't you come back?'

Jane hadn't been able to answer that and she'd continued staring out of the windscreen into the dark night, wishing she could have been enveloped in its blackness.

Rubbing her hand over the painful lump on the back of her head, she'd explained she'd come round on the floor to find Davis on top of her with his hands around her throat. The next thing she recalled, after a searing flash of pain, was the other guy on her. *For a split second, she'd also seen Maggie out of the corner of her eye.*

Lurching towards her, Seth's hands had tightened around her throat and pulled her over the gear stick. The green of his eyes were ringed by a thick outline of deep burning black anger. 'You stupid, *stupid* bitch!' He'd shaken her hard. 'I *told* you I didn't want you to go!'

Tightening his grip further, he brought his face an inch away. 'You were too pissed. What the fuck did you expect?' Seth shook Jane again. 'You did this to *yourself*!'

Jane hadn't attempted to fight back. She'd felt dead. *Wiped out. Numb.* Her sobs had caught in her throat and she'd felt she would black out. She'd wished she had. At least she'd have had some peace. *Some oblivion.*

Seth had thrown her back in the seat, her head hitting the glass of the driver's door. Opening the passenger door, he'd turned to her once more. 'I shouldn't have let you fucking go!'

She'd then watched Seth storm around the car park, kicking the fuck out of anything and everything in sight.

Jane had remained stock still in the driver's seat, trying to work out what else she could have done to change what had happened. She'd summoned up the strength to claw at the second man's face with all her might. Her nails had gouged his flesh as he'd frantically thrust into her. Twisting her body, she'd rolled out from under him, where he'd tried to grab her ankles, but she'd kicked him square in the face.

Rolling backwards and to the side, he'd screamed obscenities whilst she'd taken the opportunity to run. She'd found the others crashed out on the grass, smoking and from there, she'd silently watched Davis and his mate quickly make their way back towards town.

Jane scowled at Maggie as she clattered around putting something in one of the little cupboards. In the small confines of a caravan this was just too loud. She wanted to smash Maggie's fucking head in. Wanted to take her anger and pain out on someone. *Anyone.*

She turned her head slightly so Maggie wouldn't see the tears forming in her eyes.

Jane had needed Seth to hold her, tell her he loved her. To wrap her in his heart and tell her it would be ok. *It wasn't ok, though and it wasn't going to be ok either.*

Despite not wanting to go back over the sting of Seth's

earlier rejection, Jane couldn't stop her mind from replaying it over and over and *over*.

She'd eventually got out of the car and walked towards him. He'd been sitting on a tree trunk at the edge of the car park with his head in his hands. Brushing the hair out of his eyes, fat tears had rolled down his cheeks. The pain in his eyes was so tangible, she could have tasted it.

Smacking her hand away, Seth had angrily wiped his cheeks with the back of his hand. 'Get the hell away from me!' he'd spat. 'This is all your fault. How the fuck can I screw you now?'

Jane had stared at him hollowly. 'Is that all you care about?'

Seth had stood up, his voice icy. 'No. That's *not* all I care about, Jane. Far from it. Now leave me the fuck alone.' Turning, he'd walked towards the road and hadn't looked back.

Slowly walking back to her car, Jane had put her head on the steering wheel and cried.

'Are you alright, babe?' Maggie asked in a small voice, breaking the silence.

A single tear rolled down Jane's face. 'Not really, no.'

Maggie sat down forlornly next to Jane on the caravan's narrow bench seat and burst out crying. It was obvious she was thinking about what had happened. *What she, herself, should have stopped, instead of watching.* 'I'm sorry, babe. I'm *so* sorry for letting you down.'

Jane looked at the floor. *There wasn't anything to say.* Unscrewing the red top of the vodka, she took a swig and let the hot burn of the spirit numb her mouth.

*If only it could numb her mind.*

. . . .

SETH WAS READY. Acknowledging that although he wasn't in the best of states physically or mentally at this precise moment, he knew if he didn't take advantage of getting at least one of the bastards, he'd have to wait maybe another week before getting the chance again. *And he couldn't wait that long.*

The engine of the Senator ticked over quietly at the end of

the road and he'd been gripping the steering wheel so hard and for so long, his knuckles were white. The bastard better hurry up because he was fast running out of time.

Taking one hand off the wheel, Seth grabbed the whisky from the passenger seat and took a long gulp. Once this was done, he'd drink the second fucking bottle as well.

Clenching his jaw, Seth tried to steady his heart. It felt like it was going to drop out of his chest. How dare the bastard do that to Jane. *His* Jane.

He wanted to torture the fuck out of Davis, but knew he hadn't the patience to orchestrate that. This needed to be dealt with immediately. It was the only way he could cope right now.

Seth smacked the steering wheel angrily. He knew he'd been awful to Jane when she'd needed him. He should have reacted differently, but his anger had made him impotent to behave any other way.

What had happened to her had hurt. Hurt intensely. It was like a knife to his heart, so he'd wanted to hurt her like she'd hurt him and he reckoned he'd achieved it because she'd looked broken.

He shouldn't have done it. It was wrong. He should have made Jane feel *better*, not worse. However, hopefully what he was about to do would at least go *some* way to make amends.

• • • •

DAVIS WAS GLAD TO get out of the Barrels for the night. Despite the outward bravado, he'd felt a tad uncomfortable after seeing Jane. He didn't think he'd feel bad, but he did. *A little.*

At least he'd finally fucked her though, plus getting one over on Seth for making him look like a wanker had been an added bonus. Not that he'd ever find out about it. It wasn't like Jane would tell him. He hadn't expected his mate to have a go though.

Glancing over his shoulder, Davis stepped out onto the road, grateful he was almost home.

He was a foot from the other side of the road when he was suddenly blinded by headlights and the roar of an engine. 'What the fu…'

As the grill slammed into Davis' legs, sending him onto the bonnet, he had no time to react. The expression of shocked terror on his face froze for ever when his head smashed against the windscreen.

Seth slammed his foot savagely on the brake and the body fell sideways onto the road. Slamming the car into reverse, he backed up, the engine screaming. Crunching the car into first gear, he focused on the immobile figure lying awkwardly, before stamping his foot back on the accelerator.

He carefully lined up the wheels to ensure a direct second hit and as the car jolted up and ran Davis over for the second time, Seth laughed loudly, resisting the urge to jump out of the car and stab the fucker until every drop of blood had drained from his treacherous body. *The job was done.*

Quickly speeding away, Seth sparked a fag up. *One down, one to go.* He didn't know the other guy's name, but one thing was for sure and that was he would definitely find him.

*Soon.*

# TWENTY SEVEN

'YOU OK?' SETH ASKED, squeezing Jane's hand. He glanced towards her, watching as she unscrewed a bottle of pills and placed a couple into her mouth. 'Any for me?'

Silently handing the brown glass bottle over, Jane reached for the vodka rolling around in the foot well. Her dark eyes focused in concentration at something unknown far in the distance as they sped towards the city.

Throwing a couple of tablets into his mouth, Seth swallowed them dry. 'It will over soon, baby,' he murmured, overtaking a van creeping along at a snail's pace.

Jane stared ahead. *Would it really be over?* Sometimes she doubted that very much. She reached for her gold case, thankful that at least they didn't have to bother finding money for coke for a while.

She took a pinch from the powder and when her nostrils began to burn, decided maybe they should have cut it down with something, like they'd done with the half they'd flogged.

*Sod it. Another nose bleed didn't matter on top of everything else.*

Taking another swig of vodka to wash away the bitter taste making its way down the back of her throat, Jane felt the coke work its magic in her brain and she gazed back out of the window.

'Jane?'

Seth's deep voice snapped her from her thoughts and she turned towards him, just able to make out his eyes in the dark.

'It will be alright, you know.'

'Yeah…' Sighing, Jane returned to stare back out of the window. She knew Seth was attempting to gee her up, but she just wanted this over with. It was almost a week since that night at the park and she still felt raw about the whole thing.

Well, not actually the whole thing. She'd found she'd easily switched off and bypassed the physical side of things, but it was what Seth had said which had got to her. That and what the others had done, or rather *hadn't* done.

She silently cursed herself for the thousandth time for being oversentimental. She was as tough as old boots, after all. *At least, that was what everyone thought.*

Maybe, just *maybe*, she was sick of having to be tough and pretend nothing bothered her, when *everything* bothered her. Sometimes she just felt like running away and screaming. Screaming, screaming, *screaming* and never stopping.

The fundamental flaw was, although she could easily run away from everyone else should she choose to, she couldn't run away from herself. However, she could at least drink and take enough drugs to enable her to forget what and who she was for a while. She'd been doing it for long enough and was exceptionally good at it.

Seth frowned and tried to remove the lump forming in his throat. He could still picture Jane's empty face when he'd finally located her after his outburst. He hadn't meant what he'd said. He'd just been cross by not being in the position to protect her.

Holding her close, he'd stroked her hair and flicked his mind off. He was gutted about what had happened, but he was damned if Jane would see him cry again. *Once was more than enough.*

When he'd informed her that Davis wouldn't be returning to the Barrels and she probably wouldn't see him again, her face had remained expressionless.

Seth narrowed his eyes and focused on an articulated lorry ahead blocking the road. It had been a dead cert she wouldn't be seeing that wanker again. When the news had flown round the town a day later about the 'awful hit and run accident,' she'd put two and two together.

So close to where he lived as well.

*Yeah, terrible.*

Pulling off the main road onto a network of smaller side roads, they headed into a less-built up part of the city. Flicking the headlights to full beam, Seth searched for the turning he wanted and when the sign for the caravan park came into view, he dipped the lights to sides.

It had been a stroke of luck on Tuesday that Spooner had come in the Black Eagle looking for Jane. He'd leant on their sticky table, causing Seth's pint to slop out over the top of his glass and smiled. 'San said to tell you he's sorry.'

'San?' Jane had been confused.

'Davis' mate,' Spooner had continued. 'He'd obviously heard about the accident.'

Jane had felt Seth go rigid.

'Poor guy,' Spooner looked from Seth to Jane sadly. 'He said they were mates from college and asked me to pass on a message to you. He said it was important.'

Jane felt sick and had glanced at Seth, whose expression remained neutral.

'What's it about, then? Didn't realise you knew him? I'd never seen him before.'

Jane had smiled at Spooner's chubby face as the lies tripped off her tongue. 'I don't know him at all, he must have me mixed up with someone else.'

'Where is he now?' Seth had asked quietly, his fist clenching underneath the table.

'No idea, mate. He had to go because his Astra was parked on the double-yellows.'

Bidding them goodnight, Spooner had disappeared out of the

thick old wooden door on to the high street and in the space of two days Seth had located the man. *He'd done well.*

• • • •

SQUEEZING JANE'S HAND, Seth looked at her in the half-light. 'Here we are.'

Jane's stomach lurched as the car slowed to a halt in front of a group of large trailers standing on concrete bases. An Astra was parked out the front of the one on the left. 'Just remember I want to be the one to finish it,' she muttered quietly, a steely resolve in her eyes.

Seth nodded as they got out of the car. Shrugging his jacket on, he banged loudly on the door with his fist. Jane stood at the base of the steps behind him, her heart beating like the clappers. She hadn't wanted to see this guy again. *Ever.*

As the silhouette of a figure appeared behind the frosted glass door, Jane took in a deep breath.

Seth looked deceptively calmly at the slim woman with dark blonde hair scraped into an unflattering ponytail. She held a toddler in her arms. 'San there?'

Jane glanced at the woman. *A kid? This complicated things somewhat.*

'Yeah?' San said in a gruff voice as he made his way to the door, trying to work out who the visitors were.

Placing one steel toecap in the doorframe, Seth turned to Jane. 'Is this him?'

When Jane stepped to the side and faced San full on, recognition flooded his face. His skin paled as the situation became clear.

'Yep,' she said confidently, only resentment in her eyes as she stared at the guy in the door.

'J-Jane! Er, Hi. Did you get the message? The one I sent from my mate?'

'Your *mate*?' Seth sneered, grabbing San around the neck. Pushing him backwards into the trailer's lounge area, he beckoned Jane to follow with a nod of his head.

The woman who'd been standing stock still and confused-looking, suddenly came to life. 'What the hell are you doing? What's going on?'

She looked towards her boyfriend who was wide-eyed with terror, his hand grasping at his throat. 'San? SAN? What the fuck's this about?'

The toddler took this opportunity to scream in a loud, high-pitched wail and Jane clenched her teeth.

'Do you want to tell your missus or shall I?' Seth snarled. 'Get yourself and the kid into the bedroom, lady and stay in there until I say otherwise.'

'*What*? Are you mad? I'm going to call the police. You can't barge in here like this!'

As the woman moved towards the door, Jane blocked her path and smiled icily. 'I suggest you do as he says.'

Looking into Jane's cold eyes, the woman's confidence faltered. She glanced back at her boyfriend. 'San…?'

'Do as they say, Maria, for fuck's sake. I'll sort this out. It's a misunderstanding.'

'If only you were that considerate towards other women,' Seth growled.

Jane watched the woman nervously move into the bedroom with the child and close the door behind her.

'I guess you, rather than your *mate*, knows my wife?' Seth muttered, before head-butting San square on the nose.

'I-I'm sorry. I'm sorry! I don't know what came over me.' San's eyes watered as blood flowed onto his white Nike T-shirt. 'Davis told me to do it.'

'A coward to the end,' Seth snarled. 'Don't lie!' He tightened his vice-like grip on the man's throat. 'Easy to blame him, even though he's equally as much of a wanker as *you*.'

With his free hand, Seth reached into his pocket and pulled out a roll of duct tape. Ripping off a piece with his teeth, he quickly bound San's wrists together.

'P-Please! *Please* don't hurt me!' San gibbered, seeing Seth's hate-filled expression and realising resistance was futile.

Pulling the man to his knees by his slicked back hair, Seth kneed him hard in the face, then threw him backwards onto the grubby, beige blood-splattered carpet.

Sobbing in pain, San looked pleadingly at Jane. 'Please. I'm sorry. I'll do *anything. Please...* I've got a child.'

Jane returned San's gaze unfeelingly. 'Maybe you should have thought about that before you raped me.'

'I-I didn't rape you... I didn't...'

Seth's fist exploded the man's lip, along with a couple of teeth. 'You normally knock someone out and force yourself on them, do you?'

San stared up in terror.

'DO YOU?'

'No. *No*! I shouldn't have. I shou...'

'You cunt!' Seth ripped another length of duct tape from the roll. 'I've had enough of your whining.' Effortlessly gagging the man scrabbling around on the floor, he laughed. 'It's for your own benefit. You'll wake your neighbours the rate you're bleating. You wouldn't want them to know what you are, now would you?'

Weird squeaking noises came out of San's mouth as it was forced into a hideous grimace. Swiftly undoing the black leather belt around the man's jeans, Seth wrenched them down in one movement. The panicked sounds sounded almost cartoon-like and San's eyes bulged with abject horror.

Jane stifled the urge to laugh when Seth pulled a large hunting knife from his inside pocket. She smiled, knowing *exactly* what was coming.

Seth winked at Jane and spun the knife around in his fingers. 'Time for divine retribution.'

Stepping forward, Jane looked San directly in the eyes. 'Enjoy!'

Choking garbled noises escaped from San's mouth as he thrashed about pointlessly on the floor, the reality of what was about to befall him seeping into his panicked mind.

'Don't really want to touch it,' Seth muttered. His nose

wrinkled up as he grabbed the end of San's flaccid cock roughly. 'Needs must, I suppose.'

Holding it taut, he quickly cut it off at the base and blood sprayed everywhere. He slit the tape across the man's mouth and animalistic howls and hyperventilating choking sobs escaped, silenced only by San's own cock being rammed into his mouth.

Jane's expression remained blasé as she watched Seth wipe spattered blood from his face. Removing San of his balls, he threw them nonchalantly onto the carpet.

'Won't be doing that again, will you?' Seth raged, grabbing San around the throat and repeatedly banging his head against the floor, all cool demeanour now blown apart. 'YOU FUCKING BASTARD!'

The man started fitting horribly. Raising the knife, Seth plunged it deep into San's chest. Once, twice, three times. The frenzied stabbing upon the inert body continued, whilst the carpet pooled with dark blood.

'SETH!' Jane interrupted, grabbing his arm. 'It's done!'

Wild-eyed and with his mind elsewhere, Seth ignored her and continued to plunge the knife into flesh.

'SETH!'

With a jolt, Seth finally snapped out of the trance and ran his dripping hand through his hair. He slowly turned to Jane, his cold eyes unseeing. Shaking his head to clear it, he pushed away a long curl stuck to a thick streak of blood across his cheekbone. His green eyes, ringed with black, drilled into hers as he rocked back on his haunches.

Jane scowled. *Some wash load this was going to be... And he'd promised she could finish it. It was her argument after all, wasn't it?*

Wiping the blade of the hunting knife down his blood-soaked jeans, Seth glanced at the sticky fingerprints he was leaving over the sheath. 'For fuck's sake, the messy cunt!'

Pulling himself to his feet, he surveyed the carnage of the completely smashed broken object that no longer resembled a human being. 'Right, one second.'

Jane's eyes followed Seth as he disappeared out of the trailer. She then returned her gaze back to the end of the bastard's cock. It was still half-poking out of his slack mouth and his glassy unseeing eyes stared sightlessly at the ceiling, pebble-dashed with his own blood. She felt nothing apart from annoyance.

With a flash of frustration, she moved over to the mess in front of her and stamped on San's face, relishing the sound of the crunching bones under her boot.

An arm grabbed her from behind and pulled her away. 'Come on.'

Jane watched Seth unscrew the cap of a petrol tin and douse the body with the pungent liquid. Throwing the remains over the television and some items on the floor, her attention was drawn to a small blue ride-on tractor sitting in the corner. 'The woman? The baby?'

Seth glanced backwards. 'Oh yeah. Forgot about them.' He flicked the lights off and the room fell into darkness with only the moonlight outlining their silhouettes. Feeling his way to the bedroom door, he opened it.

The woman sat on the bed with the sleeping toddler in her arms and stared with wide-eyed shock at the blood-soaked man in front of her, before letting out a blood-curdling scream.

'Shut the fuck up!' Seth hissed, pulling the woman roughly to her feet.

'What have you done? What the *fuck* have you done to him?' she shrieked, peering blindly around in the dark whilst she was pulled from the bedroom and ushered towards the front door. 'San? SAN...?'

Seth's teeth glinted in the moonlight as he smiled at the blonde woman. 'You won't be seeing him again, love. And your kid here,' he looked towards the sleeping child, 'no longer has the stigma of having a *rapist* as a father. Unless you wish to tell him, of course.'

'A rapist?' the woman whispered.

'Yes. A fucking RAPIST!' Seth pushed her towards the

door. 'Now get out of here. As far away as possible.'

The woman stared at Seth incredulously. 'But where? What am I supposed to do?'

Seth laughed. 'Personally, I don't give a flying fuck, lady, but I *do* know you're not going to want to be here.'

Pulling out a small packet from his pocket, he stared deeply into her eyes and shook the matches in her face. 'I do know though, if you so much as breathe a fucking word about *anything,* I promise I'll hunt you down and destroy you. NOW GO!'

The extent of the situation finally sank in. Slowly nodding, the woman shakily walked down the metal stairs into the night.

Watching her retreating figure fade into blackness, Seth turned to Jane. 'Time to go. Start the car.'

Jane took one more look behind her and then left. Sitting with the engine of the Senator running, she watched Seth flick a match before he walked towards the open car door.

Slipping into the passenger seat, Seth smiled, the orange glow from the raging fire behind them lighting up his face. He grabbed Jane's hand as he sparked up a fag. 'We'll get that weekend away now shall we, baby?'

# PART TWO

## TWENTY EIGHT

GLANCING DOWN AT HER watch for the fourth time in approximately three minutes, Jane disappointingly found the time had not moved forward marginally enough. Had it stopped?

Shaking her wrist, she looked at it again. It was still 9.57. *This was a nightmare. How many more hours?*

Dizziness enveloped over her in waves as she cracked open the second can of Fanta of the morning. Maybe taking a few more tablets might waste a bit more time?

Three long months now she'd worked at the warehouse and could honestly say she'd never been so bored in her entire life.

Trying to focus her hungover eyes on the job sheet in front of her, Jane grated her teeth to stop herself from slamming her fist down on the workbench. She poked the fresh purple bruise on her arm painfully with her finger before pulling the sleeve of her tight black jumper down over it.

• • • •

'SHUT UP!' SETH SNARLED at the whining dog, before slugging down the remains of his cold tea. Wiping his mouth with the back of his hand, he rubbed at his sore temples and glared at the animal deftly positioned in front of the door.

Shoving a cigarette in his mouth, it snapped in half and he

stared at it in disgust before throwing it onto the floor. He eyed the big hole in the lounge door and slowly closed his eyes. He'd put the door back on its hinges, but hadn't repaired the hole or the splintered wood and it had been *months* now. Which reminded him, he hadn't fixed the fire yet either, had he?

Seth exhaled slowly. He was not in a good mood. Jane had been itching to pick a fight with him last night, making snotty bloody comments about everything he'd said. Every time he'd spoken, she'd moaned and then she'd disappeared for ages, leaving him sat like a twat to be bored shitless by some old bastard with a back to front shirt on and a weeks' worth of breakfast down it.

When she'd finally returned, she'd said she'd been talking to a couple of girls she used to work with. *A likely fucking story.* She'd have been talking to some bloke or shagging in the toilets.

Seth clenched his teeth. It was probably that bloke with the brown hair Stuart kept going on about. Of course, Jane had denied all knowledge when he'd asked, insisting she'd no idea what he was talking about. *Well she would, wouldn't she?*

They'd ended up having another screaming row. He knew he shouldn't have yanked her arm, but what was he supposed to do when she'd tried to smack him in the face?

He frowned. Things had been getting back on track since they'd had that weekend away in the country, but during the last few weeks they'd been back on each other's cases again.

Seth accepted he hadn't stuck to his promise of stopping the constant stream of fuckheads drifting in and out of the flat, but then Jane hadn't stuck to her side of things either, had she? Still, he needed to sort it out. He wanted things to be as they were when they'd been away.

He glared at the man lying face down on the floor who had wandered in last night. The twat had stuck his head around the bedroom door, interrupting his shag to ask if he could buy some dope. He'd been told to fuck off and wait in the lounge, but the guy must have got tired of waiting because he'd helped himself.

Seth eyed the small bag on the table suspiciously. Ok, so

he'd forgotten to sort out the gear because he'd much preferred staying in the sack with Jane, but by the looks of it, this wanker had smoked half of what had been there last night.

He nudged the man with his steel toecap, figuring now was as good a time as ever to wake the fucker up and get the brass off him for what he'd smoked. 'Get up, you fucking lazy bastard!' he growled, booting the man hard in the ribs.

With a yelp, Mike sat up like a shot, but was pulled quickly to his feet by his throat. 'S-Seth, mate,' he stuttered. 'What's happening? What have I done?'

'What you've done,' Seth pushed Mike's head towards the coffee table, 'is help yourself to my stuff, look!'

Mike's bewildered eyes searched the contents of the low wooden table. 'But, I...'

Yanking him back to an upright position, Seth pulled the man close to his face. *He was sick of these people. Fucking SICK of them.* 'You've smoked half my dope, you wanker!'

Mike's tangled dark hair caught in the collar of his denim jacket. 'Y-You said to go in to the lounge and help myself?'

Seth raised an eyebrow. 'Did I hell!'

Mike stood limply. *What was he going to do now?* He could see the rabid look in Seth's eyes. Going totally fucking tapped, he was. 'I-I'm sorry,' he mumbled. 'I must have misheard. I must ha...'

'I'm *sick* of people like you!' Seth grabbed Mike's lapels. 'Thinking you can take the fucking piss?'

'I wasn't taking the piss mate. I wa...'

'SHUT UP!' Seth screamed. 'I'm bored of excuses. *Very* fucking bored!'

Mike crashed over the edge of the armchair as he was launched backwards and backed away on his elbows. 'OK! OK!' His hands came up in a gesture of submission as Seth stepped towards him. 'I was going to pay you, mate, I promise. I only wanted a bag of something.'

Ignoring his pleas, Seth pulled Mike to his feet and slammed him hard against the wall. A large piece of plaster fell off the ceiling and crashed loudly to the floor. 'Now look what you've done!' he roared, glaring at the ragged hole. *Fucking dump. Fucking shit, fucking CRAP hole.*

'Here. *Here*!' Fumbling in his pocket, Mike tried to find some money. He knew he had twenty quid in there somewhere. He needed to get away from this.

*Everyone* knew Seth was losing the plot. It was common knowledge that even his good mates walked around on eggshells these days. Not that anyone would dare say anything about it, but it didn't leave much hope for mere acquaintances like him, did it?

Pulling out the twenty from his pocket, Mike held it up. 'Here Seth, sorry mate.'

Seth snatched it out of his hand. 'Don't be taking the Michael, *Michael*! I don't like it.' Wrenching the lounge door open with one hand, he dragged Mike down the hallway and opened the front door. 'Now sling your fucking hook!'

With a final shove, Mike tumbled down the stone steps and landed in a heap at the bottom. He sat for a moment, attempting to catch his breath and rubbed the back of his head, making a mental note not to push his luck again. He'd be giving Seth a wide berth from now on. He didn't want him on his back.

Stomping back into the flat, Seth sparked up another fag and perched on the windowsill. Feeling the rage rising up from his feet as he looked down on the people going about their business below, he spun around and grabbed his coat from the back of the sofa.

He'd had enough. He was going to find out exactly who the bloke with brown hair was that apparently Jane was so fascinated with.

## TWENTY NINE

JANE LAY BACK IN the stone cold bath. It was freezing, but she couldn't face getting out just yet. The raucous laughter, along with Stuart's nasally voice coming from the lounge, only served to strengthen her resolve. *When was Seth going to wise up about that idiot?*

Teeth on edge, her eyes moved to the peg on the wall and sighed, seeing the towel had disappeared.

'Alright, Janie?'

Jane jumped as Lee barged into the bathroom and walked past her on his way to the toilet. She rolled her eyes. *Could she get no peace?*

The sound of Lee relieving himself against the enamel of the toilet bowl echoed in Jane's ears and made her want to smash the place up.

'Had a good day?' Lee turned his head, his eyes roaming over Jane's naked body.

'Not really, but what's new!' Jane snapped.

Raising his eyebrows, Lee decided he'd best just concentrate on finishing his piss. Jane obviously wasn't in the mood for conversation.

'Alright?' Seth muttered, glancing at Jane as he walked in

the bathroom. Edging Lee out of the way so he could reach the toilet, he burst out laughing. 'Do you come here often?'

'Well, I would, except Janie keeps telling me to fuck off every time I try to wank over her!' Lee laughed.

Seth shoved Lee playfully into the wall, causing him to drunkenly stumble forward almost into the bath.

'Watch it!' Jane shrieked, wishing they'd all go away.

'Besides,' Lee continued, 'don't think she's in the mood, so your luck ain't going to be in later, mate. Right miserable bitch she is, tonight.'

'My luck's *always* in!' Seth grinned. 'But haven't got a clue what's the matter with her lately.'

'HELLO? I am here!' Jane snapped.

Seth raised his eyebrow. 'See what I mean?'

'Seth,' Jane called as the men walked out of the bathroom laughing. 'What have you done with the towel?'

Stopping, Seth turned back, indicating to wait a moment before walking off.

Sitting up in the bath, Jane soaped her body down. Was she miserable? Probably, yes. She couldn't seem to pull herself together the last few weeks and things felt like they were falling apart. When it was good it was fucking fantastic, but when it was bad, it was worse than awful. With a shiver, she realised the bad times were far outweighing the good lately, by a long shot.

The beginning of tears pricked the backs of her eyes. Things were so much better the less she felt.

Sighing, she pulled herself out of the bath, deciding she'd find a towel herself. She needed another drink anyway.

As Jane stepped out of the bath, Seth appeared and threw a crumpled towel at her. 'Here you go!'

Jane glared at the wet muddy towel at her feet. 'What the fuck is this?'

Walking over with a lopsided smile, Seth squeezed her breasts. 'The dog got soaked today and I had to use it to dry him.'

'Get the hell off me!' Jane snapped, batting his hand away.

She pointed towards the grubby towel. 'You expect me to use that?'

'There aren't any other clean ones left, baby.' Seth pulled her towards him. 'Come here. I'll dry you off.'

'No you fucking well won't!' Jane twisted away from him. 'Get out of my way!'

'For fucks sake, you miserable bitch!'

'Get back to your mates!' Jane flounced naked out of the bathroom. *Bollocks to him and to it all.* She'd just dry herself on his clean clothes.

Hearing Seth storm off towards the lounge, muttering to himself angrily, Jane sat on the edge of the bed and burst into tears.

• • • •

PRETENDING TO BE interested in Lee and Stuart's pointless conversation, Seth personally didn't give a shit what they were banging on about. All he knew was that he was fed up of being made to look a fool by Jane and wanted to know what the fuck the matter with her was. He swigged from the whisky bottle, getting drunker by the minute.

'Fuck me, Seth! Cheer up!' Stuart quipped. 'Letting birds get to you again?'

Seth gritted his teeth, his fingers fumbling for a lighter. 'My wife's *not* a 'bird,' Stuart.'

Helping himself to one of Seth's fags, Stuart laughed. 'I'm surprised her mates aren't over more often. You know that Eliza bird and the other one whose name I can never remember? Maybe that's why she's pissed off?' A sly grin passed fleetingly over his face which Seth was too drunk to notice. 'Or what about that new friend of hers - the bloke with the brown hair? The one whose car she was in the other day.'

Seth stiffened. *What the fuck was this, then?*

Stuart smirked, knowing he'd hit the target. Watching the fire burning behind Seth's eyes he fully intended to stoke it further.

Seth tried to act nonchalant. 'When was this?'

Lee watched closely. Since when had this Stuart become such good mates with Seth, anyway? Helping himself to his fags and making snide comments about Jane? What was his game?

'Don't know. Can't remember. A few weeks back, maybe? It was pretty late.'

Seth's jaw set hard. *He knew it. He just fucking knew it!* That must have been where she was when she'd been back late and given him bullshit. Well he wasn't having it. Thanks to Stuart's description and Phil's digging, he knew who this bloke was and he was going to sort it.

• • • •

JANE LAY IN A black satin wrap on the bed, chain-smoking and drinking vodka straight from the bottle, her eyes red and swollen from crying. She could still hear them in the lounge but she just wanted to go to sleep. Eyeing the almost empty bottle and grateful for the gradual fuzziness enveloping her mind, she reckoned she was half way to switch-off.

Despite her terrible mood, she smiled, recounting the time they'd had last month away from all the bullshit. It had been so nice. Like *really* nice.

When she'd finished work, Seth had surprised her dressed in his suit and looking gorgeous. He'd packed for her, including a beautiful red velvet dress he'd bought and then he'd whisked her away to a stunning manor house with beautiful grounds in the country. Their room had a four-poster bed and the thickest, most luxurious carpet she'd ever seen. Although they'd planned to go to the restaurant for dinner, they hadn't got that far - just ordered room service and copious bottles of champagne.

Even though it was cold, they'd strolled hand in hand in the hotel grounds, where Seth had placed flowers in her hair. Pulling her to the ground, he'd taken her on the river bank in the broad daylight. That weekend she'd fallen in love with him all over again and it had served to remind her why they belonged together. So much so, she'd even finally agreed to a date for the church wedding.

Sparking a fag up, Jane glanced at the ashtray full of red-lipstick tipped butts balanced on the duvet cover. *Her sixty-a-day habit was getting out of hand.* Taking another long gulp of vodka, she brought her legs up and rested her chin on her knees.

Why were they so fucked up? Couldn't they just be normal? *Maybe neither of them were capable of it.*

Since they'd returned home and despite all of their joint promises, things had gone back to normal. Well, that wasn't true. Things hadn't just gone back to normal, they'd got a *lot* worse.

Looking at the mildew-stained ceiling, she felt sick. Life had been even more of a huge blur than usual. Even by her standards, she knew their drinking and quest for obliteration had gone from ludicrous to one step beyond.

Reality had taken a complete back seat. Half the time they didn't even get to bed and just crashed out wherever they were. Furthermore, she couldn't remember the last time they'd eaten anything and had lost count of the number of times they'd woken up with no knowledge as to what day it was, let alone month. How she was managing to work was a mystery, being as she could never remember going, let alone what she'd done whilst she was there.

Their world had turned into an ever present loop of madness and she just couldn't shake the horrible feeling of foreboding that had lurked on her shoulder like a succubus for the last few weeks.

*Maybe she'd got PMT? When was she due?* Peering at her packet of contraceptive pills, a wave of fear washed over Jane as she realised it should have been three weeks ago. Reality slowly dawned through her drunken mind.

*Oh no. NO FUCKING WAY!*

· · · ·

'WHY DON'T YOU JUST shut the fuck up?' Seth screamed, upending the coffee table across the room.

Stuart stared at him in shock. 'I was only trying to help,' he lied.

'What by telling me my wife's shagging everyone else? Just get out.'

Lee nudged Stuart's arm. 'Come on, mate. Think it's time we made a move.'

Seth turned on his heels and stormed down the hallway. He kicked open the bedroom door. 'Is it fucking true?'

Jane drained the last drop of vodka from the bottle before lazily raising her eyes. 'Is *what* true?'

Stepping towards her, Seth whacked the bottle out of her hands. As it smashed against the wall, Stuart and Lee let themselves out of the flat. Neither he nor Jane noticed the satisfied smirk on Stuart's face as he walked down the steps into the night.

Their argument moved from the bedroom into the lounge, with Seth ranting about the guy with the brown hair. Jane had no idea who this bloke was, but was sick to the back teeth of hearing about him. She launched a clock which crashed through the window and sailed five storeys down to smash on the high street below.

Seth climbed out the window, teetering on the edge with a bottle of whisky in his hand and a wild look in his eye. 'Why don't I just kill myself for you? You want my death? I'll die for you, Jane, shall I? Maybe *that'll* prove how much I love you?'

Jane smiled. 'So you'd die for me? How nice.'

'Would you die for me, Jane?'

Raising her eyes slowly, she locked them on to his. 'You're not special. I'd die for anyone.'

The front door was soon kicked in by the police and they swarmed into the lounge, wrestling Seth back through the window. Jane and Seth were both arrested for drunk and disorderly along with breach of the peace.

'This is the third time in two weeks,' an officer had muttered with complete disgust as they were dragged into the police van.

As the cell door slammed shut, Jane shook her head and stared at the muddy footprint on the dirty white ceiling. She turned over on the hard metal ledge that served as a bed and pulled the itchy blanket over her, trying to ignore Seth roaring in rage from the cell next to her and mindlessly wondered what excuse she'd give at work for being late this time.

# THIRTY

AS JANE FINISHED work for the day, she realised she really had to get another job. She just couldn't stand it anymore. Rounding the corner towards where her car was parked, she was surprised to see Maggie sitting on the wall outside.

'Can I come back to yours for a bit, babe?' Maggie asked nervously, twiddling her hair.

'Course you can,' Jane smiled. 'We'll go down the Dragon later as well if you fancy?'

Maggie faltered, her nerves showing. 'Oh I don't know…'

'Look,' Jane said sternly as they walked to the car. *She knew full well what Maggie was worrying about.* 'Have you seen him since?'

Maggie shook her head. 'No…' It was true she hadn't seen Ian since the night he'd grabbed her. Jane had said he wouldn't be bothering her again, but how did she know for certain?

Glancing sideways, Jane was aware Maggie was ignorant of most of the stuff that went on behind the scenes, but Digger had a one hundred percent success rate in getting through to people. No one yet had disobeyed him and being as he'd had a word with Ian, she was confident he'd keep his distance.

The trouble was, Maggie just wasn't made of the same

fabric. She'd die a death if she knew what really went on, therefore it was hard to reassure her without having to explain everything.

Firing the car engine into life, Jane slammed the accelerator down and veered the car heavily off the kerb.

'Bloody hell!' Maggie shrieked, grabbing hold of the hand grip near the car's roof, only for it to come away in her hand.

Laughing, Jane sped down the road and then braked sharply as a green Metro trundled out of a side street. Temper flaring, she drummed her fingers impatiently and pressed down on the accelerator.

As they shot forward and steered sharply into the right hand side of the Metro's bumper, Maggie wondered what else she could hang on to inside the car. The green car span violently to the left and Jane swerved out of the way, barging past and leaving the other car to mount the kerb.

'BABE!' she screamed. 'What are you doing?'

Lighting another cigarette, Jane smiled, 'Getting home. What do you think I'm doing?'

Maggie squirmed in the seat as they floored it towards the flat.

• • • •

STUART WANDERED TOWARDS his flat with a smug smile on his face. He'd just met up with Paul and explained things were going well with the latest part of the plan. Judging by the other night and what he'd heard through the wall, it looked like Seth had finally begun to show signs of cracking.

He peered towards the door of his flat as he walked up the third flight of steps leading to the courtyard. *What the fuck was that?*

Continuing across the concrete quadrangle, Stuart stared in disbelief. *No, it couldn't be? It bloody was! Was this a joke?*

He stared closely. It was definitely a chicken. Some fuckwit had nailed a chicken to his door. Peering at the head hanging limply on its long neck with a six inch nail sticking directly through its chest into his wooden door, he grimaced and poked the chicken with his finger. *It was fucking horrible.*

'Oh that's classic, that is!' Jane laughed, unable to contain her amusement.

Spinning around on his heels, Stuart glared at her. He'd been so busy scrutinising the mangled bird, he'd failed to notice Jane and Maggie crossing the courtyard.

'You think it's funny, do you?' Stuart took a step forward, snarling. 'Is this something to do with you, you silly bitch?'

The laughter froze on Jane's face as she glared at him with hatred. 'Don't talk to me like that, you piece of shit!' She smiled nastily, enjoying the rage bubbling up on Stuart's face as he tried to think of a suitable retort. 'I'd say that's a fucking warning. Who've you upset now or is the list too long to narrow down?'

'You nasty little tart!' Stuart spat. 'Seth will eventually see you for what you are.'

Maggie paled when Jane stepped forwards and jabbed her finger hard into Stuart's arm. 'Fuck you. From where I'm standing, it looks like *you're* the one that's been exposed for what you are.'

Stuart pulled his arm away sharply with a smirk on his face. 'Get your hands off me. I don't know where you've been.'

Jane glanced at Maggie. 'Come on, let's leave this dickhead to fester with his thoughts. That's if he's capable of having any!'

Quickly scuttling across the courtyard, Maggie tried to avoid looking at Stuart. Her legs were still shaking from when Jane had purposely rammed that car on the way home. And now *this*.

'BITCH!' Stuart screamed, only to be rewarded by sarcastic laughter.

Maggie felt a shiver of apprehension run down her spine and risked a quick look at the dead chicken. *She didn't like that sort of stuff. It gave her the creeps.*

With a face like a slapped haddock, Stuart ripped the chicken from his door and stormed into his flat. He was on edge.

Breathing heavily, he dumped the chicken in the bin in the corner of the kitchen and then paced silently around his flat, unsure of what to do. He admitted he was a bit worried.

Actually, he was *very* worried.

Rage seethed inside him. How typical that stupid cow had turned up just at that moment. *She'd be loving this.* Walking to the cupboard, he grabbed a can of lager and yanked at the ring pull with shaking fingers. He plonked himself down on a wooden chair and tipped the can into his mouth.

He knew he shouldn't have been saying things about those city blokes he was running dope for, but he was pissed off running around all over the place at all times of night for them and never getting any thanks. Besides, all he'd said was they'd get replaced the way they carried on, treating everyone with such indifference.

Anyway, it wasn't like they'd send someone down this neck of the woods for him, was it? He was just being stupid.

Finally relaxing, Stuart leant back in the chair.

• • • •

SETH WASTED NO TIME trussing up the man. He would give Jane the chance to tell him the truth and nail this crap once and for all. By the look of this bloke, he'd quite easily spill the beans. Especially when given a little persuasion.

He smiled, his dimples showing. He'd get the cunt to admit exactly what had been going on in front of her so she couldn't deny anything. She wouldn't be able to make a fucking fool of him then, would she?

Feeling better than he had in a while, Seth accelerated, happy the coke was working and tapped his fingers on the steering wheel along to AC/DC. He hoped Digger had got his message because when he'd finished with this twat in the boot, Digger could get rid of him, freeing *him* up to deal with Jane.

He raged inwardly. Did she really think he wouldn't find out she'd been fucking around? It made sense now why she'd been acting funny. This trying to cause arguments all the bloody time was just a fucking excuse!

A rush of cold dread ran through his body. Jane was

planning on leaving him and binning him off for this bastard, wasn't she?

Over his dead fucking body would he let her. He'd kill her first.

With his concentration elsewhere and his mind out of control, he overshot a junction narrowly missing a red car.

*Shav*. What sort of fucking name was that anyway? He was going to fuck the bastard up. Psyching himself up into frenzy, the vein in Seth's neck throbbed at a dangerous pace, in line with his heart crashing in his chest.

He hit the steering wheel with his fist. 'I will *not* let you go, Jane!' he roared.

. . . .

SITTING ON THE SOFA, Digger absentmindedly stroked the dog as he waited. He wasn't sure what he was waiting for, but he'd had a message from Seth to be here for 7. It had only been 6, but he'd figured Jane would be back from work shortly and if he was lucky, he could cadge some grub. And he hadn't been wrong.

He glanced towards Maggie as she sat nervously on the sofa in silence, waiting like him, for Jane to rustle up some food.

Digger frowned. Seth and Jane had gone completely off the rails lately. He knew something had happened a few months back which had put the cat among the pigeons, but when he'd asked what was going down, he'd got his head chewed off, so he'd left it.

Maybe Seth had found out about what had happened with him and Jane a while back?

He shrugged his huge shoulders. Seth was a loose cannon at the moment and a very dangerous one at that, but he'd just have to cope with that if it happened.

Stomach rumbling, Digger glanced at his watch and hoped Jane would hurry up with whatever she was doing.

Pushing open the lounge door, Jane walked through with plates and smiled. 'Here we go.'

She plonked herself next to Digger on the sofa and handed him and Maggie their food. It was only a bit of chicken and rice, but that was all she'd got. Besides, it was quite apt given tonight's theme of chickens.

She'd been surprised to find Seth absent, but when Digger explained he'd been asked to come at 7, she'd put his plate in the oven to keep warm.

Hearing the theme tune of 'Emmerdale' start, Jane sat back in the chair and began to relax. At least Seth had replaced the smashed TV with one of the many stacked in the spare room. *Bloody things had finally come in useful. Well, one of them at least!*

Digger rolled his eyes. 'I can't *believe* you watch this crap!'

'SSSHHH!' Jane laughed, nudging him in the ribs, whilst shovelling a forkful of rice into her mouth. Despite her best efforts, her mind wandered back to the issue burning in her mind.

She'd missed a second period and the test she'd done the other day had confirmed what she suspected. She was definitely pregnant. Deciding she'd worry about that tomorrow, she cracked open another can of lager.

Maggie was so engrossed watching Zak Dingle on the TV, her plate nearly shot off her lap as the sound of the front door slamming took her off guard.

'Seth's back then,' Jane muttered, feeling Digger's body tense next to her.

As Seth kicked open the lounge door, dragging a man with bound wrists and ankles into the room, Maggie jumped out of her chair, screaming.

Jane frowned as Maggie's plate and its contents smashed noisily on the floor. She'd only bought them the other week to replace the ones she'd launched at Seth. Sighing, she looked back at the television and continued to eat her dinner.

Maggie stared at Seth. He looked feral. His eyes gleamed and sweat ran down his face. Looking at Jane, she felt panic quickly rising in her chest. *Wasn't she going to say anything?*

*What on earth was going on here?*

'Calm down, Maggie,' Digger said quietly, before turning to Seth. 'What's going down?'

'This,' Seth pulled the man further across the lounge, his bound ankles dropping noisily with a thud at Jane's feet, 'is the bloke my wife's been fucking behind my back!'

Jane nearly choked, her head shooting up. '*What*?'

'Don't try and deny it, woman.' Seth roughly ripped the piece of duct tape off the man's mouth, taking the top layer of skin with it.

'NO! NO!' Shav howled and stared up with frightened eyes. 'I haven't done anything!'

'Babe?' Maggie screamed. 'What the hell's happening?'

Jane stared into Seth's manic eyes as he stood behind the man on the floor. 'What the fuck is this about?' Sighing, she looked back down to her tea and then across to the TV. 'I'm trying to watch the bloody television!'

Maggie stared at Jane as if she was mad. *Watch the television? Was she serious?*

Lurching forward, Seth swiped the plate from Jane's lap and it smashed into the wall. 'You'd best start telling me the truth.'

Jane was angry. Her tea was bloody ruined and now another plate was knackered. 'Oh fuck off, Seth. You're off your rocker.'

Digger sat forward in the chair, confused. He'd expected a normal job, not this.

'Let's hear from him, shall we?' Seth roared, giving Shav a heavy kick to the ribs. 'Well, Shav, how long have you been shagging my wife?'

*Shav? Did he say Shav?* With horror, Jane recognised the man to be the brother of one of the factory girls. She'd chatted to him several times down the pub and suddenly it all began to make sense.

*This* was the guy with the 'long brown hair' Seth had been badgering her about for weeks. Absolutely nothing had gone on with him and she had no idea where he'd got the idea from.

Stepping forward, Jane grabbed Seth's arm. 'Don't be

bloody crazy! I haven't been shagging him.'

Yanking away, Seth narrowed his eyes. 'That's not what I've heard.' He leant in Jane's face. 'You must think I'm fucking STUPID!'

'Calm down, mate.' Digger stood up and reached towards Jane.

Seth spun around. 'Don't you touch her and keep out of it. She needs to give me some fucking answers.' He glared back at Jane. 'You're planning on leaving me for him, aren't you?'

'Leaving you?' Jane asked incredulously.

'Oh my GOD!' Maggie screeched, as Seth delivered another swift kick to the man's face, watching as blood and teeth sprayed over the floor. She backed herself up against the far wall.

'That's why you've been acting fucking weird. Because of *him*!' Seth pulled the sawn-off from his inside pocket.

'NO!' Jane shouted. 'You're totally wrong! Fucking leave it!'

Seth pointed the gun at the man. 'Start talking to me, Shav,' he lowered his voice. 'Last fucking chance.'

'I-I haven't touched her!' Shav garbled. 'I haven't laid a finger on her.'

'He *hasn't*!' Jane interjected. 'Who the hell said otherwise?' Pulling Seth's arm sharply, the sawn-off veered blindly across the room. Maggie let out another high-pitched wail as the barrel passed across her.

'Stop this *NOW*!' Jane shouted, as Seth aimed the sawn-off back at Shav.

Seth glared at Jane, his eyes narrow slits. 'Think you can fucking laugh at me, do you? Well your lover will pay the price.' Turning back towards the shuffling figure on the floor, he quickly pulled the trigger and watched as Shav's kneecap exploded over the underlay.

'JESUS!' Maggie screamed hysterically. Pacing around on a patch of floor, she raised her hand to her mouth and gagged.

Bending over the writhing man, Seth spoke quietly, his voice loaded with menace. 'Don't go near her again or I *promise* I'll finish the job.' He nodded to Digger. 'Get him out of here.'

Poking the barrel sharply in Shav's throat, he smiled. 'Take this as a friendly warning.'

Dragging Shav roughly to his feet, Digger pulled him towards the door, the man's shattered left leg dragging behind him whilst Maggie stared wide-eyed, her body racked with loud gasping sobs.

Jane's eyes glowered. 'I can't believe you've done this, Seth! For what? *Nothing!*'

Seth looked at her coldly. 'Don't fuck with me, Jane.'

Jane trod through the blood and sinew spattered on the underlay and yanked at Seth's arm as he leant against the wall. 'What the hell are you doing?' she spat. *It was ridiculous. He'd got it all wrong.*

'Why have you been acting weird then?'

Jane stared blankly. What was she supposed to say? *'Actually Seth, it isn't because I'm sleeping with anyone else, it's because I'm pregnant. Isn't that nice? We're so well-adjusted, aren't we? We'll make great parents!'*

Swinging away from the wall, Seth pulled Jane towards him and crushed her into his body. 'You're mine, Jane, *mine.*' He grasped her face with his other hand. 'You're *not* leaving me.'

Jane stared with contempt into Seth's flashing eyes, wanting him to kiss her. *Hard.*

Reading her thoughts, Seth crashed his mouth down onto hers, his tongue forcing its way into her mouth. Jane felt her body betray her brain as the familiar and intense longing surged through every fibre of her body. She wound her fingers in his hair as he pushed her back against the wall.

'Oh God,' Seth groaned as Jane freed him from his jeans. He wasted no time in shifting her skirt up and pulling her leg up around his waist. 'I won't let you leave me.'

Slamming her against the wall, he sank his teeth into her neck, his cock pushing deep and making her blind to anything but the waves of pleasure starting to quickly course through her body. 'I love you, Jane. Until the end of time, remember?'

As the credits for Emmerdale rolled, Maggie sobbed on the floor with her head in her hands. Wrapping her arms around herself tightly, she rocked back and forth and began humming a tune to drown out Jane screaming Seth's name.

## THIRTY ONE

IN THE CORNER OF the Green Dragon, Maggie shook like a leaf, her half pint of lager slopping over the table as she raised it to her mouth. She watched Jane laughing on the wooden pew opposite. *How could she be laughing after what had just happened?*

Seth's arm was draped loosely around Jane, his fingers kneading her shoulder. His eyes were now clear and the manic lunatic Maggie had witnessed an hour earlier had gone. He now looked like the Seth she knew. Or rather the Seth she'd *thought* she knew.

Catching her studying him, Seth winked and Maggie quickly looked away. Thrown and confused, perspiration beaded on her brow and she fanned herself with a beer mat. It gave her shaking hands something to do, other than spill her drink.

She was scared. She'd seen enough of Seth and Jane's arguments to know about their tempers, but that poor man. That poor, *poor* man.

With a horrible creeping dawn of realisation, Maggie realised there was *no way* Jane would be so matter of fact if this sort of stuff wasn't a normal occurrence and her mind questioned exactly *how* involved she was in all of this sort of shit? And the way they'd been at it afterwards, like they got off on it?

Finally managing to get the glass up to her lips, Maggie slugged down the entire drink in one go. Oh, she didn't like this. Didn't like it one little bit. She'd heard the rumours about the things Jane had supposedly done long before she'd been involved with Seth, but had put them down to gossip-mongering and small-town mentality. Jealousy even. She hadn't given it a second thought, but now…?

She'd also heard the rumours about both Seth and Jane, but surely in the four years of knowing them, she couldn't have missed stuff like that happening all the time, could she?

She *had* missed it though and this realisation was fucking her head up. Snapping back to reality, Maggie jumped as Seth lightly touched her arm.

'Same again?' he asked, smiling. Picking up her glass, he made his way towards the bar.

• • • •

JANE BENT OVER THE cistern, snorted a couple of lines of coke from the enamel and leant back against the cubicle wall.

Poor old Maggie. Oh well. She couldn't hide everything from everyone all of the time, could she? As for Seth, well, he was out of order and she wasn't sure whether he believed her about Shav, but it didn't matter anyway. He'd think what he wanted regardless.

Taking a deep breath when the coke picked up speed in her head, Jane heard Eliza's and Maggie's voices as the outside door of the Ladies toilet opened.

Eliza smiled. 'Don't know what's wrong with this one tonight,' she laughed, nodding towards Maggie.

Jane peered in the reflection of the cracked mirror to check no tell-tale signs of coke were lurking and sniffed hard, swallowing down the familiar sour taste.

'You should slow that down now. Baby might not like it.' Eliza giggled.

Maggie's eyes shot into focus. 'WHAT?' she cried, trying to

sound lighter than she felt.

'Only gone and got herself up the duff, ain't she!'

'Thanks!' Jane snapped, glaring at Eliza in the mirror. 'Thanks very much!'

'Oh my God, Jane!' Maggie moved closer. 'You're pregnant?'

'It appears so.'

'You're *pregnant* and things like tonight? Things like wh…' Jane cut her short. 'Shut it, Maggie…'

'But Jane, if you *are*, then yo…'

Jane gave Maggie a look that stopped her in her tracks. 'I'll deal with it. I don't want you breathing a fucking word to *anyone*, you hear? *Especially* not Seth!' She stared at Eliza. 'That goes for *you* as well.' Grabbing her bag from the wash stand, she walked to the door.

Maggie was amazed. 'You mean he doesn't know?'

Jane span around. 'No he doesn't and that's the way I want to keep it. Now leave it!' Pulling the door with such force it slammed hard against the wall, she gave them both a stare for good measure before stalking out of the toilets.

Eliza shrugged and tipped a mouthful of cider into her mouth. She glanced at Maggie's bewildered face. 'You know what she's like…'

Maggie felt thoroughly exhausted, but began to think she finally *was* starting to realise what Jane was like.

Jane could have killed Eliza. She'd expressly said she didn't want anyone to know. Now, because she'd had a few ciders and opened her fat fucking trap, Maggie knew as well. For fuck's sake. This was all getting too complicated.

*Far* too complicated.

Walking quickly down the uneven tiled corridor to the main bar, Jane passed a small room housing the pool table when someone caught her eye from deep in the shadows.

What a piece of luck, she thought, launching herself into the room.

Jumping over a fat bloke with vomit dribbling out of his

mouth on the floor, she swiftly grabbed Debbie tightly around the neck and didn't bother explaining why, when she smacked her head into the corner of the cigarette machine.

Jimi Hendrix continued playing from the jukebox as Maggie and Eliza stuck their heads into the room to see what the commotion was, just as Debbie's head was smashed into the machine for the second time.

Ignoring Owen, Mudflap and Clint with their drinks stuck half way between the table and their mouths, Jane dug her nails firmly into Debbie's pudgy neck and smiled.

Debbie wailed as Jane's fist smashed into her nose and blood poured down her fringed top when her head was whacked on the side of the machine for the third time,

With one final punch, Debbie's eyes rolled and she dropped heavily to the floor. Hitting her head with a thud on the quarry tiles, a small pool of blood pooled underneath her hair.

Wiping her bloodied hands down her skirt, Jane winked at Clint who was staring in rapt amazement. She opened her bag and casually lit a cigarette. 'Do us a favour,' she smiled, turning to Owen. 'Drag the fat bitch outside, will you?'

'Me?' Owen spluttered, his beer spilling on the table.

'Yes, you.' Smiling sweetly, Jane moved closer and lowered her voice. 'I could always make things awkward for you otherwise, couldn't I?'

Owen paled, knowing Jane was referring to their brief time together. He'd been amazed he'd escaped without a visit from Seth and he wanted to keep it that way. Nodding reluctantly, he pulled himself up from the seat and moved towards Debbie.

'Cheers!' Jane smiled. Walking away, she passed Eliza and Maggie's ringside seat. 'Alright, girls?'

*Fuck it. Let them gawp. She was on a roll.*

• • • •

SETH HAD ALMOST forgotten where he was. His world consisted only of the feel of Jane's mouth. Continuing to kiss her hungrily, his hand made its way up her skirt.

When someone suddenly poked him on the shoulder, he pulled away angrily and glared up at the perpetrator, then smiled. 'Alright, Digger? I wondered who the fuck that was then for a minute.'

'I could see that!' Digger muttered, noticing Seth was already quite drunk. For how long he'd be in a good mood was anyone's guess. Now he wouldn't be able to get him to level as to what all that business was with that bloke earlier. It was obvious nothing had been going on with Jane and that guy at all.

'All sorted?' Glancing up, Seth watched Digger nod almost imperceptibly. Grinning bashfully, he stood up and adjusted his jeans to disguise his arousal. 'Let me get you a beer.'

Shaking his head in resignation, Digger smiled and plonked himself down next to Jane, who was watching Seth intently as he walked away. He didn't understand these two one iota, but thought maybe if this madness was what it was like, he was probably lucky Jane didn't feel the same way about him that he did about her.

Jane smiled, recognising the girl opposite. She'd just had a brainwave. A complete and utter, amazingly astounding brainwave! This was just *too* good not to take advantage of.

Ok. Let's do it, she thought.

*And... GO!*

Flicking on her death stare like a light, Jane yelled in the red-headed girl's direction. 'WHAT DID YOU SAY?'

The bar fell silent and people gingerly glanced around to see who was going to cop it. Turning from the bar, Seth wondered what Jane was up to and slowly took a swig of his fresh pint. He'd prop the bar up a while longer rather than make his way back over. Judging by the look on her face, it was likely it would get spilt if he returned.

'YOU!' Jane roared, pointing at the girl.

'I didn't say anything,' the red-head said quietly as her friends shuffled away up the bench. She looked warily at Jane and tried to work out why her dad had employed her in the first place.

Launching herself towards the table, Jane screamed in the girl's face. 'Did you just call me a *tart*?'

'W-What? I, no, I didn't sa…'

Deciding that was enough drama, Jane pulled the girl out of her seat and head-butted her. Reeling, the girl crashed heavily back onto the wooden bench, a shocked sob catching in her throat as she clutched her bleeding nose.

Coming to the conclusion that was all that needed doing for what she required, Jane folded her arms across her chest. 'Now, fuck off!'

Scrabbling around for her bag, the girl didn't need telling twice and from his position at the bar, Seth raised his eyebrows at Digger, who looked towards the ceiling in despair.

Jane walked calmly back to the bench and everyone resumed talking. Making his way back from the bar, Seth handed out the drinks and frowned, waiting for an explanation.

Jane stroked Seth's thigh. 'You know I said I couldn't face working at the warehouse anymore?'

Seth looked confused. 'Right…?'

'Well,' she smiled, 'I don't need to worry now.' Necking the vodka, Jane winked conspiratorially. 'That was the boss's daughter!'

Seth burst out laughing and pulled her onto his lap, his mouth searching for hers.

Digger groaned and reached for his pint while Maggie sat speechless in the corner, feeling the iron fist of panic clenching further around her heart.

• • • •

BY KICK OUT TIME Seth was roaring drunk and Jane was wired to the eyeballs. Half-dragging her up the road to the flat, he wished she'd get a move on. He wanted another drink and needed to bed her again.

He grabbed Jane's arms and pinned them down by her sides, goading her. 'What's your reticence to get home? Rather fuck Shav, would you? Hate to tell you but he probably won't feel up to it tonight!' His fingertips dug hard into her flesh and his manic laughter echoed around the empty street.

Jane was spoiling for a fight, all the earlier good mood having long since evaporated. She twisted out of Seth's grip and launched herself at him.

Staggering back, caught off guard by the force of her punch, Seth raised his hand to his face and wiped the back of his hand over his mouth. Focusing on the smear of blood from his cut lip, his eyes narrowed at Jane staring defiantly at him.

Pain seared through Jane's back and head when she was slammed through the nearest shop window. As her body crashed through the plate glass, the alarm sounded, its wailing screaming loudly into the night.

Lying on her back amongst shards of glass in the pitch black, she tried to get her bearings. Through the mess of her addled mind and the silhouettes of flowers in buckets of water sitting on racks along the walls, she worked out she was in the florists.

Sticky blood trickled from cuts in her arms. 'You've cut me, you bastard!' she screamed.

Seth stepped through the broken window and yanked frantically at his shirt. Ripping it from his shoulders, the buttons pinged off like little bullets and ricocheted around the dark room. 'You want the shirt off my back as well as my heart, Jane?'

Glowering, he threw the shirt at her and began undoing his jeans, then pulled his steel toecaps off and launched them through the remains of the smashed window.

'Here!' Seth raged over the sound of the screeching alarm. 'Have it ALL!' He kicked his jeans to one side and picked up a large shard of glass, Jane's cold laugh only fuelling his anger.

'Come on, then.' Seth held the glass against his chest. 'Cut me!'

Staring at his naked figure from her position on the floor, Jane wanted to run her tongue down the line of hair from his navel. 'That would be *far* too easy,' she smiled.

'Fine. I'll do it for you.' Seth dragged the pointed shard down the ridged muscles of his stomach, the thin cut

226

immediately weeping blood. 'I'm bleeding for you, Jane, so we're even!'

Turning, he stepped through the gaping hole in the window and stalked naked up the road.

Jane would have laughed if she wasn't so angry. Her hand moved to her stomach where his baby was silently growing and she drunkenly pulled herself to her feet just as a police car screeched to a halt outside.

## THIRTY TWO

WOMEN STROLLED WITH young children in pushchairs and people walked their dogs around the wide expanse of neatly trimmed grass and manicured flowerbeds of the park.

Phil studied Seth's pensive expression intently and watched as the wind blew his hair across his face, glad he'd got a shaved head. Having hair stuck to him all the time would drive him up the bloody wall.

Shifting his weight slightly on the less than comfortable bench, he did a quick check of his pride and joy and relaxed seeing his bike's chrome glinting in the sunlight in the distance, next to Seth's Senator.

'So, what do you think?'

Seth didn't hear Phil's question. He was too busy staring at a remote spot where the trees were thickly populated on the hill. *The forest, where all was cool and calm, uninterrupted and clear.*

He smiled sardonically. What it would be for some salvation. *Unfortunately, that had left a long time ago.*

'Seth?' Phil wasn't sure what was going on in Seth's head. He'd been acting rather strange lately, but thankfully, whatever was eating him, wasn't having a negative impact on his work. He was one of the best in the business and if anything, was even better than usual recently. 'Are you ok?'

'Yes mate,' Seth turned slowly towards his friend and smiled. 'Just thinking about what you said.'

Phil waited for Seth to elaborate, but he just pulled out his cigarettes and slackened his grip on the dog's lead, lying on the tarmac path next to their feet.

'Well?'

'Well…' Putting a cigarette in his mouth, Seth flicked his Zippo and cupped his hand to shield the flickering flame from the breeze. 'I think it's a goer.'

Phil quietly breathed a sigh of relief. He wasn't sure if the job could be pulled off without Seth.

'Who else is alongside?'

Phil had a few ideas but would let Seth have the final say. 'I was thinking Digger for one and Wazza?'

Seth nodded. *Digger for definite, he was a dead cert. Wazza? He hadn't worked with him but had heard he was good.*

'Tony, perhaps?' Catching the frown on Seth's face, Phil corrected his suggestion. 'Ok, maybe not Tony. Adrian?' He took a swig out of his pewter hip flask. 'Although, he can be a bit of a liability.'

'Liability? That doesn't sound too good. In what way?'

Passing the flask to Seth, Phil squinted his eyes against the low sun. 'Going too far at the wrong time.' He savoured the hot burn of the rum in his throat. 'He's a great one to have on board but needs to be kept in line. You get the drift. I trust you'll have no problem telling him what's what?'

Seth took a long slug out of the flask and smiled lazily. 'Consider it done. Ok, we'll have a meet and discuss the finer details.'

'Also,' Phil glanced at Seth, unsure how he would take this. 'We want Jane.'

Seth's head snapped up. 'Jane? What for?'

'She's gold dust mate, you know that and she's *more* than capable.' Phil studied the emotions running over his friend's face. 'That's why she's privy to all the info.'

Seth's face set in a stony expression. 'I don't want her involved.'

Phil took another slug of the spirit and met Seth's eyes. 'We want her as the decoy. Plus, if the shit *did* hit the fan, you know as well as I do, that she'd do the business.'

Seth studied Phil in silence. He was right on everything he'd said. Everyone did trust Jane. *He* trusted her but still didn't like her being brought into this kind of stuff. 'I'll talk to her. If she's ok with it, then I guess it's fine by me.'

Phil laughed. 'Like you'd have any fucking choice if you liked it or not! You know what she's like!'

Despite himself, Seth couldn't help but smile. 'Leave it with me.'

· · · ·

WALKING INTO THE KITCHEN, Jane decided she may as well eat the tin of indistinguishable soup she'd spotted in the cupboard a few weeks ago. Bending down, she moved a box of ammunition out of the way and sighed. She wished Seth wouldn't put things like that in there. She'd spent ages picking bullets off the floor the other week after they'd tipped out a cereal box.

Finding the one saucepan they possessed, she eyed its sheared-off handle and scowled. Fuck it. She'd have to use it as it was. Grabbing the soup, she walked towards the cooker and promptly stopped. One week on and she *still* forgot they no longer had one, thanks to Seth. Her head was scrambled. She glanced down at her stomach.

*The sooner this was all sorted the better.*

Jane gritted her teeth, still angry about Seth's stunt of chucking her through that window last week. The cops had wrestled her to the ground before slinging her in the back of the police car. Unsurprisingly, they hadn't bought her pathetic excuse that she'd put herself through the window, nor had they been convinced the pile of clothes on the floor had been hers.

All they'd had to do was follow the trail of blood from the shop back to the flat and leaving her cuffed in the back of the car, they'd gone in for Seth.

Jane scowled. They'd really have to get a new door now. It had been crappy enough in the first place, but now it had been kicked in twice, it just wasn't worth having any more. *Not that it ever seemed to be closed.*

As Seth had been shoved in the back of the police car, he'd launched into a volley of abuse at her, so she'd head-butted him. The cops hadn't been able to wait to get them into separate cells and add another couple of charges to their seemingly never-ending records.

To make matters worse, when they'd finally been released, they'd returned home to a terrible acrid burning smell which proved to be Seth's tea from the night before, charred to a crisp in the bottom of the oven.

Jane had angrily stomped into the bedroom whilst Seth had ripped the oven away from the wall and launched it down the stairs, where it still remained, buckled and smashed in the courtyard.

• • • •

IN MCDONALDS, ELIZA EYED Maggie warily. Flicking her cigarette in the small foil ashtray on the table, she sipped her root beer.

'I don't like it, Eliza,' Maggie moaned, her eyes glistening with unshed tears. 'I *really* don't like it.'

'So you keep saying,' Eliza muttered uninterestedly.

'She *has* to tell him.'

Raising her eyes from the plastic cup, Eliza glanced at the clock on the far wall. *How much longer was she going to have to listen to this?* 'Why?'

'What do you mean, *why*?' Maggie gripped Eliza's arm and a lump of ash fell to the table. 'It's Seth's baby, isn't it?'

Eliza glared at Maggie. 'Of *course* it is!'

'Then we should tell him.'

Eliza pursed her lips. 'Less of the 'we'! It would be the *last* thing we did on this mortal coil!'

She felt like screaming. If Seth found out, Jane would go loco. After all, it was only thanks to her big gob last week that Maggie knew about any of this. She'd dropped herself right in it yet again. 'Look Mags, it really isn't any of our business.'

Maggie gritted her teeth. It *was* their business. Jane was their friend and they, more than most, owed it to her to be there for her this time.

Biting her nails, she admitted she'd been horrified when she realised the true extent of the weird shit going on in Jane and Seth's life. She didn't want to even *think* about the rest of the stuff Jane had done or what she was involved in. The bit she'd seen with her own eyes was scary enough.

*And now a baby.*

Maggie groaned inwardly. Ok, with their combined genes the kid would be beautiful, but it would also be a fucking *psychopath*. It didn't bear thinking about.

• • • •

*OH GOD. SHE JUST couldn't do it. Come on*! Breathing in, Jane attempted once more to force the zip up on her size eight skin-tight jeans and wiped away the tears pooling in her eyes. Swallowing down another wave of nausea, she popped a few more tablets.

She couldn't cope with this. Seth would notice soon. She willed herself to snap out of the emotional turmoil relentlessly thundering through her head. *Concentrate, Jane*!

'You ok in there?' Seth called through the bathroom door, giving it a light tap. Time was ticking for getting to the Bluebell where he'd arranged to meet a guy who should prove a nice contact for a shipment due next week.

He'd returned from his meet with Phil after a quick detour to the Oak Apple for a lunchtime pint, which had turned out to be several and then some. As a result, by the time he'd got back to the flat, he'd been feeling rather mellow. Finding Jane curled up on the sofa, he'd tried to kiss her, but she launched into him about busting a bloody saucepan or something!

He wished she would just cheer the fuck up! Recently she'd been acting so strange he didn't know what to think anymore. He knew he'd been hard work lately but fucking hell, so had she.

Trying to change the saucepan subject, he'd broached Phil's request, of which Jane had immediately agreed to. He still didn't like it, but was determined to stay in a good mood.

He knocked the bathroom door again. 'We've got to be on the road in half an hour!'

Painfully squeezing her swollen breasts into her bra, Jane pulled her T-shirt on and tried to make her voice normal. 'Coming now.' Quickly yanking the jeans off, she scuttled out of the bathroom.

'Going out like that?' Seth laughed, watching as Jane's half-dressed figure retreated into the bedroom.

'Jeans are dirty,' Jane called breezily as she rummaged around for something else and cursed inwardly for only owning mainly skin-tight or fitted clothes that accentuated the new roundness of her belly.

She'd thought she'd have several more weeks before she showed and by then it wouldn't matter because the abortion was booked for next week. Even though she was only nine or ten weeks gone, it was beginning to become obvious.

Running her hand over her little bump, a lump formed in Jane's throat. What was the matter with her? There was no time for emotions. Fear began to rise. Seth *couldn't* find out. He'd be over the moon, but they couldn't do this the way they were. It was all too fucked up. However, there was only five days to go before it would all be over and the sooner it was sorted, the better.

Jane jumped out of her skin when Seth unexpectedly came up behind her and grabbed her hips. The towel around his waist fell to the floor and his erection pressed against her back. 'Not now, Seth. We'll be late,' she snapped. The last thing she wanted was him looking at her.

'Oh well, looks like we'll be late then,' Seth murmured, his fingers reaching around and slipping inside her.

Letting out a moan of pleasure, Jane felt helpless to protest when Seth pushed her backwards. She wanted him too badly to refuse. Pulling her T-shirt off, his mouth greedily teased a nipple into a hard aching point and as he entered her, waves of pleasure crashed through her body.

Thrusting in long, slow strokes, Seth grinned when Jane came almost immediately. Watching her orgasm, he quickened the pace. 'You're on heat, baby. Let me give you some more.'

As her body immediately ramped up again, Jane realised with a wry smile it was exactly *this* that had got her into shit in the first place.

Switching positions, Seth entered her from behind, one hand touching her with feathery circular movements and when his hand ran over her belly, Jane stiffened but was too in need of further release to worry.

• • • •

LYING IN A SPOON POSITION afterwards, Seth pressed his body close and wrapped his arms around her. He'd finally worked out what was going on and was *extremely* happy about it.

Jane was pregnant. He just knew it. He'd wanted this to happen since he'd met her and now it had. Closing his eyes, he let his happiness and the afterglow of sex wash over him.

Suddenly a rush of cold flooded him as the memory of throwing Jane through the window seeped into his mind and sank like a brick in water. His arms tightened around her.

If anything happened to this baby because of his fucking temper, he'd top himself. He wanted this child more than anything. He wanted to be a father, but more importantly wanted to be the father of *Jane's* child.

That was it. He was going to put this right. *All* of it. He'd do this last job and then get them out of here. They'd go straight and he wouldn't lose his temper anymore.

Seth's brows furrowed. There was *no way* she was being the

decoy on that job now, nor was she going to be even marginally involved in *anything* from now on. He'd tell Phil as soon as he could that Jane was off the job. He wouldn't let her or his child down. He'd take care of her and protect her.

As Seth's fingers started gently probing her again, Jane's breath hitched, knowing it wouldn't take much to bring her up again. She turned towards his mouth as he moved his body between her thighs and smiled. 'Aren't you done for a while?'

'I'm never done,' Seth grinned, bringing his lips down onto hers.

Entering her gently, he brushed hair out of her eyes and picked up a slow leisurely pace. 'You're beautiful, Jane. Even *more* so now you're pregnant...'

*Oh shit. Shit. SHIT*, Jane thought, panic rising.

'When were you going to tell me?' Seth's mouth brushed hers, gently biting her bottom lip. 'I know a fair bit about women, but more importantly, I know *everything* about you!'

'How long have you known?' Jane whispered, her hips moving to meet his. She groaned as his cock reached even deeper.

Seth ran his finger over her lips, swollen from his kisses. 'I didn't until just now.' Raising himself up, he ran his eyes over her body. 'Furthermore, I know your body better than you do.'

Resting one hand lightly on Jane's slightly rounded belly, Seth increased his pace slightly. Rotating his hips, he ground into her and ran a finger softly down the contour of her face.

He stared into her eyes, feeling her body start to pulse around him. 'My baby. *Our* baby. It's amazing and I love you, Jane.'

Jane cried out as she climaxed again. Looking into the green eyes of the man she loved so fiercely, she managed to trick herself for one moment that it would all be alright.

# THIRTY THREE

IT HAD BEEN QUITE a while since Jane had been in the King's Head, but Benny had greeted her as if she'd never been away.

Wrapping her in a massive bear hug, his big beer belly strained further against his shirt buttons than it had done the last time she'd seen him. Insisting she have a drink on the house, Jane wasted no time in getting it down her neck.

'*Please* tell me you've told Seth?' Maggie whispered, pushing her cheese and onion roll around the blue chipped plate.

Sitting down, Jane scowled. Why the fuck did Maggie have to remind her? She'd been desperately trying to forget about the pregnancy, which was easier said than done. In the past two days since he'd found out, Seth had been unable to contain his excitement and she was scared she'd start feeling something other than numb. *She couldn't afford to get attached.*

Fishing a bottle of pills from her bag, she quickly slipped a couple into her mouth and washed them down with the remains of her pint.

Lighting a fag, Jane walked to the bar for a refill and forced herself not to turn to look at Maggie who she knew was staring at her. She leant heavily against the bar and hoped Lee would hurry up with her pint.

She hadn't been able to wait to get out of the flat earlier, thanks to another six drugged up bastards lying around the lounge waiting for Seth to sort out their deals. *He was supposed to be getting rid of all that sort of shit, not ramping it up*!

Yesterday the biggest load of dope, pills and coke they'd ever had arrived and it was now all in the spare room with the televisions. And the guns. It was also a guaranteed fact that if the cops raided them, they'd be dead in the water, but she didn't care anymore. It was only a matter of time.

Why couldn't Seth see they couldn't possibly have a child like this?

Almost snatching the fresh pint out of Lee's hand as he placed it on the beer towel, Jane slugged half of it down in one go before walking back to the table.

'So, when are you due?' Maggie smiled brightly, speaking just that little bit too loudly.

Jane quickly glanced around to see if anyone had heard. 'Will you shut up!' she hissed through gritted teeth.

'I bet Seth's over the moon, isn't he?'

Jane cringed. *Did Maggie just not get it?*

'You're starting to show a little bit already, aren't you babe?' Maggie continued blindly as Jane self-consciously pulled her top down further over her skirt. 'I can't *wait* to be an auntie,' she gushed. 'I know I won't *really* be its auntie, but you know what I mean.'

*Please stop going on about it. PLEASE*, Jane thought, fighting against the unwelcome emotions she couldn't afford to have.

'Imagine it! You and Seth being a mummy and daddy. It's all ve…'

'SHUT THE FUCK UP, MAGGIE!' Jane roared, grabbing her bag off the table.

Maggie stared open-mouthed. 'W-What have I said?'

Leaning across the table, Jane spoke quietly. 'I'm getting rid of it.'

'W-What?' Maggie stuttered, confused. 'Why?'

'If you have to ask that, then you *really* don't understand a fucking thing!'

Maggie looked horrified. 'But you *can't,* Jane!'

'Watch me,' Jane snapped, anger replacing emotion.

'B-but that will make you a murderer?'

'Nothing new there then?' Jane hissed. Fixing Maggie with a stare she stood up. 'Got to go.'

Walking away from the table and out into the late afternoon sunlight, Jane darted into an alley. She leant up against the cool brick wall, took some deep breaths and rested her head back to stare unseeingly up to the sky.

A single tear ran down her face. Of course she wanted this baby. She could already picture its black hair and bright green eyes, but it just couldn't happen. She wouldn't bring a child into a life like this and she'd just have to live with that decision.

*End. Of. Conversation.*

Switching off her emotion like a light, Jane wiped away the tear and stepped back out into the street.

• • • •

MAGGIE WAS STILL in shock. She turned to Eliza and eyed her scornfully. 'And you knew about this? I can't *believe* she wants to get rid of it!'

Eliza smiled sarcastically and fiddled with a loose tooth. 'Their lives are a just a little bit fucked up for babies, Maggie.'

'Where's she getting it done?'

Eliza shrugged. 'Don't know exactly. Some clinic near the hospital.'

Maggie stared at the floor. 'What time?'

Swigged from her cider, Eliza belched loudly. 'Think she said 11? I wish *I* was pregnant. No one would expect me to bloody work then, would they!' She laughed to herself. 'Why are you asking, Mags? Do you think we should go with her?'

Maggie's blue eyes glistened with tears. 'No I don't.' She wiped her hand shakily across her mouth. 'I'm telling Seth.'

Eliza sat bolt upright. 'What? You *can't!*'

'He's got a right to know. It's *his* child.'

'Maggie,' Eliza grabbed her arm. 'You can't, you *really* can't. He'll go MAD!' Truthfully, she wasn't bothered whether Seth would go mad, but more concerned that *yet again* she'd dropped herself in it. Wouldn't she ever learn?

Seeing the resolute expression on Maggie's face, Eliza knew she was going to have to do a damn fine job of talking her out of this. Sighing, she walked to the bar. *It was going to be a long afternoon.*

Maggie watched Eliza leaning unsteadily against the bar and knew she'd be trying her best to talk her out of getting involved, but realistically she didn't know *what* to do.

*Surely Jane wouldn't go through with an abortion?*

She rummaged in her bag for her cigarettes. She'd tell Eliza that she wouldn't say anything and keep out of it, but she had to do *something*.

Seth and Jane would thank her for it in the end, wouldn't they?

Maggie shrugged. Either way, she'd got until tomorrow to decide, so she'd think about it again when her head was clearer.

• • • •

SETH FIDDLED IMPATIENTLY with his Zippo as he sat at the Chapter House table, listening as the finer points of the upcoming job were discussed.

As it was, he wasn't remotely pleased his instructions to Jane not to be involved had fallen on deaf ears. She'd gone berserk, accusing him of treating her like a leper.

Leper? He wasn't treating her like a bloody leper! Was it unreasonable to say being as she was pregnant, she shouldn't be involved in an armed robbery? Apparently it was, because she'd insisted she was doing it whether he liked it or not.

*Well, he didn't like it.*

He'd said everyone would understand why she couldn't be involved if he told them why, but this had only made her even

239

angrier and she'd screamed that if he told anyone, she'd leave him.

Seth smiled. If Jane thought he'd let her go, then she had rocks in her head. Furthermore, if she thought he'd let her walk away, pregnant with his child, then she had fucking boulders in her head!

Eventually he'd backed down. He needed to keep Jane calm. Besides, he'd got two weeks to ensure she was nowhere near when it happened, but in the meantime he'd let her believe she was part of it. She'd be none the wiser until the last minute.

Wazza's long beard dragged on the surface of the table as he reached for his beer. 'So what you're saying, is we wait for the other lot to take the security van out and then jump them?'

Phil nodded. 'That's *exactly* what we're saying, yes.'

Digger smiled and leant back in his chair. 'And Jane will distract them by being the breathtakingly stunning and alluring 'damsel in distress' at the side of the road?' He gave her a wink from across the table.

'Indeed!' Phil smiled.

Jane smiled as best as she could whilst her hand ran self-consciously over her small bump. She didn't feel stunning or alluring one jot. *More like a heifer.*

'It's extremely unlikely they'll stop,' Phil continued. 'But Jane will be enough of a distraction to slow them down so we can block them at either end.'

'I don't want Jane doing anything else, though. Not with th...' A sharp kick from under the table made Seth quickly recover the situation. 'Erm, not with all these people involved.'

Phil glanced at Seth. *What was the matter with him?*

'Then we shoot them and take the cash?' Adrian piped up from the other end of the table, his manic eyes lighting up with excitement at the prospect.

'NO shooting unless it's unavoidable!' Seth snapped, studying Adrian's long dirty blonde hair, messy goatee and large biceps bulging out from his sleeveless leather waistcoat. 'The less attention we draw, the better.'

Phil smiled. 'This is a *massive* heist, guys. If we can pull this off, we make ourselves a tidy 10k a piece, whilst the other dim fuckers get the blame.'

They all laughed and Wazza signalled for another round of drinks.

• • • •

FLICKING THE LIGHTS ON as he shut the front door, Seth pulled Jane into his arms. 'Now,' he murmured, bending his head to kiss her. 'How about we take half an hour to ourselves before getting a drink?'

Jane reached her arms around Seth's strong neck, feeling his hunger pressing hard against her.

She felt dreadful. The appointment at the clinic was hanging over her head like a black cloud and Maggie's earlier comments had thrown her more than she cared to admit. Fuck. It would break Seth's heart. It would break *hers* too, but she'd have to get over that, wouldn't she?

'Seth, I...'

'Ssshhh.' Putting his finger gently to Jane's mouth, Seth replaced it with his lips.

As Seth's hand made its way up her skirt, Jane began unbuttoning his jeans, until an almighty crash from outside stopped them in their tracks.

Seth's head snapped round in the direction of the front door. Quickly doing up his jeans, he moved forwards. 'Stay here.'

Jane righted her skirt. *Who was he trying to kid? She was stopping nowhere.* She ran out of the front door just as Seth disappeared down the first set of steps in to the courtyard.

Rounding the corner, she was met by the sight of Stuart spread-eagled on the floor being kicked and punched repeatedly by two large men. 'Finally caught up with you, did it?' Jane warned, failing to hide her happiness. 'Keep out of it, Seth!' she called, watching him move towards the group.

'You bitch! Is this down to you?' Stuart spat through his bruised and bloodied mouth

Seth stiffened. He'd been about to jump in and help Stuart, but now he froze. 'What's going on?'

The large black man turned to Seth. 'Keep out of it, mate. Nowt but our friend here who's brought this on himself.'

'You thick cunt!' Stuart screamed at Seth. 'Can't you see *she's* done this?'

Flashing fire, Seth stepped forward to join in giving Stuart a kicking. For a start he'd do a much better job than these pair of jokers. They hadn't done much damage at all yet.

Jane grabbed Seth by his arm. 'Leave them!'

'Enjoying this?' Stuart shouted, his eyes blazing. 'I'll get you for this, bitch. That I promise.'

Seth was not happy. This prick was threatening Jane and he was supposed to stand here and take it? 'Either you sort him out, or I will,' he snarled to the men, giving them one final chance to do it properly.

He was bewildered by the situation but did what Jane asked. Standing to one side, he couldn't help noticing the smug smile on her face as Stuart received a further swift kick to the side of his head.

Seth decided he'd be asking Stuart *very* clearly what his problem was. He also hadn't forgotten the cheeky bastard called him a thick cunt and was beginning to see why no one liked the man.

• • • •

STUART WAS A MESS by the time the men had finished and was curled into a foetal position with blood tricking from his ear. Groans came from his shattered mouth and it looked like that blow from the hammer had shattered his left kneecap.

Giving him a final message not to show his face in the city again, the two men nodded to Seth and Jane and departed into the stairwell.

Jane could not hold it together any longer and burst into loud laughter. Moving forwards, she leant over Stuart and smirked. 'What a shame!'

'Leave it, will you,' Seth growled, pulling Jane backwards. He looked at her sternly. 'It's not worth it. You're pregnant remember?'

*How could she forget? He didn't stop reminding her.* Glaring, Jane shook herself from Seth's grip and stalked towards the stairs. 'If you help him, don't bother coming back!'

Seth had no intention in the slightest of doing *anything* to help Stuart after what he'd heard coming out of his mouth. Quickly turning away, he followed Jane up to their flat.

## Thirty Four

MAGGIE HAD BEEN AWAKE all night worrying and by morning she was still unsure about what to do. She'd walked past Jane's flat a hundred times and smoked a thousand fags before glancing at the clock on the wall of the Town Hall.

Finally, before she could talk herself out of it, she ran up the steps. Standing in the doorway, she couldn't quite summon the courage to knock, but the decision was taken out of her hands when the door flew open.

Seth stood with a towel wrapped around his hips, his wet hair dripping down his bare chest. 'Thought I heard something.'

Maggie tried not to look at him, her nerves getting the better of her.

'Jane's not here,' Seth motioned for Maggie to follow him. 'She's gone to see about some work.'

Robotically, Maggie followed Seth into the lounge, only to stop on seeing blood splattered everywhere. Her hand quickly rose to her mouth and her eyes darted towards Seth.

Seeing her shock, Seth winked and gestured her to a chair. 'Don't worry about the mess. I was just about to sort it out. Bit of business last night, that's all. Sit yourself down.'

Maggie hesitantly lowered herself into an armchair, her legs like jelly. She watched Seth casually whip the towel from his hips and step into his jeans.

'So,' Seth smiled lazily. 'What's up?'

Maggie closed her eyes not knowing where to start, but nevertheless began to speak.

Seth listened to the words that came out of Maggie's mouth, finding his emotions were scrolling through disbelief, rage and sadness, through to pure unadulterated fear.

Finally, it had sunk in that this was *really* happening and he needed to sort it. *Like, sort it now.*

He shook Maggie hard. 'Tell me where the fuck she's gone!'

'I-I…'

'NOW, Maggie.' Seth's eyes pierced into Maggie's and he listened intently as she reeled off as much as she knew.

'And what time is this happening?'

'I-I'm not sure. I….'

Gripping Maggie's arms harder, he shook her again, his voice raw. 'Stop stuttering, you silly bitch. Tell me what time or I'll fucking *kill* you!'

'11. Eliza said 11,' Maggie sobbed.

Seth's head snapped to the clock. 'WHAT?' *It had just gone 10.30.*

Throwing Maggie roughly into the chair, Seth shoved his feet into his boots and pulled a shirt off the clothes horse. He grabbed his car keys, shrugged the shirt onto his shoulders and pointed his finger in her face. 'If I'm too late, I'll hold you entirely responsible.'

When the door slammed behind him, Maggie put her head in her hands and shook uncontrollably.

*Eliza had been right. She should have kept out of it.*

• • • •

JANE FIDGETED IN THE waiting room and glanced at two women sitting opposite, staring silently at magazines, trying to pretend they weren't all there for the same reason. She'd been faltering over the last few days and felt perhaps she could make it work after all, but last night had been the straw which had broken the camel's back and cemented her decision.

She'd been in the lounge when Seth had crashed in with Digger at 2am, dragging a guy with them. Sitting astride the man, Seth beat him unconscious and the stranger's blood had sprayed all over her, like a loose showerhead.

Staring at the wild animal who'd fathered the child inside her, Jane had turned around and left the room. In the bathroom, she'd wiped the blood away and retched into the toilet for what seemed like hours.

She'd still been leaning against the cool tiles to try and stop her mind from reeling when the door slammed as Digger removed the unfortunate man from the flat.

Seth had staggered in smiling. 'What's the matter, baby?' Cupping Jane's face with his hand, he'd taken a swig out of the whisky bottle he clutched. 'Are you not well?'

'I'm fine,' she'd lied and eyed the bloody handprint he'd left on her face in the mirror's reflection.

Jane tried to concentrate on the old dog-eared copy of 'Readers Digest,' but she'd read the same sentence a thousand times.

*Was she making a hideous mistake?* Waiting gave her time to think and that was dangerous. It always had been.

She ran her hand over the little bump and immediately wished she hadn't. She needed her mind to be blank.

*There was still time.*

No. She'd made her decision and she'd have to stick to it. *It was the right thing to do, wasn't it?*

Swallowing down the overwhelming urge to run away, Jane set her jaw in a straight line and held her ground.

• • • •

SETH GUNNED ALONG the road, his knuckles white from gripping the steering wheel. His eyes stared straight ahead as he blindly fumbled for his lighter and sparked up the eleventh cigarette since he'd got in the car.

Swerving past a car, he glanced at the time on the dashboard clock. Almost 11. *Fuck. Fucking hell. COME ON! Time was running out.*

'Get out of my way!' he yelled, overtaking another car. If he didn't get there in time, he was finished and so, he thought with a savage expression, was Jane.

Silent tears coursed down his face as he pushed harder on the accelerator, the needle on the speedo hovering at just over 140mph.

Swallowing down bile in his throat, panic rose like a phoenix in his chest. Breathing in quick and ragged bursts, he wiped beads of sweat away from his forehead with his sleeve, feeling like he'd pass out any second.

'HOW COULD YOU DO THIS TO ME JANE?' he roared, slamming his fist on the steering wheel.

• • • •

JANE STARED AT THE off-white blinds hanging in strips over the side window in the small room. Although it was over-hot, she was cold and shivery.

The nurse sat talking in front of her holding a clip-board, but Jane didn't hear a word because her eyes were fixed on a wheeled trolley holding a collection of implements. Maybe she shouldn't be looking, she thought, spotting curved things with thick handles, something that looked like an electric toothbrush and a metal dish.

Without warning, her stomach heaved. Grabbing the nearest thing to hand, she vomited hard into a cardboard bed pan. With shaking fingers, she then accepted the tissue from the stony-faced nurse and quickly wiped her mouth.

'Do you understand everything I've told you?'

Jane nodded blankly and took the paperwork waved in front of her. She'd still no idea what the woman had said but cared even less.

The nurse pushed a black biro across the desk. 'Sign here and get on the bed. It won't take long.'

Jane stared at the words spinning on the paper like a kaleidoscope.

Just do it and get it fucking over with, she thought numbly.

• • • •

SCREECHING TO A HALT half-on the pavement, Seth threw himself out of the driver's door and took the steps three at a time. He crashed through the door into the waiting room and ignored the expressions of the women at the sight of a crazed long-haired man barging past them. His eyes frantically searched the room. *Jane wasn't here! Where the fuck was she?*

The woman behind the reception desk stood up. 'Excuse me, you can't g…'

Roughly pushing the woman sideways, Seth lurched past and shoved at the door of the treatment room. Finding it locked, he kicked it with full force.

Jane stared in shock as Seth crashed wild-eyed into the room, but before his presence properly sank in, he'd dragged her from the metal bed by her hair.

'Who the *hell* are you?' the nurse screamed.

Ignoring her, Seth slammed into the metal trolley, scattering the instruments all over the floor. He pushed Jane up against the wall and yanking her chin up, stared into her eyes. 'Have you done it?'

Jane looked at Seth mutely, her dark eyes expressionless. *How the hell had he found out?*

*No - she hadn't done it. She'd changed her mind.*

'HAVE YOU DONE IT?' Seth screamed.

'You can't come in here!' the nurse wailed.

Seth glared at the woman. 'I CAN DO WHAT THE FUCK I WANT!' Turning back to Jane, his eyes scanned hers. 'TELL ME! *Please* tell me, Jane. Have you killed our child?'

Seeing the pain in Seth's eyes, Jane's heart broke into a thousand pieces. She shook her head and watched his shoulders sag with relief.

'Right.' Grabbing Jane's bag, Seth picked her skirt off the

chair and shoved it into her shaking hands. 'Put it on. We're leaving.'

'Seth, I…'

'Shut up. Just shut the *fuck* up, Jane!'

• • • •

CHAIN-SMOKING, JANE PICKED at her fingers during the silent drive home, glad Seth hadn't spoken because she'd have had to answer him and she'd no idea what to say.

She was relieved when the car finally pulled up in the parking lot. She needed to drink something hard and then go to bed for a while.

Stepping into the flat, Jane walked into the lounge and began to pull her shoes off whilst Seth closed the door behind them.

Spinning Jane around, Seth drew close to her face. 'Now you can tell me what the *fuck* you were thinking!'

'I'm sorry,' she whispered.

'Sorry?' Seth screamed, 'You're *sorry*?' He yanked her head back by her hair. 'You decide to kill our child without even discussing it with me?' He shook her like a rag doll. 'How dare you. How fucking *dare* you!'

'Get off me, Seth! *This* is why we can't have a child. Because of all *this*!' Jane waved her arm wildly around the lounge - from the bloody splatters up the wall, to the patches of congealed blood over the underlay. She pointed to the upturned table, her voice sounding stronger than she felt. 'You promised me all this would stop!'

'Oh, so it's *my* fault?' Seth raged. 'Nothing to do with *you*, then?'

Jane shook her head in despair. She just wanted to lie down. She was too mentally and physically exhausted to argue and the tears were threatening to fall. The last thing she wanted was to give him the satisfaction of seeing her cry.

As she turned to walk away, Seth swung Jane back to face him and backhanded her hard across her face. The force of the slap knocked her backwards, but he pulled her on top of him onto the sofa, his hand splaying over her belly.

'You're having this baby, Jane,' he growled.

Prising Seth's hands away, Jane pushed off the sofa and ran from the room. Grabbing her car keys, she got half way up the hallway before he caught up with her.

'Where do you think you're going?' he raged, slamming her against the wall.

'Away from YOU!' Jane screamed.

'You think I'll trust you to go *anywhere* now, do you?' he laughed, opening the front door.

Watching Seth step through the doorway, Jane panicked. 'What are you doing?'

'I'm going OUT!' Slamming the door, he turned the key in the lock from the outside.

Jane tried the door handle, shaking it. *He'd locked her in the fucking flat!*

'I'm keeping you where I know what you're doing,' Seth called from the other side of the door.

As his footsteps faded away, Jane screamed with rage and tried the door again. 'SETH!'

Shaking with anger, she ran into the lounge and paced around the floor. She yanked the few framed photographs they possessed off the wall, along with anything else she could get her hands on and launched them through the window onto the street below.

· · · ·

SETH HADN'T GONE FAR. In fact, he'd only gone next door. He wasn't sure why, only that it was the closest place. He needed some breathing space to fight off the impotent sense of dread that still remained when he'd thought he hadn't reached Jane in time and that his child was dead.

Letting himself in, he found Stuart lying on the sofa, his face still bruised.

Hearing Jane screaming and smashing things from next door, Stuart glanced towards the wall and smiled. 'Everything alright?'

he asked sarcastically.

Seth glared. *Was he taking the piss?*

Stuart grinned. He still had one bargaining chip to play with. Although he'd been unable to remember a lot of what had happened the other night when those two dorks had jumped him, he *could* recall what he'd heard directly before slipping into unconsciousness. *This would either make or break it.*

Trying to read Seth's mood, which didn't look too good, he decided nevertheless to chance it. 'Jane needs to chill out a bit now she's pregnant, doesn't she?'

Seth's eyes narrowed. *This really wasn't the best topic right now.*

'Or has she let it slip it isn't yours?' Stuart let out a nasty chuckling laugh, cut short when Seth gripped him round the throat and pushed him deep into the sofa.

Needing to take his frustration and rage out on someone, Seth decided it may as well be Stuart. He owed the fucking wanker one anyway. 'You never learn, do you?' he growled, bearing his weight down onto Stuart's damaged knee.

Stuart's mouth flapped open and closed, gasping for breath as his windpipe was crushed. *Bollocks. He'd misjudged that one.*

'*Don't* insult my missus again,' Seth seethed, watching Stuart thrash his head from side to side, attempting to loosen the hand from around his throat. Relaxing his grip, he rocked back onto his haunches, then stood and steadied himself with one hand before getting to his feet.

Stuart pushed himself upright and smiling falsely, rubbed his throat. 'I was only joking,' he lied.

Seth pulled a hunting knife from his pocket and with one flick of his wrist, the sheath dropped on to the carpet. Launching himself back onto Stuart, he pressed his knee into his chest. 'Think it's funny, do you?' He lined the knife horizontally against Stuart's mouth. 'Let's give you something to *really* smile about, shall we?'

Cutting through the skin from the edge of Stuart's lips to halfway along his cheek on both sides of his mouth, Seth laughed. 'There you go, wanker. A permanent smile!'

• • • •

IGNORING THE WEIRD howling coming from next door, Jane launched one of the televisions from the spare room with all her might against the lock on the front door. As it smashed off its hinges for the third time, she grabbed her bag and with her heart beating like a drum, ran down the steps from the flat.

Slipping on a piece of wood half-way down the stairs and whacking her head, Jane righted herself and ran out into the courtyard. She wiped the blood trickling into her eye off with the back of her hand and took the next stairwell two steps at a time.

Hearing Jane's heels clattering across the stone courtyard, Seth's head shot up. *Damn. He hadn't finished with this wanker yet.*

Glancing at the gaping wound pouring blood from Stuart's face, he wiped the knife on his jeans. 'You can wait,' he hissed, then raced from the flat.

Firing the car engine, Jane yanked at the stiff handbrake seeing Seth run towards the back of her motor. *Come on. Come on.* Finally releasing it, she slammed into reverse and stamped down on the accelerator.

As Jane shot backwards, Seth leapt on to the boot and clung on whilst the car smashed into the wall at the side of the parking lot.

Jane glanced into the rear-view mirror as he tumbled onto the floor and she scraped the car into first gear.

Seth dived into the back seat as the car lurched forward. 'JANE! STOP THE FUCKING CAR!'

With tyres screeching, Jane swerved onto the road. 'Get out, Seth. Just GET OUT!'

Unable to stop the floodgates from opening, tears poured down her face. Overshooting the junction, she swerved across the road as Seth clambered over into the passenger seat, grabbing at her arms. 'Get off me!' she yelled, the car swerving again amidst much blaring of horns.

'For fuck's sake! STOP THE CAR!' Seth roared, tears rolling down his face. 'Please, Jane. *Please*. I'm begging you.'

Jane couldn't do this anymore. She'd had enough. Stopping abruptly at the side of the road, she put her head in her hands and sobbed harder than she had in a very long time.

Dragging her shaking body across the seat, Seth wrapped Jane in his arms and held her tight as she cried, pulling her face deep into his chest. He lifted her head up and brushed his mouth against hers.

Twining her fingers in Seth's hair, Jane clung on to him. 'I'm sorry. I'm so sorry. I wasn't going to go through with it, but I still don't see how we can do this. My head's so fucked up. I don't know what's going on anymore.' She looked into his eyes. 'I don't know who we are anymore.'

Resting a hand on the side of her face, Seth whispered in Jane's ear. 'You're you and I'm me.' He placed his hand gently onto her belly, a trace of a smile running over his mouth as he kissed her eyelids in turn. 'I love you, Jane. More than anything. We *can* do this and our baby will be beautiful. Just like you.'

Ignoring the people walking past the car haphazardly half-parked on the pavement, Jane unbuttoned Seth's jeans whilst he licked the blood from the cut on her head.

# THIRTY FIVE

DEBBIE SLIPPED HER HAND underneath the table and stroked Paul's leg through his tight ripped black jeans. She couldn't understand why he wasn't jumping at the chance to get it on with her.

Over the last few months they'd been working together to sort Seth and Jane out, she'd become more and more attracted to him, but he hadn't taken her up on any of her hints. *Maybe she needed to be a bit more obvious?*

Necking the remains of her cider, Debbie winked and waved the empty glass at Paul. She needed something to get her mind off things. Not only had her plan to set Jane up with Davis failed miserably because he'd gone and fucking died, but her brother's sexual demands had gone through the roof since she'd moved back in with him.

Not that she minded. Ian even made her come sometimes. It was more to do with Teddy. He was a bit fat for her liking, but it wasn't just that - it was the news Paul had given her a couple of weeks ago. He'd heard on good authority from his cousin that Jane was pregnant and since then, she'd felt horribly depressed.

Initially she'd tried to ignore it as a rumour. After all, no one else had mentioned it and that sort of stuff usually spread around town like wildfire, but since seeing Seth and Jane in the bakery last week, she could no longer pass it off as hearsay.

She'd concealed herself behind a tall shelving unit when they'd come in and stared in shock when Seth had put his arms around Jane from behind, lovingly spreading his hands over her quite obviously rounded belly. Jane had tugged her top down over her bump before turning around and kissing him passionately.

Oh, she'd seen the love in Seth's eyes as he'd looked at Jane and now they were having a fucking baby, which meant there was much less chance of breaking them up.

Gritting her teeth with jealously and rage, Debbie glared at Paul. He was taking *far* too long at the bar getting her refill.

Returning to the table, Paul carefully sat out of reach of Debbie's wandering hands and passed her a fresh pint.

'About time!' she snapped, snatching the drink. 'Listen. We really need to act. Especially on Jane.' Debbie smiled savagely, revealing her crooked teeth. 'I have a plan… Although we need to be clever how we do it, I think we should poison the bitch.'

Paul nearly choked. He hated the thought of Jane having another man's baby more than anything, but he wanted to *marry* her, not kill her. 'Can't we poison Seth instead?'

Debbie stared at him uncomprehendingly. *Was he stupid or something?* 'Seth? What the fuck for? He's not pregnant is he, you thick bastard!'

Paul didn't like where this was going. 'Well we can't be completely sure she's pregnant. Only Stuart has said that.'

Debbie scowled. *There was no mistaking what she'd seen last week.* 'However much Jane's trying to hide it, I saw her belly. She's pregnant alright, but she won't be by the time I've finished.'

Paul grimaced. This was getting out of hand, but he was unsure exactly what to do about it.

• • • •

STUART SHUFFLED ACROSS the bathroom, his bad leg stiff

as ever and peered into the small plastic-framed mirror on the windowsill. He scowled at his reflection. *For fuck's sake, what a bloody state.*

Wincing, he bared his teeth and counted five missing, including both his front ones. He ran a finger over the long scabbed scars at the corners of his mouth and winced for the second time. *He looked like Worzel bloody Gummidge!*

Pushing his hair out of his grey eyes, he studied the rest of his face and wondered whether growing a beard would hide the scars.

Stuart pushed his tongue around his mouth, feeling the stitches. He'd had no choice but to take himself to the hospital, but he'd got twenty questions from the doctors. It had been *so* tempting to tell them who had carved his fucking face up, but he'd found himself making up some cock and bull about getting mugged on a canal towpath.

He knew they hadn't believed him, but he didn't care. He was going to frame that cunt, Seth, with bells on. In fact, he'd kill the pair of them and didn't give a shit if that didn't fit into Paul's stupid plans.

Gingerly sluicing water on his face, Stuart realised he'd have to venture out at some point soon. Gritting his teeth, he promptly wished he hadn't, when pain shot from the raw nerve endings. The bastard had proper tucked him up.

'Yes Jane, no Jane…' he mimicked, 'and you're supposed to be a hard case, Seth? Taking orders off that bitch?'

Realising he'd degenerated into talking to himself, Stuart shook his head. *Jane, Jane, Jane. Bloody Jane!*

He threw his toothbrush onto the windowsill angrily. What was the fucking point? He had hardly any teeth left. He'd have to find a way to get rid of Seth and Jane once and for all and he would concentrate on that whilst his face healed.

• • • •

'CLEOPATRA! CLEEEEOOOOPATRAAAAA!' Ian groaned, watching as his length slid in and out between Debbie's ample buttocks.

Holding onto the side of the sofa, Debbie winced as her brother pounded harder into her. She wasn't a great fan of anal, but if that was what Ian needed today, then she'd oblige.

As his thrusts became more urgent, she repositioned her feet slightly. Her balance was still dodgy since the bout of concussion from Jane's bashing, but the bitch would get hers soon. *And her stupid baby.*

'Tell me, slave,' Debbie panted, playing into Ian's fantasy. 'Have you prepared my bath of milk?'

Why on earth he'd wanted her to pretend she was Cleopatra was a little confusing, but she didn't really care one way or the other. She actually quite fancied herself as the beautiful Cleopatra. Bathing all day in the milk of asps without a care in the world, apart from running out of eyeliner of course.

Hearing a groan, Debbie opened her eyes and glanced towards the fat ginger man on the chair. With jeans round his ankles and grubby stained pants half-way down his white mottled thighs, Teddy's thick hand pumped furiously.

Locking eyes with him, Debbie ran her tongue over her fat lips and looked at the thin trail of saliva hanging from the corner of his mouth.

'Going to make you bleed, Cleopatra!' Ian shouted suddenly, one hand grasping and twisting her pendulous breasts, the other pulling her hair.

Debbie grimaced, the soreness of her scalp reminding her that the stitches were due to come out of the back of her head later today.

• • • •

DRINKING STRAIGHT FROM a flat bottle of coke, Jane pulled a face. Her mind was speeding and the lack of vodka was not doing much for her mental or physical state. Plus she was bored and getting more frustrated by the minute.

In the three weeks since the abortion attempt Seth had refused to let her go anywhere on her own, even though she'd assured him *countless* times she wouldn't do anything. Now, with no job to go to, she was completely trapped and felt like she was slowly suffocating. This, coupled with refraining from drink-fuelled oblivion, meant her mind was as wired as an over-tuned piano teetering on the edge of the Grand Canyon. At least this job was on tomorrow so she could get out of the bloody flat for once.

She glanced at the men sitting around the Chapter House table and self-consciously ran her hand over the bump which had expanded further in the last three weeks. She knew it was only a matter of time before everyone guessed, but at least her morning sickness had stopped. Although it was odd not to have a flat stomach anymore and she felt horribly fat, she was getting more comfortable with it.

'So, the fine tuning is this,' Phil said, watching Adrian pick a fresh scab on his knuckle. 'Wazza drives the smaller van with Adrian in the back, Ok? And Digger, you'll be driving the larger one with Seth in the back.'

'And Jane?'

Phil glanced at Seth, who up until this point had been silent and hadn't seemed even like he'd been listening. Taking a swig from his beer, he turned his packet of cigarettes on its end. 'I was getting to that. Jane will go in the small van with Adrian and Wazza and they'll drop her at the layby once we've had word the security van has been done. That way w…'

'I want her in the van with me,' Seth interrupted. Staring intently at Phil, he picked up his tumbler of whisky.

Phil held Seth's gaze. 'That won't work. Wazza's van is positioned to pull in front of the blue one once it slows by the layby.' He focused his eyes. 'Jane can't go in your van because you'll be blocking the other end.'

Leaning back, Seth put both hands behind his head and sighed. 'Then I ain't doing it. Or *she* ain't. One or the other.'

'Seth!' Jane was getting more frustrated by the second. She'd thought it weird he hadn't griped when the message had come in for the final meet and now she knew why. *He was trying to get her off the job.*

Phil clocked the surprised expressions of all those seated. 'What's this about, Seth?' *It wasn't like him to play games.* 'Jane's got to go in that way, you know that.'

'I'm doing this the way that's needed,' Jane snapped, glaring at Seth. 'Stop being so fucking ridiculous!'

Digger exchanged glances with the others, knowing Seth wouldn't appreciate being spoken to like that in front of them. Adrian, however, hadn't noticed any of it and was busy picking at something in his teeth with a flick knife.

Folding his arms, Seth cut Jane a withering look. A muscle twitched in the side of his neck but he remained silent.

'Look.' Phil knew he needed to turn this around. *He didn't want Seth and Jane kicking off.* 'I know you're worrying about her getting involved in…'

'I can handle myself, thank you!' Jane griped.

Phil clenched his teeth and placed his hand over hers. 'I know you can, babes. Seth just wants to look after his woman.' *Hopefully that would placate them? For fuck's sake. He needed both of them on this job.*

'I don't need looking after!'

Phil forced a smile. *He wasn't going to win either way at this rate.* 'She's more than capable, Seth.'

Scraping his chair back, Seth banged his fist on the table. 'I *know* that! It's just a bit different now sh…'

'ENOUGH, Seth!' Jane screeched.

Phil had had enough. *What the hell was going on?* He looked from Seth to Jane. 'This is a big job, guys and I can't afford any weird fucking domestics! Leave it at home, eh?'

Glaring, Seth planted himself heavily back down on the chair whilst Jane shot daggers at him. 'Carry on.'

Phil looked around slowly. 'Like I was saying, Jane gets dropped at the layby once we've had word the van has cleared. It will then be around a minute before the blue van arrives.' He smiled at Jane. 'Best togs girl, short, *short* skirt. Stockings. The works, yeah?'

Ignoring Seth's eyes burning into the side of her head, Jane absentmindedly wondered whether anything like that would fit by that point.

'As soon as you see the blue transit, step as close to the road as possible. Wave your arms about and look suitably upset, but fucking lovely, yeah?'

Jane nodded. *That bit was relatively easy at least.*

'Now,' Phil continued. 'The van won't stop, but courtesy of Jane's distraction, it should slow. Digger and Seth will tail the van and Wazza, as soon as Jane steps towards the road, floor it and swerve in front, yeah? Digger, once Wazza blocks the front, you block from the back.'

He paused to make sure he had everyone's attention. 'Only Wazza and Adrian to jump.'

Phil turned back to Digger. 'You and Seth empty the lovely cargo and Jane, you get in the back of Digger's van.' He glared at Adrian. '*No* shooting unless you have to. Everyone clear? Collect vans at 5.30 from here and wait for the off.'

· · · ·

DEBBIE ARCHED HER BACK and lifted herself into position whilst Teddy lined himself up behind her. Grimacing when the soft folds of his fat belly rested against her arse cheeks as he pushed into her, she forced herself to concentrate on giving Ian deep throat.

As Ian thrust further into her mouth, she gagged before reaching down to rub her clit. It didn't look like either of those lazy bastards were going to bother to make her come, so she'd have to do it herself.

'Maggie, oh Maggie,' Ian groaned. 'Suck me. *Suck me!*'

Debbie froze and pulled her head up sharply. 'You what?'

'What the fuck are you doing, you useless cow?' Ian looked at Debbie incredulously, his erection throbbing. 'I was just about to come!'

'You said 'Maggie,'' Debbie whimpered. *She hated Maggie almost as much as she hated Jane.*

Slipping out, Teddy pulled his pants up and looked thoroughly pissed off. Muttering to himself, he took a packet of tobacco from his jeans pocket.

'What's the fucking problem?' Ian hissed.

Debbie scowled. 'I'm *not* Maggie!'

Ian slowly stroked his erection. *He refused to lose it because the silly bitch was bleating on.* 'I wish you fucking were!' Grabbing Debbie's head, he pulled her back down. 'Now get on with it!'

'NO!' Debbie snapped, pushing herself off the sofa and pulling her skirt back in place. 'Just get over her. She doesn't want you!'

Lurching to his feet, Ian grabbed her by the hair and pulled her sharply towards him. 'Shut the fuck up, you ugly cunt!'

As Ian began raining punches into Debbie's face, Teddy rolled his eyes and flicked on the TV, deciding he may as well watch 'The Magic Roundabout.'

Ian stepped over his sister on the floor and paced around the room. The fucking stupid, fat, fucking slag. How dare she moan about Maggie. Who the fuck did she think she was?

He didn't give a fuck anymore what that overgrown twat, Digger, said about leaving Maggie alone either. He wasn't scared of that threatening prick, or that gorilla, Seth.

*What was the worst they could do?*

He *would* get Maggie back. She loved him, he knew she did and that was all that mattered. Being dead was better than not being with her and *no one* was going to tell him otherwise.

• • • •

SETH COULD HAVE SWORN he'd seen Stuart smirking at the window when he'd stormed across the courtyard, but he'd more important things to concentrate on right now. *Like making sure Jane stayed pregnant.*

Even though she'd been uncooperative and had made him look a prick at the meeting, he was slightly more relaxed since putting away the best part of a new bottle of whisky. It didn't, however, change the fact that he'd no choice now but to let her do the job and that had *definitely* not been part of the plan.

Watching Jane out of the corner of his eye as she poured herself a shot of vodka, Seth stared at the book he was attempting to read. He knew he wasn't helping matters by driving her crazy and keeping her under lock and key, but he couldn't help it. He was driving himself crazy as well.

Taking another slug out of the bottle, he reminded himself to slow down. He couldn't be hungover for tomorrow's job because at this rate, he'd lose his work if he didn't curb his drinking. He knew people were beginning to question his rationality and he didn't like it one little bit.

*He was Seth and did not fuck up. Ever.*

Seth admitted he'd struggled with a lot of things lately, starting with that shit at the park and then the abortion stuff and knew he needed to sort it all out. Running his fingers through his unruly hair, he glared at Jane and felt like whacking her. He refused to fuck this up but couldn't seem to get his emotions into gear and it was starting to bother him.

Eyeing her tight skirt straining over her growing belly, a rush of both love and desire suddenly washed over him. Flashing her a lopsided smile, he beckoned her over and began unbuttoning his jeans.

No matter how much she angered him he couldn't help his all-consuming love for her.

Seth groaned with need as Jane straddled him in the chair. If he had his way, he'd give her kid after kid after kid.

## THIRTY SIX

JANE STARED OUT OF the front window of the small white Escort van as Wazza sped down the road negotiating the headlights rushing towards them. Soon they'd be in position.

Flicking cigarette ash out of the slightly open window, she was glad for the break from Seth, safely caged in the back of the white transit tailing them.

Earlier, as they'd made their way to the Chapter House, he'd insisted on pulling over every five minutes to do coke and was wired to the eyeballs.

She was to get *straight* in the back of the van the *second* Wazza and Adrian jumped. No messing around. No ifs and no buts.

None.

*Yes, she understood.*

This was to be the *last* job she'd be involved in until after the baby was born.

*Yes, ok. Fine.*

Once this job was done, they'd take a break from all of this shit.

*Yes, of course they would, like all the other stuff he'd promised...*

It was different this time.

*Sure. Wasn't it always?*

Staring at Seth's serious face, she'd found it difficult not to laugh out loud. Of course, it was different this time. It always was…

Unable to see Digger's face in the van behind, Jane could still clearly imagine his expression and knew that Seth would be counter-balancing each corner from within the cavernous hulk, the muscle in his neck twitching and the vein in his temple throbbing furiously.

When the white transit behind suddenly veered off down a side road, Jane knew they must be close to the off, but Wazza continued for another mile and a half before dipping the headlights and pulling over. Her heart raced as adrenalin pumped through her veins in anticipation. All they had to do now was wait for the nod.

She was dolled up to the nines in sky-high stilettos, a skirt barely longer than a wide belt, which grazed the tops of her fishnet stockings and a basque top with a long lace frill that concealed her pregnancy.

All in all, she felt pretty damn hot, which was nice, as at fourteen weeks gone, she'd been feeling decidedly unattractive, even though Seth was unable to keep his hands off her. She was still shit scared of bringing a kid into their madness, but was slowly coming around to the idea.

Smiling, she placed her hand on her swollen belly, accepting they'd have to tell everyone the news after this.

'You ok, girl?' Wazza asked, patting Jane's hand.

'I'm fine,' she smiled and pulled her mind back to the job in hand.

Seeing the signal they'd been waiting for, Wazza grinned. 'Game on!'

· · · ·

IAN HAD MADE HIS mind up. It was worth one last stab, surely? Stopping, he tried to make sense of the purple shapes following him, unable to decide whether they were actually there.

The voice in his head had said anything purple represented negative entities which didn't have the power to show their full bodies. He thought the voice may be his brother, Nigel, warning him about the forces of evil, but when he'd told Debbie this, she'd laughed.

Nigel was dead, she'd said, so how could he be talking?

Ian scowled. Debbie had *never* liked Nigel, even though he was her brother too. It was probably because he'd got on better with him that she had, the jealous cow. In fact, he was beginning to think she was a bit mental because she'd been acting weirder than usual lately and he'd just about had enough of it.

Glancing around at the familiar landmarks, Ian gauged there was about a mile left to walk.

Shrugging his shoulders, he decided he didn't care if Debbie, Teddy or *anyone* disapproved of him and Maggie and he'd carve that fat fucker Digger up, if he had to.

Smiling and exposing his blackened teeth, Ian quickened his pace, impatient to see the surprise on Maggie's face when she realised he'd come back for her like he'd always promised he would.

• • • •

MAGGIE HAD ALMOST pulled her big toenail off from her right foot. Her nerves were well and truly shattered and she felt like an animal waiting to be shot. She hadn't dared go out for almost three weeks in case she'd seen Jane.

The one and only time she'd attempted to venture out, her heart had raced at such a pace, it felt like it was going to erupt through her chest wall. She'd been sure she was going to die.

*The question was, did Jane know it was her who'd told Seth?*

Maggie swallowed nervously. *She'd fucked up big time.* However, at least Jane was keeping the baby, or so Eliza said when she'd popped round, but that didn't solve how she was going to face either of them again.

She put her head in her hands and cried, only to freeze when a knock sounded at the caravan door. She'd ignore it. *Yes, she'd just ignore it. It probably wasn't real anyway.*

Since the panic attack, she'd relied on Zed and the other travellers to share food and dope with her, but the drugs were making her worse. She couldn't even sleep, she was so paranoid.

Rolling her glazed eyes towards the roof of the caravan, Maggie inhaled, her breathing ragged. She was *so* bloody lonely but what else could she do?

She had nowhere else to go and it was her own fault.

The knock sounded on the door again. *Maybe she should open it?*

What if it was real and she wasn't hearing things after all? It might be Zed? Even though, when he'd brought stuff round for her, she'd been purposefully touchy-feely with him, he hadn't appeared interested. Surely any red-blooded man would have taken the hint?

Wringing her hands together, Maggie shakily reached for a cigarette as the knocking continued. Getting off the seat, she walked towards the door. At the end of the day she didn't have anything to lose anymore.

• • • •

'ARE YOU SURE YOU wouldn't just rather come with us instead?' the tall man leered, encircling Jane's waist whilst his shorter mate moved closer.

Even though Jane hadn't expected the blue transit to stop, she had it all under control and eyed the two men in front of her, deducing quite fairly that they were grotesque specimens.

'Come on, love. Don't play games.' The taller man's tongue ran over his lips as he pulled Jane sharply towards him, crushing her up against his front. 'Hop into the van, come on.'

His accomplice's eyes roamed up and down Jane's body, dribble escaping from his mouth and her eyes narrowed. She wasn't going to be treated like a piece of shit by these dickheads.

'Now wait a minute,' she hissed, hearing a van coming to a

halt nearby. *Thank God for that. About time. These two were seriously getting on her tits.* Come on Wazza! Take these fuckers out so we can all disappear, Jane thought angrily as a hand crept its way up her leg.

As the man's fingers brushed the edge of her lacy thong, she clenched her teeth, gearing to knee the freak in the groin.

· · · ·

SETH KEPT AN EYE out of the peephole from the back and watched intently as Digger tailed the blue transit. They were hanging far back enough to not cause suspicion, but not far enough to lose the target van. *It was all about timing.*

Clenching his jaw, he checked his sawn-off was loaded for the third time. He exhaled slowly, grateful that for once his head was as clear as a mountain stream. He knew Jane didn't believe this would be the last job for a while, but he'd meant it. He wanted more than anything to turn this around and sort everything out.

Reaching for his gun, he realised he was going to have to check it again. *Bloody hell, was he going fucking stupid or something?*

'Oh shit!' Digger muttered.

'What?' Seth yelled. 'What's the problem?' Peering through the peephole again, he saw two men with their hands on Jane. 'Stop the fucking van!' he roared.

Digger fully intended to stop, but first he needed to get to the bloody layby and there was one car still left to overtake. Swerving around it, he spotted Wazza's van appear in view at the top of the road. 'Wazza and Adrian jump first, remember?' he called over his shoulder.

White with rage, Seth banged his fist loudly against the van's metal divider. 'FUCK THAT! If you expect me to wait, you're fucking mad!' *He knew something would go wrong, he just knew it. Now it had and needed to get out of this van.*

'Calm down,' Digger yelled. 'You'll fuck it up if you jump first.'

'You don't get it!' Seth raged, his face panicked. He *knew* he should have put his foot down and stopped her involvement. 'Jane's almost four months pregnant!'

Digger paled. *Pregnant? Oh shit.* Screeching the van into position, he blocked the blue van off. 'We're here now. Just don't do anything stu…'

His words fell on deaf ears. Seth had already ripped open the side door of the transit and jumped out.

Jane leapt back in shock as the shot rang out of nowhere and blood splattered across her face.

As the tall man crumpled heavily to the floor, Wazza and Adrian raced from the other direction. Spinning around, she saw Seth standing next to the white transit with smoke coming out of his sawn-off, his eyes wild with rage.

'GET IN THE VAN, JANE!' Digger shouted, scrambling out of the driver's side.

The short man wasn't sure which way to turn as men surrounded him from both directions. He pulled a pistol out of his waistband and quickly blasted Wazza in the face.

Wazza crashed to the floor and three more men piled out of the back of the blue transit. Hearing Adrian roaring at the top of his voice, Jane willed him to shoot, unaware his gun had jammed.

Digger's eyes switched from one man to the other, to the other, to the fucking other. *This was a disaster. A total fucking disaster.*

Raising his gun towards the three men scrabbling across the layby, he was grateful they were totally unorganised. His face contorted into a savage grimace as he fired two shots in quick succession into the back of one man.

'JANE! GET IN THE FUCKING VAN!' Seth yelled, taking aim once more.

The short man's eyes bulged in panic, seeing another one of his mates hit the deck and he raised his pistol again, but without any hesitation Jane kneed him in the groin. Bending over, winded and howling in pain the man was unable to stop her grabbing his pistol arm.

'FUCK YOU!' Jane screamed, trying to keep her balance as the man locked his hand around her wrist and pulled her sideways.

Twisting the man's arm around, the barrel of the pistol pointed precariously close to her chest. Hearing a shot, she blinked. It wasn't her.

*Ok. Keep going.*

Trying to regain possession, the man yanked again, but Jane's high stilettos were no match for the surface of the gravelly layby and she fell heavily to the floor, dragging the man and the gun with her.

As his knee dug hard into her belly, a jolt of pain ripped through her. 'Get the fuck off me!' she screamed, pushing her thumb into the corner of the man's eye.

Roaring, he raised his hands to his face, giving Jane full control of the pistol and with her heart thudding painfully, she pulled the trigger.

The bullet blasted straight into the man's chest at the same time as another shot from behind blew away the back of his head like an eggshell, exploding blood, skin and fragments of bone everywhere.

As bullets flew, Seth threw the dead man off Jane and dragged her across the layby. She pushed herself to her feet and staggered towards Wazza lying motionless on the floor. Seeing most of his face was missing, she reached for his neck. *There was no pulse. There was no fucking pulse.*

'GET IN THE FUCKING VAN!' Seth roared, pushing Jane towards the transit.

Jane drew in a sharp intake of breath as another jolt of pain ripped through her belly and she tried to concentrate instead on the wide beatific smile across Adrian's face. Like a man possessed, he fired consistently into the bodies of the men scattered on the layby with his now unjammed pump-action.

'He's dead,' Jane murmured, automatically moving back towards Wazza.

'I can see that,' Seth hissed, pulling her away sharply. 'How many more times do I have to tell you to get in the van?' He yanked her arm. '*Now,* Jane!'

As Seth dragged her towards the transit, Jane noticed blood seeping through his jeans. 'Your leg! What the fuck's wrong with your leg?'

Seth glanced uninterestedly at his thigh. 'Took a bullet.' His eyes were cold and hard. 'It's only a graze. Now get the fuck in.'

Scrambling into the van, Jane surveyed the bodies lying in twisted piles everywhere. *Wazza. Poor fucking Wazza. Shit. SHIT.*

Shakily lighting a cigarette, she watched Digger pass cases from the blue transit to Seth, who launched them in the back of their van.

'ADRIAN!' Seth roared, a case in either hand. 'Get Wazza in the van.' *They needed to get out of here before the cops turned up.*

He gritted his teeth, desperately trying to ignore that he'd fucked up. He'd royally fucked up, but he couldn't have stood there whilst those wankers groped Jane, could he? *It was her bloody fault, this was. He'd told her. He'd fucking told her.*

Sweat poured down his face as he grabbed the last case and stuck his head inside to check they'd all been lifted. 'Digger, take the small van with Adrian. I'll take this one.'

Jumping into the driver's seat, Seth threw his sawn-off down by Jane's feet and glared at her. 'Happy now?'

• • • •

MAGGIE CLOSED HER EYES, tears of relief coursing down her face as she clung onto Ian. *She'd got him wrong, hadn't she?* All this time she'd been trying to run away from him when he'd changed. *She was so stupid.*

She'd nearly collapsed when she'd opened the door to him, but his contrite expression and the way he'd softly kissed her hand had overruled her fear. She'd let him in. She'd wanted the company. In fact, she'd *needed* it.

Smothering her neck with kisses, Ian had told her how much he loved her and how he'd never stopped. That she was the most beautiful thing he'd ever seen and that he wanted her to marry him.

She'd fallen back into his arms. She'd been so lonely. So, *SO* lonely.

Maggie smiled. Now he was making love to her like she'd always wanted, rather than fucking her like a beast. As the rush from the joint flowed through her brain, the change in Ian's eyes as he looked down upon her went unnoticed.

# THIRTY SEVEN

'WHERE THE HELL'S WAZZA?' Phil shouted, studying Jane's expression. Seth looked positively manic as he leant against the side of the van, swigging from a bottle of whisky, whilst Adrian wandered off in the direction of the Chapter House with a big grin on his face.

'So what the fuck happened?' Phil asked, unsure whether he really wanted to know. He knew Digger hadn't had any choice but to level with him. It was quite obvious something had gone horribly wrong and he'd done his best to explain how the blue van stopping in the layby and the extra blokes had affected the plans somewhat.

He cautiously eyed the blood seeping from Seth's thigh, Jane's bloodied knees and Digger's face and swallowed. 'I'm taking it you used the shooters?'

'We didn't shoot Wazza, if that's what you mean!' Seth snapped. 'Let's just say the fuckers didn't escape.'

Phil looked between them all in turn as he learnt all the details. 'Where are these guys now?'

'All over the layby,' Digger muttered.

'WHAT?' Phil screamed. *Fucking hell, could this get any worse? The cops would be all over them like a rash.* Without any time to lose, he sent Jane and Seth off in the Senator to stash the guns, whilst he and Digger drove the vans around the back.

Throwing a match to set the vans and Wazza's body alight, Phil retreated to a safe distance and wiped his forehead with the back of his jacket sleeve.

He wasn't sure whether it was sweat from the heat of the flames or the way he was feeling, but either way it wasn't good. *Wasn't good at all.*

. . . .

MAGGIE LAY FACE DOWN on the caravan bed and attempted to muffle her sobs with her pillow. Opening one red swollen eye, she peered cautiously into the gloom and watched Ian pace up and down the tiny walkway. *How could she have been so totally and utterly bloody dense?*

Ian stared at the wall. 'The purple will do the job,' he muttered under his breath. 'How many will I need?'

Maggie couldn't make any sense of what he was saying. She was far too busy trying to turn her body around into a more comfortable position, but doubted whether anything would be slightly comfortable for a very long time to come. *If ever.*

'I'm going to take you down, you piece of shit. You evil *bastard*!' he screamed.

As she hadn't uttered a word, Maggie sorely hoped Ian wasn't talking to her. Her eyes darted around the dimly lit interior of the caravan, but she couldn't see anyone, apart from him.

Burying herself further in the pillow, a fresh wave of sobs threatened to engulf her. *Why had she fallen for it? Why?*

Suddenly feeling Ian's weight on top of her once again, Maggie stiffened. She felt paralysed and powerless to move as his hands irritably yanked at the itchy blanket she'd attempted to cover herself with.

Feeling searing pain as he roughly pushed himself into her and began pounding relentlessly, Maggie nearly choked on her own vomit.

Ramming her head further into the pillow, Ian pulled her hips high and waves of red hot pain swirled through her brain. After the fisting, she hadn't thought she could bear any further agony, but it appeared she'd been wrong.

When Ian started screaming obscenities in what seemed to be a foreign language, Maggie was still amazed she hadn't passed out and instead tried to concentrate on something other than the muttering madman that was in here with her.

• • • •

CLAMBERING INTO THE SENATOR, Jane closed her eyes whilst Seth piled the collection of guns haphazardly into the boot.

'You stupid bitch! You put yourself at risk!' he screamed at the top of his voice. 'I was right all along!'

Inspecting her fingernails, Jane sighed. If she heard that one more time, she'd go crazy. Besides, he'd conveniently forgotten it was *him* who'd ballsed it up. 'No Seth, if *you* hadn't jumped, then Wazza wouldn't be dead!'

Seth nearly crashed the car as he wrenched Jane out of the seat by the top of her arm. 'You wanted me to stand there like your fucking mates whilst you got raped, did you?' he yelled. 'Or was that your fucking plan? Am I not enough for you in the sack anymore?'

Prising his hand off her arm, Jane felt like slamming his face into the steering column. 'It should have been *you*, Seth, not Wazza.'

A horrible loaded silence dragged on as Seth veered all over the road and Jane couldn't wait to get home. She winced as another sharp pain shot through her belly and she bit her lip, willing them to subside.

Seth had finished the whisky by the time he'd parked up. Coupled with the adrenalin still raging through his body, he felt wasted. By the time they'd got to the top of the steps to their flat he'd launched back into Jane full throttle.

Losing it, Jane smacked Seth in the eye, but the loose heel

on her stiletto gave way and she crashed down the steps to the bottom. She watched Seth storm off into the flat holding his hand over his bleeding eye and an expression of contempt across his face.

She tried to ride the fresh bout of searing pain that shot through her and pulled herself slowly to her feet, but as she steadied herself against the wall, a burst of water rushed from between her legs. *Christ, had she wet herself?*

She tried to work out what was going on, but another massive bolt of pain wrenched through her belly and by the time she reached the top of the steps, with an almost strange sense of detachment, she realised she was losing the baby.

Doubling over, Jane dropped her handbag on the floor and inched along the hallway while blood made a thin trail down her inner thigh, soaking into the top of her fishnet stocking.

As the next stomach-crunching contraction hit, she dropped to her knees.

Realising she'd little chance of being heard over the 'Black Sabbath' album banging at full volume from the lounge, she ignored the cuts on her knees and crawled slowly up the hall as another wave of pain ricocheted through her.

Retching up a string of bile onto the strip of underlay, beads of sweat formed on her forehead and her breathing became ragged when the contractions upped their pace.

'SETH!' Jane screamed, silent tears coursing down her cheeks. *There was no going back now.*

Receiving no answer, she pulled herself up, using the bathroom door as a prop, the waves of pain coming back to back. With one arm against the wall and the other against the sink, she managed to get on the toilet, where sweating and gagging, she waited for the inevitable.

• • • •

DI CHARLES RESTED HIS feet on his desk, a lukewarm cup of coffee in his hand and eyed the over-flowing ashtray. He was pissed off. *Really* pissed off.

His brows knitted together as he pushed a thick pile of untidy paperwork to one side. *Five dead all over the fucking road and no trace of anyone.*

Taking another sip of coffee, he placed the cup down loudly on his desk and glanced slowly around at his officers. 'And so, gentlemen, not *one* 999 call about people getting shot to fuck on the main road?'

A young policeman scanned his notepad. 'Apparently not. It was a routine patrol who spotted the abandoned van and the bodies.'

Turning his gold-tipped ballpoint pen over in his long fingers, DI Charles sighed. Twenty years' service and all he'd got was a fucking pen. He couldn't wait for the next present, perhaps for thirty years' service, or better still, retirement.

*What would he get then? A ruler, perhaps? A jar of paper clips?*

Continuing to twiddle his pen around, he wished he'd chosen to work on a farm or something. *Anything* rather than this bullshit.

'Well, I bet I know at least *half* the people involved in this, even if not directly.' DI Charles looked from one face to the other. 'Mark my words.'

'Do you think it was to do with drugs?'

'What makes you say that?'

'Well, I think I know who you're referring to and it, well, since we got information in from that bloke yesterday… About the drugs, I thought th…'

'I'm not saying it's connected,' the Inspector interrupted. 'I want to check out the prat that came in spilling his guts first.'

'Apparently he lives next door and hears stuff through the walls. He seemed ok to me.'

DI Charles sneered. 'That shows how fucking green you are then, doesn't it!'

He'd made his mind up. There was nothing else for it. He'd organise a raid and catch Wright and Ellerton red handed. Having waited so long to have those two fuckers on something, *anything* they got would be better than what he'd got on them now. *Which was fuck all.*

There would have to be *something* of interest in that dump they lived in to pin some decent charges on them, surely? If there wasn't, then he'd just make sure there was. He'd had enough. They were taking the bloody piss.

• • • •

STOMPING ACROSS TO the stereo, Seth slammed his fist down on the turntable. With a teeth-curling grating sound, the sticking record ground to a halt. He couldn't stand that bloody click, click, click, fucking *click* sound that had been repeating itself for the last five minutes. *For fuck's sake. Something else he would have to fix.*

Ripping the LP off the turntable and snapping it angrily in two, he threw the two halves into the corner of the room. *Bloody crap, useless waste of fucking space.*

Feeling his rage mounting yet again, Seth swiped the stereo off its tea crate onto the floor with a loud bang. He brought his boot down heavily on the side, causing a splintering sound as the plastic windows of the double tape deck popped out.

Bending down, he ripped the turntable arm off for good measure and flung it into the corner.

Hearing something else smash in the lounge, Jane tore a long piece of toilet roll off the holder and wiped the blood from her thighs as best as she could.

With the pain now finally subsiding, she remained on the toilet. She couldn't get up, because if she did, she'd have to look at what was in there. She'd see her tiny dead baby and she just couldn't.

Swallowing, she ignored the raging waves of panic threatening to engulf her and took some deep breaths.

*Just do it.*

Concentrating on breathing, rather than the unwelcome images rolling through her brain, Jane bunched up the toilet paper and pushed it between her legs into the bowl.

Turning the cold tap on full blast, the noise of the water almost matched the rushing in her head, but not quite.

Humming a tune to drown out the noise in her mind, she reached around. Taking one final deep breath, she pulled down on the flush.

*She needed a drink. A large one.*

· · · ·

SETH DRUNKENLY FELT for the sofa and allowed himself to fall back on to the cushions. His hand gingerly traced over the swollen mess of his eye. *The fucking stupid bitch*. He was going to look like a bleeding warthog for the next few days because of her.

What a shit night. It was all Jane's bloody fault. If she hadn't insisted on going against him about the job, he wouldn't have reacted the way he had.

Taking another swig of whisky, he scowled harder. He'd almost finished the second bottle and contemplated whether to put another record on or get more to drink. Remembering he'd just smashed the stereo up, he realised he'd have to get himself up and find some more whisky. Then he'd find Jane and give her a piece of his mind.

Tipping the dregs down his throat, Seth chucked the empty bottle into the corner and laughed as it smashed into lots of little pieces. *Now he'd go and deal with that miserable cow.*

Hearing Seth moving around, Jane was glad she'd got from the bathroom into the bedroom before he'd appeared.

She perched on the edge of the bed in the dark and desperately tried to dull the pain with vodka. Just a white line remained in her shut-down mind, fuzzy around the outside like a dreadful BBC2 test card. Her insides felt like they'd been stamped on, put through a mangle, turned inside out and then shoved back in again.

Suddenly hearing Seth stomp up the hallway, Jane closed her eyes and waited.

Kicking open the bedroom door, Seth swayed in the

doorframe, his narrowed eyes glaring at Jane. 'What the hell are you doing?' he slurred.

Jane hadn't the energy to argue. It was too difficult. *Everything was all too difficult.*

'*I said*, what are you doing?' Seth snapped, the purple swollen flesh of his eye visible even in the gloom. 'Sulking? Sitting in the fucking dark?'

Taking another swig out of the bottle of vodka, Jane shook her head.

'Then what's the matter?' Seth's voice softened slightly as he stepped towards her.

'I'm not sulking.' she replied flatly, grateful the half bottle of vodka she'd tipped down her throat in the last ten minutes had kicked in. Thankfully the edges of everything were starting to lose clarity. She'd been beginning to fear everything would remain in sharp focus for ever.

As Seth flicked the light on, he saw Jane's hair plastered to her face with sweat. Her makeup was smudged and there was blood down the insides of her thighs.

A fleeting expression of shock passed over his face. 'What the fuck?' he exclaimed confused, before realisation washed over him in slow motion. 'Oh shit! SHIT!'

Tipping his head towards the ceiling, he roared. 'WHAT THE FUCK HAVE YOU DONE, JANE?'

'What have *I* done?'

Rushing forward, he knelt down and scanned her face, his hand reaching for the bump that was no longer there.

'GET OFF ME!' Jane pushed his hand away. She didn't want him touching her. Not *there*.

'NO!' Seth howled, tears of anguish rolling down his face. Glancing at the blood stains marking the sheets of the bed, he grabbed Jane by the shoulders and shook her roughly. 'Tell me what's going on.'

Jane stared at him, expressionless. *Tired. Worn out.*

'Have you lost the baby?'

This time Jane managed to nod. She wasn't going to cry. If

she did, she wouldn't be able to stop. Oblivion wasn't anywhere near an acceptable level yet.

Seth rocked back on his haunches, his head in his hands. 'This is *your* fault, Jane!' he screamed, launching himself to his feet in front of her. 'YOUR FAULT!'

Blinking slowly, Jane looked at him coldly. Overriding the pain, she leapt to her feet. 'No Seth, the baby's dead and it's *your* fault,' she snapped, her eyes wild. 'What are you going to do now? Still go fucking straight?'

Jane prodded him hard in the chest and Seth glared at her as best as he could with his good eye. 'You going to sort it out? Again? This is *your* fault! YOURS!'

'I tell you what I'm going to do…' Pushing her backwards, Seth unbuttoned his jeans. 'I'm going to give you another baby.'

'Are you mad?' Jane yelled, trying to sit up. 'I've just had a miscarriage!'

'I'm not mad,' Seth whispered, parting her thighs with his knee.

Jane's face screwed up in agony as Seth pushed himself into her. 'You're hurting me!'

*Maybe this was what she needed?* Trouble was, she didn't know what she wanted anymore, apart from oblivion. Tears rolled down her face, realising even *that* had gone.

'I'm not hurting you, Jane. I'd *never* hurt you.' Seth lowered his mouth towards hers. 'I'll put this right. I'm going to put all of it right…'

As his tears dripped on to her face and mixed with her own, Jane wondered exactly how her life had descended into this total and utter chaos.

'I'm going to make us another baby. I'm going to make us another baby, Jane…' Seth panted.

*Oh no you won't*, Jane thought silently as Seth released himself into her. She wasn't going through that again.

*Not even for him.*

## THIRTY EIGHT

STANDING IN THE STAIRWELL shaking with fear, Maggie knocked the door of Jane's flat and waited, her teeth chattering.

Seth answered the door bare-chested, so drunk he could hardly stand and sporting the remains of possibly the biggest black eye she'd seen in a long time. He said nothing, just jerked his head for her to follow him before stumbling back towards the lounge.

Maggie stood motionless, eyeing the doors yet again ripped off their hinges and lying in broken, splintered piles. Gathering her courage, she slowly followed him, desperately hoping there would be no one trussed up on the floor. The less she thought about the last time she'd been here, the better.

Her eyebrows knitted together. She didn't pretend to understand what was going on, but then it seemed she very rarely had anyway. Self-consciously rubbing her bandaged wrist, she pulled the sleeve of her velvet jacket down and decided she would try to act normal. *Well, as normal as possible.*

Looking up, Jane knocked back the glass of neat vodka and before she'd even swallowed it, refilled her glass from the virtually empty bottle. She glanced at Seth sprawled on the sofa watching rubbish on the television. 'Who was at the door?'

'Maggie.'

Jane looked around. 'Maggie? Then where is she?'

Seth shrugged, his eyes not moving from the screen.

Eliza studied Seth, wondering what it would be like to run her tongue down the ridges of his stomach. A guilty red flush crept over her face and she pulled her eyes away reluctantly. 'You stay there, Jane. I'll go and find her.' She guzzled the remains of her can of Strongbow and pushed herself out of the armchair. 'I need to get another drink anyway.'

She also needed to update Maggie about the baby before the dozy cow waltzed in and said something that would kick everything off again.

Eliza found Maggie hyperventilating in the hallway and motioned her into the kitchen. 'Don't ask anything about the baby!' she hissed.

'What? Why?' Maggie asked, wincing as Eliza grabbed her bad arm.

'They lost it last week. Seth's in a right fucking state. Gone off his rocker, by all accounts.'

Maggie raised her hand to her mouth. 'Oh God. What happened?'

'Not sure. They haven't said much.'

'Maggie!' Jane said loudly as she walked into the kitchen, knowing full well they were talking about her. 'How you doing?'

'I-I, er…' Maggie's eyes roamed over Jane's now tellingly flat stomach. 'I'm sorry about the baby. Eliza's just told me.'

'Yeah, well,' Jane snapped, 'these things happen.' Moving so they couldn't see her eyes, she opened the fridge and grabbed a beer. 'Where have you been hiding? It's got to be a month since I last saw you.' Turning, she stared pointedly with narrowed eyes. 'Thought you might be avoiding me?'

Maggie thought she might pass out. *Jane knew*. She leant against the work surface to support her wobbling legs. 'I-I'm sorry. Really, I am. I shouldn't have interfered.'

'No, you shouldn't have,' Jane hissed, then smiled – a smile which didn't reach her eyes. 'Doesn't really matter now, does it?' Placing a can in Maggie's hand, she walked back into the lounge.

Maggie glanced towards Eliza, who shrugged.

Following into the lounge, Maggie curled up in an armchair, hoping to make herself as small as possible. When she'd got out of hospital earlier, she hadn't known what else to do but go to Jane's, even though she was worried about how she'd react.

She was also terrified of facing Seth again, but she really needed to talk to Jane about Ian. She certainly didn't want to discuss it with Eliza. The trouble was, Jane didn't seem the full ticket and as for Seth, well he *definitely* wasn't.

Maggie wasn't sure she could handle any of their weird shit right now. Furthermore, how could she ask to stay here now, with what had happened with the baby?

Seth lay languidly on the sofa and scowled as Eliza consistently droned on from the other chair over the programme he was trying to watch.

Jane glanced at the television and frowned. There seemed to be a load of foreign people running around dressed up as toilet rolls. 'Aren't you supposed to be meeting Phil?'

'Shit. Yeah…' Glancing at his watch, Seth swung his legs off the sofa and shoved his feet into his boots. 'I'm fucking late!'

Eliza felt another flush creep up her face as she watched Seth shrug his shirt on.

· · · ·

STUART PACED AROUND his flat. He'd been staring out the window overlooking the courtyard when that dappy cow had turned up next door. Seth and Jane always had people turning up - just not the *right* people.

Having spent virtually all week positioned by the window so he wouldn't miss any of the action when the cops showed up, he was getting frustrated. He'd been *so* looking forward to it, but had it happened? No, it fucking well hadn't and he wanted to know why the hell not.

After all, he'd given the pigs enough information to sink a

bloody battle cruiser and it was starting to look like they weren't going to do anything with it.

He seethed inwardly. If they weren't going to raid, then he'd have to jump to his next plan - which he might just do anyway. That would wipe the smile off the smug cow's face.

Stuart slammed his hand down sharply against the table. It was no good. There was no way he could hang around any longer without knowing. It was driving him mad. He'd have to go back up the cop shop and ask what the crack was. He'd have to be careful though. He didn't want to be recognised.

• • • •

PHIL HAD BEEN waiting at the park in the cold for an hour and had just been about to give up and leave, when he'd heard the Senator screech into the car park.

Watching Seth stagger across the grass, he realised he'd definitely made the right decision. Not only was Seth late, but the man could barely stand up and was still slugging from a whisky bottle like it was a can of pop.

He was sad it had come to this, but what choice did he have? Right now, Seth was too unreliable and none of them could afford that.

Plonking himself heavily down on the bench, Seth smiled coldly.

'What's going on?' Phil asked, genuinely concerned. He waited patiently while Seth clumsily fiddled in his pocket, trying to locate his fags. He'd known the man for over ten years. Although he'd always been a loose cannon, he'd always been one of the best, if not *the* best, but he'd never known him to spiral out of control to this extent. That shit on the job last week had been the last straw.

He pushed again, determined to try and at least scratch the surface of what was eating at his friend. 'Mate,' he placed his hand lightly on Seth's sleeve. 'You need to tell me what the fuck's going on.'

Seth's eyes filled with tears. 'Jane lost the baby.'

Phil frowned. 'Shit. I'm sorry to hear that, I truly am. I didn't even know she was pregnant until Digger told me after you got back from that job.'

Seth put his head in his hands and leant forward unsteadily, saying nothing.

'I can see now why you didn't want her doing it.'

'She lost it that night, Phil,' Seth sucked in his breath. 'We were arguing… I didn't know that she was going to… that it was going to happen.'

'It wasn't your fault,' Phil attempted to console Seth as best as he could. 'These things happen.'

'Not to *me*, they don't!' he hissed. 'I wanted that kid. *Really* wanted it.'

'How's Jane?'

Seth's eyes narrowed. 'Oh, she's fine. She doesn't give a shit.'

'Don't be crazy! Of course she does.' Phil was perplexed. 'She loves you. *Everyone* knows that.'

'She doesn't tell *me* that!'

Phil looked down at his hands. This was a nightmare and would be harder than he thought. *He was a biker, not a fucking counsellor.* 'Women, mate, ain't it. I've never pretended to understand them.'

'I know I fucked the job up.' Seth changed tack, interrupting Phil from his thoughts, '…and I'm sorry.'

'Two things,' Phil turned to face Seth. *Now was the time.* 'One is that I got wind this morning your gaff's on line for a raid.'

Seth raised an eyebrow. 'Right. When?'

'Don't know, but if you've got any gear, then get rid tout suite!'

Nodding, Seth suspected he knew what was coming next. 'And the second?'

'You need to take a break for a bit, mate.' Phil looked into Seth's glazed eyes, hoping he'd remember the conversation when he sobered up. 'Just until you get yourself sorted.'

'I don't need to.' Seth sparked up another fag. 'I'm fine.'

'You need some time to sort your head out about the baby and everything.'

'Are you binning me off?'

'No, I'm telling you that you need to take a break. All the shit going on is impairing your judgment and you're intelligent enough to know that makes things dangerous.'

The last thing Phil wanted was to lose Seth, but he couldn't afford any more mistakes. The job last week had shown *exactly* how things could fuck up if emotions got in the way. Now one of them was dead and the cops were sniffing around. It didn't mean he didn't want Seth back once he was back to normal, because he did. *If he ever got back to normal, that was.*

'Well, that's me fucked then!' Seth muttered angrily. 'Thanks a lot!'

'Don't take it personally. You'd do the same if you were in my shoes. It's for your sake as well as everyone else's.'

Seth stood up unsteadily. 'So, you're saying I'm a fucking liability?'

Phil grabbed Seth's arm, not wanting him to leave like this, but it was wrenched away. 'I mean it,' he smiled. 'Have a week or so to yourself and we'll talk again. Get yourself home, cut back on the gear and booze then we'll see how the land lies.'

'Don't dictate to me, you cunt!' Seth roared.

Phil sighed. He wasn't going to rise to it. 'Jane needs you.'

Seth laughed. A horrible empty laugh that echoed around the deserted park. 'No she doesn't.' Turning, he began to walk away. 'She never has…'

• • • •

JANE WASN'T HAPPY, yet unsurprised to hear that Phil had binned Seth off. Everything was going tits up quicker than she could keep track of and when he'd muttered something about clearing out the spare room, she knew what that signified. *At least they'd got some warning.*

She sighed. She needed to find another job. Ok, they'd got

their pay-out for the botched job, but that wouldn't last for long the way they got through it. Besides, Seth had got no reason to keep her under his scrutiny anymore. She'd go loopy if she was stuck inside for much longer - especially as he was hell bent on getting her pregnant again and she had to make sure that didn't happen.

Jane frowned. It had been bad enough he'd lamped the vicar during the christening they'd gone to at the weekend. She knew it had been a bad idea to go two days after the miscarriage, but Seth had been adamant.

He'd been unusually jovial, but she'd known he was pretending because she could see it in his eyes. After the never-ending service, everyone had gathered near the font to exchange pleasantries and Jane had glanced at the door, trying to work out when she could leave. She'd needed another drink.

Even when she'd been passed the baby, she'd managed to make the right noises, until Seth took the kid from her arms.

'Oh, she's beautiful!' he'd slurred drunkenly. 'Ours will be beautiful too, Jane.' Smiling, he'd placed his other arm around her shoulders and pulled her close, pretending to stare adoringly from her to the baby and back again.

Jane had stiffened, not needing shitty game playing. 'Stop this!' she'd hissed, trying not to draw attention to them and hoping no one had heard.

Unfortunately, they had because the vicar had wandered over. 'Ah…!' he'd exclaimed. 'Did I hear there's going to be an addition to your family?' His smiling face had beamed benevolently at Jane.

*Go away. Please go away…*

'You can always have your little one christened here after y…'

The vicar had hit the floor with a thud following Seth's swift upper cut to the side of his jaw. Casually stepping over the man, he'd walked towards the door of the church and Jane had quickly followed, ignoring the stunned faces of the rest of the congregation.

• • • •

SETH DIDN'T UNDERSTAND what Dodge's problem was. He only wanted to use the lock up until the cops had gone cold.

*Yes, he knew the guns were still there from the other week.*

*Yes, he'd said he'd shift them.*

*And yes, he knew he hadn't done so yet.*

Gritting his teeth, he'd realised he mustn't lose his temper - he needed the favour.

After promising to shift both the guns and the drugs by the end of next week, Dodge had reluctantly handed him the keys.

Sparking a fag up, Seth sat in the driver's seat and smoked it in peace, a grin spreading across his face. The generous amount of coke he'd got through whilst clearing out the spare room had removed his earlier drunkenness and he was feeling a lot clearer.

Even though that earlier shit with Phil had upset him more than he cared to admit, he knew what had been said was true. He *was* a fucking liability right now. He was embarrassed and ashamed. He didn't appreciate feeling like a cunt, but that was *exactly* how he felt.

Seth rubbed his hand across his face. He'd thought for a while they could be normal, but maybe Jane was right and it just wasn't possible?

He didn't know anymore. Actually, he didn't know much of *anything* anymore, apart from that he needed to pull himself together soon and that was exactly what he would do.

*Besides, once Jane was pregnant again, everything would be alright.*

Turning the key in the ignition, Seth gunned the engine and made his way towards the lock up. He'd offload this shit and then he was going home to fuck his wife.

## THIRTY NINE

OPENING HIS EYES PAINFULLY, Digger attempted to focus in the dim light. *What on earth was going on?*

He tried to concentrate on the fuzzy shapes around him, but everything was in triplicate. With rising panic, he desperately tried to recall where he was and how he'd got there, realising he'd got no memory of anything recent. The last thing he recalled was being on his bike, but even that was a dim recollection - lost in time and space.

*What was that?*

Something was moving across the other side of the room. Trying to raise his head, Digger found he couldn't. It felt like it was made of lead.

A weird, disembodied voice emanated from the shape moving in the shadows.

*The shape that was getting closer.*

He squinted, adjusting to the pointless glow from the twenty-watt bulb somewhere in the room and blinked, unable to believe his eyes. He appeared to be in some shit-hole flat with a bloke wearing a dress, who was chanting weird stuff. *Had he gone mad and ended up in the local loony bin?*

Glancing at something that looked like a huge sack of spuds

covered in green velvet, he'd have laughed if he hadn't been so fucking angry. It had only got more depressing when he realised he was handcuffed and spread-eagled on filthy carpet.

*For fuck's sake. His life was weird at the best of times, but this really took the biscuit.*

Struggling to take any of it seriously, Digger decided to pretend for the time being, until he'd planned his next move. When he'd worked out who these fuckers were, the shit was going to hit the fan.

• • • •

JANE LOOKED AT THE list in front of her with a bored expression. The second day at the new warehouse job was going as slowly as the first and her hangover wasn't helping. Even the two cans she'd necked at lunchtime hadn't touched the sides, but at least the coke and pills had woken her up a bit.

Glancing at her watch, she realised with relief there was only another half an hour before she could go home.

When she'd left this morning, Seth was still laying face-down in the lounge where they'd spent the night. It seemed not getting to bed these days was becoming a habit.

Jane sighed, accepting they were no nearer to getting their lives into a better state. There had been a temporary respite when Seth had returned from the lock up the other night. It was almost as if someone had waved a magic wand because he'd been full of life. They'd had a really good night down the Dragon, spending the evening laughing and messing about. It had been so good, even Maggie and Eliza had made themselves scarce.

After the Dragon had closed, Seth had dragged her by her hand up the High Street and pushed her into a shop doorway where he'd frantically pulled her skirt up and taken her there and then. *It had been good. Real good.*

They'd then gone home and had the best conversation in ages, as well as a night of mind-blowing sex. They'd made the decision to move out of town to start afresh - away from the people, the shit and the bad stuff.

Unfortunately by the morning, they'd both forgotten their promises and lurched back onto the roundabout of self-destruction.

She smiled sadly. It was impossible to pretend their lives were alright for more than a few hours and both of them knew it.

'Are you going to finish that or what?'

The gruff voice snapped Jane out of her thoughts and she looked up to find the manager cutting her death stares. How long she'd been sitting staring aimlessly at a sheet of paper, she wasn't sure, but judging by the man's face, it must have been a while.

Begrudgingly, she walked over to the pile of boxes and tried to work out which ones needed to go for despatch. Quickly sorting them into order, she glanced at her watch once again. *Sod it. That would do for today.*

Picking up her bag, she walked into the toilets to waste the last few minutes.

Jane neatly scraped together a line of coke on the top of the warehouse's toilet cistern and effortlessly hoovered it up with the help of a rolled-up fiver. Taking a deep sniff, she closed her eyes and felt relief as the drug entered her bloodstream.

Despite her general lethargy and everything else that had been going on, she was in the mood to have a decent burn out. Perhaps Tony's party tonight would fire both her and Seth out of this fucked up mood they'd both been in and give them a decent break from their feelings. If nothing else, at least they'd get off their tits in different surroundings before having another row.

It didn't take long to finish off the quart bottle of vodka she'd fished from her bag. Flushing the chain, Jane grabbed her bag from the hook on the toilet door and walked across the car park, relieved to get out of the dump for the day.

• • • •

MAGGIE WAS UNCOMFORTABLE. Eliza's family always wanted to chat. That in principal sounded good, but being as she struggled being in the same room with herself, let alone with a host of over-friendly people she didn't really know, it wasn't. She just wanted to hide and work out what the hell she was going to do, but then again, she couldn't handle being on her own either.

After going to Jane's and quickly realising she wasn't going to be able to stay there, she'd had no choice but to accept Eliza's offer of getting the fuck out of there. They'd left Seth and Jane to it, but with each hour that passed, she'd got more and more edgy over what she was going to do if Ian found her.

Correction. *When* he found her.

Maggie sighed. Slitting her wrist and nearly bleeding to death hadn't been the most intelligent thing she'd ever thought of, but that night at the caravan, it had been the only option that might have got her a ticket out of there.

She'd counted on Ian having to let her go to hospital, but once she'd sliced the bread knife across her wrist, she'd begun to wonder. As the blood had poured out, Ian had paced up and down for what seemed like hours and the thought had seeped into her mind that her plan might not work after all.

Although, at the end of the day, she'd stood to win either way. If he hadn't let her go to the hospital, then she'd have died, but as long as she'd got away from him, she hadn't cared.

Finally, he'd left her propped up against the side of a telephone box on the main road where a stranger had called an ambulance.

She hadn't breathed a word about Ian at the hospital or what he'd done. She'd just acted suicidal - which hadn't been difficult.

After a week of convincing the hospital's shrink she didn't know what had come over her, she'd been released. But now she was out again and therefore available for Ian to find.

Feeling herself edging towards hyperventilating, Maggie forced herself to think of something else.

She glanced over to Eliza. 'Do you think he likes me?' she asked tentatively, hoping she wasn't going to get her head bitten off for speaking during the crappy sci-fi serial Eliza had been glued to all day.

Momentarily pulling her eyes away from the screen, Eliza stuck her fingers into the packet of peanuts resting on the arm of her chair. 'Who?'

Rolling her eyes, Maggie pulled a face. 'Zed! You know the one I've just been telling you about?' She hadn't actually said a word about Zed, but Eliza never listened to anything she said *ever*, so it wasn't like she'd notice.

Shrugging, Eliza reached down for her can of cider then returned her gaze back to the television.

Maggie took this to mean the conversation was over and started picking at the edge of her bandage on her wrist.

If Zed was at the party, she'd make her interest more obvious. She may as well.

· · · ·

EVERYONE STOOD AROUND the wall-mounted board during the last meeting of the shift and stared at the various pieces of coloured paper stuck to it, signifying positions.

'There hasn't been any unusual movement today,' DI Charles said in a gruff voice. He pinned yet another piece of paper up. 'I'm pretty confident Wright and Ellerton will be caught off guard when we roll up at 5 in the morning.'

A rare smile broke out across the Inspector's tired face. He couldn't *wait* to pull those two in and finally detain them. 'Make sure you all know your required positions for the off.'

Several officers edged nearer to the board. They all knew this garbage was a mere formality and when it all kicked off everyone would just randomly go for it. As long as they got a result, it didn't matter where anyone stood to start with and everyone knew it.

'Right. Get yourselves home for a bit of shut eye. I want you all back here by 3am on the dot!' DI Charles narrowed his eyes. '*No one* to be late! We'll have one last briefing at 4 before we move for the off at 5.'

Glancing around the sea of faces, he looked for signs of confusion or lack of attention, but found to his satisfaction that everyone seemed to be alert. 'Are there any questions?'

There was a slight pause, until one officer piped up. 'Will there be any surveillance on the flat tonight in the meantime?'

DI Charles' brow furrowed. It was a question he'd thought about at great length. 'I thought about putting someone in place to keep tabs, but as there's very little going down of late, I made the decision to go with the raid as is, rather than waste resources watching a dark stairwell for six hours.'

Several heads around the room nodded in agreement.

'They'll probably go out somewhere to get rat-arsed, but will be back in their filthy pit by the time we kick their fucking door down.' DI Charles chuckled to himself. 'If that's all gentlemen, then I'll see you back here at 3.'

• • • •

SITTING ON THE FLOOR in the bathroom, Seth rested his forehead against the cool wall and popped another couple of pills into his mouth.

Nothing was doing the trick. He felt like he was on a roller coaster running out of track and it was only a matter of time before his carriage hurtled off the rails at breakneck speed and plummeted towards the ground.

With shaking fingers, he lit a cigarette and took a long drag. He screwed his eyes shut, but everything continued to play on repeat in slow-motion in the back of his mind.

Taking a long gulp of whisky from the bottle by his side, he swallowed another two pills. He leant his head back and a lone tear escaped against his will, running slowly down his unshaven cheek.

What the fuck was happening? They'd lost the baby. He'd lost his job. Everyone thought he was losing his mind and he was sure he was losing Jane. Running his hand through his hair, he sighed. He wanted it *all* back.

He was on edge and angry with everything and everyone. The net was closing in from all directions on every angle of his life and he was beginning to feel like he was running out of oxygen.

Pushing himself quickly to his feet, Seth slammed his fist hard into the wall, smashing a gaping hole. He wiped the blood from his knuckles down his jeans and wished to fuck he could find some oblivion.

*If only for a few minutes.*

· · · ·

TEDDY WAS HOT. *Come on Ian, do something!*

He'd been told to stay under this green thing and say nothing until he was told to. The problem was, he'd been under here for *ages* and not only was he bored shitless, but he was sweating like a pig in an abattoir. *How much longer would this go on for?*

He wasn't even sure what Ian was trying to achieve. Apparently, the plan was to freak Digger out so that he'd break emotionally. Then it would be easy to curse him, he'd said. All of his body hair would then be plucked out with tweezers to use as stuffing for a voodoo doll.

Teddy wasn't sure why, but presumed Ian knew what he was doing? He knew he was livid that Maggie had got away again because apparently they'd been having a great shagging session, until she'd slit her wrists.

She was bloody mental, that girl, Teddy thought, trying to ignore the overwhelming itch developing on his hairy chin.

Try as he might, he couldn't quite see Ian's fascination with her. Ok, so he wouldn't have said no - not that he'd ever been allowed to have a go, but he preferred Debbie, because Maggie was more unstable that a two-legged chair and it did his head in.

Apparently once Digger had been sorted, Ian would get Maggie back. There were only so many places she could be, he'd said. Fucking hell, he'd been *raging* when he'd discovered the thick cow was no longer in hospital.

Teddy secretly reckoned this was what had triggered the Digger thing, although Ian had assured him he'd been planning it for ages because his brother had told him to.

He frowned, sure Ian's brother had died years ago.

Shrugging, he then froze, remembering he was supposed to remain stock still under the green thing which was covering him.

• • • •

JANE FELT IN A rather extraordinarily good mood by the time she'd parked her car. Humming a tune, she ran up the steps to the flat and even the familiar figure of Stuart peering out of the window, wasn't enough to irritate her.

Giving him the finger, she laughed as he retreated behind his curtain.

Shutting the front door, Jane dropped her bag and listened for any movement. 'Seth?'

Pushing the bathroom door open, she noticed a new hole in the wall. Rapidly swinging around she saw Seth lying in the bath with his clothes on, his eyes staring into space.

'Hello Jane,' he slurred.

An unexpected but overwhelming rush of love for the man in front of her washed over Jane. 'What's the matter?' Sitting on the edge of the bath, she dipped her fingers into the freezing cold water. 'Seth?'

Seth's eyes watched Jane pull the plug out. 'I'm sorry, babe.'

'Sorry? What for?'

'Everything…'

As Jane turned the hot tap back on, Seth stared at the water rushing into the bath and felt himself warm up. He hadn't even noticed it had gone cold, but then he had no recollection of even getting in there. He sniffed both lines of coke Jane handed him. 'Jane, I…'

'What's wrong, Seth? Like I mean, I *know* what's wrong, but oh, you know what I mean…' Tipping a glass of vodka down her throat, she slipped off her clothes.

'What? Apart from everything? I'm losing you and I'm losing *everything*.'

Frowning, Jane turned the tap off. 'You're not losing me,' she whispered.

Grabbing her hand, Seth moved his legs to make room as she

stepped into the bath. Pulling her down, he breathed deeply as the coke buzzed through his mind. 'Jane?'

Jane couldn't discuss what he wanted to discuss. If she did, she might fall apart and she couldn't take that risk. Her life was fucked just like his and she didn't need to ask him what was going through his head to know that, because they were two halves of the same person.

Seth dealt with things by going in on himself, whereas she went out of herself and no amount of *anything* would change that. She wanted obliteration. He wanted annihilation.

*Same difference, wasn't it?*

'Shh…' Putting her finger to Seth's lips, Jane pressed her mouth onto his, her teeth nibbling his lip.

Coming back to life, Seth's tongue greedily pushed into Jane's mouth and he fumbled with the buttons of his jeans under the water. Pushing himself out of the bath, he lifted her out easily and carried her down the hall while she slipped in his wet arms, giggling.

This was the Seth Jane knew and loved. The depressed Seth scared her because they lived off each other's moods. If he was down, then she was too and she feared she'd drown. She needed to keep wired and take him with her.

Jane was thrown onto the bed and gasped when Seth buried his face in her, his tongue working its magic inside and around her. She moaned loudly as the familiar sensations built within her.

As she wrapped her fingers in his long curls, he pulled his head away from between her legs and transferred his tongue to her mouth. Pushing himself into her he picked up a fast pace.

'I love you, Seth,' Jane whispered softly.

Seth smiled as he slammed into her over and over. All he wanted now was for her to say it when he wasn't making her come.

Lifting her hips higher, he upped the pace further. 'Not as much as I love you.'

MAGGIE WATCHED THE MAN standing like a statue in the corner of the kitchen. His chin touched the lapels of his green velour jacket as he lost himself in the kaleidoscopic colours of the acid trip hurtling through his mind at the speed of light. A woman, naked from the waist down leant against him for support whilst another man ran his tongue between her legs.

Blinking slowly, Maggie centred herself on the relaxation she was happily experiencing since toking on a large bong. Eliza had made sure Ian wasn't lurking anywhere, but then neither was Zed, so she'd focused her attention on Tony who propped the wall up in the lounge.

Stuart, meanwhile, had skulked out of the party the same way he'd got in - with no one noticing. He wasn't in the mood for sex and it seemed that was all that was happening tonight.

After seeing Seth and Jane arrive, he'd realised he'd had the perfect chance to act. As he limped down the street, even his knee giving him jip wasn't enough to remove the smile off his face.

He shook his head with amusement. Just how much coke that pair had done was anyone's guess. They'd lit up the room with the excess energy emanating from them and would be so fucked by the end of the night, they wouldn't notice jack shit!

Smiling, he headed back to the flat where he knew Jane's car was parked, ready and waiting for his attention. After he'd dealt with that, he was going to bed to watch that new porno he'd bought from the strange bloke down the market with the extra finger.

• • • •

FEELING RELATIVELY CLEAR-HEADED, apart from the throbbing pain pounding at the back of his skull, Digger had regained sufficient clarity to act. What he'd initially presumed to be handcuffs restraining him, was in fact rope, which would be easy to snap from brute force alone. *He just needed to wait for the right time.*

He'd now spent several hours listening to the continued ramblings of the hooded fuckhead in the black dress. The gimp had loped back and forward across the room, waving his arms to summon up his 'inner incubus.'

*'Yes, he's scared. Yes, he knows he'll pay for his sins to eternity. Yes, he's almost ready to be taken over…'*

Digger presumed that it was *him* the freak was referring to, but hadn't liked to point out that not only was he not remotely scared, but was also quite happy to pay for his sins. Furthermore, he wasn't being taken anywhere!

After careful consideration, he decided the green lump on the sofa wasn't worth expending much energy on. It still hadn't spoken, but it had proved it wasn't an inanimate object by coughing several times and a hand had appeared to scratch at what he'd presumed was its head.

Suddenly everything fell into place. Digger was ninety-nine percent sure who these dickheads were and he was going to kill them both. As Black-Dress moved closer, chanting and holding a pair of tweezers, he knew it was the right time.

Snapping the rope, Digger yanked his arms and legs free and delivered an upper cut to the man's jaw, sending him sprawling onto his back.

Enjoying himself, now he'd got his meaty hands around the scrawny fucker's throat, he crushed down harder and ripped the black hood away from the man's head. *He'd been right. It was Ian – that stupid, bloody freak!* 'Do you like purple, you cunt?' he hissed, grinning savagely. 'Well you'd just fucking *love* the colour of your mug right now!'

Hearing a shuffling noise, Digger turned to see the green shape attempting to move off the sofa. 'Oh no you don't!'

Smashing his fist into where he thought the thing's face might be, the lump flopped back unconscious onto the sofa.

Digger grinned, pleased his shot had been a damn fine guess and resumed his grip on Ian's throat. 'Don't know what you were trying to achieve, but you and your mate have made a very, *very* big mistake…'

A gargling sound escaped from Ian's mouth and his eyes bulged out of their sockets, reddening as the blood vessels began to break when Digger pushed down further on his windpipe.

As the pressure increased, Ian tried to scream, but nothing came out. Through his watering eyes, he attempted to focus on the grinning lunatic pinning him to the floor.

How dare this cunt rip his hood off! It was a sacred item of clothing, charged with power in *exactly* the way Nigel had explained. In fact, he'd followed the instructions to the letter, so how come this monster was still living? He didn't understand it. *More importantly, where had Nigel gone?*

He could hear nothing in his mind now, apart from a loud rushing sound. Calling silently for his brother, he waited for the answer that would no longer come.

Colours flashed behind his eyes and the roaring in his ears was completely distracting him, making him feel panicky. He had no air left at all and just couldn't drag any from anywhere. The rushing was getting louder and the weight on his neck heavier, but someone was *still* screaming at him.

Ian tried to smile, but his muscles had locked. A heartbeat thundered away inside his head.

*It was getting darker now, really dark.*

. . . .

JANE WAS BLITZED. Putting the pipe of the bong down, she swallowed another glass of neat vodka and watched Maggie unsuccessfully drape herself over Tony.

Accepting the random kiss from a girl sitting next to her, Jane wondered where her bag was. She needed a smoke and some more pills.

Seth lay on the floor with his arms behind his head, watching Jane. He was finally starting to lose the grating edge and it seemed the pills were finally working. Smiling, he opened his mouth and someone chucked two small triangular orange pills in. *Bring it on*, he grinned and swallowed them dry.

'Hey, baby!' Kneeling down, Jane kissed Seth hard on the lips. Giggling, she flicked her tongue across his teeth, letting his hands run over her bare breasts. 'I'm going to have a bit of fun with Clint, ok?'

Seth raised an eyebrow. He'd noticed it was turning into one of *those* parties again. Tony had already fucked some blonde bird next to him and now the man had got Maggie all over him. There were plenty of other bodies scattered around engaged in various acts, but to his surprise he was so mashed and relaxed, that for once he was up for whatever Jane wanted.

Winding his hand in her hair, he reined her in closer. 'Whatever you want, Princess. Just come back to me!'

'I'll always come back to you, Seth.' Jane kissed him again. 'Oh, and Eliza wants a piece of you.'

'Does she?' Seth laughed. 'And you want me to do that?'

Jane shrugged, her feet tapping to the drumming music. The rushing in her head was getting strong. *Really* strong.

Clint appeared, standing guiltily behind Jane as she pushed herself to her feet.

'No tongues now, do you hear?' Seth winked, silently wondering why the fuck he wasn't smashing the prick in the face. He slipped a couple more pills into his mouth and watched as Clint took Jane's hand.

Jane shoved Eliza towards Seth. 'Your turn...'

'Don't tempt me!' Eliza laughed.

'Just go for it!' Jane swayed against Clint. 'It's fine.'

When Jane disappeared, Eliza faltered, not knowing what to do. She wasn't sure how to take her tonight. Jane had already turned her down for a threesome again, but then she'd seen her snogging a woman, so was she serious about offering Seth to her or not? *She couldn't tell.*

Eliza sat down next to Seth, who smiled lazily. 'Are you ok?' she muttered, uncomfortably aware that he was enjoying her embarrassment.

'Hear you want to kiss me, Eliza,' Seth laughed, watching her blush.

Glancing across the room, a jolt of jealousy ran through him seeing Jane wind her arms around Clint's neck. Quashing it, he forced himself not to be jealous.

*Don't stress remember,* he told himself. He wouldn't let anything spoil tonight. They were supposed to be having a good night with no shit. Ok, so he hadn't realised that meant they'd be messing with other people and if he was honest, he'd rather not, because he was fine just chilling out.

Shrugging his shoulders, he knew he was in no state to argue. If that's what Jane wanted, then he'd have to handle it.

Sneaking another glance as Clint's mouth explored Jane's, Seth wondered whether he *could* handle it. Forcing his hands from clenching into fists, he stared at Eliza. Grabbing her by the hair, he pulled her sharply towards him.

Eliza almost fainted when Seth plunged his tongue into her mouth and felt her heart thundering in her chest now pressed against his.

Pulling away, Seth smiled and took a swig of whisky. 'There you go. Will that do?'

'Shit!' Eliza panted. 'No! I want more!'

Seeing Seth's body crushed against Eliza's, Jane shut her eyes and opened herself further to the rushing flooding through her body as the overload of drugs and drink coursed through her veins.

Maggie, however, wasn't getting as far as she wanted. She'd managed to get a kiss out of Tony, but that had been about it. It had been a bit half-hearted in all honesty and her drink-fuelled confidence was faltering.

She backed off, under the excuse of finding another drink and quickly popping a cigarette into her mouth, asked someone avidly watching two girls kissing on an armchair, for a light. Without even moving his eyes in her direction, the man waved the lighter at her.

*Was she that irrelevant?*

Sulkily moving back towards the lounge, Maggie stepped over a bloke inconveniently lying unconscious across the doorway and her eyes were suddenly drawn towards Jane heading upstairs with Clint. Her nervousness returned. *What the hell was Jane doing and where was Seth?*

Maggie scanned the room, only to see Eliza mauling Seth on the floor. She sighed, knowing everything would kick off sooner rather than later and she needed more drugs to calm her down before that happened.

• • • •

LYING BACK IN BED, Stuart was very pleased. He'd found Jane's car *exactly* where she'd left it. It hadn't taken long and all he had to do now was sit back and wait.

He smiled. Paul could definitely go fuck himself. Yet again he'd had to put up with his bleating about not doing anything to Jane, just Seth. As far as Stuart was concerned, it was *well* past that. It was personal from his side now, not just Paul's.

Anyway, he didn't give a flying fuck what that retard wanted, but to shut him up, he'd nodded politely. After all, if Paul knew what he'd got planned, he'd go even more loopy.

*If that was possible, of course.*

Grinning to himself, he watched as a man took some ginger bird hard up the arse. Yeah, the video was a bit corny and he could have done without it being in German, but it wasn't like he was going to miss an in-depth storyline by not understanding what the fuck they were saying, was it?

Pushing his hand under the duvet, Stuart rummaged around in his boxer shorts and took hold of himself.

• • • •

ELIZA GUIDED SETH'S HAND between her legs, but he pulled away. *Why was he ignoring her?*

Seth scowled. He didn't want to kiss Eliza and certainly didn't want to fuck her. Feeling extremely uncomfortable, he propped himself on his elbow and shook his head to try and clear the fog enveloping his mind. When Eliza's hand snaked up his thigh towards his groin once more, he yanked her hand away again.

'What's the matter? Don't tell me you're going to leave me frustrated?' Eliza whined.

Seth attempted to give her some form of smile. 'That's *exactly* what I'm telling you.'

Eliza was too drunk to think rationally. She was gagging for Seth, but all he'd done was kiss her. *Jane said she could have him, so what was his problem, for God's sake?*

Her eyes narrowed. She wasn't in the mood for this. 'What's wrong with you?'

'Nothing's wrong with *me,*' Seth hissed, the smile disappearing and his previous good mood evaporating. He took another long swig of whisky. *That was it.* He'd do a couple more lines of coke, find Jane, then go home. He'd had enough of this bullshit.

Eliza tried to pull him towards her again. 'Leave it, will you!' he slurred angrily, wishing she'd just fuck off.

Huffing, Eliza straightened her hair and pushing herself angrily to her feet, staggered off red-faced in Maggie's direction.

Seth glanced around the room but couldn't focus on anything. *Shit. He needed to go home.*

Shoving two loose pills from his pocket into his mouth, he hoped they'd do something. They had to. He had to straighten up because he felt like he was in treacle.

Unsteadily pushing himself to his feet, he slugged down the remains of the whisky and tossed the empty bottle to the floor as he lurched across the other side of the room.

*Was that Jane on the stairs?*

Seth tried to make his way over, but the walls were closing in and the floor was moving in opposite directions with each step he took. Blinking rapidly, he concentrated his tunnelled vision on the figures in the dark and a wave of rage roared through him, realising it *was* Jane with Clint.

The skinny twat had Jane's leg up around his waist, his free hand grasping at her breasts and he panted heavily as he pushed into her against the wall.

Seth leant against the wall at the bottom of the stairs to keep himself from hitting the deck and took a deep breath. He was far too fucked up to do anything with the anger that washed over him like a tidal wave. An overwhelming feeling of panic enveloped him and he stumbled towards the front door.

'Seth?' Maggie grabbed his arm. 'Are you ok?'

Seth saw sixteen copies of Maggie circling around slowly in a large haloed arc and his feet sank into the carpet as if it was quicksand. 'Going home,' he muttered in a virtually intelligible slur. 'Get Jane!'

Maggie's stomach sank with dread as she watched Seth crash against the kitchen work surface, rip open the front door and disappear into the night.

## FORTY ONE

JANE SWAYED UNSTEADILY and looked around. She'd *no* idea how she got back to the flat, but knew something was wrong as soon as she did, because it was deserted. *Why had it taken Maggie an hour to let her know Seth had left the party?*

She wondered how she'd managed to be so fucking stupid to think he'd be ok about her and someone else. She'd been so wired and after she'd brought him out of his earlier downer, she'd thought he'd be alright with things. Panic rose within her. He'd better not have done something stupid. She should have known he'd *never* share her.

Taking the stairs three at a time, Jane ran faster than she thought possible, whilst trying to stop the floor from moving.

Nearing her car, she saw Clint. 'What the hell are you doing here?' Jane screamed.

'Hey baby,' Clint smiled, reaching to touch Jane's hair. 'Thought you might want to carry things on?'

Jane focused on his handsome face and pushed his hand away. 'Are you *mad*? Get out of my fucking way!'

Clint followed as Jane staggered towards the car. 'Hey, what's the matter? Are you ok?'

Turning, Jane scowled angrily. 'Does it look like it?' Tears threatened as she pulled at the door handle. 'Seth's disappeared.'

Grabbing her arm again, Clint smiled. 'Don't worry about him, he'll be alright. Stay with me.'

'Get off me, Clint!' Jane ripped her arm away. Seth wasn't ok. He wasn't with *her* and she needed to find him.

'You can't drive like that!' Clint yelled, as Jane fell into the driver's seat.

'Fucking watch me!' she screeched and fired the engine.

Screaming down the road, Jane hadn't a clue where to start looking for Seth. She could barely stand, let alone drive and had already successfully driven up several kerbs and over the top of a roundabout.

Trying several places she'd thought he might be, there had been no sign of him and for the first time in ages she was scared. *Really* scared. She didn't want to lose him. *How the fuck could she live without him?*

Knowing this place was her last shot, she screeched into the wooded clearing, slammed the car door and ran unsteadily towards the wood.

Her heart lurched seeing Seth leaning against a tree. Reaching him, she touched his face and relief coursed down her face in hot tears. 'Where have you been?'

'I don't know,' Seth slurred. Wandering blindly away from the party, his anger had abated to be replaced with pure, raw desolation. He'd just needed to escape, but from what and to where, he hadn't known, so he'd just walked.

He tried to focus on Jane's face. *She was here though, wasn't she? She'd come for him.* Feeling another wave of nausea rush over him he turned and steadied himself against the tree trunk with both arms as his stomach heaved.

'Jane,' Seth muttered, his hair hanging over his face. 'You're going to leave me, aren't you?' He raised his head. 'I can't do this anymore,' he whispered. 'I saw you with Clint against the wall.' He tried to focus but was too doped up. Too drunk. 'Jane don't leave me. I can't bear it.'

Jane attempted to concentrate her rolling, spinning mind, but watching tears roll down Seth's face as he struggled to stay upright, she felt sick with guilt. 'You and Eliza were doi…'

'Nothing happened,' Seth slurred. 'It was just a kiss. I can't be with *anyone* but you, even if you want me to be.'

Jane didn't want him to be. Watching him with Eliza had made her feel sick. It was her own fault and she wondered how it was possible to love someone beyond anything, but hate them with a vengeance at the same time.

Reaching up, she grabbed Seth's face and kissed him, tasting a combination of salty tears and vomit. *She didn't care about that – she loved him.*

Seth put his hand over hers. 'Do you love me, Jane?'

Looking into his bloodshot eyes, Jane laughed hollowly. 'You think I'd be here if I didn't?'

'Why won't you just say it? What's your problem? I need to know.'

Jane rubbed her hand over her forehead and sighed. She didn't know why she felt unable to tell Seth how much she loved him. Maybe if she spoke about how she felt it would make her weak, or leave her open to being hurt?

She smiled wryly. Whether she spoke her feelings out loud or not, she knew full well he was her weak point.

Taking a deep breath, she brushed Seth's hair away from his face. 'I'm *never* leaving you.' She smiled as best as she could. 'And just for the record, I love you more than anything.'

Closing his eyes, Seth gripped onto Jane hand. The shit had to stop from both sides.

*All of it.*

• • • •

DIGGER TOOK A DRAG of his fag as he walked down the dark road towards town. Rubbing the lump on the back of his head for the third time, he still had no idea what he'd been coshed with. He wouldn't find out either now, not that he was in the least bothered. He smiled, content in the knowledge that the weird fucker, Ian, wouldn't be chanting anything at *anyone* anymore.

The memory of Ian's mouth jabbering silently as the last breath of air was squeezed from his body flitted into his mind and he grinned. It was amazing how little time it had taken to wipe the greasy fucker off the face of the planet.

He'd wanted to smash the wanker's face into an unrecognisable pulp, but due to the fast-spreading pool of shit emptying from Ian's bowels, he'd disappointedly admitted he should move on. Besides, there'd been the other fuckwit lurking under the green tablecloth to deal with.

Once he'd given Teddy a swift slap to bring him round, the spineless bastard had started bleating like a lamb, banging on about how he'd had nothing to do with it. He *had* however, blabbered something that had been rather interesting, of which he'd *definitely* be following up.

However, regardless what had been said, there was no way either of them could be allowed to walk away, so he'd slowly and very enjoyably wrapped his hands around Teddy's hairy, smelly fucking throat, strangling the life out of him as well.

Clenching his jaw, Digger quickened his pace, glad there wasn't far now to go. Only the thought of the expression on that dirty fat whore, Debbie's, mug when she got home after her night shift, to find her fuck-buddy brother and his bender sidekick dead in the middle of the flat, pulled him from his annoyance.

Traipsing up the high street, he realised how much his feet hurt. He could do with a couple of stiff drinks. Maybe he could nip into Seth's and grab a couple of beers?

He glanced at his watch. Just gone 4.30. Seth and Jane would probably still be up, but even if they weren't, they wouldn't mind him nipping in.

Turning the corner, Digger clocked the car opposite and smirked inwardly to himself. *That was a fucking copper if ever he'd seen one!*

Continuing into Ash Street, he then spotted the white roof of a riot van behind a hedge and almost laughed out loud. *Seth had*

UNTIL THE END OF TIME

*been right about the raid. This lot were so fucking obvious it was unbelievable!*

The temptation to walk over, knock on the window and ask which one of them wanted to earn extra Brownie points by finding a couple of dead bodies was strong, but he refrained.

Continuing casually up the road, Digger pretended he'd no idea he was being watched. Scowling, he flicked his fag butt into the road and carried on. He'd have to go to the all-night garage to get his beer now because of them.

• • • •

FROM HIS CAR, DI CHARLES swigged from the coffee in his flask and his nose wrinkled with distaste.

When he'd arrived for the final briefing earlier, the groups of faces surrounding his desk has looked distinctly half-asleep, which hadn't filled him with much confidence, but at least they'd all turned up on time for the raid.

He raised the cup of coffee to his mouth, bracing himself again for the revolting acrid taste to assault him and silently wondered why he continued to drink it.

He hoped to God they could pull this off tonight. He'd waited long enough for this moment.

And then there was PC Ginning. He'd watched the expression on the man's face as he'd greedily slurped from a polystyrene cup. He was a weird one, but then as long as he did his job, he didn't much care.

He knew the bloke wasn't liked around the station, but the more bodies they had on this job, the better. Besides, apart from himself, for some reason Ginning appeared the only other really enthusiastic one out of the lot of them.

Glancing at his watch, DI Charles looked back out of the window, scanning the road ahead, before pressing the button on his radio. 'Does anyone need to go through anything once more or are we good to go?'

His senses suddenly spiked, spotting a large man wandering up the road. 'Hold what I just said,' he barked into the radio.

'There's a man heading towards the target location.'

Fidgeting on the uncomfortable bench seat in the back of the riot van, PC Ginning could hardly contain his excitement as he listened to the inspector's voice on the radio.

Smiled smugly, he rubbed his sweaty palms down his black trousers, knowing he stood a very good chance of getting another grope of that Ellerton bird, if he was lucky. He didn't give a fuck if the others didn't like him. Besides, they wouldn't drop him in it, the bunch of pricks.

DI Charles' voice crackled over the radio yet again and broke the highly-charged silence. 'Watch that man. He's now out of my vision, so will be in yours anytime now. I need to know if he goes into Wright's stairwell.'

Everyone trained their eyes on the big man coming into view at the end of the road.

'This guy's one of Wright's cronies,' DI Charles continued. 'He could be going there now and if he does, then we'll dive in early. If he walks past, then we'll wait a bit longer.'

Seeing the size of the man, Ginning frowned as he drew level and then smiled when he continued past. *That was lucky and certainly less to have to deal with.*

• • • •

JANE WAS SHATTERED. She watched Seth stare through the windscreen, watching the coming dawn. To sober up, they'd spent the last couple of hours sitting in the car doing coke, but her hangover and comedown had kicked in without even sleeping.

She didn't know how she'd manage to go to work in a couple of hours, but then she did most days on little or no sleep - so this one wasn't really an exception. Putting her head in her hands, she sighed and stroked Seth's arm absentmindedly.

Seth glanced over as Jane did the last of the coke. 'I would have just slept it off, you know.'

'Really?' Jane snapped. 'Why don't you just take less fucking pills instead?'

Seth's green eyes flashed. 'Why don't you stop fucking other people, then I won't have to.'

*Not this again.* Angrily getting out of the car, Jane walked away with Seth in hot pursuit.

'JANE! Don't you dare walk away from me!'

Jane's mind span as she tried to get away from his shouting. She just needed five minutes out.

'Jane! *Stop*!' Seth roared, close on her tail.

Ignoring him, Jane realised with a sad sense of resignation that things were seriously out of control.

Would anything stop them destroying themselves and each other, except death?

*Maybe that was the only way?*

# FORTY TWO

'GO! GO! *GO!*'

Hearing DI Charles' voice crackle over the radio, the cops rushed up the stairwell and slammed the battering ram against the flimsy front door, then stormed into the brightly lit hall. 'POLICE!'

A loud barking, accompanied by a flurry of white fur launched itself towards the officer at the front. The dog sprang up from his hind legs, his teeth bared and sank his fangs into the man's thigh, locking on for grim death.

The cop kicked out and whacked the dog's skull with his truncheon. Several others joined in, raining down thud after thud until the dog collapsed in a pool of blood.

'I don't believe this,' DI Charles muttered from the bedroom doorway, glaring at the scene in front of him. He'd forgotten about the dog. *How could he have forgotten about the fucking dog? His neck would be on the chopping block for this.*

'Where the fuck are they?' one officer shouted, wiping the dog's blood from his hands down his trousers.

DI Charles felt like throwing himself out of the window. He'd been *so* looking forward to seeing the shock on those bastard's faces and they hadn't even got the bloody decency to be in.

Trying to ignore his dented ego and the crawling sensation that opting for no surveillance had been an *extremely* bad decision, he instead concentrated on what to do next.

He barked at an officer to radio for an ambulance, then faced the rest of the group. 'OK, search the place. Rip it to pieces!' His eyes narrowed. 'Find anything you can.' *He would still get them. He had to.* 'I'm having these cunts if it's the last thing I do.'

DI Charles stomped from the flat in a rage, leaving two cops upending the mattress and chucking clothes to one side, whilst others busily pulled the kitchen drawers to the floor.

PC Ginning stared at the mess in the living room. *Jesus Christ! Did people really live like this?*

His eyes moved to a large framed photograph of a scantily-clad Jane draped over the tank of a shiny black motorbike, which reminded him to look in her knicker drawer.

*He may as well do something half-enjoyable.*

· · · ·

ON THE DRIVE BACK from the woods, it hadn't taken Seth long to revert to arguing about Clint and Jane had just about had enough, but as she swung the car into the space next to the Senator, the steering wheel span on the column.

Yelling with shock, she slammed the brakes on, but the car still scraped down the side of Seth's Senator.

Opening the passenger door, Seth eyed the thick gouge running down his paintwork. 'What the hell have you done, you stupid fucking cow?'

'The steering went!' Jane yanked the key from the ignition and stormed off in the direction of the stairwell. 'Drive it and see for yourself if you don't believe me!'

Seth followed, his face like thunder, but seeing the front door to their flat lying on the floor, he quickly moved Jane to one side and rushed in.

The first thing Jane saw when she followed, was the dog lying in a pool of blood and she quickly knelt down to tend to him, but Ginning appeared and grabbed her.

Spinning on his heels, Seth's eyes narrowed into slits. He knew *exactly* who this cop was and what he'd done to Jane. He'd been waiting a long time to catch up with the bastard. 'You CUNT!' he screamed, hammering his fist repeatedly into Ginning's face. He may have spent all night drugged up to the eyeballs and chucking his guts up, but was still capable of packing a quality punch.

With blood streaming out of his nose and a gash over his eye, Ginning flailed around, pointlessly trying to shield himself from the relentless blows crashing into his smashed face. *The fact his colleagues were nowhere to be seen hadn't escaped his notice either.*

Hearing the commotion as he placed various bits and pieces into evidence bags, PC James glanced at the other officers, knowing none of them were making any attempt to go to Ginning's aid. He pressed the button on the radio and smiled, hearing further shouting and bangs coming from the hallway. 'They're back.'

One of the officers glanced at him. 'Do you think we should go and help?'

PC James nodded reluctantly. Although none of them wanted to admit they were enjoying that Ginning, the slimy wanker, was getting a pasting, they'd have to be seen to be doing *something* when the DI returned, otherwise they'd have to explain themselves.

• • • •

WHEN DEBBIE TURNED the key in the lock, she felt a funny prickling sensation, like she was being watched. Glancing over her shoulder, she looked up and down the deserted road. These weird night shifts finishing at 5.30 in the morning were clearly fucking her head up.

Satisfied she was being stupid and imagining things, Debbie pushed the door open and stepped into the dark hallway. She flicked on the light then stopped. It was quiet. Ian and Teddy must have gone to bed for once, rather than crash out on the sofa. That was ok. It would give her a bit more time to think.

Since hearing on the grapevine that the psycho-bitch had lost Seth's baby it meant that there was little point in putting her latest plan in action. Although it may still be worth poisoning the stupid slag just for the fun of it, rather than purely to offload the fucking kid.

Debbie smiled as she sparked up a fag. Yes, she'd think about it a bit longer before deciding whether she needed a new plan. Kicking off her shoes, she walked into the lounge, deciding she'd just have a quick drink before hitting the sack.

It took a few seconds for her brain to digest the carnage in front of her before hearing a dreadful high-pitched wailing noise. It was several more seconds before she realised the horrible noise was coming from her own mouth.

• • • •

DI CHARLES BURST THROUGH the doorway, pleased to see Ellerton lying face down on the underlay with her hands cuffed painfully behind her back. According to PC James, the psychotic little bitch had fought like a tigress, punching and head-butting him when he'd tried to cuff her. Apparently it had taken three of them to finally take her down.

He winced looking at James' watering eyes and broken nose, then glanced back at Jane who was studying him with contempt.

Turning his attention to the wheezing bloodied body of Ginning propped against the bedroom doorway, he shrugged. That twat was irrelevant in the scheme of things. Providing they could get the shit to stick on this pair of low-lives he didn't give a fuck who got caught in the cross-fire.

He was even happier to see Wright manacled and held down by more officers, whilst another whacked him with a truncheon. 'Seth Wright and Jane Ellerton.' DI Charles' voice was clear and loud. 'I'm arresting you both on suspicion of possession of controlled substances with intent to supply, handling of stolen goods and assaulting a police officer.'

Seth laughed. 'WHAT? Yeah, right!'

'You do not have to say anything, but it may harm your defence if you do not mention when questioned, something you later rely on in court.' DI Charles continued, ignoring Jane rolling her eyes in boredom.

'You've killed my fucking dog!' Seth growled, straining against his cuffs. 'I'll mention that, shall I?'

Jane almost laughed as an officer moved forward and placed a boot firmly on the small of Seth's back. It was funny how it took seven of them to take him down, but now he was shackled, they were acting like trophy hunters.

• • • •

STUART'S HEAVY AND erratic breathing steamed up the thin glass in the window as he pressed himself against the pane. His throbbing erection was almost painful as his hand pumped faster and faster along the length. *Oh, this was so fucking good.*

He'd listened intently to every word coming clearly through the thin wall as the police had ransacked next door and he'd happily snuggled further down under his duvet. *At long fucking last! Busted!*

As time went on, he'd realised Jane and Seth weren't there. He could have sworn he'd heard them return earlier and unable to stop himself fidgeting, he'd padded over to the window, glancing out into the dim light of the dawn, seeing straight away that Jane's car had been missing.

A wide smile had spread over his weasily face, not quite able to believe she'd taken it out so quickly. That meant it had been more than feasible that she could have already been wrapped around a fucking lamppost, along with Seth.

*Two birds with one stone and all that…*

However, that hadn't happened because they'd returned. But it was still good as they'd walked straight into the pile of coppers waiting for them inside and Stuart had more than enjoyed listening to the chaos.

Focusing his gaze back out of the window and savouring the

feelings coursing through his body, the smile plastered across his face widened as Seth and Jane were dragged across the courtyard. Unable to contain himself, he felt his legs begin to shake.

Seth glanced up at the window and his eyes connected directly with the man pressed against the glass, but as Stuart's hot fluid spurted out like a geyser against the anaglypta wallpaper, he was too far gone to notice he'd been seen.

• • • •

THE DUTY SERGEANT looked towards the ceiling, realising in retrospect it hadn't been a great choice to bung Wright and Ellerton in the same cell this time.

Admittedly he'd done it before because it tended to shut them up. Like a pair of weird co-joined twins, they made more noise when they were separated. Plus he enjoyed watching them shagging. It livened up the boring shifts which got repetitive with the usual steady stream of glue-sniffers and crap burglars. Not tonight though. There had *definitely* been no shagging tonight. They'd been at each other's throats for a good hour and it was getting worse.

Although *one* good thing had come out of tonight, he thought, smiling. He hadn't been able to hide his joy when he'd heard about Ginning and felt like shaking Wright's hand for that one. *It was about time the greasy pervert got a slap.*

Another bout of shouting and screaming finally pushed him over the edge. Stomping towards the cell door, he banged loudly with his fist. 'SHUT THE FUCK UP, WILL YOU!'

He yanked the metal grill open just in time to see Ellerton whack Wright round the head with the cell chair. Sighing, the sergeant rushed back to the desk to answer the phone, only to be told there was some fat bird in reception, rattling on about dead bodies.

Another fucking nutter, he didn't doubt, but now he'd have to send some of his guys to investigate regardless. This meant *he'd* have to attempt to split Wright and Ellerton up on his own and he wasn't looking forward to that one little bit.

## FORTY THREE

DODGE WAS LIVID. He eyed Seth's gear, piled up one side of the lock up and scowled. It had been *weeks* now and if the man hadn't shifted it by the end of the week, he'd get it out himself and dump it on the steps outside Seth's bloody flat.

He didn't want the fucking cops sniffing around his gaff. Not with all the ringed motors he pulled off. He wasn't as lucky as that jammy bastard and would get sent down quicker than two shakes of a duck's tail.

He was well aware that the Highwaymen's lawyer had come up trumps again and all the charges lumped on Seth and Jane had been dropped, due to lack of evidence. Well, *he* didn't have people like that to rely on and if he was pulled in, he'd be straight back in nick and he didn't want that. It was fraying his fucking nerves.

Raising his eyes up to the leaky ceiling, Dodge brushed his hair off his forehead and picked up one of Seth's crates. Impotently moving it on top of another, he sighed.

· · · ·

MAGGIE WASN'T SURE she'd heard correctly and blinked rapidly. '*Dead*?'

Jake nodded, his lank hair flapping around his face. 'Last

week. Both of them. Found by Ian's sister.'

Maggie was sure she must be hallucinating. 'Debbie?'

Jake nodded. 'That's the one. Went berserk, she did.'

'What happened?'

'No one knows. It's all very weird. Word has it that it was some type of satanic ritual gone wrong.'

Maggie knew well enough it wouldn't have been that. *No, someone had done this.* A tear ran down her cheek. 'I need a drink.'

Putting his arm around her shoulders, Jake steered her towards the bottom end of the high street. 'Come on. Let's go to the Kings.' If he played his cards right he might be on to a winner.

• • • •

SETH THRUST THE VIDEO camera into Jane's hands. 'Film it!'

Jane eyed the heavy camera. 'Where have you got this from?'

'Doesn't matter,' he mumbled, 'just film it.'

'You want me to film it?' Jane glanced across to Clint whose stoned eyes were staring straight at her.

'Yes Jane,' Seth hissed, staring hard into her eyes. 'I want you to film it. Did I not just say that?' As he brushed his lips on hers, she curled her arms around his neck.

Feeling Jane's body against his, Seth realised he could quite easily forget the whole thing and just take her here and now. 'Later,' he murmured, pulling away. He needed to do this first to get some bloody self-respect back.

Jane scowled as Seth walked over to where Clint was trussed up against a tree with rope. She was unable to see what he was planning to gain by any of this and wished he'd just get over what happened at the party. It was more than a week ago. *Did he really have to be so melodramatic, for God's sake?*

She studied Seth leaning against a tree, fiddling with his revolver and admitted, even after years and far too much shit, there was *still* something about him she found utterly irresistible. On the flip side, she also found him equally aggravating and her feelings constantly alternated between wanting to fuck him or kill him.

Although Clint was stoned off his bonce, panic was rising and threatening to mess up his chilled demeanour. *Seth wouldn't actually do anything stupid, would he? This was to prove a point, right?*

He'd been told far too many times Seth and Jane were fucking nutters and to stay clear. His eyes moved to Jane who was messing with something. *What was it? It looked a like a video camera.*

An involuntary smile passed across his mouth as an idea formed. *Maybe they were all going to fuck and film it?* Looking at Jane, her legs encased in skin-tight black denim, he felt his groin tighten. There was something about that woman that flicked his switch.

He tossed his head, trying to get a long curl out of his eye and wished he could move his arms. It was all starting to get a tad uncomfortable.

Clint saw Jane smile as she spotted the bulge in his leather trousers and he smiled back, feeling a lot less paranoid. He savoured the heady rush of the dope rolling through his brain and breathed in the sweet scents of the woodland.

Suddenly snapped out of his reverie by a clicking sound, he opened his eyes to the barrel of a gun and his mouth fell open. He had no time to register anything more before he was punched hard in the stomach. Crumpling over as much as the ropes binding him would allow, he heaved and gasped for breath.

Hard green eyes stared into his. 'I did say, 'no tongues,' now didn't I, Clint?' Seth growled.

'W-What?' Clint stuttered, trying to override the crushing pain in his torso. He began to think he may have slightly misread the situation. 'Oh, c'mon man, you were all for it!' He smiled, ever hopeful. *Maybe this was all part of the game?*

Seth gripped Clint's face and pushed his head back sharply

against the tree trunk. 'I didn't say you could fuck her!' he snarled. 'You took the piss.'

'I wasn't taking the pi....'

'YOU FUCKED MY WIFE!' Seth roared. 'You must think I'm some sort of cunt, if you think I'd be ok with that?'

Clint's eyes darted towards Jane as she leant against a tree, the camera resting on her shoulder. Her eyes met his and she shrugged. 'You're joking, right?' he gibbered.

'Do I look like I'm joking?' Seth muttered.

• • • •

PHIL FROWNED, PRETENDING he was interested in what Dodge was going on about, when really he wished he'd shut the fuck up. He'd only come to the King's for a quiet pint when he'd been accosted by this bastard, which only served to remind him why he hadn't been in here for ages.

Dodge's arms waved around, his voice rising. 'But Seth's *got* to move that stuff, it's been there for weeks and I don't want any attention on me.'

Phil gritted his teeth and gripped Dodge's arm hard. 'Keep the noise down, you stupid cunt!'

Dodge's eyes darted around the bar to see who was listening, but there was only a bunch of half-conscious hippies and some fat bloke. The only person staring at him was one of Jane's mates, but she looked like she'd lost the plot anyway. 'Sorry. Sorry!' he muttered and tried to winkle his arm out of Phil's vice-like grip.

'Chill out,' Phil whispered under his breath. 'I'll sort it.'

Nodding, Dodge quickly scuttled out of the pub before he was grabbed again. He knew his every move was being watched by the biker's steely blue eyes.

Nodding to Lee, signifying a refill, Phil placed his empty glass on the beer towel and turned around. Picking up his fresh pint, he leant against the bar with his elbows and gave Maggie a wide manic smile.

He'd pop round Seth's later and remind him to shift the gear.

He didn't trust that Dodge. He was far too fucking jumpy and the way he was playing his trap he'd drop them all in it.

At least Seth seemed to be getting his act together, so maybe he'd be ok to do some work again? He'd weigh it up later, Phil thought and smiled to himself. This beer was going down far too well.

He shouted up another. *One for the road maybe.*

Maggie felt like she was speeding. Her brain thundered along like an express train and she couldn't concentrate on what Jake was saying.

She'd seen the look on Dodge's face and even though she hadn't heard much of the conversation, she'd heard Seth's name mentioned. As for Phil, well - he was just mental and scared the life out of her.

Her hands shook as she picked up yet another drink. She needed to leave, but couldn't will herself to move. If she stood up, her legs might turn to jelly and she'd collapse on the floor, then *everyone* would stare at her and she couldn't cope with that.

A wave of nausea flooded her. Why had Jane been so sure she wouldn't get any more grief off Ian? Were Ian and Teddy's deaths something to do with Seth?

Feeling tears welling in her eyes, she glanced back to the bar, feeling even worse as Phil grinned at her again. *This was like a bad dream and she needed to talk to Jane. She'd know what to do.*

Swallowing hard, Maggie felt wretched and could no longer stop the hot tears from falling down her face. Neither did she have the energy to move Jake's arm away when it snaked around her shoulders.

• • • •

SETH STUDIED CLINT CLOSELY. Abject paranoia and fear of losing Jane coursed through him and rage at being taken for a mug, beat on a path that was not going to be quashed. Clint was a nice-looking guy and he could see why Jane found him attractive, but he didn't like it one little bit.

'B-But wait,' Clint stuttered, wishing he wasn't so stoned. 'I'm sorry if I went over the line, but Jane was up for it. It wasn't just me.'

Realising too late this was the worst thing he could have said, he watched Seth's eyes narrow into slits, then his head was slammed harder into the trunk than before.

'So what are you saying?' Seth roared. 'That I'm not enough for her?'

'No, NO!' Clint looked pleadingly towards Jane.

'Come on, Seth,' Jane said amiably. 'That's enough now.'

Seth's head flicked around and he smiled savagely. 'You're right, Princess.' His voice was strangely calm. 'It *is* enough…'

A quiet sigh of relief escaped from Clint's mouth as Seth stepped back a few paces. 'What say I buy you guys a drink?' *He knew he could definitely do with one.*

'No thanks.' Spinning around, Seth raised his pistol and fired a single shot into Clint's chest.

Jane continued filming as Clint's body went rigid against the tree trunk, his head flopping forward and a stream of thick purple blood pouring from his mouth. She wondered whether they were going to be much longer here because she needed some more coke.

Placing the pistol back in his inside pocket, Seth gave Jane a wide, bright smile. She stopped recording and gratefully pulled the heavy camera down from her shoulder.

He untied Clint, who fell in a heap at the base of the tree.

Tossing the rope on top of the body, he fished a can of petrol out of nowhere and gave it a shake.

Jane made her way back towards the car, watching Seth chuck a liberal amount of fuel around and concluded she may be slightly responsible for all of this. *Did she feel bad? Did she fuck.*

*She felt sod all.*

'Sorry about that,' Seth smiled, grabbing Jane from behind. Swinging her around, he kissed her.

'Urgh, you stink of petrol!' Jane prised Seth's hands off her as he pushed her playfully into the car. 'Feel better now?' she asked as he jumped behind the wheel.

'That I do,' he grinned.

'Not think you went slightly over the top?'

'No I don't!' Seth raised an eyebrow and fired the engine. 'This is what happens when you decide to fuck someone other than me. Now let's get home. There's more stuff I want to film.'

Taking a swig out of the vodka from the glove box, Jane laughed.

· · · ·

'I'D SAY HE'S PRETTY much back to normal.' Digger said, taking his place next to Phil at the Kings Head bar. 'Well, as normal as he ever was.'

Handing Digger a pint, Phil grinned. 'She's staring at you.'

'Who?' Turning to meet Maggie's bloodshot eyes, Digger smiled. *Just who he wanted to have a word with. He'd been beginning to think she'd emigrated.* 'Bear with me a moment, mate.'

Maggie thought she might pass out when Digger beckoned her over. She was astounded her legs were still holding her upright as she followed him outside.

Digger's eyes drilled into hers. 'I think you owe me an explanation?'

Maggie leant shakily against the wall. She'd got enough problems as it was and more than bitterly regretted allowing Jake to buy her so many drinks. In fact, there wasn't much of her life right now that she *didn't* regret.

Digger sighed and folded his arms. *Maggie's shrinking violet act was getting on his tits.* 'Stop playing the Virgin Queen,' he scowled. 'I was asked to warn Ian off, which I did, but you decided to fuck him again, right? Would you like to tell me why?'

Maggie went cold. How did he know about that and who had asked him to warn Ian off? *Jane... Oh shit. Jesus fucking Christ. Shit!*

Digger studied the emotions running across Maggie's face and slowly blew the smoke from his cigarette over her. He bent lower, speaking quietly into her ear. 'Ian took umbrage at me sticking my nose in.'

Maggie hardly dared move, let alone look at Digger.

'Especially when he thought you were taking him back.'

She started shaking involuntarily. 'I... I...'

'AND he and his stupid fucking mate tried to *kill* me!' Digger hissed, his eyes vicious slits.

Maggie very nearly choked on her own tongue as realisation dawned. 'You? It was *you*...?'

Placing a large arm either side of her, trapping her against the wall, Digger smiled nastily. 'It was me, what...?'

Maggie said nothing, the words sticking in her throat.

Digger moved away. 'You need to have a good look at yourself, love. Shafting people who stick their necks out for you never has good consequences.' He gave her a long look. 'For *anyone*...'

Turning on his heels, he walked back into the bar, leaving Maggie to heave into the gutter.

• • • •

'SHH,' JANE WHISPERED. 'Don't talk. Just fuck me. Hard.'

*No problem*, Seth thought, checking the video camera balanced on the shelf behind them. Holding both of Jane's arms over her head, he bit one nipple viciously. Hearing her gasp in pain, he smiled.

Quickly parting her thighs with his knee, he slammed deep into her, silencing her cries with his mouth. *She wanted it rough, did she?*

Biting her bottom lip and tasting blood as his teeth cut into her flesh, he held Jane firm and thrust hard. 'Keep still!' he growled, pulling himself onto his knees and dragging her with him. Rolling his hips, he upped the pace.

Smacking Jane's hand away as she traced a hard line down his chest with her nail, Seth flipped her over, pushing her face down into the mattress. He delivered a stinging slap across her buttocks, his fingers bruising her hips as he gripped her and then slammed hard into her from behind.

Jane hadn't chance to take a full breath, before her arms were twisted painfully behind her back whilst Seth slowed his pace, drawing each stroke out with precision.

Her body shuddered with the need for release and as the eye of the camera behind them filmed, she turned her head to the side, watching Clint silently die for the second time on the small television Seth had rigged up next to the bed.

Grabbing Jane around the throat, Seth threw her onto her back then crashed his mouth onto hers. It only turned him on further when she clawed his back, drawing blood.

His thumb circled her, his fingers probing deep and she groaned, trying to pull him into her, but resisting, he held her down.

Jane's hips tried to escape Seth's teasing fingers, but he mercilessly continued. Feeling her body shaking, he smiled and pushed her legs up towards her shoulders, burying his mouth in her wetness. Tasting her need for him, he flicked his tongue hard.

'Oh God, Seth!' she cried, as he sucked and probed faster.

Feeling hair rip from his scalp as Jane yanked and twisted it, arching her back beneath him, Seth's arousal was now unbearable. He raised himself up to look at her, his cock feeling like it would explode.

Dropping Jane's legs, Seth quickly rammed himself back inside her up to the hilt and ramped up the pace to a breakneck speed.

Sweat poured down his face as Jane writhed underneath him crying out for release. He knew he was about to blow. 'I'm going to make you come now,' he growled, changing his stroke slightly.

Jane couldn't do anything, apart from scream Seth's name as she came hard around him.

Riding the wave of orgasm as long as possible, Seth finally

exploded into Jane and collapsed heavily on top, kissing her softly. She tensed her most intimate muscles hard around him, making him groan loudly as the final drops were squeezed out of him. Licking the sweat from his face she clutched onto him, her breath ragged.

'We should have come around earlier, Digger!' Phil grinned as they stood watching from the bedroom doorway.

## FORTY FOUR

PAUL DIDN'T LIKE THE Oak Apple, but Debbie was insistent they met there rather than the Black Eagle. When she'd offered to buy the drinks, he'd been amazed. It was usually *him* who forked out.

He watched her leaning casually against the wooden bar, her short top exposing part of her flabby back and cringed. Why he'd shagged her last week, he didn't know - apart from that he'd had too many and finally succumbed to her persistent advances.

She'd been really cut up over Ian's death and so he'd tried to help her drown her sorrows, but one thing had led to another and now she was acting as if they were a couple.

Hearing Debbie's nasal voice resonate loudly around the large open-plan room, Paul blanched, realising why she'd offered to go up the bar.

'I'm telling you,' Debbie spoke to the group around her. 'I've been in a right state. My poor brother *butchered* by that murdering bastard.'

Paul glanced from left to right, watching more people's ears prick up. *Shit!*

'Everyone knows Seth Wright did it. I even told the police it was him. They know what he's like - as do all of us. Let's face it, he wanted to get me back after what I did…'

Paul hastily pulled himself from his seat, aware that several pairs of eyes were now on him. *What the hell was the stupid bitch doing?*

'And that's not the worst of it. Paul watched Seth leave Ian's flat that night. He'd been planning to surprise me when I got back from work, but when there wasn't any answer he left. When I got back, I found my brother and Teddy… *Dead.*'

Paul watched Debbie lean dramatically over the bar and sob loudly. He knew she was putting it on. Frowning, he stumbled haphazardly through the crowd with panic etched on his face. *Why had she said he's seen Seth leaving? He hadn't seen anything! He'd get shit for this.*

Debbie made a show of composing herself. 'Only a couple of days ago, the psycho threatened me. He said he'd kill us both if we breathed a word, but I'm not scared of Seth and neither is Paul. This time we'll make sure he gets locked up for what he's done.'

Reaching the bar, Paul grabbed Debbie's arm. 'What the fuck are you doing? No one's said anything to you,' he hissed into her ear.

Before Paul could say anything further, Debbie flung her arms around his neck and kissed him passionately. Pulling away, she smiled widely. 'I'd also like to announce that we're getting married!'

Paul stopped trying to rectify his smudged makeup and stared at Debbie in horror. *This was getting ridiculous.*

• • • •

SETH WATCHED LEE top up the gin in the bong. 'I need to move the stuff. It'll be ok at your mate's, yeah? I need to keep things clean here a while longer.'

'Don't see why not. He's safe. Besides, you've got to shift it somewhere.'

Seth nodded. Setting the bong going, he took a deep pull and held the thick smoke in his lungs. 'Phil said Dodge was flapping his gums down the King's.'

Lee raised his eyebrows and poured himself a shot of rum. That was the *last* thing Seth and Jane needed. He'd been worried about Seth, but thankfully it seemed he was getting himself back together again. *On the outside at least.* 'Things ok now?'

'Yeah, we're ok,' Seth answered dismissively and fiddled with the brightly-coloured bong pipe, hoping his expression hadn't been noted. They were *far* from alright, if truth be known, but he wasn't discussing his feelings with anyone. *Even himself.*

Every time he mentioned the wedding, Jane would change the subject and he was worried she was getting cold feet. He knew she took his lack of motivation to move away to be because he couldn't be arsed, but that was far from the truth. The truth was, it was taking all his power to maintain a façade of being sorted, when really he was still drowning.

His brow knitted together and he took another pull on the bong, feeling the effects creeping into his brain. *Turn it down... Turn it off...* He didn't want to feel. Feeling was dangerous.

Lee interrupted Seth from his thoughts. 'You sharing that or what?'

Pushing the bong across the table, Seth frowned. Maybe they *should* just go? It was probably the right thing to do, but he wasn't sure whether he could take it at the moment.

He took a deep breath. He'd speak to Jane again about it later and make a final decision before they got too drunk.

• • • •

TIPPING A FEW PILLS into her mouth, Jane washed them down with a mouthful of lager. 'I'm telling you it was *him*!'

Eliza sipped from her pint of cider and raised her eyebrows. 'Are you *sure*? I mean, would he really do that, after what Seth did to him?'

'Look it's been confirmed my steering was tampered with,' Jane seethed. 'It had to be that cunt and yes, he's that fucking thick he'd do it *regardless* of Seth.'

Maggie picked at her chewed fingernails. She still hadn't

broached the conversation she needed to have with Jane about Ian. She had to say something soon, although the tap room of the Black Eagle wasn't exactly the best place to ask her friend if she had any part in her ex-boyfriend's murder. Wiping her face with the back of her hand she reached for a cigarette and nervously turned her lager round on the table.

'AND,' Jane continued. 'I reckon he set us up for that raid. I've told Seth over and over, but he won't have it.'

She rapidly necked the rest of her pint. 'He'll have to listen about the car though. I'll have that bastard, if it's the *last* thing I do. With or without Seth!' She felt like she was going to blow a gasket and all she wanted now was to get pissed. 'Another?'

Reaching the bar, Jane watched Maggie sidle up next to her, fiddling with her hair. 'You alright, Mags?'

*No she wasn't. She wasn't alright at all.* Maggie's eyes tracked over to Eliza who was now giggling with a wizened gap-toothed geriatric. She had to say something before she lost her nerve or before Eliza came over. 'Just wondered if I could speak to you about something?' she muttered, following Jane's eyes as Paul shuffled through the pub door. 'Jane?'

*Great. The one opportunity she'd had all day to speak to Jane alone and now it looked like she was going to flip out.*

The usual chant kicked off from a group of men at the far end of the tap room. 'Alice. Alice. Who the fuck is Alice?'

Jane stared at Paul. She hadn't seen him for *ages* and by Christ, he looked even worse than before. She watched him spot her, then hastily retreat the way he'd come in. Only after the heavy wooden door had closed behind him, did she pick up her fresh pint from the beer towel. 'What did you say, Mags?'

'I need to speak to you,' Maggie whispered.

Jane raised an eyebrow and took a large swig of her pint. 'I'm listening.'

Maggie glanced around. 'Not here. I meant somewhere on our own.'

Jane sighed. 'Ok. Come to the flat.'

Maggie lingered at the bar whilst Jane walked back to the

table and tried to ignore the leering man next to her who smelt strongly of horse shit.

She wrung her hands in desperation. What if Digger was there? Seth would undoubtedly be, so how the hell was she supposed to speak to Jane in front of *them*?

. . . .

'DON'T BE SO fucking stupid!' Seth snarled. He leant back in the armchair and blew a long stream of cigarette smoke out up towards the ceiling.

'I'm telling you that Stuart tampered with my fucking motor,' Jane snapped, standing in front of Seth with her arms folded. 'It's a fact.'

Rolling his eyes, Seth laughed. 'What, because some bloke said so? Come on, that place would say *anything* so they could fix it!'

'The guy's a bloody mechanic! Are you saying there's nothing wrong with the steering?' Jane temper spiked when Seth smirked at Digger. She was sick of being made out to be melodramatic. *Why couldn't he see the wanker had tried to kill them?*

From her position in the corner, Maggie tried not to look at anyone and hoped she'd blend in with the wall. It was bad enough coming here in the first place, plus Digger hadn't taken his eyes off her - *daring* her to look up or move. She'd done neither, but was fast running out of places to stare and now it looked like Jane and Seth were going to have another row.

Maggie closed her eyes, trying to control her impending panic and hoped it would all go away, but it didn't.

'Jane,' Seth laughed. 'Do you *really* think Stuart would dare to pull a stunt like that?' Accidentally dropping his cigarette end on his jeans, he jumped up quickly and flicked it to the floor, causing yet another torrent of stoned laughter from Lee.

'Yes I do!' Jane grabbed the vodka and shoved some more pills into her mouth.

Seth held his hand out towards her. 'Come here, baby and

kiss me. That's if you don't crash on the way and blame some conspiracy theory!'

Jane scowled. *Oh, it was all so funny, wasn't it.* Bollocks to him! She wouldn't get a word of sense out of him tonight, he was so stoned.

Taking a final swig out of the vodka, she slammed it down and headed towards the door. 'Come on, Mags!'

Seth stood up unsteadily. 'Where the fuck are you going now?'

'Out!' Jane snapped.

'But you've only just got back.'

'And what does *that* tell you?' Jane pushed the lounge door so hard, it slammed against the wall and rebounded back onto Maggie who was following.

'Things definitely going well then, I see!' Lee quipped sarcastically as Seth slumped back into the armchair.

## FORTY FIVE

MAGGIE WAS PLEASED by Jane's decision to go out of town for a drink. The chances of having an uninterrupted conversation down the Dragon, King's or Oak Apple were slim.

She hadn't broached the subject of Ian until they'd been safely ensconced at a wooden farmhouse table in the lounge bar of a village pub and when she'd blurted it out, it hadn't gone down too well. Now she began to wish she hadn't said anything at all.

'You did *what*?' Jane roared, ignoring people staring at them from around the bar.

'I was lonely,' Maggie whined, trying to justify why she'd slept with Ian again. 'I thought he'd changed. He…'

'*Changed*? Are you crazy? People like that don't change!' Jane interrupted, her dark eyes flashing.

Taking a gulp of her pint, she narrowed her eyes, unable to believe Maggie had been so stupid. 'You think *I* don't get lonely? It's possible to be around people all the time and still feel on your own, you know and yes, I *did* ask Digger to warn Ian off.'

'But…'

Jane's muscles tensed with anger. 'But *nothing*. What did

you want me to do?'

Maggie hung her head and shamefully explained what had happened the night she'd let Ian back into her life.

'Well I'm glad Digger finished the pair of bastards.' Jane's voice dripped with venom. She stood up. 'You can't wonder why he's cross though, Mag. He did what I asked and then you hop back in with Ian.'

Tugging at Jane's arm, Maggie pulled her back down. 'I know, I know... I'm sorry.'

Jane placed her hand over Maggie's, feeling her flinch. She frowned. *There was more to this than Ian.* She studied her friend's face. 'Maggie, what's going on?'

Maggie looked at the table. That was the problem. She didn't know. All she knew was that she didn't want to feel like *this*. 'I don't know.'

Jane rolled her eyes. She could do without a fucking pity trip. Had Maggie any idea of the problems she'd caused? 'Just tell Digger what Ian did.'

Maggie searched Jane's face. 'NO! I can't tell him. Don't tell anyone, Jane! I couldn't bear it!' Her eyes darted around. 'You're the only person I've told. I don't want anyone else to know.'

Jane nodded, 'Ok, don't worry, I won't say anything.'

· · · ·

SETH WAS FAR from happy. He'd been round three pubs so far and no one had seen hide nor hair of Jane. He was getting fed up of running around town all night looking for the stupid woman.

'Chill out!' Lee muttered, getting fed up. 'Just let her get on with it. She's probably gone out of town.'

'She *never* goes out of town,' Seth seethed, his anger increasing with each minute that passed. 'If she's with someone else, I'll fucking *kill* her!'

Looking towards the dark night sky, Lee hoped for something to get him away from this. *Aliens, perhaps?* 'Let's just go and get another drink.'

Seth suddenly stopped, a manic grin on his face. 'There's one place we haven't tried.'

Lee looked at him questioningly.

Seth grinned. 'The Bull's Head!'

'She doesn't go in there much, does she?' *Please* not the Bull's Head, Lee thought, already getting depressed at the prospect of wading through sawdust-covered dog shit and listening to Leonard Cohen on the jukebox.

'No she doesn't,' he smiled, 'so it'd be the last place she'd expect me to look.'

Seth looked so pleased with himself, Lee didn't have the heart to say if that was the case, then maybe Jane just wanted some time out. Instead, he grudgingly followed him up the road.

• • • •

JANE RETURNED FROM the bar with a couple of double vodkas and sat back down, waiting for the conversation to continue.

'I don't know why I'm so upset?' Maggie whispered, her eyes staring vacantly at a picture of a haystack on the wall.

'Nor do I!' Jane laughed hollowly.

'I'm not like you, Jane.'

*Ah, now they were getting somewhere. Was this about Ian or her?* 'What's that supposed to mean?'

Maggie paused, her heart beating loudly in her chest. 'The things you do. The things Seth does. It's not *normal*, is it?'

Jane clenched her jaw. She didn't need a lecture.

'Why do you do this stuff?'

Leaning back in the chair, Jane turned her cigarette lighter around in her fingers. She tipped the vodka down her throat and placed the glass gently back on the table. '*Why* is the operative word, isn't it?' She looked pensive. 'Why does there have to be a *why*?'

Maggie didn't understand. Surely there had to be a *why*? The stress and confusion of the last few days ran over her like an avalanche. 'You scare me, Jane.'

Jane frowned and signalled to the barman for more drinks. 'No need to be scared. Besides…' Stopping mid-sentence when the barman set down more drinks on their table, she smiled and waited until he'd left. 'It's probably all for nothing anyway.'

'What is?'

'Life? The world? Everything? I don't know. If you believe any of it, that is?'

'Believe what? I don't understand.'

Jane drifted off somewhere else. What was the real point of life? Was there a point? Everyone was searching for an in-depth reason for their existence, but did anyone consider there may not be one? It may just be as it was and then it was over.

She quickly swallowed the fresh drink. 'Don't think things don't get to me. I just deal with it by shutting my feelings down.'

Maggie listened carefully to what Jane was saying. She'd never heard her talking like this before, but then she'd never asked any questions.

Signalling for another drink, Jane trained her eyes on Maggie. 'Everything is disposable, Mags.'

Maggie sipped at her drink nervously. 'Even people?'

A slight smile twitched at the corners of Jane's mouth. '*Especially* people. They're the ones that cause the problems.'

Maggie didn't know what to think. This was doing her head in. 'But how do you justify it? Doesn't it keep you awake?'

Jane laughed. 'Oh, for God's sake. I take pills to stay awake and pills to go to sleep! What's the difference?'

'You make it sound so simple.'

Nodding and smiling as the barman deposited another double on the table, Jane turned back towards Maggie, the smile leaving her face. 'Nothing's simple, but nothing's hard either. It's what you want it to be. Look, I don't profess to have all the answers.'

Taking a long pull of a cigarette, she exhaled slowly. 'The only way not to hurt, is not to think.'

Maggie's eyebrows knitted together. She was still confused. *Was Jane saying the answer to everything was just to take enough shit not to care, notice or what?* 'That's fucked up!'

'*Life* is fucked up!' Jane laughed.

Maggie frowned. Surely it all caught up with someone in the end, didn't it? 'Aren't you scared of going to hell?'

Looking at Maggie incredulously, Jane tapped the end of her cigarette into the ashtray. 'How can I be scared of going somewhere I've already been?'

'But Seth? He's…'

'As I'm sure you've heard, I was like this *long* before I met him.' Jane raised an eyebrow when Maggie looked away. 'I've just found someone the same.'

'But I'm worried about you.'

Getting a little bored, Jane picked up her bag. 'Don't worry about me, Mags. There are more important things to stress about. Come on, I need some powder.'

'That's another thing. You do too much stuff. The drink, powder, pills. I don't want you to die.'

Jane laughed again. 'I'm not scared of dying. It's the only thing that's guaranteed. I'm no different to anyone else.'

Maggie sighed. Jane *was* different to everyone else though. Apart from *Seth*.

• • • •

LEE'S EYES DARTED up and down the main road keeping an eye out for the cops, whilst Seth grabbed Paul by the scruff of the neck and pulled him up from where he lay in a pile of glass.

Zed watched with a confused grin over his stubbly face as he leant against the wall. He wasn't sure what was going on, but this sure beat watching a scruffy mongrel on a piece of string have a shit in the corner. That had been the most interesting thing that had happened tonight by far, until that weird bloke with the make-up on had turned up just before last knockings.

He stared with morbid fascination and relit his joint as Seth dragged the man to his feet by his jacket collar and head-butted him repeatedly.

'Seth, come on. Leave it!' Lee stepped forward. *For God's*

*sake, he didn't need this.* All the mellow undertones from the afternoon's bong had long gone and he just wanted to go home, but Seth was in the zone.

Pent-up rage was etched all over Seth's face, his square jaw clenched into a hard line as he weighed up the situation. Staring at Paul who he was still holding firmly by the lapels with his head lolling on his chest and blood running freely down his shirt, he growled in frustration.

He'd already heard on the grapevine about what had been said down the Apple and this twat had got off too lightly before, considering everything he'd done. He just wanted to kill him, like he should have done ages ago and was quite happy to do so. Right *now*.

Only Lee's constant pleading to leave it because there were too many people watching, finally snapped him from his anger blackout. Reluctantly dragging Paul around the side of the pub, he threw him roughly to the floor and left him amongst a pile of rubbish near the trade bins.

Returning to the front of the Bull's Head, Seth wiped his hands down his long coat and shouted brightly to the amassed crowd. 'Show's over, folks!'

Without even glancing at Lee, he headed off down the road.

• • • •

JANE GLANCED IN THE rear-view mirror. She'd put far too many drinks away, but thankfully the coke she'd just taken had brought her back up. 'I'm taking it you'll be keeping schtum about Digger?' She glanced towards Maggie, who seemed reluctant to answer. 'It's the *least* you can do, considering.'

She was getting irritated with Maggie's reticence to play the game. If she chose to get involved with people like Ian, then she needed to take the rough with the smooth, not live in a fucking dream world. 'Life isn't a bed of roses, Maggie?' she snapped. 'There aren't knights in shining armour and there aren't any fucking happy endings.'

'I won't be saying anything about Digger,' Maggie mumbled

quietly. 'But what about Debbie?'

'What the fuck's she got to do with it?' Jane didn't want to even *think* about that fat bitch.

'According to Jake, she went to the police.'

'The cops don't give a flying fuck when wankers like Ian drop off the twig or go missing.'

'Is that how you two get away with so much?' Maggie snapped.

Jane shot her a look, feeling her nerves jangling. She didn't have to explain anything to anyone, except herself and if Maggie was going to start having digs, then she could fuck right off. She'd put up with an entire evening of questions as it was. She'd obviously forgotten the only reason Digger had had a word in the first place, was for *her*.

'I heard Debbie was spouting off down the Apple earlier,' Maggie continued. 'She said it was Seth who killed Ian.'

Jane's head snapped round. 'What? He had nothing to do with it!'

Maggie tried to backtrack. 'I'm not saying he did, babe. Just telling you what she's saying. I'm worried she'll drop everyone in it,' she lied, shuddering involuntarily. She really didn't care what happened to Digger *or* Seth.

Turning into a road near town, Jane pushed the accelerator to the floor, causing Maggie to slam against the window.

'Slow down a bit, babe,' Maggie screeched.

'Oh, shut the fuck up!' Jane snapped. She needed to put a stop to this Debbie shit. She'd thought she'd got the message through to the dirty bitch last time, but obviously not if she was still trapping off. She'd have to sort the slag out once and for all. *Enough was enough.*

'Are you coming to the flat, Maggie, or will being in our presence offend you?'

Maggie regretted the whole of the nights' conversation. She didn't want to fall out with Jane, but she just didn't get any of it anymore. 'I'd better head back to the caravan. Can you drop me off?'

'Sure,' Jane muttered through gritted teeth.

Continuing along the road, the headlights lit up a figure walking on the left-hand pavement and Jane's eyes shone. She quickly knocked the car down a gear and slammed her foot down harder on the accelerator.

*Fucking bonus. Absolute fucking bonus!*

'What are you doing?' Maggie yelled, scrabbling to hang on to something as the car mounted the pavement.

Jane didn't answer, her concentration focused as she drove at the rate of knots. *Payback, bitch!*

Feeling a bone-shaking thud, Maggie's hand flew to her mouth as a body slammed onto the bonnet. She clawed against the chair and fruitlessly attempted to back away from the bloodied face of Debbie squashed against the windscreen.

Jane laughed maniacally and tried to fathom how to get the fat fuck off her car before she dented it further.

Swerving violently, she dislodged Debbie from the bonnet and glanced in the rear-view mirror, seeing her body crash heavily onto the pavement behind. Eyeing the cracked windscreen, she smiled at the minor inconvenience.

Flicking the window wipers on to remove the blood splattered over the screen, Jane accelerated and turned the tape player up to drown out the noise of Maggie vomiting into the foot well.

## FORTY SIX

LEE WAS GLAD TO sit down. After everything, there was still no sign of Jane. He watched Seth pacing up and down.

Abandoning his glass, Lee drank straight from the rum bottle. 'So, who was the freak?' He'd seen that strange bloke around, but had never taken much notice, presuming he was one of the many oddballs released from the local mental hospitals.

Walking over to the large window overlooking the high street, Seth leant on the sill and frowned at the blood stains on his coat. He stared vacantly down at the dark street below. 'Just someone I heard was speaking out of turn. Nothing for you to concern yourself with.'

In the reflection, Lee saw the wisp of a sarcastic smile pass across Seth's mouth as he stomped over to the stereo, the tails of his coat flapping. Roughly pulling the lid of the turntable open, he dropped the needle on the record, making a loud scratching sound.

'Where the fuck is Jane?' Seth suddenly barked, wild-eyed. 'She can't just disappear!'

*Not this again.* Lee decided he'd have to make his excuses and fuck off home. No amount of rum could make him cope with listening to another one of Seth's bloody rages.

'I need to know where she is!' Seth roared and picked up a large tea mug from the table. He launched it at the wall and Lee ducked as shards of china ricocheted around the room.

* * * *

MAGGIE WAS RELIEVED to hear Jane's car engine getting fainter as she sped off into the distance. Shakily, she made her way over the field towards her caravan, feeling she would throw up again as the image of Debbie replayed in her mind.

The noise when Debbie had hit the metal bumper... The face with eyes wide in abject terror squashed against the window and the mouth wide in a silent scream... *All the blood...*

She wished it would just go away.

A shiver ran through her as she pulled out her cigarettes and lit one with trembling fingers. Had she imagined the whole thing? Jane had acted as if nothing had happened and had merely reminded her about a party tomorrow, before speeding off into the night.

Maggie swallowed down the uncomfortable lump in her throat. No. Unfortunately it had very much happened and she couldn't handle it anymore.

'You alright, Mags?'

The voice from nowhere made Maggie almost choke on her tongue, before relief washed over her as Zed's face loomed out of the darkness. *Keep the tears in check, Maggie. Keep the tears in check.* 'Bit of a shit evening...'

Zed grinned, his long blond dreads flapping around his shoulders. He waved an unlit joint in her direction. 'Fancy a smoke?'

Maggie smiled gratefully. 'I'd love to.'

*Thank God.* With any luck she'd be able to erase tonight from her brain.

* * * *

'JUST STOP GOING ON!' Jane screeched. She wouldn't admit something she hadn't done.

Standing in front of her, Seth's face was red with rage and

the veins in his temples throbbed. Glaring, he lurched forward. 'Just tell me who you've been with?'

'Get the fuck out of my face!' Pushing Seth hard in the chest, Jane began to walk away.

'I'll kill you if you've done the dirty on me again!' Seth snarled. He grabbed Jane's arm, his eyes black with anger. 'I won't ask you again. Now TELL ME!'

Lee tugged Seth's shirt sleeve in an effort to calm him down. 'Come on, mate.'

Spinning around, Seth yanked Lee's hand away. 'And *you* can fuck off and all! Why are you still even here?'

Lee angrily stomped into the kitchen. He didn't appreciate being spoken to like a piece of shit. Seth's jealously and paranoia was a fucking obsession and it was pissing him right off.

Shaking her arm out of Seth's grip, Jane attempted to follow Lee to the kitchen.

'Oh no you don't!' Grabbing her with one hand, Seth upended the table with the other and smashed Lee's bottle of rum into pieces.

He stared deep into Jane's eyes as he slammed her against the wall. 'Just level with me. Tell me where you've been.'

'For your information, I've been with Maggie, Seth. Not that I should have to explain myself to *you*,' Jane raged.

'You must think I came down on the last fucking branch.' Seth tightened his grip on Jane's arm, unable to decide whether to kill her or fuck her. 'And yes, you do have to explain to me. You belong to *me*.'

Jane laughed hollowly. 'I belong to no one.' Wrenching out of his grip, she stared at him coldly. 'I'm *sick* of you.' With rapid precision she delivered a stinging slap to the side of his face, the red imprint immediately visible. With a roar, Seth turned on his heels.

'Walking away, are you?' Jane sneered, fuelled to have a full-blown row. Catching up with him as he reached the lounge door, she pulled his arm. 'If you think I'm marrying you again, you're off your bloody head!'

Touch paper fully activated, Seth shook her roughly by the shoulders. 'Oh yes you fucking will!' His eyes flashed with fire. 'You *will*, Jane, even if it's the last thing you do!'

'Threatening me now?' she laughed, determined to rile him. 'You piece of shit. I'm not scared of you. You're a fucking joke!'

Grabbing Jane's face, Seth yanked her head around. 'A joke, am I?'

Kneeing him hard in the stomach, she grabbed his hair and pulled his head up. 'I wish I'd never laid eyes on you, Seth Wright!'

Seth stared at Jane icily for a couple of seconds, then pushed her away and walked out of the lounge door, banging it hard behind him.

As the front door slammed, Jane's shoulders sagged and tears of frustration rolled down her cheeks. She wiped the back of her hand across her face and pulled her cigarettes out of her pocket.

. . . .

MAGGIE FELT BETTER the second she'd inhaled the first drag of the joint. 'What? *Tonight*?'

'It was hilarious,' Zed laughed, helping himself to a swig of cider from a bottle on the tiny work surface. 'He whacked him and then chucked him through the bloody window!'

Chuckling to himself, Zed could still picture the expression on the weird guy's face when he'd sailed through the glass and landed with a thud on the pavement.

He took the joint that Maggie offered back. 'It carried on outside and I thought Seth was going to kill him, but he ended up dumping him around the side with the rubbish!'

Maggie sighed, longing to unburden herself about Debbie. She wished Zed would hurry up and pass her the joint back so she'd have something to concentrate on. Furthermore, she needed to get stoned. *Very* stoned.

'Shame about Clint, though,' Zed muttered, eyeing Maggie.

*She was a nice-looking wench. Now Ian was out of the way, he wouldn't be treading on anyone's toes.*

'What about Clint?' Maggie gratefully took the smoke and raised it to her mouth. *Seth hadn't given him a slap tonight as well, had he?*

'I saw Mudflap earlier. He's right upset.'

Moving to the edge of the seat, a horrible feeling of foreboding crept over Maggie.

Wondering at the expressions he saw fleeting across Maggie's face, Zed continued. 'Haven't you heard? Clint's body was found in the woods last week.'

Maggie took a sharp intake of breath. *Dead? He was dead?*

'Burnt to cinders. Only identified by dental records.'

Feeling sicker than ever, Maggie shakily took another drag of the joint, noticing there wasn't much left and hoped Zed had more where that came from. She tried not to picture the blackened, charred corpse of what had once been Clint. The lovely looking, quiet Clint. *No! Don't think about it!*

'He'd been tied up and shot.'

'Who did it?' The words left Maggie's mouth before she could stop them.

'No trace at all,' Zed shrugged and looked straight at her. 'He'd obviously pissed someone off, but I expect it'll go down as unsolved.'

Maggie stared at her feet. *She* knew who'd done it. She didn't need to be told, nor did she need any evidence.

*Jesus Christ.*

• • • •

'DON'T WORRY ABOUT SETH,' Lee soothed, trying to placate Jane as she stormed around the kitchen.

'I'm not *worried* about him!' Jane snapped, shaking with rage. 'I'm pissed off with his fucking tantrums!' Locating the vodka bottle, she took a long slug and tossed a pill into her mouth.

'Yes, he does go a tad over the top sometimes!'

'Sometimes?'

'It's *you,* woman!' Lee laughed. 'I've known Seth for donkey's years and he hasn't been like this over any other bird. You're a bad influence!'

Jane scowled. 'Oh, so it's *my* fault as usual, is it?'

'Hey, come on,' Lee smiled, 'I was only joking!' Pulling her towards him and feeling her tense body, he stroked her hair. *Jeez, if he had a woman like her, he wouldn't be trying to drive her away. Quite the opposite…*

'It all gets too much sometimes,' she sniffed, the threat of more tears rising. As Lee pulled her into his chest, she felt herself relax for the first time all evening. It was nice to feel arms offering comfort for once.

It took a few moments to register through Jane's vodka-dulled mind that Lee had pressed his mouth down onto hers. She pulled away and stared at him in disbelief. 'What are you doing?'

'Come on girl!' Lee smiled, moving towards her mouth once more, his hand pushing roughly between her legs. 'Seth won't find out, besides he's a stroppy bastard. I won't give you grief.'

Jane pushed Lee away with revulsion. For God's sake! He was supposed to be one of Seth's friends! Why did people think they could do what the hell they wanted? Who did they think they were? For one stupid minute she'd actually thought he *cared* about her feelings, but he'd just wanted to get in her knickers. *Like everyone else.*

'I think you'd better go.'

Lee looked at Jane disparagingly and straightened his shirt. 'Suit yourself, you miserable bitch!'

• • • •

MAGGIE LAY BACK on the caravan bed and happily yielded as Zed gently thrust into her. She ran her hand down his back, enjoying the sensations flooding through her. Sensations she hadn't experienced for a long time. Feelings that made her feel wanted.

Slightly overwhelmed by the torrent of emotions rushing through her stoned brain, she began sobbing quietly.

Zed stopped, his grey eyes filled with concern. 'What's the matter? Don't you want to do this?'

Maggie looked into his worried face. Ok, so he wasn't the best-looking bloke in the world and his dreadlocks did honk a bit, but he was the first person in ages to treat her with any form of respect.

Panic began to overwhelm her. *What if he wanted to leave? She couldn't be on her own tonight.* 'No!' she cried quickly. 'I do want to!' Gripping Zed's buttocks, she pulled him deeper and tried to smile. 'I do want you, it's just...'

'Just *what,* babe?' Zed muttered, picking the pace back up.

'I-It's just that...' Maggie knew she shouldn't say it, but couldn't help herself. '...I think I love you.'

Zed tensed. *Holy God. He liked the wench, but only wanted a shag. He was into free love, not relationships!* Deciding that kissing her tenderly would save having to answer, he shrugged inwardly and got on with the job in hand.

Maggie took Zed's kiss as confirmation that he felt the same way as she did and a warm glow emanated from within her. Clinging onto him, she relaxed and began to move.

• • • •

'YOU'RE BACK THEN?' Jane slurred, glancing up from the television when Seth crashed drunkenly through the flat.

Not bothering to answer, he slumped in the armchair opposite and began messily rolling a joint.

'Don't think you need anymore!' she muttered hypocritically, having finished the bottle of vodka after Lee had left.

Seth eyes swivelled over but remained silent. *Wasn't she going to even bother asking where he'd been?* His fist clenched. 'Where's Lee or have you pissed him off too?'

With difficulty, he pushed himself out of the chair and staggered over to the television. 'Turn this shit off!'

Misjudging the distance between the power switch and his hand, he fell heavily against it and with sparks flying from the back of the unit, the television landed with a crash on the floor.

Jane raised her eyes towards the blood-splattered ceiling in frustration. 'Nice mates you've got,' she sneered, watching as Seth stumbled towards the chair.

'What's that supposed to mean?' Seth clumsily righted the coffee table he'd tipped over earlier. *Surely she could have picked that up, the lazy bitch?* Eyeing Jane suspiciously, he knew she was spoiling for a fight, but he'd now calmed down and didn't want another row.

Deciding not to give her a chance to answer and spoil his train of thought, he concentrated his mind in the hope he could still form an understandable sentence. 'Jane, I've been thinking.'

Jane couldn't even be arsed to look at him. Raising a can of lager, she tipped it into her mouth. What was he going to accuse her of now? Should she tell him about Lee?

Probably not. He'd go mad and she'd got to go to work in a couple of hours.

Having not elicited any response, Seth took Jane's silence to mean she was listening. 'I think we should try for another baby.'

Choking on the mouthful of lager she'd managed to get into her mouth, Jane spat it over the sofa. 'WHAT?'

'I thought you'd be pregnant again by now,' Seth slurred, disappointment audible in his voice.

Jane really didn't want to be having this conversation. *Was he crazy?* 'Seth, I'm on the Pill!'

'Well you were on the Pill last time, weren't you? Besides, I thought you weren't taking it anymore?'

'No,' she snapped. '*You* said I wasn't going to take it anymore.'

'But…'

'I don't want a baby, Seth. How many more times? *Look* at us, for God's sake!'

As Seth stared at her uncomprehendingly, Jane realised she had the perfect way to change the subject. 'By the way, your mate stuck his tongue down my throat earlier, but I told him to leave, ok?'

*There. She'd said it. That would get him off the baby conversation.*

'Come on, Jane. If you're trying to piss me off, surely you can do better than that?' Seth laughed.

Jane scowled. *Why was he laughing?* 'What?'

'Lee's my *mate*. He wouldn't do something like that! Grow up and stop lying!'

Getting out of the chair, Jane slammed the can on the table. 'You're fucking mental, Seth. The only person who's lying to you is *yourself*!'

Grabbing her cigarettes, she walked towards the door. 'Oh, and by the way, I mowed Debbie down tonight, but then I'm probably making that up for effect as well, right?'

'Whatever you say, Princess,' Seth chuckled, watching Jane stalk from the lounge.

## FORTY SEVEN

AT THE PARTY the music was at ear-blowing point and the walls reverberated with every beat of the AC/DC track that screeched from the stereo.

Stuart leant against a wall, pretending to be interested in the stupid tart gyrating in front of him and reached over to grab his can gingerly balancing on a small ledge. He glanced into the next room and seeing Seth, laughed to himself. Did the stupid bastard really think he was ok about being cut up? *If only he knew, the fucking idiot!*

Sneering, he watched Jane snort coke over the other side of the room and realised she hadn't even noticed him. The silly bitch was probably too off her head to focus. With a snide smile, he thought about the row he'd heard the previous night through the wall. Although it had stopped him getting any kip, it had given him a warm feeling to know that Seth and Jane's relationship was still well and truly fucked up.

He scowled. He'd been disappointed the raid he'd engineered hadn't resulted in getting them removed for the foreseeable future. He was even more pissed off that his car tinkering exploits hadn't had the desired effect either, but he hadn't finished yet.

To top it all, Paul was really pushing his fucking luck. The dickhead had risked everything by staggering around to his flat in a right mess after taking a kicking from Seth the other night. He'd started shrieking that Debbie was dead and that everything needed to stop.

For a start, he'd been less than amused that the gibbering fuckwit had turned up in the first place and as for Debbie, well he didn't give a flying fuck. He'd told Paul in no uncertain terms that he'd no intention of stopping *anything* for him or anyone else. Hoping no one was about, he'd dragged Paul from his flat and instructed him to stay the fuck out of his life from now on.

*Game over!*

Fixing his attention back to Eliza, Stuart suddenly realised this unexpected show of wantonness from Jane's horrible friend would do nicely as an entrée. He stared into her stoned eyes as she traced her finger down his chest and swung her lithe body suggestively.

He forced himself to smile, even though he couldn't stand the cheap slag. Her association with that hellion was enough to put anyone off, but fuck it. If it pissed Jane off then he'd happily screw the tramp.

Chucking a malevolent stare in Jane's direction, Stuart willed her to notice as he reached to touch Eliza's hair.

• • • •

MAGGIE MOVED HER eyes around the dimly-lit room, struggling to see who was there and felt uncomfortable from those she could see, let along the ones she couldn't.

Raising a bottle of beer to her mouth, she took a swig and sparked a fag up for something to do. She'd got completely off her head last night, but had *still* been unable to blank her mind. So much for Jane's pearls of wisdom of how to remove unwanted feelings. *It didn't bloody work!*

Maggie flinched as beer sloshed down her black leggings, thanks to a naked man covered in tomato sauce running past. Making chicken noises, he raised his hand in apology and she smiled weakly, trying not to question what he was doing.

Well so much for true love. Zed had buggered off and she hadn't heard or seen him since. She'd spent *all* day making excuses, but by kick out time at the Barrels with still no sign of him, she'd begun to think he'd binned her off.

Her eyes darted around the room again in the hope he'd arrived in the five seconds since she'd last looked, but he was still nowhere to be seen. She'd played last night back so many times in her head, she couldn't remember what was real and what wasn't any longer.

Jane swigged down another gulp of vodka and smiled, watching Eliza dancing drunkenly, but when Stuart's face became illuminated by a cigarette as the recipient of Eliza's attention, her smile froze. *What the fuck was she doing?*

'Hey, babe!' Maggie shouted as she walked over, causing Jane to almost drop her gold case of powder on the floor. 'Heard about Clint?'

'When's the funeral?' Jane muttered uninterestedly, her eyes fixed on Stuart, who was now staring directly at her while he kissed Eliza.

Maggie searched Jane's face for any tell-tale sign of involvement, but found none. 'Funeral? How did you know he was dead?'

'Funnily enough because I heard he was!' Jane hissed, her eyes narrowing. 'Why else?'

'Nothing,' Maggie mumbled and scurried away. *Maybe her gut feeling was wrong, but she doubted it somehow.*

• • • •

DESPITE HIS BETTER judgement, Stuart was enjoying himself immensely. The feel of a woman's flesh around him was a nice change from his hand. Even if it was this skanky whore. He was also getting off on the glowering snarl plastered across Jane's face.

'Harder!' Eliza shouted as she clung to Stuart's neck, trying to bite it.

Grimacing, Stuart moved his neck out of the way in the hope that the tart didn't get her rabies-infected molars into his flesh. He slammed into her harder and smiled. The tramp was totally off her tits and wondered whether he should get in a sheep dip after having his cock in it?

This idea was promptly forgotten when Jane made her way over.

'Jane! Hi!' Eliza yelled.

'I need a word with Stuart.'

'Can't it wait?' Eliza whined, grasping onto Stuart's buttocks.

'Not really, no.'

Disgruntled, Eliza hastily pulled her knickers up and tripped off unsteadily in the direction of the kitchen, while Stuart pushed himself back into his jeans, more than aware Jane's eyes were lingering on his exposed private parts.

'Dear, oh dear…' Jane sneered, her eyes travelling from Stuart's groin up to his face, which to her amusement had gone red.

'What the fuck do you want?'

Moving closer, she peered at the scars around his mouth that showed through his patchy beard. 'Listen, you cunt, I know it was you who fucked with my car.'

Stuart smirked sarcastically and leant back against the wall. 'I don't know what you mean?'

'Oh yes you do!'

Moving forward, Stuart grinned. 'Think what you like, but you can prove *nothing*, bitch.'

Jane felt rage bubbling. What she wouldn't give to blow this fucker's face off at point blank range.

'Doesn't appear anyone else thinks the same as you though, does it?' Stuart glanced in Seth's direction. 'Even Lover Boy thinks you're fucking unhinged!'

'I don't give a shit who thinks what! I know what I know,' Jane glowered and pointedly took a swig out of her vodka bottle. She stared at Stuart with level eyes. 'AND I'll repay you fourfold.'

'Are you threatening me?' he laughed, slowly blowing smoke into Jane's face, proud that so far he'd resisted the urge to smash the bottle into her teeth.

'No, you piece of shit. I'm *promising* you.' Jane turned to walk away, but Stuart grabbed her arm. She swung around, her eyes blazing. 'Don't touch me!'

'I was just going to say how very sorry I was to hear you lost the baby.' Stuart's cold voice dripped with sarcasm and his eyes danced seeing pain jolt behind Jane's eyes. 'At least that's one less genetic fuck up the world has to deal with!'

Jane smacked him hard around the face. 'You bastard.'

Forcing herself to stalk away from Stuart, she felt Seth's eyes burning into her from the other side of the room.

· · · ·

JANE STOMPED INTO the garden. She needed some air. She couldn't believe Seth had whacked the guy she'd been talking to.

Leaning up against the cool brickwork, she was thankful no one else was around and took several deep breaths of cold night air in a bid to slow down her thumping heart and raging anger. As for him accusing her of fancying Stuart - if anything could have insulted her more, she didn't know what it would be.

She was so preoccupied, she didn't notice anyone approaching until a hand was around her throat.

'Listen, hell cat,' Stuart hissed, his face inches from Jane's as he pinned her to the wall. 'Don't *ever* try to humiliate me again!'

Jane didn't flinch, just stared defiantly into his face. 'Get the fuck off me!' She gripped at Stuart's hands around her neck which were beginning to hurt. 'I know what you are, even if no one else does,' she hissed through clenched teeth.

As Stuart applied more pressure, Jane hawked and spat into his face. In shock, he released his grip and raised his fist.

Jane stood unmoving. *Let him hit her. That way everyone would see him as she saw him. Bring it on.*

'What the fuck are you doing?' Digger roared, pulling Stuart backwards by his collar and slamming him against the wall. 'Well?' he snarled, baring his teeth.

'She needs a fucking slap the nasty little…'

'That's ENOUGH!' Digger screamed, his voice hoarse. He didn't like this dickhead at the best of times, but *really* disliked him right now, the greasy skinny little shit.

'It's ok, Dig.' Jane smoothed down her hair and smiled sweetly. Only her eyes showed the hatred she felt. 'Stuart and I disagree on a lot of things, but I think he'd just decided to leave, hadn't you?'

Glaring, Stuart yanked his collar down and tried to rid himself of Digger's grip, his face a mask of rage. 'You bitch!'

Digger released his grip and jutted his bull-head forwards menacingly. 'Fuck off out of here then, you cunt!'

Smiling sardonically, Jane laughed in Stuart's face, knowing full well he'd take it up the arse and leave.

• • • •

SETH GLANCED AT his knuckles, seeing that silly fucker's teeth had cut them. Scowling, he wiped his bleeding hand down his jeans and stared dispassionately at the man who'd gone down like a sack of spuds. If the prick had wanted to keep his front teeth, he shouldn't have been talking to Jane, should he?

*She was his wife. No one else's.*

He'd been happy to finally get away from the bloke in leopard-skin spandex who had been trying to wrap a python around his neck. He'd been leaning against the wall, wondering why he kept getting accosted by weirdos and it had only been then that he'd noticed Jane with Stuart.

He snarled inwardly. All this time she'd banged on, accusing him of all sorts and it was because she wanted *Stuart*, wasn't it? It explained her obsession. Pretending she hated him, indeed? There was *no way* she'd be so obsessed with the man unless they had a thing going. She'd probably only whacked him around the face to try and cause a diversion from what she really had planned.

He was sick to death of it. Sick to death of Jane taking the fucking piss. What the fuck was wrong with her? Why was she trying to turn him against all his friends? Did she just not want him to have any?

She'd then moved on to a group of freaks who'd been lying on the floor, Seth's teeth clenched. *She'd been fucking laughing at him, hadn't she?*

When he'd gone over, she'd seemed to prefer to continue talking to that bloke amongst those weirdos rather than listen to anything he'd got to say, so he'd had no choice but to sort it. *People just didn't learn.*

The vein in his temple throbbed, his mood getting worse by the second and he snorted angrily.

Squinting harder he ground the joint out on the carpet and pushed himself away from the wall. Even after making his point clear she'd gone and done it again. He couldn't see her anywhere.

Several people were staring at him and he sighed, clenching his jaw tightly. He'd find Jane first and have it out with her before even thinking about sorting them out.

'JANE?' Seth roared over the music and roughly pushing someone out of way, clumsily stumbled from the room.

• • • •

'WHAT IS THAT FUCKWIT'S problem?' Digger muttered.

'Me and Stuart don't like each other,' Jane said quietly. She was feeling drunk now the adrenalin was wearing off as well as thoroughly exhausted from the constant stress and grief that followed her around. 'Seth's now accused me of having a thing with Stuart!'

'Oh, you know what he's like!' Digger smiled. 'You should have stayed with me.'

Jane laughed, despite her annoyance. 'Maybe I should have.' Swaying slightly, she stumbled towards the wall, realising she needed the boost of some more coke because the vodka was fast catching up with her.

'Whoa!' Digger caught Jane before she tripped into the wall and pulled her into his barrel chest. 'You know I didn't like what that twat was doing to you just then.'

'Oh, don't worry about him,' she smiled up into Digger's stern face as he wrapped his arms around her. 'I'm tougher than I look and let's face it, I'm used to it!'

He guffawed. A big belly laugh that vibrated through her. 'I know for a fact you are!' Digger's face washed with concern. 'But you shouldn't have to be used to it.'

Unable to help himself, he gently brushed his lips against hers. *It was no good. He wanted her. Fuck Seth.*

The combination of vodka, coupled with strong arms around her was too tempting. Winding her arms around Digger's thick neck, Jane raised her face towards his and as he brought his mouth down fully onto hers, neither of them noticed Seth leaning against the doorway.

• • • •

'JANE!' ELIZA SHOUTED. '*JANE*!'

Digger was frantically unbuttoning his jeans, his cock desperate to be inside Jane when she suddenly pulled away from him.

Jane tugged her tight black top down over her exposed breasts and angrily turned towards Eliza. 'WHAT?'

'You need to sort this out,' Eliza yelled. 'It's Seth, he's gone off on one again!'

Jane glanced apologetically at Digger before taking off back into the house.

'Seth, always Seth!' Digger muttered to himself, his balls aching.

Eliza glanced over her shoulder as they rushed up the hallway. 'He threw some stuff around and stormed out. I tried to stop him…'

Jane sighed and stumbled out the front door, the glare of the streetlights hitting her full bore in the eyes. Staggering along the driveway, she squinted up and down the road but could see nothing.

Maggie and Eliza watched Jane from the doorway. 'Just let him get on with it!' Eliza shouted.

Maggie sighed. She couldn't be doing with this. She didn't want to be here anyway and shouldn't have come. That was it. She was leaving.

Hearing a horrible screeching of tyres, she swung her head around just in time to see a car lurch around the corner, its headlights on full beam amid a plume of smoke and exhaust fumes.

Before she had chance to register what was going on, the car sped at a breakneck pace along the road straight towards Jane. 'JANE!' Maggie screamed at the top of her lungs, whilst Eliza ran down the driveway.

Seth gripped the steering wheel, his bleeding knuckles white as he bombed down the road. His eyes were fixed on Jane who was conveniently illuminated in the blinding headlights of the Senator.

He'd had enough. She'd taken liberties one time too many and it was game over. First that shit with Stuart and now Digger. Digger was supposed to be his friend, for fuck's sake. In fact, what she'd said about Lee the other night was probably true as well.

Everyone was taking the piss out of him. *Everyone*. And *she* was the common denominator. Well it all stops here, he thought, fixing his glare on the figure in front of him.

Pushing his foot down harder on the accelerator, the smell of burning rubber from his tyres made his eyes water. 'No one else is having you, Jane!' he screamed as the car mounted the kerb.

## FORTY EIGHT

SETH WIPED THE SWEAT from his brow as he slumped heavily into the driver's seat, grateful that was the last lot. Dodge would pay for doing this to him, but first he was going home to see if Jane had turned up. If she hadn't, then rest assured, he'd find her.

Squinting against the sun streaming through the windscreen, he felt like crap. As well as the raging hangover, he hadn't got to bed last night because of her and then he'd had to move this fucking gear.

He'd been in a bad enough mood returning from that party without finding the flat's entrance piled sky high with all the stuff from Dodge's lock up.

The fucking stupid, *stupid* bastard. The silly cunt had left bags of coke, guns and God knows what else, in full view of all and sundry.

Pushing his Beretta under the seat, Seth turned the key in the ignition. He'd be blowing Jane's fucking head off with that if he found out she'd been with some bloke instead of coming home to him.

He pursed his lips, finding it hard to believe that he'd overreacted about both Digger *and* Stuart.

Digger had looked hurt when he'd cornered him this morning and questioned him over what he'd seen last night. Digger had been *adamant* what he thought he'd seen was wrong. He'd said that he'd been *hugging* Jane, not kissing her and he must have misread it if he'd thought otherwise. He was his *friend* after all, he'd explained.

Seth wasn't sure. It hadn't looked that way to him, but admittedly the night was a bit of a blur. He frowned, *sure* Digger had been kissing Jane. *Was he was going mad?*

Then he'd been filled in about what Stuart had said and done, so it looked like he'd got the wrong end of the stick over that situation too, which meant that was something *else* he'd have to rectify. *Again.*

Pushing his foot to the floor, Seth roared back towards the flat. He could do with getting in a couple of hours kip before they went out tonight. *That's if Jane turned up, of course.*

• • • •

SETH WATCHED JANE walk into the lounge and shrug her leather jacket off. 'Where have you been?' he asked, eyeing her suspiciously.

'Do you ever ask anything else?' Jane snapped, feeling a strong urge to knock the whisky bottle out of Seth's hand.

Propping himself up on his elbows on the mattress in the middle of the floor, naked apart from a sheet draped across his waist, Seth eyed Jane, his green eyes piercing. 'Ok, I'll make it easy for you. Who did you fuck last night, because it wasn't me!'

Despite his intentions to smooth things over after his spate of apparently jumping to the wrong conclusions, he was unable to stop the diatribe of accusations from spewing out of his mouth.

Instantly enraged, Jane swung around to face him. Stripping off last night's clothes, she threw them onto the floor in a messy pile. 'You mean apart from that wanker, Stuart, who, according to you, I'm having an affair with? Or perhaps Clint again?' She glared at him. 'Oh, wait! It couldn't be him, being as you've already offloaded him!'

She sighed. She wasn't going to mention Digger. Ok, so he'd been a close shave, but Seth was like a stuck record. On and on and fucking *ON*. What did he expect in the end? Being as he was so hell bent on assuming the worst, she wasn't about to make him feel better by telling him she'd stayed at Eliza's. He probably wouldn't believe her anyway.

Reaching for a bottle of vodka, Jane chucked a couple of heavy-duty painkillers into her mouth. She'd taken loads already, but still felt like shit, so therefore a few more wouldn't hurt.

Her eyes narrowed. 'Let's get this straight. *You* try to kill me and now you're asking me why I didn't come back and who I've been shagging?'

'For a start I didn't try to kill you and yes, that's about the extent of it.'

Jane looked at him incredulously. 'You tried to run me over, for God's sake!'

Seth tried not to laugh. He'd completely forgotten about that, but now she'd said it, he remembered. He hadn't planned it. She'd just been standing by the road and it had been too much of a good opportunity to pass over.

For fuck's sake, he couldn't even remember driving home, so how could she expect him to remember every other detail? 'Alright, but where've you been the rest of the time?'

'Fuck you!' Jane screamed, launching a book. Sailing across the room, the corner of the spine hit Seth squarely on the cheekbone.

Yelling in shock, he flew off the mattress. Gathering Jane's clothes and boots, he stamped angrily to the window and threw the pile onto the street below.

'What the hell are you doing?' Jane screeched, whilst Seth dragged her down the hallway by her arm.

Opening the front door, Seth shoved her outside. 'Off you go! Now you won't have to bother taking your kit off when you next see whoever you're fucking behind my back, will you!' he roared, slamming the door in her face.

• • • •

JANE SLOUCHED AGAINST the sticky seat in the Barrels. She hadn't been happy having to get dressed in the high street in full view of what seemed like half the town, but now she was almost at the point where she was incapable of thinking, thanks to the non-stop amount of spirits and pills she'd poured down her throat, nothing mattered.

She didn't care that the flashing strobe lights were hurting her eyes either and was just grateful the volume of the music removed the need to talk to anyone. *All she was interested in was oblivion. She'd had enough.*

'Are you sure you're ok, babe?' Maggie asked for the four hundredth time as she placed her hand on Jane's arm.

Nodding, Jane kept her gaze fixed on the hypnotic swirling flashing lights and robotically moved her arm away from Maggie's touch, hoping she'd get the hint and sit somewhere else. Her head was in a dark, strange place and despite trying to quell her rage, her mood was worsening.

Shoving another pill in her mouth, she shook the bottle, dismayed to see only a few left. All she could see in her mind's eye was blackness and anger for everything and everyone and she knew she was spinning out of control.

Should she go back to the flat? No, she'd drive somewhere. It didn't matter where and would keep driving until all of this shit had stopped and she wasn't angry anymore.

*Until it was over.*

Watching Eliza staggering towards her with a wide grin and her drink spilling down her black fishnet tights, Jane sighed. *Would no one leave her alone?*

• • • •

SETH WALKED SLOWLY up the road towards the Barrels. 'Jane reckons she's not going ahead with the wedding,' he muttered savagely. 'Said she'd rather be dead.'

Digger sighed, having heard it all before. 'Why don't you two just sort things out?' he snapped impatiently. 'Either that, or go your separate ways?'

Seth stopped and glared drunkenly at Digger. 'Separate ways?' His eyes narrowed suspiciously. *Was this a plan so Digger could step into his shoes? Had he been right about what he'd thought he'd seen, after all?* He put his hands into his deep pockets. 'Why would we want to do that?'

'I meant if you're both unhappy, then call it a day?'

'I'm not unhappy!' Seth hissed, his eyes flashing menacingly. *Well, he wasn't. He'd be unhappier without her.* 'Do you think Jane's unhappy? Are you saying I'm making her unhappy?'

Digger fidgeted uncomfortably. *There was no reasoning with this guy.* 'No, you said she wanted to call the wedding off.' He decided to backtrack and say something useful. 'Besides, why are you getting married again anyway?' *Let her go so I can have her. I'd treat her better than you,* he thought resentfully.

'Oh, this is just the church one. You know, the legal stuff,' Seth muttered, waving his hand dismissively. 'You know I don't want to be with anyone else,' he said quietly. 'I love her.'

'I know you do, mate,' Digger put his hand on Seth's shoulder, suddenly feeling guilty yet again for his overwhelming feelings for Jane. 'You need to sort out this anger issue, though.' He hesitated. 'And your paranoia. It makes you kind of mad.'

Seth carefully scrutinised Digger. 'I can't help it. Besides, Jane's just as bad.'

Digger laughed. 'Well, I won't argue with that. You're both pretty fucking mental, truth be known.'

'Come on. Let's just get in there,' Seth smiled and took the steps to the Barrels two at a time. Giving Spooner a friendly slap on the back, he jumped the queue.

• • • •

SETH HELD JANE UP against the wall in the toilets. 'Let's fuck it all away, baby.'

Jane's brain was rolling. She'd no idea where Seth had come from or how he'd got her into wherever she was. All she could see was ten copies of him. Her head lolled to one side and she shook it in an attempt to clear it.

Tonight the pills had even managed to overshadow the effects of the coke, however her body still worked, even if her mind didn't. Somewhere through the fog of narcotics and alcohol the stirrings of an orgasm rose.

'You and me, baby. You and me,' Seth groaned, his pace relentless.

Millions of tiny coloured stars danced in the blackness of her mind as the multiple world in front of her eyes rotated on its axis. A flashback from the annals of time popped into her head from when they'd been doing just this many moons ago.

It wasn't like that anymore. *Nothing* was like that anymore and she wanted it to be. *Needed* it to be. She wanted to be back in that other universe where everything was shiny, happy and new. When it was pretty.

*Alive.*

· · · ·

DIGGER LAY BACK in his bed and stared at the ceiling. He felt like shit for betraying Seth again, but felt even worse now he knew for certain he wasn't going to get Jane back under any circumstances.

When she'd knocked on his door earlier, he'd hoped she'd finally come to her senses and left Seth. He'd glanced around for a suitcase, but there had been nothing.

She'd been totally off her head and in all the years he'd known her, he hadn't *ever* seen her that wasted. When he'd finally sat her down and fetched her a vodka, she was still popping pills like they were Smarties. *She'd worried him.*

Running a hand over his head, Digger sighed. He shouldn't have done it, he knew that. Jane had been in no fit state, but he hadn't been able to help himself. He so desperately wanted her, but not only had he done her wrong, he'd also completely humiliated himself.

Leaning over to grab his cigarettes from the bedside table, he cringed. When Jane had responded to his kisses, he'd wasted no time in getting her clothes off, but he'd only succeeding in making a prize fool of himself. He'd wanted to make love to her, but she'd only wanted hard and frenzied fucking.

Involuntarily covering his face with his hands in embarrassment, he could have strangled himself. He'd begged, yes *begged*, Jane to leave Seth and be with him instead. He'd then told her how much he loved her. And then even worse - he'd asked her to *marry* him.

Digger groaned. Ok, so it was true. It's what he wanted, but he should have just kept it to himself.

Jane had looked at him in a strange unfocused way, but instead of taking the hint, he'd kept on. *'I'm in love with you for God's sake, Jane. I need you. Marry me!'*

Jane had staggered off the bed, crashing into the bedside table. 'Didn't realise you felt that strong, Digs,' she'd slurred. 'Sorry babe, but I'm with Seth - you know that and that isn't going to change. I need to go. I shouldn't be here.' Picking her knickers off his bedroom floor, she'd lurched from the house.

He hadn't been able to let her walk around in that state, so he'd run after her, but before he'd been able to stop her, she'd flagged a car down and jumped in.

He wished to God she'd agreed to what he'd asked. The aftermath with Seth wouldn't have been pretty, but it would have been worth it to get her back. Now he'd probably ruined a perfectly good friendship because he couldn't keep his feelings to himself.

Digger sighed. With any luck Jane might not remember what he'd said.

• • • •

'WHERE THE FUCK have you been?' Seth screamed as Jane fell through the front door. Spotting her knickers in her hand as she staggered up the hallway, his teeth felt like they were going to snap.

Suddenly noticing a man standing at the bottom of the steps out of the corner of his eye, he rushed towards the short, greasy guy shifting from foot to foot uneasily. 'And who the hell are you?' he roared, grabbing the man savagely by the collar. 'Have you been fucking my wife?'

'No. No!' the man squeaked. 'She flagged me down! I gave her a lift, that's all.'

'A *lift*?' Seth stared at him, his eyes rabid. 'Where from?'

'I-I don't know. Some house out of town. I don't know whose. I just brought her here. I didn't kn…'

'Why would you have agreed to that, unless you were intending to get some?' Seth yelled.

'B-Because she asked me to drop her here an…'

'You didn't know *I* was here, you mean?' Seth raged, furiously. 'DID YOU TOUCH HER?'

'No. No, I…'

'I don't believe you, so shut the fuck up.' Seth crashed his head down onto the man's nose.

Screaming in pain and shock, the man scrabbled around in an attempt to get out of Seth's grip, while punch after punch rained down onto his head.

Somehow resisting the urge to crush the bloke into the concrete, Seth dragged the bloodied man across the courtyard to the stairway and then launched him down the dark steps. Hearing the man thud to the ground out of his view, he wiped his hands down his jeans and quickly stalked back inside the flat.

Jane swayed unsteadily against the kitchen work surface thankful there were more pills in here she could take. Clumsily unscrewing the vodka, she tipped it into her mouth.

'I don't believe this!' Seth raged, stomping into the kitchen. 'What the fuck have you been doing? Who was that man and why did you disappear when the Barrels kicked out?'

He'd thought things were ok again between them, but then she'd fucked off and now *this*. Seth scowled, contempt written over his face. He wanted to smash her head in. 'Look at the fucking state of you! What the fuck are you on?'

Jane laughed and shrugged her shoulders, spilling vodka down her front. *She'd no idea where she'd been, or who with.*

*She didn't care anymore and just wanted to go to sleep.* 'Fuck off and leave me alone,' she slurred, unscrewing the bottle of pills.

'I'll leave you alone alright, you bitch!' Seth turned away, too angry to deal with her right now. 'I'm going to bed.'

## FORTY NINE

CLINGING ONTO THE metal rail, Seth feared his legs would collapse from under him. Alternating waves of nausea and freezing cold rushed up and down his body like moving stripes. *This couldn't be happening.*

'We're losing her. Give me some power.'

The machine sprang to life, beeping loudly and Seth's heart lurched, seeing Jane's top being ripped open, exposing her breasts. He grabbed the paramedic's arm kneeling at the side of the stretcher. 'DO SOMETHING!'

'Sir, calm down. That's what we're trying to do!' Yanking Seth's arm away, the paramedic continued to line the flat plates of the defibrillator above Jane's chest.

'CLEAR!'

There was a loud crack as the electric current rushed into Jane's heart, her whole body jerking stiffly. The paramedics eyed the monitor, the line flat and the tone static. The dial was turned, raising the electrical charge further. 'CLEAR!'

The machine continuing its unbroken whining.

'Come on, Jane! Fucking *come on*! Don't you *dare* leave me!' Seth gulped in large mouthfuls of air to stop himself hyperventilating. 'BRING HER BACK!'

'Sir! *Please!* Step back!'

Sitting down heavily on the stretcher opposite, Seth put his head in his hands. 'Don't leave me,' he whispered again whilst Jane lay grey and lifeless on the stretcher. Her makeup was smudged and her hair matted. *He'd give anything to take her into his arms and bring her back to life.*

He could no longer look as the defibrillator delivered another electric shock into Jane's still body and his eyes darted around the interior of the ambulance parked out the back of the flats. Why weren't they taking her to hospital? Why were they still sitting on the side of the fucking road?

*What was he going to do? This was his fault.* If he'd paid more attention, she'd be alright, but now she was fucking dead.

He'd always been able to sort things one way or another, but he couldn't sort this out, could he? The only thing he wanted and he could do *fuck all.*

Seth wiped the thick film of sweat off his forehead. *Why the hell hadn't he noticed?*

Getting up halfway through the night, he'd been angry to find Jane lying on the bedroom floor in front of the portable gas fire. Picking her up, he'd thrown her roughly onto the bed in her soaking wet clothes and had thought no more about it. He hadn't even taken any notice this morning when she was still flat out, he'd just stomped into the kitchen to find a drink.

Waiting impatiently for the kettle to boil, he'd glowered at the mess she'd left. *Why couldn't she bloody well tidy up?*

As he'd scanned the empty bottles and blister packs of tablets on the work surface, a horrible sense of dread had run through him. Rifling through Jane's handbag, he'd found another empty bottle. Throwing them to one side, he'd raced back into the bedroom and tried to shake her. *Nothing.*

He'd shouted her name to get a response, but there was still nothing. If she'd been breathing, it had been so shallow he hadn't been able to hear it. Trying not to panic, he'd pulled on his jeans and raced bare-chested down the road to the phone box.

Finally the paramedics had rushed into the flat and worked

on Jane unsuccessfully for what seemed like years and then they'd taken her by stretcher to the ambulance.

Snapped back into the here and now by the silent atmosphere, Seth looked frantically from one paramedic to the other. Why wasn't anyone telling him anything? Was Jane dead? He had the right to know for fuck's sake.

'WHAT'S GOING ON?' he roared, grabbing one of the paramedics.

'Shh!' the paramedic hissed, glaring at Seth. Angrily pulling his arm away, he desperately tried to insert a line into a vein on Jane's arm. 'Her veins have collapsed,' he muttered, 'I can't get the needle in.'

Seth felt his mind racing, getting faster and faster like a roundabout. *Fuck. FUCK!*

Eventually getting the needle into a vein, the paramedic breathed an audible sigh of relief. He attached a drip bag and hooked it to a clip above and the monitor started beeping. 'We've got a heartbeat.'

Seth slumped back on the seat, relief washing over him. Fresh tears spilled down his face as he pulled his cigarettes from his pocket. 'So, she's ok?'

The paramedic smiled grimly. 'Not necessarily. We need to get her to hospital.'

'I'm coming with you,' Seth said quickly.

'I thought you might be,' he muttered. 'Hey! You can't smoke in here!'

Seth took the fag out of his mouth. *His brain wasn't working.* 'Sorry. Sorry.'

• • • •

THERE WAS NO SIGN of life from Jane the entire way to hospital and Seth perched at the side of the stretcher refusing to let go of her hand. The machine monitoring her heart was keeping up a steady beeping, the green lines peaking and troughing on the monitor.

'You scared me, baby,' a weak smile played at the corner of

his mouth. 'Don't be doing that again.'

The paramedic rolled his eyes. He was sick of people like this. Looking at the woman lying motionless in front of him, he grimaced. Pretty young thing as well. Wasting her life on drugs and all that sort of shit.

Glancing at the blood sample readings, his eyes widened and he silently wondered how this one had managed to get through the night. 'If I can take some details, Sir?'

Seth gave the information as clearly as he could. His mind was that scrambled, he struggled to remember what his own name was, let alone all of Jane's details.

'Has she taken an overdose before, Sir?'

Seth stared at him blankly. 'She hasn't taken an overdose. She must have just lost track of how many pills she'd had.'

The paramedic raised his eyebrows, noticing the strong smell of alcohol emanating from the long-haired man. 'She must have *seriously* lost track to have readings like this!'

Seth felt slightly irritated. *Was this dick calling him a fucking liar?* He tried to calm himself down. Punching the guy who'd just brought Jane back from the dead wouldn't have been his finest moment.

'Listen, she wouldn't have *purposefully* taken an overdose,' he kept his voice level. 'We erm, sometimes take quite a few pills.'

The paramedic eyed Seth suspiciously and scribbled on the paperwork. *Obviously a pair of druggies. The guy looked like he'd got a sandwich short of a picnic as it was.*

'Next of kin?' he glanced back at Seth who looked up puzzled. 'Jane's next of kin, Sir?'

'Well, it's *me*, isn't it?'

'Your *name*, Sir?' The paramedic was starting to lose patience with this bonehead.

'Wright. Seth Wright.'

• • • •

JANE'S CONSCIOUSNESS flew down spiralled multi-coloured

corridors of an undetermined shape and a loud thrumming noise ran in the background. She wanted to open her eyes, but couldn't because they didn't work. She could hear a voice which sounded like Seth's and she felt hideous, but strangely calm. She was floating and it was quite nice, apart from her mouth felt it was stuffed full of wet, stringy cotton wool.

'We can't do anything else, Sir,' a voice said.

*Whose voice was that?* Jane thought. Who were they talking about? Probably someone who'd wandered into the flat during the night. She decided this was another good reason not to open her eyes so she didn't have to look at the collection of drongos lying on the floor around her bed. *Why couldn't Seth lock the bloody door?*

'But if you pumped her stomach?'

*Seth, who are you talking to?* Jane asked silently having no energy to form words out loud. Her mind was a total and utter blank. *Had she even been to sleep?*

The flashes and sparks from the kaleidoscopic corridor continued and she wished they'd stop. It was starting to make her feel sick and something was squeezing her arm really hard. *What the fuck was it?*

'Like I said Sir, the pills have been in her system all night. There's nothing to pump.'

'Blood pressure's still sky high,' the nurse muttered.

Jane felt panic stirring. Something was wrong and she wished someone would let her into the conversation.

'It's a case of seeing if her liver will cope, but the threat of failure will stay for some time. A few weeks, but especially over the next few days.'

Jane had had enough. She didn't know what the hell was going on, but she intended to find out.

• • • •

SETH WAS GLAD WHEN the doctors finally left them alone. Sitting back in the plastic chair, he fidgeted and wondered what to do with his legs.

Wedging one boot across his knee, he perched on the edge of the chair uncomfortably and wiped his face with his grubby T-shirt, suspecting he looked even worse than he felt.

The relief Jane was alive was replaced with a weird sense of anger at the thought that she should have died. *He'd* put her in bed and if she'd died, he'd have woken up next to her corpse. He didn't give a shit about dead bodies, but he did if it was *hers*.

Feeling a strong urge to punch her, he instead angrily slammed his fist on the table next to the bed, feeling totally and utterly impotent. *He needed a drink.*

A nursed poked her head around the shiny blue plastic curtain surrounding Jane's cubicle and smiled benevolently. 'Everything ok?'

'Yeah,' Seth nodded, his face glowering with pent up rage and waited silently for her to leave. He listened as the nurse's footsteps faded away on the tiled floor. 'Jane,' he hissed through clenched teeth. 'Why the fuck did you take so much shit?'

Jane listened to Seth muttering. Was he having a go at her? Couldn't he at least wait until she'd properly woken up? She was far too tired to have an argument.

Twisting her body slightly, she wished she'd got a drink of something as her tongue appeared to be glued to the top of her mouth. What time was it? They'd have to get up soon surely? Christ! She must have put away a fair bit away last night to feel this rough!

Involuntarily she reached over, but could only feel metal. 'Seth?'

'You're awake then?' Stroking Jane's face, Seth brushed her cheek with his lips. '*Please* don't do that to me again.'

Jane was confused. *What was she supposed to have done now?* Finally finding the energy to force her eyes open, Seth slowly came into focus, before she was blinded by the glaring light of fluorescent strip lights. *What the fuck?*

'You're in hospital…'

An expression of shock flashed over Jane's face and she attempted to sit bolt upright, stopping mid-way as a crushing pain seared though her skull. Raising her hand to her head, she stopped in her tracks. *Hospital?*

'You took too many pills.'

Jane frowned. Had she? She couldn't remember what the hell she'd taken. She couldn't remember anything.

'I thought you were going to die.'

Jane watched a single tear run down Seth's cheek. 'Don't be silly,' she slurred, trying to make light of the situation. 'I need a drink. Can you get me a can of something? Is there a machine around here?'

• • • •

WITH A SOUR EXPRESSION on his face, Seth walked down the corridor back towards Jane's cubicle, holding a can of Lilt. He hated vending machines at the best of times, but this one had been laughing at him. Not only had it been five corridors away, but it had also filched his last twenty pence.

He'd resolved this by tipping it at a forty-five degree angle then dropping it heavily back to the floor, where it had delivered the can, plus a bag of Minstrels and four quid in change.

Sighing loudly, Seth pulled open the curtain and stepped inside. 'Bloody machine, if…' *Jane had gone. Oh, for God's sake!*

Turning on his heels, he rushed back out of the room. He'd got a fairly good idea where she'd disappeared to.

Jane snatched her arm away when Seth caught up with her. 'Why didn't you wait?' he hissed.

'No time, no time…' Jane muttered, stumbling down the corridor.

'Miss Ellerton?' The doctor followed the two figures. '*Miss Ellerton!*'

Jane ignored the voice from behind. It sounded like it was underwater, echoing and bouncing off the walls. It was putting her off concentrating on staying upright and the sides of the corridor closed in, like a fish-eye lens, making her feel sea-sick.

'MISS ELLERTON!'

Jane's face contorted into a frown. *Ignore him. Just ignore him...* It couldn't be much further before she was outside. *Did she have a car here? Never mind, she'd just get a taxi.*

She needed to leave and didn't care how she achieved it. If she stopped she'd pass out, collapse or not be able to get going again and she couldn't risk *any* of those things happening. She continued walking, her legs feeling more rubbery with each step.

• • • •

SETH WATCHED JANE as she stared vacantly out of the window from the back of the taxi. Her bare legs and feet were white with cold and her small leather skirt wasn't doing much to keep out the weather.

He'd spoken to the quack himself, telling him Jane was discharging herself.

*Yes, he knew it wasn't a good idea.*

*Yes, he knew she could keel over at any time.*

*Yes, he'd take responsibility for her and of course he'd bring her back the minute anything didn't look right.*

*Yes. Yes. Yes.*

Seth rolled his eyes, knowing he'd have no chance of getting her back in hospital whatever happened. *Not unless she was dead.*

Staring at the back of the taxi driver's head, Seth willed him to drive faster. He placed his arm loosely around Jane's shoulders. 'Are you ok?'

There was a long pause as Jane's brain caught up with Seth's question. 'Yeah, great.'

Seth clenched his jaw. *She didn't need to be fucking sarcastic.*

'What time is it?'

'3.'

'3?' Jane turned to face Seth, her eyes bloodshot, the pupils dilated like saucers. *She was still well gone.* 'We need to hurry up,' she slurred. 'There's a band on down the Barrels tonight that I want to see.'

'I THINK YOU should lay off things a bit,' Seth snapped, watching Jane top up her vodka.

Jane rolled her eyes. 'Oh, for God's sake, it's been two weeks. We were getting pissed the same day I got out of hospital remember?' Taking a swig she stared at him impassively. 'On a different subject, I take it you've let Stuart get away with trying to fuck us over?'

Seth grimaced. Jane had been nagging him about why he hadn't done anything for weeks and he was sick of it. He knew he'd have to do something, but he'd had other things on his mind lately. *Like her.*

There were a few people he wanted to pay a visit to and Stuart was most *definitely* one of them, but it would be on *his* terms, not Jane's. Couldn't she see it was bad enough having to accept people that he'd thought were friends, weren't, without her reminding him constantly?

Jane lit a cigarette. 'Don't you care that everyone's mugging you off?'

Draining his can, Seth placed the empty tin loudly on the coffee table and looked at her, wishing she'd just shut up. Sick of being treated like a twat, he raised his eyes to the ceiling and concentrated on a damp patch.

All those wankers Jane had shagged behind his back - like that cock sucker Owen, who'd thought he'd stood a chance. Coming in the chippy bold as brass with her on his arm. He'd only let that one go because he'd needed to sort things out with her.

Then there was that Clint prick and they were just the ones *he* knew about. Furthermore, he'd never believed there wasn't something going on with that Shav cunt either. Seth grated his teeth. Not that he'd since him since.

As for Paul, well he'd got a score to settle with him too and he'd pull that one in soon. *The hard truth was that none of them were mates.*

In fact, Seth didn't actually think he'd even got any anymore. Dodge turning him over and then Lee taking the fucking piss. *That's if what Jane said was true.*

He'd also more than clocked the way Digger looked at her. Then there were the things he was sure had happened, plus some things he'd said recently made him think that he really might be trying to get him out of the way. Phil was probably waiting for his turn too.

Seth scowled. They all tried to make out it was *his* paranoia, but he just wasn't sure anymore and it was making him angrier and more resentful by the day. He cracked his knuckles in frustration. He wanted to kill the fucking lot of them, truth be known and as for Stuart...

'You don't give a toss that bastard tried to kill us, do you?' Jane's voice rose. 'Or that he started on me at that party.'

Seth's eyes fixed straight ahead. *Yes, he did care. How many more times?*

'*Or* what he said about the baby?'

Seth's teeth clenched.

'At least Digger told him where to get off, unlike *you*!' Jane was pushing her luck and she knew it, but that wasn't going to stop her. She was on a roll. 'At least he's a *proper* man!'

'FOR FUCK'S SAKE, JANE!' Seth roared, kicking the

table over. He jumped to his feet. 'I've *told* you I'll deal with Stuart, but in MY time, NOT yours!'

Jane squared up to him. *She'd get Stuart finished, if it was the last thing she did.* 'If you're not bothered, then you obviously don't love me...'

*Oh that was a cheap trick*, Seth thought. If Jane didn't know how much he loved her by now, she never would. Walking off into the kitchen, he pulled another beer out of the fridge and cracked it open angrily.

• • • •

'I'D BEST MAKE TRACKS,' Digger winked, bending down and kissing Jane on the cheek.

Seth felt a fission of uncertainty run through him. When Digger had turned up, he'd been so jovial he'd questioned his own logic about his rising suspicions, but he'd managed to convince himself that it *was* his paranoia. At least, in *this* case and he wanted it to stay that way.

Aside from everything else, Digger had been a much-needed diversion by popping by on his way to an escort job and interrupting their escalating argument, so at least that was something to be thankful for. His presence and easy-going humour had deflected their bad moods and stopped them griping at each other. Now, half-cut and wired, they hadn't felt the need to revert to the original argument. *At least, not yet.*

Seth shook Digger's hand and laughed as he walked him to the front door. 'Don't know how you do it, mate!'

'Got to pay the bills, ain't I?' Digger grinned, jogging down the first set of steps. 'See you later!'

Smiling to himself, Seth walked back into the lounge, pleased to see Jane was setting up a couple more lines on the table. As she hoovered up her third line, he flicked through their record collection, looking for something to put on.

Choosing an album, he walked up behind her and scooped her long hair out of the way. He took the rolled-up fiver out of her hand and planted a kiss on her neck.

'Trying to deflect me?' Jane laughed, watching as Seth snorted the spare line. 'Shall we go out?' she asked, unsure of the time. She looked onto the street below, seeing a few people milling about.

Wiping the white residue from under his nose, Seth cracked open another beer. 'Yeah, why not!'

Jane hoped Maggie wouldn't be out tonight. It would only spark Seth to rant about people poisoning their relationship, whilst failing to notice that he allowed his mates to have a good run at doing just that.

She felt her temper prickle. Although it was tempting, she wasn't going to start again about Stuart. *Not today anyway.*

One thing Jane *did* agree with Maggie on was that her and Seth needed to sort things out. Her eyebrows knitted together. Whatever happened to their plans to move away? She sighed, realising like everything else, it had got waylaid in a drunken haze. *They had to make this better.*

Wrapping his arms around her, Seth rested his chin on her shoulder and Jane smiled, pushing thoughts of Maggie from her mind. 'We going out then?'

'Well, maybe later,' Seth murmured, pushing her against the window. Firstly he was going to remind her why she was with him.

Jane's breath caught as Seth's hand inched up her skirt, his hardness pressing urgently into the small of her back. When he ripped her top off with one hand and pulled her knickers to one side with the other, she closed her eyes in anticipation.

As Seth took her roughly from behind, Jane was enjoying herself immensely. Her bare breasts were exposed for all to see through the glass of the window pane as he pounded into her and she waved cheekily to the man intently watching them from the flat opposite.

Picking her up, Seth balanced her on the back of the sofa and buried his face between her legs. 'Only me, Jane, remember?'

Letting the sensations overtake her, Jane's fingers twisted in Seth's hair as she pushed herself against his probing tongue before climaxing on his mouth. After catching her breath, she dropped to her knees.

Seth groaned loudly as he buried himself as deep down Jane's throat as possible, fucking her mouth hard. Holding on to his solid thighs, she ran her teeth gently over the throbbing veins of his length and her tongue mercilessly flickered around the sensitive tip.

Seth bit down on his bottom lip as he tried to control the raging sensations rising within him. 'Wait!' he gasped, pulling her up from her knees and pushing her back against the sofa. 'I'm going to make *you* come again first, baby,' he growled.

Jane looked up at him, his muscles taut and his head tilted slightly back as he slammed deep into her. *God, how she loved him. Despite everything, she loved him more than anything.*

As Seth pounded harder, Jane ignored the man in the flat opposite who was now frantically pumping at his own cock and abandoned herself to the orgasm violently rushing through her.

# FIFTY ONE

ELIZA DRAPED HERSELF over Jake, her arm hanging loosely around his neck. There hadn't been many options tonight, so he'd have to do for now. He was a bit of a pig, but it wasn't like she had to look at him was it?

Catching Maggie's eye from where she was sitting with Bryn at the sticky table, Eliza wondered what had happened to Zed. Since Bryn had unexpectedly returned on the scene last week, Maggie had gone back to being obsessed with him. *That girl needed to make her mind up.*

Batting her eyelashes, she waved her empty pint glass towards Jake, hoping he'd get the hint. Her mouth was a dry as a bone. It had been over five minutes since she'd finished it and still he hadn't moved. *What sort of bloke was he?*

'I'm *not* going through all this again, Jane,' Seth hissed, trying to keep his voice level, fully aware they had an attentive audience. He didn't know why this lot bothered - the argument had been the same for the last two days so there was hardly anything new for them to listen to.

'You can say what you like. It's not happening!'

Seth tipped the rest of his pint into his mouth and fixed his steely gaze on Jane. She *would* marry him. It was all booked and he was damned if he'd let the fact she'd got her knickers in a twist about Stuart ruin it. He wished he'd finished the twat off ages ago. It would have saved a ton of bloody hassle.

As if reading Seth's mind, Jane swung around and faced him, her dark eyes defiant. 'I told you yesterday, it's not just about Stuart. It's *everything*!' Sighing dramatically, she poured the remains of her vodka down her throat. 'Why can't you understand?'

'So you just don't want to marry me anymore?' Seth was getting angrier. 'And keep your voice down? I'm sick of this lot listening to everything.'

Jane felt like screaming. She wanted a fresh start away from all the bullshit, like they'd promised each other.

'May I remind you that you're already married to me anyway!' Seth continued, a sneer appearing across his face.

Jane slammed her empty glass down on the table. 'Tell me why you're insisting we do it again, then?'

'Because I want to do everything properly.'

Rolling her eyes, Jane placed her hand over Seth's and looked into his handsome face. 'I just want to get everything sorted first.'

Seth pushed himself quickly away from the table, causing Eliza and Maggie to desperately grasp for their rapidly spilling glasses. 'WHAT THE FUCK DO I HAVE TO DO, JANE?' he roared, his arms outstretched theatrically.

The whole pub fell silent when Seth grabbed his coat and stomped towards the front door and Jane felt Maggie's eyes on her as she watched him leave. *She wasn't going after him.*

• • • •

DODGE WAS STARVING. How long did it take to cook a fucking sausage? He only wanted one and a small portion of chips, not a bloody three course meal. Drumming his fingers impatiently on the stained countertop, he glared at the man behind the counter aimlessly shovelling chips in the deep-fat fryer.

Tapping his foot, Dodge sighed and glanced at the queue behind him. He didn't have time for this. He just wanted to get home, well aware he'd get an ear bashing from Mary. He'd said he'd be home for tea, but he'd got involved at the King's and now it was gone 10. She was going to go mad, but he was damned if he'd put up with her ranting on an empty stomach. *Besides, he needed something to soak up the beer.*

The man behind the counter looked tired and bored. 'Salt and vinegar?'

Dodge nodded at the man paused with the salt in suspended animation over the chips.

'Sorry about the wait,' the man muttered monotonously and passed the small package over the counter.

Stomping out of the chip shop, Dodge wiped his nose on the sleeve of his jacket and glanced at his watch. He should be back in twenty minutes. With any luck, Mary would have already gone to bed, so he wouldn't get grief until the morning and if he played his cards right, he'd be out the door before she'd even have chance to get started.

Spotting a familiar figure opposite as he rounded the corner, his stomach lurched. He hadn't seen Seth since offloading his stuff because he'd done a good job of avoiding him. *Until now.*

Shoving a handful of greasy, soggy chips into his mouth, Dodge quickly digested how best to handle the situation. *Should he ignore him or act normal?*

Opting for the first choice, he kept his head trained downwards and pretended to be extremely interested in his chip paper.

Crossing the road, Seth blocked his path. 'Hello!'

'Oh!' Dodge exclaimed, acting surprised. 'Seth! How you doing, mate?'

He didn't have time to react or to save his dinner from hitting the floor as he was roughly dragged into an alley between two shops by the lapels of his jacket.

Seth smiled as he pinned Dodge against the wet brick wall of the dank alley. What a bit of luck. He'd wanted to catch up with this two-faced piece of shit and he hadn't even had to go looking. Plus, thanks to his argument with Jane, he was in just the right frame of mind.

'Thought you could fuck me up, did you? Dump my gear for all to see?' Seth's teeth gleamed in the moonlight.

'No. I-I…'

'Some mate you are!'

Dodge fidgeted and tried to move out of the stranglehold. 'I-I *said* you needed to move it with the cops sniffing around.'

'Do you realise how much shit you could have caused me, you stupid prick? *Do you*?'

'I-I needed to clear the lock up,' Dodge stuttered. 'I asked Phil to remind you.'

As Seth released his grip, Dodge jiggled his head from side to side, attempting to kick start the blood flow in his crushed veins. He seriously wished he hadn't stopped for chips. Even Mary's moaning would have been preferable to this. Seth was one of the few people he hadn't wanted to get on the wrong side of and although he'd heard he'd been losing the plot, he'd very wrongly assumed he'd also lost his touch.

'I have to say,' Seth folded his arms and stared at the man he'd once thought of as an ally. 'You've disappointed me.'

Watching Seth's eyes darken, a sickly knot of despair formed in the pit of Dodge's stomach.

'The fact you're trying to make up crap excuses makes it even worse.'

'I-I was…'

'You'd have sold me down the fucking river, wouldn't you, you cunt!' Seth snarled.

'No, No! I wouldn't have.'

Rocking back on his heels, Seth laughed quietly. 'Don't you see mate, you already *did*! The fact you spoke to Phil rather than me, was an example.'

Grabbing Dodge around the throat, he pulled him clean off the ground. 'Dumping my stuff in full view of every fucker was another,' Seth's eyes narrowed further. 'Trying to set me up, were you?'

'No. No! Of course n…'

'Thought I'd lost the fucking plot?' Seth screamed. The slight flicker behind Dodge's eyes told him all he needed to know and white fury descended like a mist. He rammed his fist down. 'You two-faced motherfucker!'

Seth rained punch after punch down upon his former friend, who crashed to the floor under the onslaught and colours and sheets of bright white lights flashed through Dodge's mind as muddy water seeped through his jeans.

• • • •

PICKING HER BAG UP, Jane glanced around the table and tipped the last dregs of her drink into her mouth, knowing she should just go home and have the argument waiting to happen. 'I'm hitting the road.' Standing up, she leant on the table for support, deciding she probably shouldn't have had those last extra few vodkas.

Eliza shifted to the edge of the seat and moved her leg off Jake's. 'Can we cadge a lift?'

Jane smiled ruefully. 'I haven't got the car tonight. Sorry.'

Eliza pouted and slinging her legs back over Jake's knees, resumed plaiting his hair.

'See you later, babe!' Maggie smiled, looking relaxed now she'd had her quota of alcohol and undivided attention from Bryn.

*Oh, for life to be simple*, Jane thought. Raising her hand in goodbye, she headed out through the front door of the Oak Apple.

As she wandered up the road, Jane glanced into the alley and through her blurred vision, saw Seth's familiar silhouette. She couldn't quite make out who was getting the pasting, but watching as his fist crashed repeatedly down upon an inert figure in a puddle, she realised he was in no rush to stop.

As she made her way up the narrow passageway, she saw it was Dodge on the receiving end and raised her eyebrows.

Spotting her, Seth gave her an imperceptible nod, before turning back to the job in hand. She could see he was zoned out, but surely he didn't want to beat Dodge to an inch of his life?

Jane touched Seth's arm. 'Don't you think that's enough?'

'*What*?' he glared at Jane with hooded eyes, watching as she glanced at the smashed-up, bloodied face lying in the mud.

Dodge's eyes were already swollen shut, his cheekbone was broken and it looked like he'd lost a couple of teeth. 'Think you've got the message across,' she said.

'I don't get the message across properly to *some* people, it seems,' Seth hissed. 'Wouldn't want to disappoint you.'

Jane stalked back in the direction of the alley's mouth. *If he was going to be an obnoxious twat, he could piss right off.* 'Save your wrath for Stuart, Seth.'

'Stuart. Oh, *Stuart*. You had to get that in, didn't you?' Seth raged, landing another blow in Dodge's now unrecognisable face. *Stuart wasn't here right now, but this cunt was.*

• • • •

SETH COLLAPSED ONTO the sofa, trying to keep himself awake by throwing empty beer cans idly into the bin. Unfortunately, he was so drunk, he was missing the target by a long shot - which only irritated him further.

Switching the television on for the fourth time, he glared at the subtitled film on Channel 4. Flicking to the BBC, it was the test card. Sighing, he switched the television off and threw the remote control on to the table with a clatter. *Three hours and still no sign of her. Again…*

All the fury he'd unleashed by giving Dodge a kicking had been replaced by anger over Jane's absence. After barging into the flat ready for a row, he'd been surprised to find her missing and as time had slowly worn on, he'd got drunker and more annoyed. Now he was ready to blow.

Inspecting the blood underneath his fingernails, Seth dragged himself off the sofa and stumbled towards the window. He gazed down into the dark deserted night. *Was Jane doing this to wind him up? It certainly felt like it.*

Feeling his whole body shaking, he stared at the remains in the whisky bottle and raised it to his lips. Maybe he should go next door and stab that Stuart cunt to death in his fucking bed? But what if Jane came back when he wasn't here? He couldn't risk that.

Cracking his knuckles, he stretched and sat back down to wait.

He hadn't had to wait long. Jane had barely got through the front door before he launched himself up the hallway in three strides and grabbed her by the jacket. The back of her head collided into the wall as he slammed her backwards.

'Who've you been with?' Seth screamed, his face inches from hers.

Jane shrugged out of his grasp. 'Fuck you, Seth!'

'How fucking dare you treat me like this!' he roared.

Jane slapped him hard around the face. 'Get the hell off me!'

As a red welt appeared on his cheek, Seth grabbed Jane's face with one hand and yanked her chin up. 'You belong to me, Jane. *Me!*'

Glowering, she yanked his hand away and shoved him hard in the chest. 'I've told you before. I belong to *no one!*'

Staggering back drunkenly, Seth crashed against the opposite wall of the narrow hall before regaining his balance. Moving quickly, he grabbed Jane's arm and swung her around. 'Don't do this to me again,' he begged. 'You're killing me.'

Jane stared at Seth stubbornly and remained silent. *Let him sweat.*

'I won't have this. You belong to *me*, not anyone else. I won't let you make a fool out of me anymore.' Grabbing her shoulders, he shook her roughly, angry that despite his wrath he was as hard as rock for her. *God, she was infuriating, but he loved her so.*

'If you don't like it, you know where the fucking door is!' Jane spat.

Seth's face was a mask of rage as he pinned her up against

the wall and crashed his mouth down onto hers with a growl.

Despite her rage, Jane's body responded with desperate longing as always. *Damn him. Why did he always have this effect on her?* Shaking her arms free, she grabbed his hair with one hand and pulled him closer towards her.

Seth pulled Jane's skirt up, easily lifting her against the wall and she wrapped her legs around his hips. 'You're not leaving me, Jane,' he gasped, unbuttoning his jeans.

Jane cried out and dug her nails into the ridges on Seth's back as he entered her, savouring the familiar feel of him inside her. His lips trailed kisses up her neck as he pumped hard.

'You *know* I won't leave you,' Jane whispered, grasping a fistful of Seth's curls and abandoning herself to the pleasure his body always gave her.

She smiled. *How could she ever be with anyone else?*

## FIFTY TWO

ELIZA HUNG THE DRESS carefully on the handle of her wardrobe and stared at it. She couldn't remember the last time she'd worn a long dress.

Running her hand over the dark purple taffeta, she smiled. At least it was tight and had a split down the side, plus it was low-cut so she could show her tits off. Whatever happened, she'd look hotter than Maggie. They might have identical dresses, but she'd look the best by far.

'It's a lovely dress, dear.' Joy stood behind Eliza, making her jump. 'Must have cost a fortune.'

'Well, I didn't pay for it, put it that way!' Eliza grinned.

'Jane must be excited.'

Eliza wasn't sure that Jane was excited at all. With less than two weeks to go until the church wedding, she seemed more fucked up every time she'd seen her. She wasn't sure what was going down, but had given up trying to find out.

'Don't know really Ma, she's been a bit weird lately.' Eliza turned the dress around for the third time and admired the back, which consisted of a plethora of criss-crossing straps.

'She's probably just nervous.' Joy smiled.

Eliza doubted that but it was easier to agree rather than

explain Jane and Seth's manic relationship to her mother.

'Have you seen her dress? What's it like?' Joy asked.

Eliza had to admit she was envious of Jane's dress. It was *truly* gorgeous. Handmade from off-white silk and ruched all the way down, it splayed out at the base into a wide fishtail. The puffed shoulders blended into lace sleeves and the entire gown was covered with hundreds of crystals that caught the light in every direction imaginable.

'Oh how beautiful!' Joy exclaimed, listening as her daughter described the dress. 'Jane will look stunning! That Seth's a lucky man.' Raising an eyebrow, she winked. 'Of course, it helps that he's extremely handsome. He'll make her happy, I'm sure.'

Eliza turned away so her mother couldn't see her expression. Oh, Seth made Jane happy in the sack alright, but as for the rest of it, she wasn't sure.

All she knew was that she wished Seth loved *her* like that. Except without all the weird shitty bits.

· · · ·

JANE STARED MINDLESSLY at the piece of paper containing the list of boxes due for shipping and popped another pill into her mouth. She needed to slow her mind down. God, she hated, hated, *hated* this job and would look for another one as soon as everything else was out of the way.

Feeling like she was on a turntable spinning out of control, she rubbed at her temples. Seth had promised they'd move after the wedding and find somewhere else. Somewhere that people couldn't just walk in. Somewhere that wasn't slap-bang in the middle of everything.

*But could either of them stay straight long enough to manage it this time?*

At least he was back on with Phil and the boys. The job he'd pulled off last week had been an *extremely* lucrative one, pulling in thousands - hence the ability to foot the wedding bill.

Jane grinned. He'd taken a huge risk ordering everything with no idea how they'd pay for it, but he'd told her not to worry and that he'd sort it. *And sort it he had.*

Furthermore, they hadn't had an argument for the last two days either, so perhaps things were indeed looking up. For the first time in a very long while she'd begun to think maybe, just *maybe*, their plan was feasible.

She hoped so because today she'd confirmed her suspicions. She was pregnant again.

Looking around the room, Jane breathed in deeply. Even though her life was even more out of control than before she was determined it would be different this time.

· · · ·

GLANCING CASUALLY AT HIS watch, Seth opened the boot of the Senator and threw the duct tape in.

With a grunt, he heaved the unconscious man from the ground and roughly chucked him inside. As the man's head collided hard with the inside of the wheel arch, he slammed the lid and wiped his hands down his jeans.

He couldn't *wait* to surprise Jane with this. She'd be back from work soon. He'd spent several days planning it and it had all come together like clockwork. Tonight he'd be finishing this shit once and for all.

*It was going to be fine now. ALL of it.*

Rubbing his hands together happily, he entered the flat and reached for the whisky. He'd just have a small one before Jane got home. No actually, he'd go and pick her up from work instead. She could leave her motor there and then he'd drop her back off there in the morning. He could then give her the surprise straightaway. This had gone on long enough as it was.

Raising the bottle to his mouth, he took a large gulp, moaning contentedly as the whisky burnt his throat. His eyes moved to his wedding clothes hanging on the rail in the spare room.

The black frock coat, trousers, purple waistcoat and matching cravat were in a suit carrier and his top hat lay in a box on the floor. Polished black leather shoes sat next to the hat box and all he needed now was the new shirt, which he was picking up from the tailors tomorrow.

He'd been determined to have stuff that fitted his shoulders properly this time, unlike what he'd had to make do with at the hand fasting and he couldn't wait to see Jane in her wedding dress. Apparently, he wasn't allowed to see it until the day. *What fucking difference would that make?*

The urge to go and peep inside the large dress carrier hanging on the wall in their bedroom was overwhelming, but restraining himself, he took another swig of whisky instead.

Jane had looked beautiful the last time, but he'd bet she'd look drop-dead gorgeous in this one. *Especially when he got to take it off her.*

Seth twizzled the ring he'd worn since the hand fasting around on his finger. Jane was happy to use the same rings again, but he'd insisted they had new ones. He'd already given the new rings to Digger because he was the one bringing them on the day.

*Second wedding. New start. New rings. It all made sense.*

Sparking up a fag, he happily took one last swig of whisky, walked out of the spare room and left the flat.

• • • •

STUART SLOWLY CAME BACK to consciousness and immediately went into panic mode. *Where the hell was he? He couldn't breathe! Oh Jesus!*

He tried to call out, but found he couldn't move his mouth and neither could he see anything. Had he gone blind? Trying to feel in front of him, he realised with horror he couldn't move his arms from under him. *Was he paralysed?*

A fresh wave of fear rushed through his body, along with a wave of nausea and he tried to calm himself down in an effort to control his breathing. Hyperventilating through his nose wasn't doing him any favours.

His mind was totally and utterly blank. Finding he could still move his teeth, he gritted them and attempted to concentrate.

He'd been going home and had reached the first stairwell when he'd heard something behind him. He'd started to turn around but hadn't got very far. A further rush of dread piled over him and he realised something was wrong. *Very wrong.*

Feeling a jolt that sounded like a door, broke him from his panicked thoughts. *It was a car door. Was he in a car?*

Suddenly the penny dropped in his fuddled brain. *He was in a fucking car boot, wasn't he? Shit!*

Trying to move his legs to kick out, Stuart found his feet were also stuck and he couldn't move enough to bang on the walls of the boot. Closing his eyes, he swallowed hard, realising he knew whose car boot it was.

*This was Seth. It had him written all over it.*

A surge of defiance rose up and replaced his confusion and fear. This was beyond the fucking pale. He wasn't having this.

*He wasn't having it at all.*

• • • •

MAGGIE WALKED HAND IN hand with Bryn towards town, feeling that she might faint with pleasure. She couldn't believe how much her life had changed over the two weeks since he'd returned. They'd picked up where they'd left off and she'd fallen head over heels for him hard. She needed a decent man and was confident he fitted the bill. *Besides, he'd be fine with her plans.*

'You are coming to the wedding with me, aren't you?' she gushed.

'Of *course* I am, babe.'

'You'll have to wear a suit.'

Bryn stared at Maggie. 'A suit?' Looking down at his faded, ripped jeans and Metallica T-shirt, which wasn't far off the extent of his wardrobe, he wondered where on earth she expected him to get a suit from.

'Yes,' Maggie eyed him suspiciously. 'It's in a church, babe. You can't go like that, can you?'

Bryn wondered why on earth not? It wasn't *him* getting married for fuck's sake, was it? Besides, if he had anything to do with it, with any luck he'd be out of here by next weekend and back with Lucy.

He'd spent a very enjoyable few months with her, that was until they'd had a stupid argument, but he felt he was starting to win her round.

When he'd sneaked out away from Maggie the other night on the pretext of buying fags, he'd called Lucy from a payphone. She wasn't as icy as previously, so he reckoned he was getting somewhere.

Besides, there was only so long he could cope with Maggie. She was nice enough, but *so* full on and he hadn't been able to think of anywhere else he could go as easily. He just needed a little bit more time.

Smiling sweetly, Bryn planted a kiss on Maggie's lips. 'Ok, honey. I'll get a suit. Don't want to let you down, do I?'

• • • •

JANE WAS PERPLEXED. Every time she looked at Seth, he was grinning like a Cheshire cat. 'Just tell me what it is!' she pleaded.

Seth's green eyes glinted with mischief and he took his hand off the gear stick, giving Jane's a tight squeeze. 'What? And spoil all the fun?' Raising an eyebrow, he returned his gaze to the road. 'You'll have to wait. Trust me. You'll *love* it!'

Jane wondered what on earth it could be. Short of a gift-wrapped kilo of cocaine, she couldn't think of much else she wanted. She loved Seth to death when he was full of life and surprises like this. Like it had been in the old days before everything else had happened.

Snorting some coke off the end of a key, she glanced out of the window and tried to fathom where they were going, but admitted she was none the wiser. It was obvious they were in the country, but that didn't tell her much. *Maybe for a change they were going for a drink somewhere out of town?*

Hearing a clunk from behind, Jane turned her head. 'What was that?'

'What?'

'That clunking noise?'

Seth glanced in the rear view mirror. 'Don't know. I heard it earlier. Think the exhaust might be coming loose,' he lied. 'I'll get it looked at.'

Swinging off the road, he pulled onto a dirt track and continued down a bumpy narrow lane.

Jane looked out of the window into the fading light. 'What the hell's this? Where are we going?'

'Patience, my dear. Patience.'

Coming to a halt, Seth opened the passenger door and pulled Jane out of the Senator. 'Come on!' he winked. Kicking the door shut he crushed her up against it and kissed her passionately. 'First,' he smiled, pulling away. 'Your surprise!'

Jane felt like a little girl when she was taken by the hand and led around to the back of the car.

Flipping the boot open, Seth revealed Stuart crumpled up against the wheel arch, bound with duct tape and sporting a large gash to his head. 'Ta-dah!'

A slow smile crept across Jane's face as she stared at the figure blinking in rapid succession when the light hit his eyes.

'This, my darling,' Seth grabbed a thick handful of Stuart's hair and pulled him roughly from the boot. 'Is my wedding present to you.'

# FIFTY THREE

AS SETH DRAGGED STUART on to the floor, Jane smiled serenely. Finally he was going to deliver. *About bloody time!* Watching Stuart jerk around like a half-paralysed caterpillar, she fought the overwhelming urge to laugh.

Seth pulled a small pocket knife from his coat and expertly slit the duct tape from Stuart's mouth. 'Let's see what this cunt has got to say, shall we?'

Stuart flinched as the top layer of his lips was ripped away, along with most of his scruffy beard. 'You fucking sick bastard!' he screamed.

Jane stood over him. 'I see you're still an obnoxious prick!'

Thrashing around aimlessly, Stuart's face was bright red with rage. 'You horrible slag!' *He knew he was finished, but it was the final insult to have her here watching and enjoying it, the fucking psycho bitch.*

Laughing, Jane leant against the boot and casually inspected her long red fingernails. 'You look ridiculous,' she smiled. 'Like a fucking *beetroot*!'

'You should be dead in your fucking car by now!' Specks of saliva sprayed from Stuart's mouth, so livid he could hardly get the words out.

Jane didn't need to look at Seth to know Stuart's words had resonated because his fist smashed straight into the man's face.

'Hang on Seth,' Jane walked back towards Stuart. 'Let me help you.' Delivering a well-aimed kick to his face, she watched with detached glee as more of his teeth smashed out. 'Whoops!'

Seth didn't need to zone out for this one and couldn't help but smile when Stuart spat out chunks of broken teeth. *The guy was fucking begging for it.*

His fist connected once more, smashing Stuart's right eye socket. 'It's a shame you won't be able to come to our wedding, but never mind.'

Grabbing him around the throat, he pulled out a small pair of pliers and pushing Stuart's head backwards, rammed them into his mouth. 'One,' Seth counted, smiling as he tossed a tooth to one side. 'Two… Three…'

• • • •

BRYN DIDN'T PARTICULARLY want to trek back to the caravan once they'd got into town, because he'd been planning on going straight to the pub, but Maggie had been insistent.

Stopping at the offy, she'd bought a crap bottle of cheap white wine which they'd shared whilst walking back to the field. He *hated* wine but had dutifully swigged his half.

By the time they reached the van, Maggie was irritatingly giggly and girly. Bryn leant against the sofa bed and wondered why she was rushing around lighting candles.

Maggie smiled and then slipped her top down, revealing her breasts. 'Hey babe…'

Bryn grinned. *Hell, if she'd wanted a shag, why didn't she just say? She didn't have to do all that crap with candles!*

Pulling her towards him, he greedily wrapped his mouth around one of her erect nipples. Releasing himself from his jeans he peeled her leggings down. Not quite as nice tits as Lucy, but nice all the same, he thought, pulling Maggie on top of him and tracing his tongue teasingly in a circle on her flesh.

Maggie groaned with pleasure as she slid down onto Bryn.

This may be the time that did the job, she thought. That's if it hadn't happened already. He'd be so pleased.

'Faster,' she gasped, riding him harder. She looked at his face. His eyes were closed, his mouth slightly open and his expression was one of pure rapture. *Yep. He was as much in love with her as she was with him.*

*Life was good.*

• • • •

'YOU,' SETH SNARLED, 'are a piece of *shit*!'

Stuart grinned sarcastically, even though moving his broken mouth was excruciatingly painful. 'And you're a jumped-up, fucking wanker, Seth Wright.' His eyes flashed in defiance. 'You're a fucking joke! You and that whore.'

Gripping Stuart's windpipe with both hands, Seth smiled at the choking sounds coming from what was left of his mouth. *This cunt thought he'd got one over on him, did he? Well not any fucking more!*

Releasing one hand, Seth twirled his blade around and flicked it into position. 'Reckon it's time to make sure you don't say fuck all, prick!'

Jane could hardly contain her excitement as she watched Seth carefully. The obnoxious, defiant look on Stuart's face was now replaced with fear.

Wrenching Stuart's mouth open, Seth quickly grabbed his tongue and yanked it forward. The knife was pushed into his mouth and a panicked, garbled noise escaped, thick purple blood spewing out as his tongue was cut through.

Jane stared in morbid fascination as the garbled noise turned into an animalistic howling.

'Shut up!' Seth barked. 'Right little diva, aren't you?' Cutting through the final sinew, he held Stuart's tongue up and waggled it comically. 'Let's clean you up, shall we? You look a right fucking state!'

Undoing his flies and with legs apart, he aimed at Stuart's face.

Jane watched contentedly as the stream of piss poured in a torrent over Stuart's mouth and nose and he thrashed around, desperately trying to avoid the hot liquid burning his eyes. 'So now what?' She wrapped her arms around Seth's waist from behind.

Turning, Seth planted a kiss on Jane's mouth. 'Now it's round two.'

. . . .

BRYN LAY BACK ON the sofa bed and sighed contentedly. Exhaling cigarette smoke, he wondered when he could safely suggest returning to town. He needed to call Lucy at some point soon.

Maggie sat cross-legged next to him and he wondered if she had any more dope. *Why was she staring at him like that? She was starting to give him the creeps.*

'What are you frowning for, babe?' Maggie purred, looking at Bryn with a concerned expression.

Bryn jumped, almost dropping his fag onto his chest. 'Was I?' He quickly tried to think of something to say. 'Nothing's wrong. Just wondering if you're ok? You're very quiet?'

*Ok. So he lied. The quieter she was, the better, but he couldn't exactly say that, could he?*

Maggie brushed her fingers lightly over his face. 'Aw. You're so sweet.'

Bryn forced a smile that he hoped looked genuine. 'Shall we head back into town?'

A pout formed on Maggie's lips. 'Really? You don't want to stay in?' She pushed her breasts forwards. 'The night's still young and there's plenty of time for more, you know…'

'Jesus, woman!' Bryn tried to make a joke, but was starting to feel slightly suffocated. He needed to get out of here and back into society.

'Ok. We'll go to town,' Maggie said sulkily, 'but I've some really good news I want to tell you about first.'

Bryn propped himself up on his elbows. 'Good news?' *Had*

*she won the pools?* That may alter his plans slightly. He could face a few more weeks with her to help spend the money.

'Yes,' Maggie gushed, her eyes shining. She stroked Bryn's arm gently. 'You're going to be *so* pleased. I know you feel the same way as I do.'

*Oh get on with it!* Bryn tried not to glance at his watch and smiled, feeling like his face was going to crack. 'Don't keep me in suspense.'

'Well,' Maggie shuffled closer and took his hand. 'I came off the Pill a couple of weeks ago so that we could try for a baby.'

The world hung in suspended animation and a slow wave of fear ran up from Bryn's feet and trickled through every vein, until it reached his head. *He couldn't have heard right, surely?*

Shaking his head, he laughed nervously. 'Thought you said something about babies then!'

Maggie's smile grew wider. 'I did.'

A clammy film of sweat broke out over Bryn's forehead and he sat bolt upright.

'I *knew* you'd be pleased!' Maggie leant forward, her lips reaching for his.

Bryn stopped her with his hand. 'Y-You're not pregnant, are you?'

Giggling, she put her hand on her belly. 'Give yourself chance! Well, I *may* be. We might have been lucky already or maybe just now did the trick?'

Bryn thought he might throw up. Wiping the sweat away from his face, he scrambled to his feet. *This was a total nightmare.* 'Are you *insane*?'

'What the matter? Don't worry. If I'm not already, I'm sure it won't take long,' Maggie reached out, bewilderment on her face.

Bryn stared at her in disbelief. '*What*?' He felt like he was going to froth at the mouth. 'Are you *nuts*? Did you not think to discuss this with *me*?'

Her face fell slightly. 'Aw, you're not cross with me are

you? Should I have waited until it's definite before saying something?'

'NO!' Grabbing Maggie's arm, Bryn pulled her heavily across the bed. *He felt like killing her, the stupid bitch.* 'You're fucked up! I don't want a fucking kid!'

Maggie looked like she'd been slapped. 'W-What?'

'I *said,*' Bryn hissed through gritted teeth, 'I don't want a fucking kid. What's so difficult to understand about that?'

Shaking Maggie with both arms, he scowled as she burst into tears. 'Shut up, you stupid cow!' he raged. 'I don't want a kid and I *certainly* don't want one with you. *Ever*!'

Throwing her roughly back onto the bed, he grabbed his jeans and quickly pulled them on. He didn't care if he had nowhere to go. He wasn't staying with this nutter anymore, that was for certain.

Maggie crumpled on the bed in a heap, sobbing. 'B-But, where are you going?'

'AWAY FROM *YOU*!' Snarling, Bryn pulled his T-shirt over his head. 'I mean it, Maggie. If you're pregnant, I'll kill you!'

• • • •

JANE PASSED SETH the stake and watched as he hammered the end into the earth with a mallet.

Tossing it to one side, he smiled and rubbed his hands together as he stood back to admire his work. 'Right. Let's get on with the final phase.'

Stuart lay white-faced, curled in a ball with vomit and thick blood pouring from his mouth.

'Not so cocky now, are you?' Jane laughed, enjoying the shaking, shrunken body that was uttering soft whimpering noises in front of her.

Watching impatiently as Seth rolled Stuart onto his back, she helped unbuckle his belt. *The quicker this was done, the quicker the fucker would be gone for good.*

Yanking Stuart's jeans down to his ankles, Seth lifted him by his underarms and pulled him upright, but his legs folded from underneath him. 'Come on, cunt!' he roared. 'WAKE UP!'

*It was no use. He was too far gone.*

Seth slapped Stuart around the face, his glazed eyes rolling and a trail of bloody saliva dribbling out of his mouth. 'Oh, for fuck's sake!' he muttered, hearing a strange whining noise. 'He's off with the fucking fairies!'

'Get on with it. Don't want him to die before the exciting bit do we?' Jane winked, unable to contain her enthusiasm. 'That just wouldn't be cricket!'

Seth smiled savagely as he dragged Stuart over to the stake. Although the man didn't have the energy or ability to put up any form of physical struggle, the whimpering noises increased as he was shoved onto the pole. With a couple of minor adjustments, the tip pushed slowly into him.

Jane stood next to Seth, her heart beating fast. *What a way to go,* she thought smiling.

'Anything else you want, baby?' Seth asked, smiling at the pleasure on Jane's face. Although he'd much rather be sticking his cock into her than shoving this wanker onto a pole, some things just had to be done.

The corner of his mouth twitched into a half-smile as Stuart's weight took the strain and a horrible guttural moan escaped as the pole made its way up inside his body. A fresh wave of vomit spewed out as the pointed end pierced Stuart's bowel and a gush of blood and shit poured onto the grassy floor.

Jane felt slightly queasy, but relieved. It was over, or would be very shortly. As the finale unfolded, she walked back to the car to get the vodka.

• • • •

ELIZA WAS STRESSED OUT. Not only was Jake determined to get her on her own, but Maggie was hysterical. Something to do with Bryn. She didn't have a clue what was going on, but hoped after a few drinks she'd stop fucking crying.

*Where was Jane when she needed her? She was supposed to*

*have been here nearly an hour ago.*

Hearing the back door to the bar slam, she looked up to see Jane walk in the bar.

'Eliza?' Jake slotted into a space on the bench next to her.

'Got to go and see Jane. She's just arrived, look.' Eliza stood up quickly. *Thank fuck for that!*

Pouring a vodka and orange down her throat, Jane grinned. 'Sorry I'm late. Got a bit held up.'

'Where's Seth?'

Jane glanced down the corridor. 'Just washing his hands.'

'Washing his hands? What you two been doing?' Giving Jane a wicked grin, Eliza winked, then her nose wrinkled up as the strong smell assaulted her nostrils. 'Christ! You fucking *stink* of petrol!'

'Ah yes, the car ran out of fuel, so we had to fill a jerry can up,' Jane smiled.

Eliza raised her eyebrow. 'Been doing something nice?'

'Actually, yes. Something I've wanted to do for quite some time.' *She'd enjoyed flicking the match, but fuck, did she stink!* 'Think I'd better wash my hands too.'

Eliza grabbed Jane's arm as she turned to walk towards the toilets. 'By the way, you're going to have to do something with Maggie. She's in a right bloody state.'

Jane rolled her eyes. *What now?*

• • • •

MAGGIE SOBBED HYSTERICALLY and propped herself against the table, not caring her shaking hands were causing her lager to slosh out of the glass.

She couldn't cope anymore. She might as well just top herself. Taking in a big, hiccupping breath, she ignored everyone staring at her.

'Hey,' Zed flopped down heavily on the bench next to Maggie. 'What's up?'

Maggie slowly raised her head up. *Zed was back?* She looked at him with teary eyes. 'Oh babe, everything's just so *awful.*' Sobbing loudly, she buried her head in his chest, bypassing that he hadn't washed for at least a week.

Placing his arm around her shoulders, Zed pulled Maggie nearer, hoping he could cadge a bit of dope. 'Come on, it can't be that bad?' He stroked her hair. 'Besides, I'm here now.'

Maggie's sobs quietened as she leant further into him and smiled. *Sod Bryn. He might have gone, but Zed was back now, so there was light at the end of the tunnel.* Sitting back, she wiped the tears from her face.

• • • •

JANE SCRUBBED HER HANDS as best as she could with the small dry piece of soap, whilst Eliza sat on the toilet and filled her in as to what was going on with Jake.

'What are you going to do?' Jane asked dislodging something unsavoury stuck behind one of her fingernails.

'I don't know, I really don't. He isn't very interesting in the sack.'

Laughing, Jane sluiced the cold water over her hands and glanced at her reflection in the mirror, smiling when Seth appeared through the door behind her.

'Happy now?' he whispered, bringing his hands up to cup Jane's face. His lips twitched into a slight smile, then crushed down onto hers.

'Jane?' Eliza shouted from the cubicle. 'Who's that? Are you still there?'

Jane was pushed roughly against the washbasin as she undid Seth's belt buckle. Pulling her quickly into the next cubicle, he slammed the door behind him just as Eliza flushed the toilet.

'Jane?' Eliza frowned, confused.

The score became clear when the partition wall began to shake violently as Seth took Jane against it, very hard and very quickly.

Returning to her seat, Eliza tried to pretend she hadn't seen Jake frantically waving at her. Although hearing Jane and Seth at it in the toilets had made her hot and she wouldn't mind a bit of action herself.

She frowned. Maggie appeared to have recovered from her total and utter all-consuming heartbreak of ten minutes previously and was smiling intently at Zed. Eliza rolled her eyes. She gave up with that girl, she really did.

*Now. What to do about Jake?* Maybe she should give him another chance in the sack before binning him off entirely?

Eliza glanced at her watch. Still two hours of drinking time to go. She could probably get several drinks out of Jake beforehand.

*Yeah, fuck it.* Smiling, she walked towards him.

# FIFTY FOUR

JANE WAS EXCITED. She'd spent the last hour rummaging through her clothes, picking out what she was going to wear later and she'd narrowed it down between two things. She held up the skin-tight black velvet halter dress.

*Would that go better with her stilettos, or the new one?*

Looking at the gorgeous iridescent emerald green sequinned dress, there was realistically no contest as to which one she would wear. It had to be that one. The green would match Seth's eyes and a shiver of anticipation ran through her as she imagined him peeling the dress off her.

When she heard the front door slam, she quickly folded up the green dress and shoved it under the bed along with the pregnancy test. She'd have one last night before accepting reality and would surprise Seth with that later.

'Hey, Princess!' Seth grinned, his eyes smiling as he entered the bedroom.

With only a week to go until the wedding, he was confident he'd got everything sorted and was finding it impossible to lose the smile that seemed to be permanently on his face.

Now that twat Stuart was off the radar, Jane was happy, he was happy, so it was all good. Plus he was meeting Digger, Phil and Tony for a drink down the Dragon tonight. Jane was going up the Barrels with Maggie and Eliza and he'd go up there for last orders. That way he'd still see her.

He glanced at the dress in her hand. 'You wearing that tonight?'

Looking at the black halter neck she was clutching, Jane feigned indifference. 'Not sure yet. Probably. When are you meeting the others?'

Seth's eyes narrowed and he eyed her suspiciously. 'Why? What are you planning?'

*Oh, don't spoil it Seth*, Jane thought sighing. 'Nothing!'

'Make sure you're not.' Seth stepped towards her. He didn't want a row. He placed his hand on the small of her back and pulled her towards him, his fingers tracing up her inner thigh. 'I'm not going *anywhere* until I've been in you,' he murmured and sat back on to the bed, pulling Jane with him.

· · · ·

'BLOODY HELL, MATE!' Digger laughed. 'Slow down, will you! You won't get as far as the Barrels, at this rate!'

Seth was knocking drinks back like they were going out of fashion. He'd also dropped several pills which had given him an edge and was in an unstoppable mood. 'Oh, I'll get there alright!'

'You must be mad going through this again, mate,' Tony laughed. 'Most blokes would try to get out of marriage the first time, let alone doing it *twice*!'

'I'd do it a thousand times over with Jane.' Seth smiled, his voice only slightly betraying the amount of beer he'd put away.

'You're too much in love with that woman for your own good,' Tony smiled. He had *no* intention of settling down. He returned his gaze back to the short-haired blonde his eyes had been following for the last ten minutes.

Digger whacked Seth on the shoulder. 'I wish you all the best.' *He meant it*. Having accepted defeat where Jane was concerned, he now hoped Seth didn't discover his previous indiscretions.

Seth tipped the remains of his drink into his mouth and smiled as he looked around the table. *They were good guys, this lot.* At least he knew where he stood with them, unlike half the fucking hangers-on and liars he seemed to attract by the bucket load.

Tony scowled as a greasy-haired bloke staggered past the table and trod on his foot.

'Sorry,' the man mumbled, then smiled. 'Alright, Seth?'

Seth nodded automatically. He didn't have the first clue who this bloke was and didn't particularly want to change that. He *certainly* didn't want to enter into any form of conversation.

'Seen your missus up the Barrels. Fuck me, she's looking good,' the man grinned, oblivious to the expression on Seth's face.

'What's that supposed to mean?' Seth barked, his eyes narrowing. *What was this dickhead trying to say? What was Jane up to that he didn't know about?*

As unwelcome thoughts flooded through his wired mind, he felt his blood pressure rising.

Phil sighed, watching Seth's instant mood change. He'd been hoping he would behave himself tonight. The man had seemed more stable lately and he didn't want anything tipping him over the edge. It had been ages since they'd all been out for a bit of a laugh and the night had been good, until now.

'I said, what the fuck's that supposed to mean?' Seth repeated, standing to his full height.

The greasy-haired man visibly shrank, realising he'd somehow said the wrong thing. He looked around the crowded bar, noticing that worryingly his mates had conveniently disappeared. 'N-Nothing. I-I was just saying she looked nice, mate. I didn't mean anything by it.'

'I'm not your *mate*! You were insinuating something, weren't you?' Seth roared, pushing the table and tipping Tony's pint over in the process. 'What's she doing?'

Digger jerked his head at the greasy-haired man, signalling

him to make himself scarce. He pulled Seth's arm. 'Come on man, leave it. He wasn't suggesting anything.'

Seth begrudgingly allowed himself to be pulled back on the bench seat and seethed as the man scuttled away whilst he still could.

'I'll get more drinks then, shall I?' Tony moaned. Picking up his empty glass, he made his way through the heaving throng to the bar. He might have known it would kick off at some point.

Seth gritted his teeth and fought to control his breathing. He should have just gone up the Barrels. He could have kept an eye on Jane that way. Why the *fuck* had he let them talk him into coming down here? *He must be fucking stupid!*

'You need to calm down, mate,' Phil muttered in Seth's ear. 'Don't ruin the night.'

'But Jane…'

'Jane, nothing!' Phil snapped. 'She'll be doing *fuck all*, apart from trying to enjoy herself. Stop being so fucking paranoid, will you? Now calm down and have a fag.' Taking a cigarette out of his packet, he passed it to Seth.

Pushing the offered cigarette away, Seth stood up, knocking the table for the second time and barged through the crowd out through the front door.

• • • •

CONDENSATION STREAMED down the walls in the Barrels as the sea of hot, sweaty bodies danced to the beat. Maggie pressed herself against Zed and Eliza was wrapped around Jake in the corner.

Maggie was over the moon. She'd spent two idyllic days with Zed. Although they'd smoked far too much dope, they'd also gone for lovely romantic walks across the fields too. And of course plenty of sex.

She hadn't given Bryn a second thought. Well, she may have mentioned him once or twice, but once Zed said he was sick of hearing about the guy, she'd decided to button it and forget all about him.

Bryn wasn't worth the bother anyhow. Besides, if he *had* got her pregnant, she'd just tell Zed it was his. He was too laid back to care either way and if she wasn't, then it wouldn't be long before she was.

As the alcohol flowed through her veins and the beat of the music thrummed through her body, Maggie gyrated to the music and looked admiringly at Jane. She looked absolutely stunning.

Jane's head was rushing with alcohol, but it would be her last night of letting her hair down and she was having a very good time. As another drink was pushed into her hand, she tipped it easily down her throat without missing a beat.

She was on a roll and couldn't wait to see Seth's face when he saw her in the new dress.

• • • •

RUNNING UP THE STEPS of the Barrels, torturing himself about what Jane was doing, Seth pushed past the queue. He stood out of breath at the top, thoughts rushing through his brain like a freight train.

'What's up, mate?' Spooner asked, watching Seth lean unsteadily against the bannister.

Seth felt wasted. 'Jane?'

Spooner winked, 'Yeah, she's in there looking mighty fine. You're a lucky man!'

Seth glared. *Why was everyone saying that? What the hell was going on?* He knew the day had been too good to be true. Why didn't he learn? She was probably screwing someone in the middle of the dancefloor right now. She'd done that with him more than once, after all.

Wild-eyed, he raced down the steps to the bar, slamming people out of the way. Yanking the double doors open, the ear-splitting music blasted him in the face as he swayed in the doorway. He scanned the room, hardly able to see anything, it was that crowded. *Where the fuck was she?*

Feeling panic rise, Seth shoved someone trying to squeeze past him into the door jamb. He needed a fucking drink, but he needed to find Jane first.

Squinting to adjust his eyes, his heart lurched seeing her standing on one of the bench seats in the far corner, dancing with her arms raised over her head. His gaze ran over her body encased in an iridescent skin-tight dress shooting tiny rainbows off in all directions.

Blinking, he cocked his head to one side. *Fucking hell!* The gleaming green material covered her body like liquid. It looked like she'd been poured into it. Jane pulled the hem of the short dress up to reveal the tops of her stockings as she danced with abandon and he swallowed quickly, a wave of love and lust rushing over him.

*She looked absolutely ravishing.*

Pulling his coat across himself self-consciously, in case the growing swelling in his jeans became obvious, Seth stepped forward into the crowd. He needed to kiss her. *In fact, he wanted to take her right now.*

Jane was well aware everyone was looking at her and she was revelling in it. A man began grinding against her as she changed position. Laughing, she continued to dance, pushing herself against him and raised her arms higher.

Feeling hands on her thighs she pushed them away, but the man quickly pushed one hand up between her legs. Eyes flashing with anger, she swiped his hand away. She was too busy scowling at the man's leering face as he attempted to grope her for the second time, she didn't notice Seth, until he was in front of her.

Without uttering a word, Seth pulled the man roughly onto the floor and head-butted him. People screamed as tables went flying and the man slumped to the floor.

Jane remained on the seat, horrified at the blood that had sprayed down her new dress. *Why had Seth gone psycho tonight of all nights? This wasn't how it was supposed to turn out.*

Stepping down from the seat, leaving Seth to continue raining punches down onto the man, she pushed her way angrily through the sea of bodies and broken glass, making her way to the door. She'd had enough.

Leaving the man to bleed, Seth turned on his heels and followed Jane. *If she thought she was disappearing to start with someone else, she'd got rocks in her fucking head.* 'Finding someone else to grope?' he screamed, pulling her towards him.

Jane's face contorted into a grimace and she made a futile attempt to shake herself from Seth's grip. 'Are you fucked up or something? What's the matter with you?'

Seth dragged her out of the double doors and onto the landing. 'Enjoying yourself? I knew I couldn't trust you!'

People tried to pretend they weren't listening as they shuffled past awkwardly. Seth glared at each one of them in turn, his eyes like daggers. He'd quite happily knock all of them out if they so much as even fucking looked at him.

*Come on. Just look. Go on…*

'What do you mean '*enjoying myself*'?' Jane spat, grabbing Seth's shirt. 'I was, until *you* turned up!'

'You stupid cow! Cover yourself up!' Seth snapped the strap of Jane's dress, exposing her breast. 'Having a good look?' he screamed in the face of the nearest person.

Shaking with rage, Jane attempted once more to rip herself from his grip.

Hearing the commotion, Spooner ran down the stairs. 'Come on, you two.' He laid a hand on Seth's shoulder and tried to smile. 'Think maybe it's time you guys called it a night.'

BOOTING IN THE front door of the flat, Seth panted like a rabid animal as he dragged Jane into the hallway. His head felt completely fucked and he couldn't cope with any more. He should have stayed in. He should have made *her* stay in and then none of this would have happened.

Finally shaking free, Jane glared at Seth, her arm already showing the beginnings of purple finger-shaped bruising. Swaying slightly, she felt the sting of tears at the back of her eyes and wished she hadn't drunk quite so much.

Snarling, Seth slammed his fist against the wall repeatedly. He wanted to beat the hell out of everything. He sucked in air through his teeth and sneered at the blood pouring from his damaged hand.

He turned to Jane with a savage snarl. 'Why do I even think about trusting you? *Why?*'

Jane glared. *The night was ruined. Totally and absolutely fucking ruined.* Stamping into the lounge, her eyes were wild with anger as she grabbed a vodka bottle.

Following her, Seth smacked the bottle from her hand in one swipe. 'You stupid bitch!' The bottle shattered as it exploded noisily into the wall, covering Jane in liquid and hundreds of tiny glass fragments.

Feeling like he was going to have a heart attack, he tried to get his breath, his words coming out in staccato bursts. 'Letting... people... grope... you... like... some... fucking... *tart*!'

Jane was sick of Seth's accusations. 'Who the fuck do you think you are?'

Seth's eyes formed narrow slits. 'What the hell do you expect? Wearing something like *that*?'

Jane couldn't believe what she was hearing. The dress was gorgeous and she'd worn it for him, the ungrateful bastard. *Why the fuck did she bother?* She'd just find someone that would appreciate her.

But she didn't want someone did she? She wanted him. *It could only ever be him.*

Seth sneered. 'Not getting enough attention? Trying to get yourself raped again?' He wanted to hurt her. Wanted to make her suffer. He wanted to see her bleed to take away his anger.

'How dare you! How fucking dare you!'

Seth closed his eyes in desperation. She looked absolutely stunning, but that was the problem. It meant everyone wanted to take his place and he wasn't having it. He was sick of people taking the piss and trying to step on his toes. Jane was his. *HIS!*

He wanted to tell her she looked beautiful and take her to bed. Tell her he loved her and that she was his life. He wanted to say that without her, he was nothing.

Seth willed himself to stop, knowing he was being way out of order, but couldn't now he'd started. He was too drunk. Too wired. Too angry. 'You're mine, Jane, *mine*. Not anyone else's. I'm sick of you taking liberties. I'll kill you first.'

'Kill me then! *Go on*! At least I'd be away from you!' Jane screamed. She watched Seth pick up the whisky and take a long slug. 'Don't you think you've had enough?'

'I've *never* had enough, Jane.' Seth leant on the back of the chair for support. 'And nor have you.'

'What you going to do?' she laughed in his face. 'Lock me

in the flat again? Tie me down? Make me walk round with a fucking bag on my head, so no one can look at me?'

Seth looked up slowly and turned his head towards her. Putting a cigarette between his lips, he raised his lighter which illuminated his face in the flickering flame. 'If I have to, Jane. If I fucking have to, yes.'

'That's what *you* think!'

'Where the fuck are you going?' Seth screamed, panic in his eyes as Jane walked towards the door. 'You're not leaving! You're married to *me*!'

'Not for much longer.'

Springing up like a panther, Seth grabbed her. 'What's that supposed to mean? Who are you seeing behind my back? Who the fuck are you seeing?'

Saying nothing, Jane shook her arm free and opened the lounge door.

'*I said*, what's that supposed to mean? Answer me *NOW*!' Seth roared at the top of his lungs, tight on her tail.

Jane glanced over her shoulder as she stormed to the bedroom. 'I'm leaving you, Seth.' *She was lying. What she really wanted was for him to kiss her and stop this shit.*

'You're going nowhere!' Seth screamed. 'WHO THE FUCK HAVE YOU BEEN SEEING?'

In her haste, Jane ran straight into the bed and knocked it to one side. Wincing, she grabbed the hunting knife from the bedside cabinet and stumbled over to the other side of the room.

'What the hell are you doing?' Seth screamed, lurching into the room behind her. Catching his foot in a bag from under the bed, he threw it to one side angrily.

'What I should have done *ages* ago!' Jane raged, her temper blown.

Pulling her wedding dress off the hanger, she slashed through the suit carrier. Yanking the dress from its covering, she was no longer able to hold the tears in as she continued to drag the knife through the exquisite material.

Seth stared in horrified fascination when Jane threw the

knife on the bed and glared at him, her eyes stony. 'Look,' she smiled nastily. 'No dress, no wedding…'

It took a few seconds for him to register exactly what she'd done. 'You fucking crazy bitch!' he roared. 'WHAT THE FUCK HAVE YOU DONE?'

Picking up the dress, he stared at the tattered fabric. It was absolutely beautiful, but it was completely ruined. *They'd never get another one in time.*

Jane wanted to stop crying, but she couldn't stop the sobs from coming in torrents. 'This is *your* fault!' Pushing Seth into the wall, she snatched the dress out of his hands. 'You just don't know when to stop, do you? Get the hell away from me!'

Seth wanted to punch her. His head felt like a pressure cooker. As she sat on the bed, clutching the ruined dress, her body wracked with heavy sobs, he glared at her and for once was totally speechless.

Jane started shoving bits and pieces into the carrier bag he'd thrown to one side and it slowly dawned on him that she was serious. *She was putting stuff together to leave.* 'Oh no you don't!' Seth cried, snatching the bag out of her hands.

'I can't do this anymore,' Jane sobbed, standing up and impotently banging her fists against his chest. She had to get out, even if it was only for half an hour.

Grabbing the bag, Seth tipped the contents on the bed. 'You're not going anywhere!'

'GIVE THAT TO ME!' Jane screamed, watching as he picked up the pregnancy test.

Moving it out of her reach, Seth pulled the used test from the box. 'You're pregnant?' His voice was little more than a whisper.

Jane heard his question, but couldn't react. Her voice box felt paralysed and a fresh wave of tears poured down her face. *What did it matter?* Everything was devastated and ruined. Her life was fucked, plus she'd trashed her beautiful dress.

Seth stared at her. *He had to know. He just had to know.* 'Jane? Are you pregnant again?'

Seeing her slight nod, a wide smile spread over his face. He took a deep breath. It was all going to be alright. He could sort this. He'd stop this shit and go to the quacks or something. Get them to get rid of his anger.

*He meant it this time.*

Jane stared blankly. She tried to delete the words from her brain before they gained momentum, but before she could do that, her anger forced them out.

Raising her chin defiantly, she looked straight into Seth's eyes. 'It might not be yours,' she shrugged, determined to hurt him as much as he'd hurt her.

Seth's mouth hung open with shock, like he'd just been slapped. He studied her face. 'Are you serious?'

Jane paused, determined to get the maximum effect. 'Deadly serious.'

Hurt plastered Seth's face as he stared incredulously at the woman he was so in love with. *She wouldn't do this to him, would she?*

Frowning, he realised she would. Jane was more than capable of doing it on *purpose* purely to get him back for everything. 'Be serious.' His voice was calm and quiet, betraying the torrent of swirling emotions rushing through his mind. 'Is the baby mine?'

Enjoying the devastation smeared across Seth's handsome face, Jane laughed. 'It might be, might not. Does it matter?'

Seth's hurt was immediately replaced with rage. 'DOES IT FUCKING MATTER?'

Jane faced him, her arms folded, the smirk on her face getting wider. *He didn't like it the other way around, did he?*

Springing forward and grabbing Jane by the shoulders, Seth shook her roughly, his eyes wild. 'Tell me whose baby it is.' Spittle formed in the corners of his mouth, his breathing heavy and ragged. 'TELL ME WHO THE FATHER IS!'

Throwing Seth's hands off her, Jane shrugged dismissively. 'It's between you and a couple of others.' *That would get him.*

'*WHAT*?' A ringing noise clamoured inside Seth's ears as he sank onto the bed and put his head in his hands. *He could take most things, but not this.* 'I'm going to kill you,' he muttered, feeling like he was going to throw up.

Jane stared at him for several minutes before picking the test off the bed. Placing it on the table, she shrugged, no longer caring. She was too tired. 'Whatever.' She slipped her stilettos off, her feet aching like mad.

'I'm going to fucking kill you,' Seth repeated, reaching under the bed.

Jane sighed, the anger diminishing. Fresh tears ran down her cheeks in a silent, hot wave. She couldn't keep this shit up. She loved him too much. 'I didn't mean it. The baby's yours, Seth.'

'I don't believe you.' Seth's voice was hollow. He wanted to believe her. Really wanted to, but didn't know what he believed any more.

Jane shrugged again. *He was the one who'd started this. It was his fault.*

Seth pulled the Beretta out, wild-eyed, his hand trembling as he aimed at Jane's chest. He knew there had been a reason he'd kept this gun under the bed and here it was.

Jane looked up, only to stare down the barrel of the gun. 'What the fuck are you doing?'

Sweating profusely, Seth wiped his forehead with his shirt sleeve, but kept the gun trained on Jane. If he couldn't have her then no fucker would. There was *no way* he'd watch her have someone else's kid. *No. No. NO!*

Jane was nonplussed, until she heard him cock the gun. *Fuck. He was going to fucking shoot her.*

She had to stop this. '*Don't*!' she yelled. Grabbing the knife off the bed, she launched herself at him at the speed of light.

Seth watched in slow motion. He wanted to shoot her, but couldn't. He loved her, even if he hated her half the time. Seeing a flash of steel, he raised the gun out of the way above his head and felt no pain when the knife sunk deep into his chest.

As the Beretta clattered noisily to the floor, Jane stared disjointedly at the handle of the blade embedded deep in Seth's chest. A torrent of blood sprayed in her face, over her dress and in a high arc over the ceiling.

She pulled the blade free and thick red blood ran down over her wrists, drenching the front of Seth's white shirt. She looked into his face as his hand moved slowly to his chest.

*Shit. Shit! Oh shit!*

'Jane…?' Seth whispered, gently touching her face.

A silent single tear slipped down Jane's face as the man she loved beyond life itself, crashed in slow motion to the floor, his big frame hitting the deck heavily.

• • • •

JANE WAS UNSURE how long she'd been rooted to the spot. It felt like hours before she dropped to her knees.

The screaming inside her head got louder, whilst everything else got quieter. In fact, it was completely silent, apart from her rasping breathing and the clock ticking on the bedside table.

*Oh come on. COME ON! Don't do this… Don't do this.*

Praying silently to a God that didn't exist, her brain picked up a breakneck pace and floods of emotions raced through her mind. *How long had she been sitting here?*

Dizziness washed over her in tidal waves as she brushed Seth's long curls off his face, her tears splashing onto his pallid cheek.

The clock continued loudly ticking. Its noise seemed even louder than before. Thunder crashed inside her head and her stomach heaved.

Totally uncaring how much time had elapsed, she remained in the pool of blood, her knees pulled up to her chest and she stared vacantly at the pile of ruined material that had once been her wedding dress.

Although she didn't want to leave, in the cold silence of the early dawn, she knew it was time to go.

From the start, they'd promised each other they'd be with each other until the end of time. They'd always promised that, but it was too late.

*It was the end of time and he'd already left.*

Moving like an automaton, she pulled herself to her knees. She couldn't look at Seth again. It hurt too much.

Forcing herself to feel nothing, she pulled the bedroom door shut behind her and robotically walked up the hallway into the lounge, trying not to look at his coat thrown over the back of the sofa or his work boots on the floor.

She knew the empty lager cans on the table would taste of his mouth and she forced herself not to pick one up. Running her hand over the life growing in her belly, she paused before taking a deep breath.

Jane took a cigarette out of her bag and glanced uninterestedly at her bloodied hands. Picking up her keys, she went through the front door and down the steps without looking back.

There was no point.

*It was finished.*

# THANK YOU!

Thank you for reading *Until the End of Time*. I hope you enjoyed reading it as much as I did writing it!

If so, please leave a review on Amazon and/or Goodreads.

Reviews from readers are SOOOO helpful and especially important to us authors and without you we would have nobody to write for!

Thank you once again and hope you enjoy the rest of my books.

*Edie xx*

# MORE FROM THIS SERIES

### #2 - ESCAPING THE PAST

'**Dark and impossible to put down...**' - *5 stars*

Things have changed and Jane has got on with her life.

Well, not *entirely...*

Embroiled in a bitter feud between two rival firms, it is clear that not everyone is who they proclaim to be.

The net is closing in and some things just can't be changed.

'**Totally addictive...**' - *5 stars*

'**...a well-written, fast-paced, gripping, edge of your seat kind of tale... This story is strongly recommended...**' - *5 stars*

'**...I am very impressed by this author and their ability to write a book that was like a mobster movie...The characters were real, believable and raw... Shocking twists and turns...**' - *5 stars*

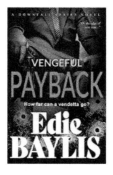

### #3 - VENGEFUL PAYBACK

'**The interweaving of characters and their schemes throughout the plot was masterful...**' - *5 stars*

There is something missing. Something *very* important and no one is above suspicion.

Past vendettas are gaining pace and it is vital that whoever is behind this never-ending stream of cleverly engineered payback is discovered before it is too late and everything held dear is ripped apart.

'**All three instalments would make a great movie...**' - *5 stars*

'**Amazing read... Whatever you are doing, please continue...**' - *5 stars*

'**On the edge of your seat...**' - *5 stars*

*\*\* These are Downfall Series books, but can be read as standalones. They contain written depictions of graphic violence, sex and strong language and also contain some themes that may be uncomfortable for certain readers.\*\**

# MORE FROM THIS AUTHOR

## RETRIBUTION SERIES:

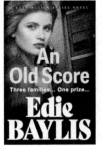

### #1: AN OLD SCORE
**Three families... One prize...**

Teagan Fraser had no idea what she was getting herself into when she took on an assignment as a live-in carer for Dulcie Adams – a retired dancer from a Soho club. Dulcie has waited forty years for a time that never came and left looking after something important, which Jonah Powell and his firm want back.

In addition to the notorious Powell firm, there are others wanting to claim what they believe is rightfully theirs and they'll do anything to get it back.

A lot can happen in the space of two weeks and Teagan might wish she'd never become involved.

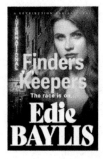

### #2: FINDERS KEEPERS
**The race is on...**

When Saul Powell is released early from prison, it causes mayhem for the family firm. His brother, Jonah, has enough problems trying to keep semblance amidst the chaos, not to mention his fast approaching unwanted marriage.

Even Jonah's problems pale into insignificance compared to what Robert Adams is discovering about his mother, Dulcie – the woman he's always put on a pedestal.

Can anyone come out of this nightmare unscathed?

### #3: THE FINAL TAKE
**The time is now...**

Even knowing Ron O'Hara is somewhere in the vicinity, Jonah Powell feels it's time to finally get rid of the diamonds which have haunted his family for decades and caused so much trouble.

However, other problems start to arrive from unexpected and additional sources, some of which Jonah didn't expect.

But what does it all mean? It may be apt to call time on the curse plaguing his family and of those around him, but how can this be achieved while so many other things are at stake?

# MORE FROM THIS AUTHOR

## HUNTED SERIES:

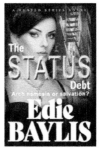

### #1: THE STATUS DEBT

Lillian Morgan would do anything to regain the status she lost by marrying beneath her and to cover the sordid details of her husband's death. This includes blackmail and the hand of marriage of her own daughter.

Tori thought her life couldn't get much worse, but someone is not being honest and secrets have the power to rip everyone to shreds.

Especially when life is built on lies.

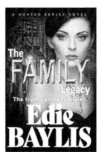

### #2: THE FAMILY LEGACY

Unsure of whether Matt or Hunter has fathered the child growing inside her, Tori's unwanted wedding to Matt grows closer, but is there light at the end of the tunnel? Unfortunately, Tori hasn't counted on another man present in her life. One who is more instrumental in her misery than she realises.

Sometimes the truth is too late in coming and makes bad things happen and sometimes a hidden legacy can cause the most horrific thing of all…

### #3: THE TARGET OF LIES

Neil Sparks has a score to settle. In fact, he has several… His first port of call when returning from France after a five year exile is to catch up with his estranged wife. Secondly, Neil wants to even a score with the people instrumental in his departure and thirdly, he wants an explanation from the man who promised his marriage would be free from hassle. The trouble is, he's not the only one with an agenda…

There are too many people about to become caught in the crossfire and everyone could become a target.

# MORE FROM THIS AUTHOR

## ALLEGIANCE SERIES:

### #1: TAKEOVER

Samantha Reynold hadn't bargained on unexpectedly needing to step into her father's shoes and take over the family casino business and known nothing about the rules of this glamorous but deadly new world. But she won't let her family down, especially when it looks like they could lose everything to their biggest rivals – the Stoker family.

Eldest son Sebastian hasn't got time to pander to pretty girl Samantha as she plays at being boss. Rumours are swirling around the streets of Birmingham that have the power to rip the Stoker family apart and destroy everything they've built.

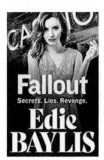

### #2: FALLOUT

With the odds stacked against her, Samantha Reynold is determined to prove she's tough enough to be the boss. But when a secret from the past threatens to ruin Sam's reputation, she suddenly feels very alone in this dark new world. There's only one man she can turn to – rival club owner, Sebastian Stoker.

Seb knows first-hand how secrets and lies can tear a family apart. He wants to protect Sam at all costs, but siding with her could threaten his own position as head of the Stoker family and risk accusations of betrayal.

With loyalties divided and two families at war – the fallout could be deadly.

# ABOUT THE AUTHOR

Over the years Edie has worked all over the UK as well as in several other countries and has met a lot of interesting people - several of whom have supplied ideas for some of the characters in her books! She has now settled back in central England with her partner and children, where she is pursuing her writing.

Edie writes gritty gangland fiction, using a combination of thrillers, suspense and romance.

She is currently signed to Boldwood Books for a 5-book gangland fiction series set in Birmingham. The first in the *Allegiance* series, *Takeover* was released in January 2022 and the second, *Fallout*, will be released in May 2022.

Edie's other series are the *Retribution* series, the *Hunted* series and the *Downfall* series - all trilogies.

When she isn't writing, Edie enjoys reading and is a self-confessed book hoarder. She also enjoys crochet and music as well as loving anything quirky or unusual.

Visit www.ediebaylis.co.uk for the latest news, information about new releases, giveaways and to subscribe to her mailing list.

# ACKNOWLEDGEMENTS

Thanks to the people that kindly read my drafts of *Until the End of Time* – you know who you are and I appreciate your time and feedback.

Printed in Great Britain
by Amazon